"I NEED YOU," SHE MURMURED.
"I AM NOT AFRAID."

He got up then. She was watching him; he could make out the gleam of her eyes in the moonlight that came from the uncurtained window. His hand touched her hair, stroked her throat, a single finger gently tickling below and behind her ear. Leonie sighed; her hand ran up his arm caressingly. Slowly, he eased down beside her. His hand slid from her neck to her breast. Leonie gasped. He knew he should have given her one more chance to change her mind, but he knew also that it would be beyond his ability to let her go now. Slowly, lingeringly, he began to make her his. . . .

Other Books by Roberta Gellis

BOND OF BLOOD
THE DRAGON AND THE ROSE
JOANNA
KNIGHT'S HONOR
ROSELYNDE
THE SWORD AND THE SWAN

THE ENGLISH HEIRESS

Roberta Gellis

A DELL BOOK

Published by
Dell Publishing Co., Inc.
1 Dag Hammarskjold Plaza
New York, New York 10017

Produced by Lyle Kenyon Engel

Copyright © 1980 by Book Creations, Inc.

All rights reserved. No part of this book may be repro-
duced or transmitted in any form or by any means, elec-
tronic or mechanical, including photocopying, recording,
or by any information storage and retrieval system, without
the written permission of the Publisher, except where
permitted by law.

Dell ® TM 681510, Dell Publishing Co., Inc.

ISBN: 0-440-12141-8

Printed in the United States of America
First printing—October 1980

A Note to the Reader

It may surprise the readers familiar with my work to find that the events of this novel take place in 1791 rather than in 1191 or 1291. However, there is considerable similarity in the problems confronting people of the Western world in these times. In the twelfth and thirteenth centuries, the techniques and concepts of government were changing from a loose feudalism to a centralized monarchy; in the eighteenth century, monarchy was giving way to varying forms of republicanism (which we call democracy).

Any examination of history shows that no political change is peaceful, and, sadly, the higher and more complex the principles motivating the change, the bloodier and more violent are the events surrounding it. In medieval times, the highest principles (aside from those of religion) were personal honor and/or personal benefit. Political events were seen through these blinders, which narrowed the range of vision. By the eighteenth century, life was far more complex. The concept of honor was not totally abandoned or even laughable, as it is now, but it was altered and overshadowed by the theories of "the common good" or "the will of the people." Events were no longer isolated in a castle, a town, or a shire. What took place needed to be considered in the terms of a nation or even the whole continent of Europe.

Although I am less drawn to describing events that are well-known to most readers of history and historical novels than those of earlier periods (and I fully intend to return again to the brilliant and magnificent tapestry that is medieval history), I could not resist this attempt to depict the tumultuous age in which our contemporary concepts and ideals of government were established. I have done my best to portray the actual historical events and personalities with accuracy. This has not been an easy task, not because of a lack of information but for exactly the contrary reason: Hundreds, perhaps thousands, of books and articles have been written about the events and people of this time—and most of them have very contradictory views and interpretations. I could not hope to exhaust the research materials available. The best I could do was to read widely and then present what I felt to be the most appropriate conclusions.

I have enjoyed writing this book. I hope you will enjoy reading it. As usual I have become so involved in the lives of my major characters (who are fictional, as are their families, friends, and servants) that history is seen through their eyes, and their personal lives dominate the historical events. This is as it should be in a novel, in my opinion. I always appreciate readers' comments on my work, but in this case I would be more than usually grateful to those who would take the trouble to write to me. I would like to know what they think of this book and whether they would like me to continue setting novels in this period as well as in medieval times.

ROBERTA GELLIS

June 1979

CHAPTER 1

Sir Joseph St. Eyre's hoarse roar penetrated the half-open doors of his study into the breakfast parlor, making his wife's blue eyes open wide and his youngest son's expressive brows rise. His grandson jumped. Philip was the only member of the third generation of a large and lively set of descendants, a credit to the old man's virility, who was currently resident in the large manor house of Stonar Magna. He was not accustomed to displays of temper from his grandsire. Over seven decades of life, encompassing three wives, a numerous and abundantly energetic family, and many joys and sorrows, Sir Joseph had developed an equable disposition.

"*Grand-mère*," the boy exclaimed, "*qu'est-ce que c'est que—*"

"Speak English, Philip," Roger St. Eyre interrupted.

There was no particular expression in his voice, but his stepmother, Lady Margaret, glanced briefly in his direction before she turned her attention to Philip, who was obligingly repeating in English his question about what had disturbed his grandfather.

"I have no idea," Lady Margaret replied placidly, and then widened her eyes again as a renewed blast of expletives curdled the air. "But I really think your papa had better go and see what is wrong before your ears are further sullied with objectionable phrases."

That made Philip giggle happily. *Grand-mère* was so different from *maman*. She said many of the same things, but *grand-mère* was only "doing the proper," and her eyes laughed. She knew that Philip was no longer a baby, and didn't wish him to be one nor to be like a perfect image of a boy in a silly novel. It was nicer here, nicer without *maman*'s shrill, sharp complaining and bitter words. The giggle cut off suddenly, and Philip bowed his head. Those were bad thoughts. He had had them many times before, but that was different. Now *maman* was dead.

Lady Margaret did not notice Philip's gesture of guilt, because Roger had thrown down his napkin and was sliding his chair back to rise. He smiled warmly at his stepmother, and she returned his smile thinking that Roger was looking much better. In the months since Solange had died, many of the lines of bitterness and worry had smoothed away from Roger's dark face. His expression had always been saturnine because of the way his brows arched in a circumflex above his eyes and because of the length and firmness of his jaw. However, as a boy the look in Roger's eyes—brightly, almost shockingly blue against his dark skin—had been gentle and kind when it did not sparkle with mischief.

Manhood had not changed that expression—until Roger had met Solange on his Grand Tour. He had courted her, loved her, sworn to be true. Unlike other young men, Roger had not forgotten her or his promises. With characteristic tenacity of purpose he had discussed the matter with his father, sensibly presenting facts and figures about his love's family background and financial expectations rather than the color of her eyes or the shape of her face. Sir Joseph could see no objections—beyond the fact that Solange was French. He pointed out to his son that the lifestyles of the two nations were very different and that a French girl from a family tied to the French court might not be happy in England. To this Roger had replied that he had discussed the matter with Solange and she understood.

Although Sir Joseph did not believe this, he did not argue the point. He was quite sure Roger had explained everything with great care and clarity; what he did not believe was that a fifteen-year-old girl understood him. Besides, there was sufficient likelihood that Solange's parents would not choose to ally their daughter to the son of a simple baronet or that they would not wish to send her so far from home. On the other hand, the girl was very young. If she loved Roger, she would adjust.

These sanguine hopes were not fulfilled. Solange's parents were only too pleased to be rid of one of their superfluity of daughters, and to be rid or her so cheaply. Roger's settlement would keep her quite well, Solange's debt-ridden father said with satisfaction, and dropped into the wastepaper basket the letter suggesting that he pay his daughter's promised dowry. Roger was concerned about her father's position; but he wanted Solange, and the marriage went off without any other hitch. Unfortunately neither youth nor love—if she felt any—enabled Solange to adjust to her adopted nation. She could not understand the relationships among the classes of society or the predilection of Englishmen for living in the country with only brief visits to London. Most of all she could not understand her husband's refusal to live beyond his means.

Roger had a handsome, if not lavish, private income from an estate settled upon him by his father. In addition, he was reading law and could expect to enlarge his private income substantially from his earnings once he was called to the bar. This latter activity revolted his wife almost as much as his bourgeois insistence on avoiding debt. All noblemen, Solange asserted passionately, lived above their means. It was crude, vulgar, and ungenteel to count the cost of anything. It was even more vulgar for a nobleman to take the "long robe."

In the beginning Roger exhorted, reasoned, and pleaded, explaining again and again that English customs were different. He had restricted his own pleasure to pay for Solange's. But it was useless. The more she had, the more extravagant she became; and the more her husband did for her, the greater her contempt for him grew. Philip's birth, three years after their marriage, brought Roger and Solange to a final parting of the ways. She hated the disfigurement of pregnancy; she hated the pain and indignity of childbirth; she hated the squalling, red-faced creature that was produced. When she recovered from her lying-in, Solange refused all sexual congress with her husband. She did not make excuses. She told Roger outright that she had done her duty as a wife and provided him with an heir; now she was through with an act she had always found repulsive.

This was more a relief than a punishment to Roger, who had struggled fruitlessly for years to overcome his wife's frigidity. He had used every form of foreplay a considerate nature and an active imagination could devise—only to be told he was disgusting. He had confined himself to the simplest form of intercourse, prolonging the act until it was

agony for him, hoping to bring her to climax—only to be
told he was deliberately torturing his wife. The inescapable
conclusion was that Solange found *him* so repulsive that
she could not respond no matter what technique he tried.

The effect of such a conclusion on a man of passionate
temperament was not happy, but it was mitigated by the
fact that Solange's behavior—out of bed as well as in it—
had long since killed Roger's love and even destroyed any
affection he had had for her. However, his nightmare was
not over. Roger could not simply separate himself from his
wife as so many husbands did. He could not set her up in a
house, furnish her with a liberal allowance, and let her live
her own life. He could not even allow her to return to Paris
and live there. Roger knew that Solange's living costs
would outstrip *any* allowance, no matter how generous,
that she would borrow on his credit, and he would be ruined. To threaten that he would not pay her debts would be
ridiculous. Solange knew he would never permit her to be
thrown into debtors' prison—and Roger knew she knew.
They had to live together so that Roger could control her.

Grimly, he set the bounds and kept Solange within them.
It was not pleasant. It was a long nightmare that wakened
Roger in the night, cold and sweating. He was forced to
create a major scandal by removing Solange physically
from the gambling tables of a public room, returning jew-
elry purchased without his permission, and going personally to inform the major modistes that he would not pay his
wife's bills.

In revenge, Solange made public scenes that left her husband sick and shaking, and when she found this was turning more people against her than arousing their sympathy,
she tried to make Philip hate and despise his father. This
effort failed because Solange was unable to provide for the
child's emotional needs. In one thing alone she succeeded.
Philip was more French than English in speech and manner. All Philip's servants were French, from his wet nurse
to his current valet. French was his first language, and he
spoke English, although fluently, with the slight accent and
the intonation of the foreign-born.

As he left the table, Roger noticed his son's bent head
and paused to squeeze his shoulder consolingly. He certainly did not want Philip to feel embarrassed about an

occasional exclamation, particularly when he knew how good a relationship existed between the boy and Lady Margaret. Philip looked up and smiled gratefully, thinking that his father had guessed the guilt he felt for being relieved that his mother was dead. His father really understood. Philip could not help knowing that Roger was more relieved than he, and also torn by guilt. The boy stifled an impulse to run after Roger and hug and kiss him. Englishmen did not do such things. He sighed as Roger entered the study and closed the door.

"I beg your pardon, sir," Roger said to his father with an amused quirk to his lips. "I'm sorry to interrupt you and to shut you in without a 'by your leave' or 'if you please,' but Lady Margaret felt your language wasn't fit for tender ears. . . ." His voice drifted off as Sir Joseph looked up. There was no answering laughter in his father's eyes. "Good God, sir," Roger exclaimed, "something is really wrong. I had thought it was Vinnie again. Is there something I can do to help?"

"I don't . . . by God, yes! You are just the man I need, Roger. Do you keep up your French connections?"

"My French—there was never much 'connection' between Solange's family and myself. They felt—"

"No, no, my boy," Sir Joseph interrupted hastily. "I didn't mean that. Sorry to bring it to mind. You used to do a lot of business with some legal firms in France, getting our wretched young devils on the Continent out of trouble."

"Oh. Yes and no, Father. Technically, we're still associated, but I haven't had much to do with them recently. Of course, most English travelers have been avoiding France, and Paris in particular, for the last couple of years. Why?"

Sir Joseph sighed. "Sit down. This is likely to be a long story. You remember Stour, don't you?"

"Of course. He died about three or four years ago."

"Yes." Sir Joseph nodded sadly. "If I live much longer, I shan't have a friend left me. William and I were good friends. Then young William—not that he was so young, really, about the same age as your brother Arthur—took a chill and died of an inflammation of the lungs."

Roger frowned. "I hadn't heard that. I'm sorry. He used to take me out with a gun when you visited with Stour.

That would make Joseph the earl. Well, he would have been anyhow since William had never married and said plainly he had no taste for it. But I don't understand how I didn't know of his death."

"It was after Solange had taken ill. With the doctors in the house and she sinking so swiftly in such pain, you had enough to bear without adding more bad news. The devil is in it, though, that Joseph won't be earl. Joseph is dead." Sir Joseph touched the letter lying on his desk to explain where his information came from.

"Good God!" Roger exclaimed. "No wonder you're upset. How did it come about? That would pass the title to little William. Poor boy! But Lady Alice will be a tower of strength. She—"

"They are all dead," Sir Joseph growled, his voice harsh with his effort to keep it from shaking.

"What!" Roger's bellow was nearly the equivalent of his father's first roar of surprise and distress. "Sir, what can you mean?" he asked, lowering his voice. Roger would have been inclined to think his father was joking—only this wasn't the sort of thing Sir Joseph or anyone else with normal sensibilities joked about. Still, he couldn't help protesting, "This isn't a novel by Horry Walpole or Mrs. Radcliffe."

"You might think it was," Sir Joseph replied, but there was so much sadness in his eyes that Roger had no inclination to smile. "Joseph was on the Irish estates. You know Stour was a good landlord and did not like always to be taking the word of the bailiff about conditions there. Besides, Joseph and Alice had no taste for the high *ton*. When William died—it was very quick—Compton wrote at once to Joseph, and he came immediately. Then, seeing everything was in excellent order, he went back to help Alice with packing and moving. She was breeding again, and he didn't like to leave the whole weight of shifting the household upon her."

Breeding or not, Roger thought, Alice de Conyers was perfectly capable of moving either a single handkerchief or a full household with the least fuss and inconvenience. Yet he understood quite well why her husband would gladly put himself out to spare her any effort. She was not a handsome woman, but had a sweetness of disposition for which Roger would have eagerly traded all of Solange's beauty.

However, he did not interrupt his father's tale with his private reflections.

"They took ship on June twenty-second on the packet *Pride of St. George*."

"The *Pride*!" Roger gasped. That disaster that had been widely reported in the London papers. The *Pride of St. George* had been hit by a sudden squall and had gone down, nearly in sight of land. "But I didn't see their names in the list of those lost."

"No, because some passengers were saved and several of them remembered Joseph. He had got his family and a number of other women and children into one of the small boats and lowered it safely. Then apparently he was washed overboard, but someone else saw him clinging to the side of the boat Alice was in. The winds were terrific and all those who managed to grab something that would keep them afloat were blown miles apart. If they had come ashore in one of the wilder areas of Wales, it might well have taken weeks to get word to Compton. He kept hoping . . ."

"But it isn't so very long," Roger offered without much conviction, "less than three weeks. They might still—"

"They have been found," his father interrupted, his voice again harsh. "The bodies of Joseph, little William, and Alice were washed up near Morfa Nevin. They haven't yet found the little girls. They may never be found."

"God rest them all," Roger sighed. "I am really *very* sorry. I know how fond you were of Joseph, and he was your godchild. How awful!"

"Yes, but I'm ashamed to say it was less grief than selfishness that gave me such a turn." Sir Joseph looked at his son and smiled ruefully. "I *was* fond of Joseph, and I was truly shocked to hear of his death, but I'm old, my boy. I've lived through many deaths. It isn't only affection that makes me wish Joseph alive again. He made me executor of his will."

"Made you . . . but Father, how could he expect . . . I mean . . ."

There was more amusement in Sir Joseph's smile now. "All right, Roger, don't confound yourself looking for a polite way to say that I can't be expected to live much longer. In fact, I think I will be around longer than you believe."

Roger laughed. "You can't be around longer than I would hope for, however."

Sir Joseph now laughed aloud also, a mischievous twinkle coming into his eyes. "Don't be so sure of that." Then he frowned again. "Compton not only wrote to tell me that he had identified Joseph, William, and Alice but to say that he has tried several times to contact Henry with no success."

"Henry?" Roger asked, then nodded. "Oh, yes, I remember. There was another brother. Whatever happened to him? I don't remember ever seeing him at all."

"You must have, as a child—or maybe not. When you were still at home, Henry must have been at school. He has ten or twelve years on you, at least."

"Yes, and by the time he was out of school, I was in. I can see how I never came across him, but why can't Compton reach him now? Where is he?"

"In France."

"Oh, lord!" Roger remarked. "What a bufflehead to go to France now. Well, I—"

"No, no," Sir Joseph interrupted. "Henry didn't go now. He lives in France, has lived there since about seventeen-seventy, seventy-two or three was when he was married, I believe."

"He married a Frenchwoman and settled in France? I see."

"Yes, and don't say 'I see' that way, as if you are confirmed that Henry is buffleheaded. He isn't at all—at least, not generally, although I don't understand. . . . Well, let me tell you in a logical way so that you will see why Compton is worried."

"If he weren't worried, with what has been happening in France over these last two years, he would be an idiot," Roger exclaimed.

"Is it so bad as that?" Sir Joseph asked, frowning. "I haven't paid much attention, you know. I've never been overfond of the French."

Sir Joseph's face was carefully devoid of expression. Roger shrugged his shoulders and gripped his father's forearm for a moment. They had never discussed Solange, although after the gaming room scandal, Sir Joseph had offered to supplement Roger's income. Roger had refused, assuring his father that in one way he had sufficient funds, and in another the income from the Royal Treasury would not be enough, since Solange's wants expanded geometrically with the ability to satisfy them. Sensibly, Sir Joseph had never offered his son sympathy; that would have smacked too much of "I told you so."

"It wasn't so bad in the beginning, except in Paris," Roger explained. "There was only a little rioting in the smaller cities and minor disturbances in the towns and countryside, but matters are growing more and more serious. The *émigrés* say that this constitution, which frees the serfs and revokes the forest laws and such matters, has provoked an orgy of license among the peasantry. Of course, they are bound to be strongly prejudiced, but I believe there is a kernel of truth inside the shell of self-pity. The central government *does* seem to have lost control of the provinces. The Prussians and Austrians have thrown the French army out of Belgium, and there is good evidence that they intend to invade France itself soon."

"Damn and blast!" Sir Joseph exploded. "I take it all back. Henry *is* buffleheaded. Why the devil did he not come home when he saw everything falling apart?"

"Perhaps he couldn't," Roger suggested. "Or he may not have realized how disordered everything was. Often when one is directly involved, one doesn't see the whole picture. What I don't like is the fact that Compton couldn't reach him by letter as early as June. As far as I know, there hasn't been such a generalized disruption in the country at large that letters wouldn't have got through. If Compton wrote more than once, as he must have done, and Henry de Conyers was living in the country, and there has been no answer . . ."

"Well, go on," Sir Joseph urged impatiently.

"He—he may not be alive, sir, or he may be in serious trouble," Roger responded reluctantly.

"But you said it was only Paris that was completely out of control," Sir Joseph protested.

"Unfortunately not, sir, although that has mostly been the case. Still, there have been serious incidents—in Caen and Mouton and a number of other cities I don't have on the tip of my tongue. Although . . . Do you know when there was last news of de Conyers?"

"Curse it, no, and Compton didn't say. I heard from Joseph pretty regularly—at least, Alice wrote, but I assume

Joseph asked her to do so. But I only heard of Henry through Stour. Naturally I have no news later than seventeen eighty-eight or so." Sir Joseph paused a moment then sighed. "Damn and blast," he repeated, but with more resignation than rage. "Something must be done. I suppose I must post up to London and speak to Compton. He will have the latest intelligence. Then I can—"

"I don't think you should, sir," Roger interrupted firmly. "London is hotter than the hinges of hell just now. It wouldn't agree with you at all. Why don't you allow me to handle this? Perhaps when Compton has told me where de Conyers was when he heard from him last, one of the firms I dealt with in Paris will send a man to give him the news or discover what is wrong."

Sir Joseph raised a brow at his son. "Trying to prove that you are not impatient to see the last of me?" he teased.

"Not at all," Roger returned briskly. "In fact, I'm bent on shortening your days to lengthen my own. Since the school holidays will last several weeks longer, I'm trying to preserve my own health and sanity at the expense of yours by leaving my son on your hands while I escape."

"I should have known better than try to draw you," Sir Joseph sighed. "I *never* had the last word with your mother, and I haven't had the last word with you since you were three—that was when you started to talk. You were late at it, but, by God, once started . . ." He laughed. "Thank you, my boy. I shall be most grateful if you will save me this journey. I hope to heaven you have some answer, but if you don't, at least you will have saved me the trip to London and back before I need to go to France."

"Father!" Roger exclaimed. "You can't mean that! Just because Joseph de Conyers named you executor . . . That will must have been written years and years ago. Joseph must have meant to change it."

"And name a younger man?" Sir Joseph said. "Yes, I suppose he did, but the fact is that he hadn't gotten around to it, and it is my responsibility. Aside from that, Roger, I wouldn't like to see Stour's lands fall into decay while the inheritance is fought out in court. In addition to the disruption caused by not knowing Henry's fate—which means that the estate will be administered by some fool of a court appointee and be run right into the ground—this is Stour's son. William would have bailed any of you out of trouble;

he hiked Arthur out of a real hole with a woman once when I was in Jamaica. No, if Stour's son is in trouble—especially trouble he hasn't made for himself—I couldn't sit idly by and do nothing."

Roger felt like shaking his father and telling him not to be an idiot. A man in his eighth decade was not the person to be thrust into a nation that—as far as Roger could tell—had gone quite mad and erupted periodically, for no rational reason, into riots. He reminded himself that his father did not know how bad the situation was, but he had no intention of describing it in greater detail than he already had. Roger knew his father. Sir Joseph had determined that Henry de Conyers and his family would be found—dead or alive—and a recitation of the difficulties would not change his mind.

In fact, Roger thanked God sincerely that he had not said more about the situation in France. If his father understood the real difficulties, he would never have accepted Roger's platitude about getting information through one of the legal firms with which he was associated. Probably Sir Joseph would have started packing already, realizing that the only way to be sure de Conyers was found was to go himself or send someone really trustworthy. Since Sir Joseph was not the man to push dangerous or disagreeable duties onto other people, and was not particularly concerned with prolonging his life—which he knew to have been already unusually long—he would have determined to go himself. Roger shuddered at the thought of trying to dissuade his father or—equally unpleasant—trying to explain to Lady Margaret why he had given his father information that had precipitated him into such an action.

Roger's mind was busy as he pointed out to his father that nothing could be done until he spoke to Compton, and he had made his decision before he finished the sentence. "I have some business in town anyway," Roger continued. "It isn't pressing, but I might as well take care of it now. If you don't mind, sir, I think I'll leave today and get matters under way."

Sir Joseph's penetrating stare rested on his son for a long moment. He understood rather more than Roger expected, although not the whole. It was at once obvious to Sir Joseph that Roger intended to go to France himself; however, he misunderstood his son's purpose. Sir Joseph believed that Roger, freed from the weight he had carried for years, was seizing an opportunity for adventure and excitement. Roger had been a most adventurous child, Sir Joseph remembered, always sticking his nose into what did not concern him. Once, he had been lucky to escape with his life when he decided to discover why a herd of horses had been down on the beach in the cove at night.

That time curiosity had not killed the cat, although it should have. Smugglers were not "gentlemen." Most of them were hard and ruthless men engaged in a dangerous and illegal trade. If they were caught, their punishment would be brutal. And it was with them that Roger had chosen to get involved. With typical cleverness and persistence, he had visited that cove every day after first seeing signs of horses, until he had figured out the schedule of when the horses would be there. If he had only asked, Sir Joseph thought, but no, not Roger—he had to find out for himself. Doubtless it had occurred to the child at once that horses by the seaside at night were a "secret." To ask about a secret—to show you knew there *was* a secret—was to warn those whose secret it was. Roger, even as a boy, could be tight-lipped as a clam.

He had waited, deduced, watched—and had been caught by the smugglers. One part of the gang had immediately produced a simple answer—drop the boy off the cliff. An accident could happen to anyone. Roger had laughed aloud. "I couldn't help it," he had told his father when describing the scene later. "They were so stupid. How could *I* have an accident on the cliff? I've been climbing there for years and years, night and day. You would have known right away that if I fell it was no accident. One of the men who recognized me said so too, and the Frenchman agreed with me."

The Frenchman, Sir Joseph had learned, was Pierre Restoir, the captain of the smuggling vessel, the *Bonne Lucie*. Pierre had intervened decisively in Roger's fate, insisting that the boy be released in exchange for a promise not to report what he had discovered to the authorities. Roger had promised readily enough, with the reservation that he must tell his father. The small group of "professional" smugglers had muttered rebelliously, but Pierre's determination and the reluctance of the local "hired" men to harm a youth so intimately connected with local authority determined Roger's fate.

Sir Joseph had taken no action, knowing that there were many alternate coves—although not quite so well suited to the purpose. Still, it was most likely that the smugglers would shift their base. In a way he was right, but he had no way of knowing that Pierre Restoir was still very young and a quixotic daredevil to boot, with an insatiable curiosity of his own. He had been greatly drawn to the brave, lighthearted boy for whom he had stood up, and had to know whether his judgment of the child's character had been correct.

Right at the agreed-upon time Pierre was at the cove, and Roger was there to meet him. It was safe enough for Pierre, who was cautious and cunning as well as curious, even if Roger had betrayed him. This trip his ship was loaded with nothing more offensive than a cargo of newly caught fish, and there were no ponies waiting to carry off illegal merchandise. If Roger had reported to the Revenue Service and their officers were in ambush, Pierre had ready a good excuse for anchoring, and the searchers would have found nothing.

There were no custom men, however, only the eager boy. As a reward, Pierre took Roger aboard the ship and showed him how they dodged the revenue cutters and coastal guard. It was not the last trip they made together, although Sir Joseph knew nothing of the development of a genuine friendship between his twelve-year-old son and the captain of the *Bonne Lucie*. When Roger was absorbed in the early joys and the bitter disappointments of his marriage, he and Pierre saw little of each other, but after Roger had been called to the bar, their contacts increased dramatically. The aristocracy soon learned that Roger St. Eyre was the man to approach if one had to leave England quietly. For example, a gentleman who had killed his man in a duel and needed to make himself scarce until a pardon could be secured found Roger's services invaluable. Not only could he arrange transport but he could also arrange transfer of the gentleman's assets through a highly respectable French law firm, secure introduction to the French court, and, in general, provide for life to continue enjoyably.

* * *

Sir Joseph did not mention Pierre Restoir—in fact, he did not remember the name of the man involved in Roger's early adventure. Nor did he connect the smuggler with Roger's profitable career. Roger never mentioned Pierre to anyone, because every person who knew of him and his trade increased the danger for him. However, Pierre was well to the forefront of Roger's mind without mention. Even before he went to tell Philip and Lady Margaret that he intended to post up to London, Roger stepped out of the house to speak to his groom, Shannon, in the stable. He told the man to leave a message at the Soft Berth, the little alehouse south of Kingsdown, that Pierre should call in at Dymchurch House as soon as it was convenient. Then he went to explain to Philip that he would be away for a day or two.

He almost missed his son, who was already on his way out dressed in rough country clothes. His news did not dim the brightness in Philip's eyes, Roger saw with relief. There was nothing left of the haunted look, the forced smile, with which Philip had accepted such news in the past. Roger smiled. The boy was perfectly happy here. Grandpapa was even more amusing than papa; the gamekeepers of Stonar Magna were well broke to child and did not mind a boy tagging along and asking questions. The same was true of the grooms and the local farmers. Best of all, Lady Margaret—called *grand-mère,* although she was totally unrelated to Philip except by marriage—never scolded over dirt or torn clothing or stable smells. With a clear conscience and a strangely lifting heart, Roger set out for London.

CHAPTER 2

Leonie de Conyers stared at the solid wooden door of the cellar that was her prison as if the pressure of her gaze could force it open. *She would not die!* She would escape. Now that mama and François were dead, the possibilities were much better. A lash of guilt made her wince, but it eased quickly. Leonie knew that if her being in prison could have kept her mother and brother alive, she would have remained patiently incarcerated forever. But they were gone and nothing could bring them back. And if she and papa did not soon escape, they would be dead also.

How? There were so many hows. Not only how to get out of this cellar, but how to rouse papa so that he would wish to escape also, how to get out of the town, possibly even how to get out of France altogether. Her mind lingered on that for a moment. At least she and papa had a place to go. Papa was not French-born. He was an Englishman, youngest brother of the Earl of Stour, and he was on good terms with his family. In fact, papa's brother had urged him many times in the last two years to "come home" and bring his wife and children. Tears rose to Leonie's eyes, but she blinked them back. There was no sense in dwelling on such might-have-beens. She glanced at her father and noticed with satisfaction that he was sitting up. Last night he had eaten willingly. Perhaps it might not be so difficult to get him to agree to escape.

The trouble with papa, Leonie thought, rising suddenly and pacing the confined space, was that he blamed himself for everything, for all the terrible things that had happened to them. That was nonsense. One could not see the future. One could only act as it seemed best at the moment. Nonetheless, Leonie's mind could not help ranging back, wondering at what point—had papa acted differently—the whole train of events would never have taken place. She paused. If papa had refused the nomination to the Estates General? Instinctively Leonie shook her head in negation and began to pace again. A de Conyers did not refuse a duty to the nation. A de Conyers always fulfilled his—or her—responsibilities.

Anyhow, what had happened had not really started with the calling of the Estates General. Papa always said the trouble had started long, long ago when Louis XIV gathered the entire government into his own hands, giving power and wealth only to those men who hovered around him. Thus, the nobles were divided from the people, and . . . Leonie stopped, shook her head again. It was ridiculous. She sank down to the dirt floor. Of course the history of France had affected their lives, but Louix XIV had acted as he had because of the history that preceded him. The abuses that had exploded France into revolution had grown slowly. One could go back and back to Adam and Eve.

Besides, it was not the trouble in France that had thrown them into prison and killed mama and François. Color fed by hate and rage rushed into Leonie's face, making her light brown eyes as fierce and golden as a she-wolf's. The lips of her wide mouth curled back, showing strong, white teeth, and the nostrils of her straight nose flared. Leonie was not, strictly speaking, a beautiful girl. Her features were too strong to satisfy the current craze for porcelain-delicate, pretty dolls. Also, the mingling of her father's blond and her mother's dark coloring had produced an odd combination; Leonie was a brunette in complexion, but with honey-gold hair.

Leonie looked down at her hands, which in her tense anger had curved into claws. She sighed and straightened the fingers. Hate was unpleasant and unnatural to her; she had inherited her mother's temperament—placid and sunny. Hate made her feel shaky and sick, yet there was no other response possible to the memory that had come to mind. Papa had made *one* mistake. Once only, he had done something that should have been done differently: When Jean-Paul Marot had tried to incite the peasants on mama's estates to rebellion, papa had prevented the people from killing him. The peasants had been enraged against the rabble-rouser because papa had offered to excuse all rents and taxes—after the poor crops of 1787 and 1788 people were already starving. Jean-Paul Marot had stood up and begun to shout that papa's offer was no favor, that it was the *right* of the people to be free of rents and duties.

Perhaps it had not been gratitude toward papa that made the peasants so angry; perhaps they had secretly agreed with Jean-Paul and had only been afraid that papa would take back his offer of relief. That made no difference. If papa had not intervened and had Jean-Paul arrested, the peasants would have torn him apart. He would have been dead. He would not have been released from prison in Dijon when, after the Bastille had fallen, the whole country had gone mad and opened all the jails.

Jean-Paul Marot was the beginning, middle, and end of all the trouble. Leonie jumped up again, breathing fast. He—so full of noble words about equality and justice, so full of vicious, evil deeds that hurt everyone. . . . She tried to wrench her mind away, but it was impossible. The whole story played itself out again.

They had come home from Paris several months after the constitution was approved, and papa had suggested that the mayor call a meeting of the electors and other responsible citizens so he could report to them. Was the mayor ignorant of the fact that Jean-Paul had been rousing the unemployed, the dissatisfied, the dregs of the town, or did he simply discount the importance of such people? Papa would not have made *that* mistake. He had seen what the mob could do in Paris. But papa did not know there was a mob in peaceful Saulieu.

All the family had come with papa to be at the meeting. They were all so proud of him and of the new hope for France. Instead of joy, violence had resulted; instead of freedom, the despotism of mob rule was created. Jean-Paul had planned it well. With all the responsible citizens in one place, his mob had only to storm the hall. Jean-Paul and his mob had seized power. Even then papa had not recognized him. It was only when the monster had reminded him . . .

Leonie shuddered and buried her face in her hands for a moment, struggling to block out the memory of that night, of herself and her mother spread-eagled on the floor, violated by man after man while her father, bound and gagged, was forced to watch. Jean-Paul had taken her first, not even looking at her, laughing in her father's face and reminding him of the "injury" papa had done him. Papa had saved his life! Leonie lifted her head, her eyes brilliant with hate again. Jean-Paul had intended to destroy her, but he had failed!

Then the flame died out of Leonie's eyes and her expression grew thoughtful. It was strange, but that horror had not been all bad. The thing itself, yes, but the results . . . She considered what she had been before that night—a person insulated from life. Nothing unpleasant had ever touched her. Even the bloody violence she had seen in Paris had seemed like scenes in a painting—dreadful, but nothing to do with her. What she had not realized was that nothing good had really touched her either. She had accepted the love of her parents, her physical comforts, the courtesy of everyone around her with mild pleasure. She had known neither love nor hate.

Now she knew both. Strangely, love had come first in a burning uprush that had seared out the pain and shame of rape. As soon as Jean-Paul and his mangy dogs had left them, mama—battered and bleeding as she was—had crawled to wrap her daughter in her arms, to comfort her, to assure her it was a passing thing, that she would be better in a very little while. It was true, too, Leonie remembered. Perhaps because she had not been alone, because mama had undergone the same horror and made light of it; perhaps because the eruption of violence, the sudden seizure, had shocked her so much already that she could feel nothing strongly. She remembered what had happened, but the memory of horror was less important than mama's tenderness and papa's wild grief. How she loved them for what they had given her! For the first time in her life, she had really loved.

Hate had come later, after her stunned mind had taken in what had happened, after Leonie realized that they would not be killed as those others in Paris had been killed and their heads paraded through the streets on poles. Perhaps that was the strangest of all, the way a love for life had grown up side by side with the hate.

Jean-Paul had come again to the cellar the next day, and after his men had subdued papa, he had laughed at them again and told them that they would not be killed—that

was too good for them. They would learn what he had
learned in the prison at Dijon—how to die by inches.

There could be no doubt Jean-Paul had done his best to
fulfill his threat, but instead Leonie had learned what joy
was. All the things she had taken so much for granted that
she had not even noticed them became a source of infinite
pleasure; a breath of fresh air or taste of wholesome cheese
was more wonderful than the most elaborate dinner.

Unfortunately, the things that bred strength in Leonie
had worked as Jean-Paul planned on the others. The dark
and filth, the slimy cold in the cellar—even though it was
summer now—had sapped strength from mama and François. The child had sickened first. Tears dimmed the glow
of Leonie's eyes, and she began to pace once more. She had
done her best to save him, inventing stories and games,
trying to make him laugh and want to live; but she had not
been able to save François or mama.

Leonie stopped again and allowed her eyes to rest
thoughtfully on the wooden door. She had been out of that
door any number of times. Possibly she could have escaped
herself, but she had never considered it—not while papa,
mama, and François were still prisoners and might be tortured or killed for her freedom. Now there was only papa,
and he was not so physically weakened as mama and François had been; escape was no longer impossible. What was
more, her lover—Leonie uttered a slightly hysterical giggle.
What an inappropriate word for Louis le Bébé. Louis loved
nothing and no one—except himself.

A disdainful smile curved Leonie's lips briefly as she sat
on the floor, her legs pulled up close to her body, resting
her chin on her knees. She did not hate Louis. After all,
their purposes were exactly alike. He used her to satisfy the
needs of his body, but she was using him also—and she
had the better of it because she knew what Louis was, but
he was much mistaken about her. He thought her weak
and stupid; perhaps he even thought she was in love with
him. Leonie laughed softly.

Then she grew thoughtful again. She could have loved
Louis; she was ripe and ready for love, and at first he
seemed so lovable with his round, innocent face. Heaven
made a great many mistakes, but Louis's soft features—
youthful, guileless—which had gained him the soubriquet
of le Bébé, must be more than a mistake. It must have

been a deliberate joke or a deliberate test of people's perceptiveness. Louis was everything his face was not. He was a thief with a keen eye for what would do him good and a heart as cold as ice. Louis sought comfort, pleasure, and advancement. He had chosen his profession deliberately and had never gone hungry or been caught. Louis never did anything without a good reason, and although he took no personal pleasure in the misery of others, he would never hesitate to use pain and misery to advance his own cause. But Leonie did not know that in the beginning.

Leonie only knew that Louis had shrunk away rather than press forward when Jean-Paul had signaled his other dogs to take their turn on her abused body. It was a small thing, but it had burned itself deeply into Leonie's mind, one tiny flicker of humanity in a black night of bestiality. Weeks later she recognized him at once when he brought them food, and her good opinion was confirmed because, for once, the meal was not deliberately made more foul. Louis, unlike the guard who usually brought the food, did not throw the stale, moldy bread into the slime on the floor or spit into the stinking soup, prepared with meat a starving dog would have refused. Made bold by desperation, Leonie whispered a plea for a drop of clean water, a crust of fresh bread, for her little brother. Louis had not answered but had given her some decent bread; he had had to be quick, for the other guard had come down the stairs to curse him for spending too much time with the prisoners.

"You were late. I thought you were not coming," the young thief had answered mildly.

"So what? Let them starve as we have starved," the older man growled, his eyes suspicious.

Leonie had turned away, sick at heart, hiding the clean bread with her body. Sometimes she could hear what went on in the courtyard through the half-window in their cellar, and she had once heard one of Jean-Paul's men threatening to accuse another of treachery, or currying favor with the ex-magistrates of the town so that if the revolution should fail, he would be safe. If the old guard wanted to get the young one into trouble, he had only to accuse him of trying to ease the lot of the prisoners whom Jean-Paul hated so much.

At first Louis did nothing to help the de Conyerses but neither did he do anything to increase their torment. Once in a while—the rarity heightening the value of what was received—he did more. He pretended fear when he brought a decent stew, fresh bread, a wedge of good cheese. He said he had thrown away the foul portions destined for the prisoners and taken the good food from his own table. He could not do it often, he whispered apologetically; someone would notice or his own family would starve.

Later, when they believed in him, he offered to take Leonie out for "exercise." He could not take the others, he said. No one would question him or look to see the face of a young girl with whom he chose to walk, but an older man or woman or a young boy would cause comment. Once—the first time—they actually did walk a little way while Louis explained what he wanted. He gilded it finely with hints of the desperate danger he courted to give Leonie's family the little ease he could. He veneered with talk of self-sacrifice the ugly fact that he was demanding that Leonie pay with her body for the favors of clean water and an occasional mouthful of unspoiled food for her mother and brother.

Louis had been clever, but he underestimated Leonie. She knew what love was—the giving without thought of recompense. She knew what honor was also. She knew a man worthy of love did not ask nor expect payment for dangers voluntarily undertaken out of sympathy or justice, more especially when those favors were bestowed on someone utterly helpless, utterly within one's power. Nonetheless, she agreed without much argument to what Louis wanted, fearing if she did not that her parents and young brother would suffer for her resistance. Leonie knew she had neither maidenhead nor reputation to protect, and she had no feeling of "wrong" attached to sexual promiscuity. Her cooperation was a matter of survival.

Later, Leonie came to realize that she had benefited from Louis's selfish desire for a cost-free and delicate bedmate. Simply to be out of the fetid atmosphere of her family's cell had helped her resist the soul-killing despair that destroyed her mother and brother. In addition, coupling with Louis had removed from the act itself the taint of torture it had held after she had been raped. Louis was not a good lover. He was far too indifferent to his partner's needs. However, he liked comfort. He had no intention of forcing or frightening his bedmate so that she would be stiff and inflexible or would struggle against him. Thus, he was gentle if not considerate. He did not bother to try to wake Leonie's desire, and he never brought her to climax. Yet he made intercourse simple and acceptable, a thing not to be feared or avoided.

Leonie could not help smiling. Louis had explained how and what to do to arouse a man. Leonie enjoyed that part so much that she invented new devices that produced quite dramatic results. The pleasure she derived came from reducing so self-possessed and calculating a creature as Louis to a sighing, moaning mass of quivering flesh. More importantly, instructed by Louis's total selfishness as well as by his lust, Leonie had learned that her body could be a valuable trading device and weapon.

Not that she tried to trade with Louis for anything beyond what she knew he was willing to give anyway. Not even lust could divert Louis from his own purposes; however, Leonie knew that most other men were different. Louis had taught her that, too, laughing about the weaknesses of others, at the gifts his companions gave their women, at the things they did for them. Leonie listened with downcast eyes, a model of dullness and docility, smiling inside herself at the weakness *Louis* displayed. Because he needed to boast of his own powers, of his own growing influence and importance, he had told her a very great deal.

Jean-Paul's grip on Saulieu was no longer as strong as it had been when he first seized power. There was serious unrest in the town that was being repressed with fiercer and fiercer measures. So far no one had been executed, but it was only a matter of time. Louis had grinned when he told Leonie that the previous night, and that grin had given her serious food for thought. Although he still retained only his position of night watch in the Hôtel de Ville, Louis was now one of Jean-Paul's confidants. Leonie suspected Louis was only waiting for Jean-Paul to go a little too far, shake the faith of those who still followed him just a little more, and then topple him and seize power in his stead.

No consideration of past service or friendship would save anyone Louis decided to sacrifice to gain that power—and that was what made Leonie gaze at the door of her prison with such fixed attention. She was convinced that Louis's grin, when he mentioned execution, signified that the sacrifice he planned to use to overthrow Jean-Paul was the execution of herself and her father. After the shock of Jean-Paul's take-over had subsided and dissatisfaction had begun to grow, Marot had used papa to pacify the people, bringing him from his prison, cleaning him and dressing him well, and forcing him to say that he was in comfortable quarters, well cared for. There was no danger that papa would not do as he was told, not while she and mama and François were in Jean-Paul's power.

However, Jean-Paul had not been able to use papa that way for more than a month. The signs of grief and deprivation were too strong. No amount of cleaning and elaborate clothing could hide the effects now. Thus, Leonie thought, it might be easy for Louis to convince Jean-Paul that papa and she had outlived their usefulness, except for being an object lesson. Some accusation could be trumped up, they could be executed, and Louis could use the anger and resentment caused by their executions to overthrow Jean-Paul.

It was a large assumption to build on the small ground of a grin and sly expression, but it was too dangerous an idea to neglect. Yet it was dangerous to act, too. Leonie had begun to hope that enough unrest would develop to topple Jean-Paul. His fall would almost certainly lead to freedom for herself and her father. No one else had cause to hate them personally, and even if the new leaders were "of the people" and did not want Henry de Conyers, the aristocrat, near Saulieu, papa could promise to leave for England.

Unfortunately, it seemed too late for that now; at least, Leonie was not willing to take the chance of waiting any longer. It might be difficult to rouse papa to the need to escape, but she had an idea that might work. If it did work . . . Leonie's eyes danced. She would use the weapon she had so long and so laboriously fashioned— Louis's belief that she was dull and docile, loving, inventive only of sexual variations to please and delight the man she adored. Slowly, patiently, she had drawn and filled in that picture of herself until Louis was convinced—convinced enough to permit himself to sleep in her presence after making "love."

First it had been a bare closing of the eyes; later had come a time of testing, when Louis lay limp and snoring.

Leonie had not known he was testing her. She had made no move to harm him or to escape because her brother was dying and her mother already sick. Nothing could have convinced her to leave—even if Louis had offered to help her escape, she would have refused because it would have meant leaving those she loved behind. She had, in fact, innocently convinced him that she had no intention of harming him or escaping by acts of dishonesty. While Louis was "sleeping," Leonie had stolen a few little things she did not think he would miss—a few crusts of bread, a leftover piece of cheese, a candle stump, a flint and tinder to light the candle. Thus, Louis felt he understood her completely, and he relaxed his guard in her presence. Then he slept naturally, silently curled into a fetal ball. Leonie recognized her mistake and her victory at the same time.

She had been careful to preserve that victory, continuing her "stealing" by taking items that, she now realized, were left out for her to take. She would not have bothered after her mother's and brother's deaths except that it gave her a reason to be moving around Louis's room. She encouraged Louis's belief in her "love" for him in every way she could—with sweet words and anxious care. Once or twice —for instance, after a particularly satisfactory climax, Louis had overslept. Dutifully, Leonie had waked him at the time he usually returned her to her cell, saying she was afraid she would get him in trouble. Oh, yes, time and time again Leonie had proved herself careful of Louis's welfare. He still did not leave weapons where she could get them, and he still secured the keys to the cellar around his neck, where Leonie could not steal them without waking him, but—within the bounds of reasonable caution—he trusted her.

Leonie grinned as nastily as Louis ever could. She had long since worked out a way to get the keys and immobilize him. . . . Then the nastiness went out of the grin. Her device would do no harm, and she was certain he would be able to work his way free and escape himself—or work out some good story that would protect him from punishment. However, whatever Louis's fate, time was running out, Leonie was sure. The very next time Louis wanted her for the night, she had better make her move. That meant she would have to make papa aware of their danger.

CHAPTER 3

The lift of spirits that had seized Roger St. Eyre when he left his father's house to embark on the rescue of Henry de Conyers persisted, although the drive to London was hot, and the news Compton had for him was all bad. As the man of business had written Sir Joseph, Henry's last letter had arrived in April, addressed to his brother William. Since William was dead and Joseph had told Compton to open all correspondence, Compton had read the letter. He produced it now for Roger, who groaned as he read.

The headlong enthusiasm of the man about the reforms to be made in France and the benefits to be reaped by all was at once appealing and appalling. Roger wondered briefly whether Henry simply did not want to be torn from his wonderful political experiment and had therefore ignored Compton's report of first one brother's death and then the other's. A moment later, Roger shook his head at himself. There was not only enthusiasm in Henry's description of the work finally produced by the National Assembly but also a strong streak of practicality in the analysis of the effects of the various constitutional provisions. There was also warmth. After a second reading, Roger had no doubt that Henry de Conyers was a man of strong affections and a strong sense of responsibility. Whatever his enthusiasms, he would not have ignored notice of his brothers' deaths. Nor would he have sloughed off his responsibility for the estate, no matter how enthralled he was by social and political developments in his adopted land.

As he reread the personal news at the end of the letter, Roger became aware of a sharp prick of anxiety mingled with excitement. "Through this difficult time," Henry had written, "Marie has been as steadfast as any ancient heroine, supporting me with her love and understanding. I cannot tell you how often my spirit faltered when irresponsible orators like Desmoulins whipped the ignorant into a frenzied mob crying for blood, and when that blood was spilled, horribly. Many times I bade her take the children to you in England, but she perceived how very unwilling I was to part with her and them. Leonie and François also set up a terrible protest and begged me not to force them to leave their country in her hour of trial.

"Now that all is over," the letter continued, "I am glad I did not permit my fears for their safety to overpower me. They would never have forgiven me, I think, if I had deprived them of this experience, of seeing the creation of a great new nation, dedicated to the right of all men to be free and equal. In any case, we are all perfectly safe now. My work is done and I have been freed to return to a quiet private life. There is no chance that I will be called upon to meddle with the government of France again. It was agreed that we of the National Assembly could not succeed ourselves. No deputy to the National Assembly is eligible to be elected to the Legislative Assembly that will soon convene."

It was obvious to Roger that Henry had guessed wrong. They had not been safe. Had things gone as de Conyers expected, he surely would have responded in some way to Compton's news. The lack of response could only mean that he—that the whole family—was dead, driven into hiding, or perhaps imprisoned. Whatever had happened had obviously happened to the whole family; if Henry had been accused of some political crime and imprisoned or even executed, his wife Marie would have responded to Compton's letters. Thus, the strongest possibility seemed to be that the family had been threatened or attacked and driven from their home. In that case, de Conyers would never have received Compton's letters.

Roger laid down the letter he had been reading and chewed gently on his lip as he reflected. It was odd that if Henry had been driven off his estate, he had not made his way to England. Perhaps he had not had sufficient money. He could have been afraid to stay in one place long enough to receive an answer to an appeal for help from England. Even so, would Henry not have written and requested funds to be sent to a place where he could pick them up? France was still in turmoil, but most of the banking houses were still functioning. In fact, Roger realized, Henry would not have needed a bank nor have needed to wait for help. An appeal to Lord Gower, the English ambassador, would have solved all his problems.

Excitement quickened Roger's breathing. The letter he had read had not been written by a fool or a coward. If Henry had not answered Compton or appealed for help from his family or the English embassy, it was because he could not. For some reason Roger did not bother to investigate, he would not believe that Henry and his entire family had been executed. He was, quite unreasonably, sure that they were under house arrest or restrained in some other way from communicating with their friends. An unholy light came into Roger's bright blue eyes.

Compton cleared his throat uncomfortably. Long years as a man of business for aristocratic families had given him a quick recognition of a "gentleman" about to indulge his fancy. What threw him off balance was the unexpectedness of seeing such an expression on the face of Roger St. Eyre.

"Mr. St. Eyre," Compton protested faintly.

Roger raised one peaked brow. Compton cleared his throat again. He had seen that expression reduce witnesses, juries, and sometimes even judges to stammering incoherence. It bespoke more than seven hundred years of uncontested "getting their own way" for the St. Eyres—a habit this particular scion of the stock was not about to change. Compton had no quarrel with Roger's ability to quell witnesses, jurors, and judges. It was one of the reasons he, as a solicitor, had briefed Roger to try difficult cases before recalcitrant justices. In fact, Compton knew Roger only as a staid, sober, and remarkably clever barrister—which was why he had been so shocked at the devilish mischief that had shone in his eyes a few moments earlier.

"My father has empowered me to look into the matter of the present whereabouts of the Earl of Stour," he said. "Do you have some objection to that, Mr. Compton?"

The voice was all it should be, rich, smooth, with just the faintest hint of surprised arrogance; the face was grave enough to convince anyone of the sobriety and reasonableness of Roger's character. Only the glint in the eye betrayed the inner emotions—a mixture of laughter and excitement. Compton looked into those brilliant eyes and shook his head. He had not risen to his present affluence and influence by being faint of heart.

"None, sir," he replied with asperity, "unless it results in finding that you, as well as his lordship, have disappeared."

A remarkably astute individual, Roger thought, stiffening just a trifle. Then the humor of the situation struck him, and he smiled. "You have a choice of me or my father," he said wryly.

Compton goggled. "Your father? Surely Sir Joseph would not consider . . . Good God! But how could he even think . . . The fatigues of such a journey at such a time . . . the . . ."

"Yes, you perceive the difficulties, but, unfortunately, Sir Joseph does not." The light in Roger's eyes grew brighter, and Compton had a horrible notion that Sir Joseph's would look just the same. "He says," Roger continued, "that, having lived so long, it is unlikely a little exertion will kill him and that he does not wish to see Stour's land fall into decay while the inheritance is in the courts."

"Neither do I," Compton snapped, "but I do not see that it will help to have me—or you, or Sir Joseph—swallowed up in France too. The area must be in considerable disorder. I wrote to the Honorable Henry's—I mean the present earl's—solicitors in Saulieu, and received no reply from them either."

Roger nodded. "I suspected as much. I didn't suppose you would overlook so obvious a move. That is why I don't propose to attempt to find him through my usual French correspondents. Since I have nothing immediately in hand and the long vacation is just about upon us, I feel this is a peculiarly propitious time to investigate the matter personally." Roger saw the objections forming on Compton's lips and rose to his feet. "There is really no sense in arguing about the matter. Either I go or we remain in ignorance—and my father will not accept the latter course."

"We could send someone else," Compton said dryly. "There are—"

"No," Roger interrupted firmly. "A junior clerk in your office perhaps? Don't talk nonsense. Such a person would know neither enough French nor enough about France and would not be the slightest use. And please have the goodness to call off any enquiry agents you have hired, if you have hired any. It would be asking for trouble to have anyone openly looking for Stour under what I fear are the present circumstances."

"Fortunately I haven't gone so far," Compton said, tacitly agreeing that if Roger were to go, the less interest shown in Henry's whereabouts the better. "I intended to suggest that method of approach to your father and obtain his approval for hiring such agents. I still believe——"

"No," Roger interrupted again. "Such men are either stupid or unfitted for an enquiry in a foreign country. If Stour and his family are still alive and in the area, I fear that they are under restraint and circumspection will be necessary to free them."

"I fear so too," Compton said a little grimly. Then he sighed. "Mr. St. Eyre, I think what you are doing is very unwise from your own point of view, very dangerous, but there is nothing I can do to stop you. From my point of view—if I can't dissuade you from taking such a risk—I can only be most grateful."

On that pleasant note they parted. Roger could have repaired to his club for a leisurely and elegant luncheon and a chat with his friends, but he was seized with a restless energy that drove him to quite uncharacteristic activity. The rest of the day was remarkably busy. Roger settled all the unfinished business that he could and committed the remainder to the hands of a competent associate. At least, he hoped he had settled his business, because his mind was half on Henry de Conyers. By the time he was ready to inform the clerk of his chambers that he would be away for a while—something the young man had already guessed without difficulty—Roger had a full plan of action outlined.

His next move was to visit his banker, where his request produced knowing glances and a slight puzzlement. Had the high-level gentleman Roger dealt with any idea that the sum he drew was for himself, he might have had to endure some protests. Roger was a valued client, nearly a friend, and an attempt like Compton's might have been made to save him from himself. However, Roger's banker was well-accustomed to obtaining funds in foreign currencies for him rapidly. The banker was a little puzzled only because he had heard of no current scandal and no one who needed to leave the country in quiet haste. The only hesitation was caused by Roger's demand for gold and silver. It would take time to gather the coin, Roger was told,

but he might have it late that afternoon or in the early
evening.

From the bank Roger hailed a hackney and told his
groom to take his own curricle and horses back to the stable. He had driven himself, expecting to need to transport
the chests of money, but he did not want to fret his excellent team by the start-and-stop pattern his next move
would entail. Roger realized that for a stranger to come
into a relatively small town in France and stay there would
require some explanation. In ordinary times it would have
been enough to say he was an English tourist—but these
were not ordinary times. An itinerant tradesman would be
the least remarkable figure. Since Roger knew nothing
about any trade at all, he had at first dismissed this notion.
Then it returned to him. He knew guns! Not only was he
an excellent shot but he had always been fascinated by the
mechanisms themselves. He could be an itinerant gunsmith! All he needed was stock.

The rest of the afternoon was spent on a round of the
major gunsmiths' shops, where Roger's purchases did raise
protests. Some protested he was stripping them clean of
parts, which were hard to obtain; others wanted to know,
laughing, whether he intended to set up a shop in competi-
tion. Finally, however, Roger accumulated what he felt
would be an adequate stock in trade—as many old and
foreign weapons as he could obtain together with a few
newer but worn pieces.

Finally, having returned to his chambers, Roger wrote
his father a full account of what he intended to do. It erred
a trifle on the side of lightly dismissing all the problems
involved and presenting the expedition in the vein of a
long-needed holiday. The odd thing was that Roger was not
intentionally deceiving Sir Joseph. No matter how he tried
to curb himself with a mental recital of the difficulties and
dangers he would be facing, Roger *felt* as if he were going
on holiday. His letter was a very accurate rendition of his
own feelings.

The sensation of having cast off a heavy load, of being
free and light, was so strong as to be irresistible. Although
it was already very late in the day when two small but
heavy strongboxes were delivered from the banker to Roger's chambers, he did not lock them in his safe and go to
his club as he had fully intended. He was aware that he

would be unable to make ordinary conversation. Either he would be too silent, inducing his friends to exhaust their inventiveness—which was considerable—in efforts to entertain him and make him forget his bereavement, or he would talk about his plans, which would be even worse. Half his cronies would insist on accompanying him and the other half would try to argue him out of going.

The solution that accorded best with Roger's mood was an instant escape. He had his curricle brought around and the strongboxes loaded. If he grew tired, he could stop at a posting house on the way; if not, he could drive through the night. It was cool and clear and the moon would be almost full.

The impulse was most fortunate. When Roger arrived at his own estate, Dymchurch House, he found that Pierre had actually been in the alehouse at Kingsdown when the groom had brought the message and had sailed his *chasse-marée* around the next day. He had discharged his cargo earlier and was anchored openly in a nearby harbor, his men ostentatiously making minor repairs. It had been an odd chance, Pierre told Roger at dawn the next day, but he had thought it worthwhile to stop because he did not expect to be back in England for several weeks. Cargoes were getting harder and harder to come by, he complained bitterly. The whole country seemed to be going mad.

"I did not care what those lunatics in Paris did," Pierre growled disgustedly. "Men are men and it seemed to me that as many bottles and kegs would get by the town communes as got by the king's agents."

"Perhaps the town officials are more vigilant or more afraid to take a little bribe," Roger suggested, concealing his amusement.

"It is worse than that," Pierre groaned. "All this talk of equality and the rights of man has gone to the heads of those who can least afford it. Do you know what my supplier from La Rochelle told me?"

Roger shook his head, not wishing to spoil Pierre's story, although he had a fairly good idea of what Pierre would say.

"That idiot," the Frenchman continued, his voice rising with remembered fury, "refused to sell me anything unless I paid the tax! He said the taxes belonged to the people now, and he would not rob his fellow citizens as he had robbed the unjust king."

"Did you not try to explain that a large portion of the revenue still goes to support the throne?" Roger asked gravely, although his lips were twitching with suppressed mirth.

Pierre threw his hands out in a gesture of hopeless revulsion. "I told him that, and he answered me that the amount was now strictly controlled to provide enough magnificence for diplomatic purposes. Then I lost my patience and told him he would rob no one since, doubtless, the major part of the revenue found its way into the private pockets of officials—as it always had. That was a mistake. The madman grew quite furious. He actually flew to strike me, exclaiming that those elected by the people had the people's interest at heart and would not be corrupt as the king's officers were."

"Tsk, tsk," Roger rejoined, unable to command his voice for a longer expression of sympathy.

"If this continues," Pierre went on dispiritedly, "I will need to deal with dishonest men—and that is always a bad thing. One cannot—"

Unable to control himself any longer, Roger whooped with laughter. "Do you mean to say that you have dealt only with honest men all these years?" he choked.

Pierre looked at him with surprise. "Now and again, I suppose, there has been a thief or two mixed into the business, but I take good care to be rid of such men as soon as they betray themselves. Naturally I have dealt mostly with honest men."

"But you are *smugglers*," Roger said gently, as if he feared to shock Pierre with an unpleasant truth.

"That is not dishonest," Pierre protested indignantly, "that is only against the law. Do not talk like a lawyer, Roger. I pay honestly for my wares and charge an honest price for delivering them. I cheat no man. I can see no reason why my labor, or any other man's, should be taxed to support a king—or a commissioner either."

This was not the first time Roger and Pierre had had such a discussion, and Roger merely laughed again. He had given up hope of convincing Pierre that government had some really necessary functions and that the cost of those functions rested rightfully on those who benefited from them. Although he did not even know the word, Pierre was a confirmed anarchist, absolutely convinced that each man should govern and protect himself and that part of governing oneself was not taking overgreat advantage of those weaker than oneself. Roger freely admitted it was a good idea—so was true Christianity—but neither philosophy was workable, except for a very few people. The rest of the world needed laws, lawmakers, law enforcers, and judges to govern them.

Seeing Roger laugh, Pierre snorted with a mixture of irritation and good humor. He recognized that Roger had been teasing him. "Never mind your silliness," he said reprovingly. To Pierre, Roger was still "much younger," and he often spoke to him as if he were a boy. "I do not know how I let you drag me into this argument again. All I wanted to do was to tell you that my trips will be less frequent. I will try to leave word when I expect to be back—"

"No, don't do that. It would be dangerous for you. In any case there will be fewer passengers unless you sail to German ports. France isn't a safe haven these days."

Pierre sighed. "Idiots! If they did not like their king, did they have to make so much fuss to curb him or be rid of him?"

"*Their* king? You're a Frenchman also, Pierre."

"Not I!" Pierre exclaimed. "I am a *Breton*. I use their language—as I sometimes use yours—for convenience in business. But I am *not* French."

That time Roger did not smile. The Scots felt the same way and had tried to make the point stick with bloody results more than once. The Welsh, too, persistently regarded themselves as a separate people, although they had been tied to England for many hundreds of years. This was no joking matter, Roger realized, even though Pierre had never spoken of it before, and Roger valued Pierre's friendship too much to make a jest of deep feelings, no matter how impractical.

"As to the German ports," Pierre continued, going back to the concrete question, "I am not ready yet to use them, although I may be forced to. Sacred Heaven, I have already been forced to *sell* several catches of fish because I could not find cargo. I will end up as I started—a fisherman! It is not only France that has gone mad. Belgium is in an uproar too, what with the French troops marching in and the Austrians and Prussians driving the French out. I have not even been able to pick up any lace." He sighed again. "I cannot deny that your message was most welcome. I can use a passenger. Where does he want to go?"

"It is I," Roger replied with a smile, "and I'm not perfectly sure where I want to go."

"You! No, my friend. Do not tell me that *you* are fleeing your government, and as we said before, this is no time for a pleasure tour of France."

"You're quite right," Roger agreed. "I will not be touring for pleasure, and my quarrel isn't with *my* government but with yours—sorry, I mean that of the French."

"There is precious little government in France right now," Pierre remarked.

"I'm aware." It was Roger who sighed this time. Then he grinned. "For a man of my profession, there's much to be said for a strong, corrupt central government. It used to be necessary for my agent only to drop a word into the ear— and an appropriate bribe into the hand—of the right man to find someone or release a prisoner. Now I must go myself."

It was apparent that Pierre was about to protest. Roger forestalled him by describing the entire problem and his father's attitude. Having heard him out, Pierre shook his head with a jaundiced expression.

"In the words of your local people, that is a fine cock-and-bull story."

"I swear every word is true," Roger insisted.

"Oh, I believe that this Henry de Conyers is missing," Pierre replied, "and I believe that your father wishes him to be found or to have good evidence that he is dead, but that you must go . . . My friend, you have been too long quiet and assisting others to escape the results of 'raising the devil.' Is that how you say it? Now you wish to raise the devil yourself. No, do not shake your head at me. I know you too long and too well to believe your mouth. I look into your eyes and I see what I see. Only for that reason do I take you—because I know if I do not, you will go anyway. But it is dangerous, my friend, very dangerous, what you wish to do."

* * *

The same evening that Roger St. Eyre landed in France, Leonie de Conyers began her attempt to jolt her father out of the passive despair that had enveloped him since the death of his wife and son. She began simply enough by announcing that in a few days they were to be executed. Henry looked at her blankly for a while and then asked slowly why Leonie should suddenly say such a thing.

"It was the way Louis looked at me and spoke to me yesterday," Leonie replied. "Papa, we must escape or we will die."

"I, not you, my love," Henry answered soothingly, letting his eyes drift away from his daughter's face. "I must die. It would be better for you if I were dead. Perhaps your friend would find a way to free you. Perhaps Marot would let you go. No one could believe that you were an enemy of the state, and—I am the one he hates."

Leonie shook her head violently. She did not know how much her father guessed about her relationship with Louis, but he must not be permitted to convince himself that it could save her. Perhaps her father knew she was Louis's whore; perhaps he had accepted the knowledge for the sake of the few glasses of wine, the few saline draughts, the apple or two that Leonie had smuggled down to her sick mother and brother. Leonie hoped, however, that her father had been too shaken up with his wife's and son's illness and with his own sad reflections to think much about the matter. Hopefully, he thought Louis as innocent as his sweet face looked. If he did, it would save a lot of trouble.

"You know it is not so," Leonie protested. "Would Jean-Paul let me go to cry aloud the horrors he has committed? And as far as Louis, you know he could not let me go. That would mean his death as well as mine. He could not even run away with me. Where could we go that Jean-Paul would not find us? I know I must die," Leonie's voice shook, "but do not condemn me to live alone until then—and then die alone."

To Leonie's relief her father looked at her again much more alertly. His mind had been jerked out of the deadly rut it was traveling by his daughter's statement. Dull despair was thrust aside by rage. Leonie die too? Not without a struggle to prevent it! Henry had not considered escape previously. All four of them could never have managed, and no one would consent to leave the others, who would surely be tormented even more in punishment. Now, however, there was only one to escape. No one would be left behind, because Henry fully intended to die to free his daughter.

This noble resolve had to be reconsidered a moment later. Leonie had put her finger on the problem when she asked where she could go. Worse than that, how could a seventeen-year-old girl without family or friends survive in the France that his "noble" ideals had created? In the past . . . Henry wrenched his mind away from the past. It was dead . . . like François . . . like Marie. . . . The numbness of despair began to drift over him again. He wished to die. At least if he died here, there was a chance he would be buried in the same grave with Marie. Henry shuddered. It was not he alone who would die. Leonie was right. Jean-Paul would never let her go, and the young guard was nothing but a child. In any case, it was a father's duty to take care of his daughter; that was more important than his wish to die. It would be his punishment for not sending his wife and children to safety that he should be separated from Marie even in death.

"No," he said strongly, startling and delighting Leonie. "You will not die."

"Oh, Papa—" she began.

"No, no, listen," Henry urged, switching to English to avoid any chance of being overheard and understood. "Let's set aside the question of how you will escape for the moment. I have some ideas, but what you must know is where to go and what to do if we should become— separated."

Although the implications of that word were ugly, Leonie could not help smiling. The impetuous tone— always more pronounced when her father spoke English— carried her back to the days when Papa rode the high horse of his dreams and his wife mischievously unhorsed him from time to time with practical observations. Not that Henry came down without a struggle. He loved a discussion and would seek with great energy and ingenuity to find a way around the practical obstacles Marie presented. Because she was not certain of how to introduce the idea that she would be able to free them, Leonie fell into the old pattern.

"But Papa, you are putting the cart in front of the horse.

What difference does it make whether I have a place to go if I cannot get out?"

Leonie's English was clear, fluent, and idiomatic. Only the slightest accent and foreign intonation marked it as being a second language. Henry had always spoken English to his children. He had always insisted that they should visit his family. Somehow, it had never been the right time to go to England. The first years of his marriage had been devoted to restoring his wife's estates to profitable productivity. By the time he had things running smoothly on the land, Henry had seen that the government of France could not continue to exist as it was and had thrown himself into the agitation for reform and into practical measures for relieving the misery of the local population. Those efforts had made inevitable his election as deputy for the district in 1789—and then it was too late.

Henry smiled at her. "The way out is simple enough, child. When someone brings us food—it's always that young man these days—I'll jump on him from behind the door. I'm not as strong as I was, but I'm still stronger than that boy."

Leonie was not at all sure of that. The muscles in Louis's small body were whipcord and steel, and her father's were soft with inactivity and weak with starvation. However, she did not argue. Her plan was better and surer, but there was no harm in having a second string to one's bow. If Louis did not soon "take her for a walk," or if Louis should be sent away or denounced—Jean-Paul might be more aware of what Louis was than the thief believed—it might be necessary to use her father's plan. There was a good chance it would work, Leonie thought. Even after the first shock of seeing his wife and daughter raped had worn off, Papa had been docile for fear his loved ones would be punished for any rebellion on his part. And since Mama's death he had been little more than a limp body. Leonie was surprised at how well he responded to her prodding. She had feared she would be unable to rouse him, even though he had begun to eat and sit up without urging the day before.

"If we must," Leonie agreed tentatively. "I could help you. Between us . . . Very well, once out of the cell there can be no trouble getting out of the building. Usually no one except Louis is here after dark. There is a side door that is barred, which we can open from the inside." Louis had shown Leonie that door—a temptation to test whether she would try to escape while he "slept." "It is after that we will have trouble. The gates of the town are locked at night, and we certainly could not escape before dark. Also, by the next morning our absence will have been discovered."

"That's all true enough, but I daren't try to get help from friends in town. If they're not already prisoners, Jean-Paul's men will look first in those places. I think we can get over the wall."

"Over the wall!" Leonie looked with blank astonishment at her father. The walls of Saulieu were nearly ten meters high.

Henry grinned at his daughter, his face losing for the moment the haggard, defeated look it had worn for so long. "I've climbed cliffs three or four times as high, and smoother, but I don't expect you to be a monkey, my sweet. In the poor quarter, there are houses built right up against the wall. If I can find a rope, I can draw you up from a roof and let you down on the other side."

"But Papa," Leonie protested, "there might be guards on the wall. And what about the people that live in the houses? What will they think and do if they see us climbing roofs and walls? Will they not cry out that we are thieves?"

"There won't be guards on the wall. Why should there be? France may be at war in the north, but there's no present danger of invasion here. As to the people in the houses—in that part of the town we're more in danger of being stopped to share what we have stolen than of being reported to the authorities. If anyone questions us, we need only say we're escaping criminals—and surely we look the part. They'll likely help us." A bitter laugh shook him. "We'll not even have to lie. It's true. To those who rule now, we *are* criminals."

Leonie was a good deal less sure of this wall-climbing notion than of her father's previous idea. She had been hoping that her father would suggest a house in town where it would be safe to hide. Apparently he did not believe that would be possible. There had to be a better way than attempting to climb the wall.

"The offices of the civil guard are here in the Hôtel de Ville," Leonie suggested. "Perhaps we could write passes for ourselves so that the guards would let us out the gates?"

"That's a good idea," Henry agreed, "but I don't know the forms they use now or what excuse anyone except a messenger could have for leaving in the middle of the night. If we were decently dressed and had a horse and carriage . . . But for a man and woman afoot and in rags . . . No, Leonie, I don't think it will work. However, if we have time, we could try to find something. Perhaps there will be passes we could copy or even steal. Perhaps"—Henry's eyes brightened—"perhaps there will be *weapons* we could steal."

Henry was catching fire at the notion of action after such a long and bitter hopeless state. Leonie was delighted to see him "alive" again, but she did not wish to be swept away by his enthusiasm and hurled into a new trap. She could see that if they could obtain weapons, they could get through the gates by killing or threatening the guards. Well, that or over the wall; she would try anything, but to make their escape successful they would need money, and Leonie did not believe her father would steal. Louis had a few francs around, and she had every intention of taking those, but it was a very small sum. If Louis had more money, either it was not in his room or it was well hidden.

"If we cannot go to your friends," Leonie said, shelving for the moment the problem of how to pass the walls and raising the new idea that had hit her, "the question arises of how to live and how to get far enough away that Jean-Paul cannot seize us again. We will need money, Papa."

"Yes, and clothes and horses—but those can be bought with money. We have money, Leonie. There's money at the château."

Leonie caught her breath and looked aside. Did her father think the château would be as he left it? Did he think the peasants had not run amok over it as soon as he had been seized by Jean-Paul?

"No, my love," Henry said gently, seeing what she feared in her face. "I'm not living in a dream world of the past." His eyes shadowed. "Of course, if they have burned it to the ground . . . Well, let's hope part is still standing. There was a secret strong room just behind the chimney in the library—that would be the last place to go even if the château was set afire. The wall slides out from behind the mantelpiece. Even if they have burned and sacked the house, I don't believe they would have found that room."

That was probably true. Leonie herself had not known there was such a room. Seeing her surprise, her father smiled.

"I didn't tell you or François because your mother—" His voice wavered and the smile died, but he took a breath and continued steadily, "Your mother had this terrible fear that you might think it was a place to play and lock yourselves in in some way. It didn't seem important that you should know."

It was not. Nothing in the past was important, except the money—if it was there—and the danger involved in getting it. "The château is the worst place to go. They will be waiting for us there. Jean-Paul and his men will run to the château as soon as we are discovered missing."

"Possibly, but there's just as much chance they'll realize we must expect them to look there for us and, therefore, that we would go in the opposite direction. I don't dare hope they won't send someone to the château, but there's a good chance that they'll send only a few men, not surround the place in force so that we can't get in."

"And if they come after we are in? Will we not be trapped there, Papa?"

"If we can get in, they'll never find us. The château was built over a much older place. There are tunnels behind the cellars—oh, yes, you never knew of those either. Even I would never have allowed that until you were older. Those tunnels are dangerous—you can be lost in them, and they are old; sometimes something falls from the roofs. In this case, however, there's less danger in using them than avoiding them. Jean-Paul could search forever and not discover those passages. The only danger is that if they *knew* we were hidden there, they could starve us out."

At that, Leonie laughed mirthlessly. "They will have a long wait before that happens."

Her father smiled at her and nodded. "We know how to starve now, do we not, my love?"

CHAPTER 4

Despite Pierre's warnings, Roger found no danger at all in his first days in France. With Pierre's help, he was able to purchase a rather worn-looking carriage. The horse that was hitched to it looked little better, but that was a deception of the eyes. Under unkempt mane and uncurried coat was a strong body, and the gelding had a real turn for speed as well. Also through Pierre, Roger changed more of his English currency for a few assignats and low-denomination French coins, so that he would not draw attention to himself.

Altogether Roger's trip from St.-Valéry to Saulieu was uneventful. Sometimes he was recognized as an Englishman by his accent. Although relations between England and the "central government" in Paris were growing more and more strained, the people in the small towns through which he passed did not care about that. They were happy to accept his francs and sous and gave him accommodations in the inns, which were emptier than usual owing to the unrest in the country. He did not stop at any of the large towns, although he could not avoid going through Amiens. From there, however, he was able to travel south and west by lanes and byways, asking his way to Dijon.

That method had drawbacks as well as advantages. Roger lost himself quite thoroughly in the mountains and traveled nearly as far as Vesoul on a miserable rainy day, without even a light spot in the sky to show the sun's position, before he realized he was going in exactly the wrong direction. All in all, the two days this cost him did not turn out to be a total loss; when he deplored his mistake in going east instead of west, a fellow guest at the inn told him of a road a few kilometers south of Langres that would take him due west as far as Châtillon. There he took the

chance of inquiring for Saulieu and found to his relief that
he could get there without even entering Dijon.

Up until this time Roger had had no need to use the
cover he had devised. The guns and gun parts he had
brought with him rested quietly in the boxes in which they
had been packed. No one had seemed interested or curious
about why he was traveling. Those who recognized him
specifically as an Englishman dismissed him as another of
the lunatics who seemed to rush all over Europe with no
aim beyond the actual traveling. Those who just realized he
was a foreigner, without guessing from where, assumed he
was intent on getting back to his native land before the war
grew more intense and closed the borders. In Saulieu, however, Roger needed a reason to stay, at least until he could
discover what had happened to de Conyers.

Having taken up residence in a modest but decent inn
frequented by middle- to lower-class artisans, Roger
broached his purpose to the group assembled in the main
room the evening after his arrival. He liked Saulieu, he
stated, and he saw there was no gunsmith in town. Was
there a place where he could set up a temporary shop to
buy, sell, and mend until the town's needs were satisfied?

He was not really surprised at the surreptitious glances
the other men in the room cast at each other. He had
guessed that the town administration must be in a turmoil
and tyrannical to boot if a member of the National Assembly had been arrested.

The silence in response to Roger's question was growing
noticeable, and he had begun to raise his expressive eyes in
simulated surprise when the innkeeper cleared his throat
uneasily and agreed that Saulieu was a good place to live.
It was so near the mountains, he said, and yet sheltered so
that the climate was excellent. There was good fishing and
good hunting, now that the forest laws were repealed.

"Ah, well," Roger laughed, "if you go on, you will make
me wish to settle here, but I do not seem to be able to stay
long in one place, even when there is sufficient business.
However, one thing at a time. I must find a place to work
if I am to stay at all, for a man like me has little in reserve,
only enough for a few days' food and lodging until I can
begin to ply my trade."

There were uneasy glances again, but one of the men by
the bar said, "You should see Maître Foucalt, *numéro*

trois, rue Gambetta. He will know better than we."

Again eyes met briefly or were lowered. Roger noticed here and there a brief angry frown, but he remained deliberately blind, as if he were too intent on his own business to care about anything else. "And is it necessary for me to get permission from the Hôtel de Ville to set up shop?" he asked, seeming to pursue his purpose singlemindedly.

"Maître Foucalt will know best about that. We are all residents here and would not be affected by such a rule" was the reply given by one of those who had initially frowned at the naming of Maître Foucalt.

Roger let the subject drop, asking next about whether there would be a good market for guns in the town and listening to the responses with half an ear. He had no way of knowing whether he had been directed to a spy of the town rulers or to a man opposed to them, but he was not much concerned about that. He knew himself to be an acute judge of men and did not doubt that his story would deceive a spy while he would be able to obtain some notion of what to do next.

Accordingly, bright and early he took himself to the address and requested a few moments of Maître Foucalt's time. He was received promptly, almost with relief, as if a once-busy man now had not quite enough to do. After Roger had stated his problem, there were a few moments of cautious fencing. Then, suddenly, Maître Foucalt asked whether Roger was an Englishman. Roger was a little surprised. In this relatively small town buried in a mountainous region, it was unlikely that the people would have much contact with English travelers. However, Roger allowed that he had been born in England and asked blandly how Maître Foucalt had guessed his origin. The elderly man looked at him for a few seconds in silence.

"It is the way you say certain words," he replied slowly at last, his eyes fixed intently on Roger's face. Then his lips tightened, as if he had decided to take a chance on something. "It is the way Monsieur de Conyers spoke."

The mention of de Conyers's name was obviously an invitation. If Roger was what he claimed to be, he would show no more interest than a polite remark on the fact that there was another Englishman in the district. On the other hand, if he had come to look for de Conyers—and that

would not be so farfetched an idea to someone who knew
Henry, knew he was the son of a nobleman, and knew that
Henry could not have communicated with his family for
nearly five months—that was a deliberate opening for questions.

It was an opening that required an instant response. To
hesitate was as revealing as to display outright an interest
in de Conyers. Roger was almost certain that Maître Foucalt was no agent of the town tyrant. The eager way the
young clerk had welcomed "business" implied a recent
diminishment. Also, even before Roger's accent was recognized, Foucalt had implied that Saulieu was not a healthy
place to set up in business. He had not said anything that
could be taken as a criticism of the governing body (singu-
lar or plural) of the town, but he had suggested subtly that
there might be problems for an honest businessman. Still,
after ten years of practicing law, Roger was innately cautious.

"Ah," he said at once, "you have an English resident in
the town. Englishmen are often interested in guns. Perhaps
I could do a little business even if, as you suggest, this
would not be a profitable place to stay."

That gave Roger his answer. There was such a look of
disappointment, of a last hope lost on the suddenly lined
and sorrowful face of the advocate, that Roger could no
longer doubt him.

"No," Maître Foucalt sighed, "he is no longer resident.
Ah, well, I am sorry—"

"Is Henry de Conyers still alive?" Roger asked, inter-
rupting what was obviously going to be a polite farewell.

Maître Foucalt's face grew sharp. "*Henry* de Conyers,"
he breathed.

He had not given the first name. Then this man,
whoever he was, must have come to look for de Conyers.
There was no question that he was a stranger to the town
and even to the district. Thus, almost certainly, he was not
a henchman of Jean-Paul Marot. Besides, Maître Foucalt
thought bitterly, since he himself was the only one who
could be implicated by this conversation, it did not matter.
His life was over anyway.

"I do not know whether he is still alive," Maître Foucalt
said quickly, his voice lowered. "The last time anyone saw
him was early in July." He related quickly the events that

had taken place—the take-over of the town by Marot, the imprisonment of de Conyers and his family (although Foucalt was unaware of the horrors that had accompanied the imprisonment), and the periodic display of Henry. "But," he concluded, "no one has seen him for about six weeks. It may be . . ."

"No," Roger replied briskly, "there is no sense in killing him secretly after all this time, if that is what you fear. It is possible that some or all of them are dead," he added more slowly. "Perhaps they fell ill. Prisoners tend to lose heart and are victims to disease."

"There is only one physician," Maître Foucalt remarked. "Do you not think . . ."

"Perhaps the physician was told to keep the matter quiet," Roger began. He saw from the fleeting expression on the advocate's face that if the physician had been summoned to attend de Conyers, he would have mentioned it, whatever he had been told. "It is also possible," he continued, "that the conditions under which Monsieur de Conyers is kept do not accord with the appearance given when he was displayed. From what you told me, it seems as if the man Marot had some personal grudge against—"

"That is so," Foucalt interrupted, "but at first he had such power—we were all so . . . so . . . If he wanted monsieur dead, why did he not have him executed? No one could have opposed him then."

"Then!" Roger picked that up. "And now it is different?"

Maître Foucalt's face closed and suspicion flashed in his eyes. Roger shook his head and raised a hand defensively. "No, I am not asking you to tell me anything that could harm anyone or betray any plan. I do not wish to know anything beyond what any man in the street would know. Remember, I am a stranger in the town. I know nothing at all."

Such information Maître Foucalt was willing to give. He described the disagreements within the ranks of Marot's followers with considerable relish. Roger noticed the man said nothing of the attitude of the upper bourgeoisie, but he did not ask about it. It was clear without being told that they would be opposed to the rule of such creatures as Marot's followers. Roger also guessed that they might be organizing a counter take-over from Foucalt's expression when the doctor was mentioned, but a moment's thought made him realize that such an action would be of no use to him.

The trouble with actions planned by responsible members of society was that they planned, and planned, and planned. It was all too likely that no action would ever be taken or that, through so much discussion, news of what they intended would come to the ears of their enemies. Even if they managed to keep their secret and actually brought themselves to act, the coup might fail. Then, Roger thought, he would be far worse off. Doubtless a torrent of blood would flow in revenge, and Henry's—if he were still alive—would be among the first to be spilled.

The best hope, Roger decided as he listened to Maître Foucalt, was to find a weak link in Marot's own chain of command. Perhaps a jailer could be bribed. . . . Roger interrupted the flow of Foucalt's narrative to ask where the prison was and whether the jailers were as venal as the usual run of such men. If so, Roger added, he might have the means to bribe one of them.

"De Conyers is not in jail. He is in the Hôtel de Ville," Foucalt replied. "I am not sure whether Marot did that to depress criticism—you must understand that Monsieur de Conyers was greatly loved and respected by many—or whether he did it for greater security. All we have discovered is that there are special guards, men who are, we believe, particularly devoted to Marot. You understand it is very dangerous to seem to be interested in Monsieur de Conyers, but I will try to find out which men guard him."

"That would be a great help," Roger agreed, but he felt dissatisfied.

It was not that he doubted Maître Foucalt's sincerity; he simply felt the need to be doing something himself rather than sit in a mock gunsmith's shop and wait for information. For years Roger had done just that—sit in his chambers reading about the actions of other people. He had worked hard, driven on through boredom and fatigue by the knowledge that each fee he received would prevent one argument with Solange. Now the old man of the mountains was off his back; he felt light as a feather, as eager for action as a boy. With an effort Roger kept his face sober. It would not do to make Maître Foucalt think he was a lunatic by suddenly laughing for no reason. Still, Roger felt like laughing. Pierre was right after all, Roger admitted to himself He did wish to "raise the devil," instead of only hearing about others doing it.

"This hatred Marot has for de Conyers," Roger said, having been struck by an idea, "does this carry over to all Englishmen?"

"Not at all," Foucalt replied readily. "In fact, it is just the opposite."

He then mentioned Marot's devotion to the ideas of Jean-Paul Marat and said that Marot often molded his actions and policies on the arguments in the *Ami du Peuple*. Roger whistled softly. He had seen some copies of that incendiary paper recently, and the passionate diatribes against the representatives of the National Assembly and against the landed aristocracy of France boded no good for Henry and his family. However, Marat had been an admirer of the English form of constitutional monarchy, and he had been treated with courtesy both times he fled to England to escape imprisonment. Marat was all for friendship with the English and was—one of his sensible attitudes—opposed to war altogether. The local tyrant, Foucalt said, followed faithfully his Parisian mentor's ideas on those subjects.

"Very good," Roger remarked with enthusiasm. "Then it would not be unsafe for me to go to the Hôtel de Ville and ask permission to set up a shop here? I would like to see the building with my own eyes and talk with some of Marot's men."

Foucalt again examined his guest closely, suspicion reawakened. However, a short reflection pointed out that there would have been nothing to stop Roger from going to see Marot secretly; there was no need for him to say he was going. Besides, a mental review of what had been said convinced Foucalt that no one but himself could be endangered, even if Roger was in league with Marot.

"I think it would be safe enough for you. The worst danger would be that Marot's henchmen might seize your stock of guns without informing him. It is not likely that Marot himself would do such a thing. He is not a greedy man, you know, only bitter and warped. That is the worst of what the *ancien régime* has done to us—turned such men, men with good ideas and what might have been noble purposes—into bloodthirsty monsters."

* * *

The high hopes that Leonie and Henry had for escaping had dimmed steadily throughout the week following their discussion. No opportunity was granted them to put either plan into action. Louis did not take Leonie to his bed and, far worse, she had not even been able to induce him to enter the cell when he brought food. The first time he simply thrust the soup and bread into her hands through the narrowest opening possible, Leonie thought little of it. Louis had done it many times before. She suspected he had more than one set of irons in the fire.

She had made no protest and no attempt to draw him into the cell. Although her father was behind the door ready to act if Louis should come in, Leonie was not at all eager to try so dangerous an expedient. She had not told Henry of her own plan. She hoped to be able to convince him that Louis had given her the keys or she had stolen them without confessing openly that she was the thief's mistress. To avoid raising this issue, she had pointed out to her father that he was weak from long inactivity. A few days of exercise could not cure that completely, but it would be of some help.

Henry agreed and began to try to strengthen himself. Leonie was well satisfied. Her father would feel he was doing something—and actually he was, because he would need strength to escape—while she would get him out in her own way in a day or two. But two days passed and then three, and still Louis did not come for her at night. On the fourth day, when he handed in the food, Leonie spoke his name softly.

"Are you angry for some—" she began.

But he did not let her finish, merely shook his head sharply and closed and relocked the door. Fear leaped up and tightened Leonie's throat. Had they been condemned already? Could someone have overheard her father and herself planning? No, they had always spoken in English, but that in itself could betray that they were planning something. Leonie strained to remember whether the cell had ever been dimmer than usual, indicating that someone was listening at the half-window and blocking the light, but she could not recall anything like that. Perhaps she had somehow betrayed her thoughts to Louis? But he never paid enough attention to her to notice even what she wanted him to notice. Leonie bit her lip. It was far more likely, really, that Louis had outsmarted himself and suspected *he* might be in trouble. If so, his first move would be to show marked severity toward the prisoners.

Immediate panic subsided as Leonie squatted down beside her father and broke the bread in half. The bread was fresh! She bent to sniff the soup—an act she normally avoided as much as possible. Not only was the aroma appetizing but what was in the bowl was thick, more like stew than soup. For an instant, panic returned. Was this the last meal? In the next instant, Leonie nearly laughed. That Marot should order such a kindness was impossible. But that Louis should think of so considerate a gesture was equally impossible. Louis would be far more likely to omit giving them any meat at all the night before they were going to die on the principle that feeding them at such a time would be wasteful.

"How good this is, Papa," Leonie remarked. She wanted her father's opinion but did not wish to infect him with her fears and doubts.

"Yes. So was yesterday's food. Didn't you notice?"

"No," Leonie said, much surprised. How could she have failed to notice something like that?

"I mentioned it to you, and you agreed. You must have forgotten." Henry sounded troubled.

Leonie laughed. "I do remember now. I was thinking of something else yesterday."

Of course, yesterday had been the day she was sure Louis would take her to his bed. Leonie had been so tense and excited, planning and replanning every move that she would need to make that she could have eaten stones without noticing. She did remember her father talking to her during supper, but her replies had been automatic. But if the food had been good last night also . . .

"I wonder why?" Leonie breathed.

"I am sure the poor man does his best to get us a decent meal whenever he can," Henry answered, obviously surprised by Leonie's reaction.

Leonie did not contest her father's statement, although she knew he was mistaken. "Perhaps he does," she said mendaciously, "but why is it suddenly possible for him to give us a really excellent stew two days in a row? That was never possible before."

Henry thought that over and shook his head. "I cannot

guess, unless my friends in town have given him money so that he can buy good food for us. Perhaps they were afraid to approach him before, or were in prison themselves, or did not know we were in need of help. . . ."

Leonie bit her lip. She could not say to her father that if anyone had given Louis money to feed them he would have put it into his pocket without a second thought. There had to be a reason. At least, she thought, soaking up the last of her share of the gravy with her last piece of bread, she did not need to worry about this being the "last" meal. Quite aside from Louis's character, two last meals in succession were not likely.

In fact, Henry had come closer to the truth than Leonie. Louis had, indeed, been paid to feed Henry and Leonie well, and the reason he did not pocket the money as Leonie believed he would was because he wished to be sure Leonie and her father would be strong enough to serve his purpose. He was not quite such a cold-hearted monster as Leonie, in her bitterness, suspected. It was true he would not endanger himself for her, nor would he have hesitated to sacrifice her if that was the only way to accomplish his ends. However, when an opportunity came up to get what he wanted *and* possibly do Leonie a good turn, he was not averse to doing it that way. Leonie and Henry were being fed so that they would be strong enough to escape. Since Louis had every intention of protecting himself by sounding the alarm for the civil guard, there would be considerable running and hiding if the prisoners were to get away. Louis preferred that they get clean away, because he knew Marot would then concentrate—to the exclusion of everything else—on getting them back. This would accomplish the double purpose of making Jean-Paul blind to what Louis was doing and of making his behavior even more obnoxious to the people of the town.

Louis had gotten involved partly because he was always on the lookout for a situation he could turn to his own use, and partly by pure accident. On the afternoon of his discussion with Maître Foucalt, Roger had gone to the Hôtel de Ville and made inquiries about setting up a business. His request had been greeted with surprise and suspicion, which Roger did not mind at all because it resulted in his being passed from one person to the other. Each clerk was afraid to admit that he did not know whether permission was needed; nor was anyone willing to accept the responsibility of giving permission.

The discussion and cross-checking took so much time that Louis had appeared on the scene ready to close and check the offices before anyone had gone home. His strong, if unofficial, influence with Marot was known, and he had been asked for his opinion on the subject of Roger's case. Roger's surprise had been masked at once behind lowered eyelids. Petty officials are too status-conscious to ask the opinion of a building janitor or night watchman. Ergo, Louis was more than he seemed, and from the repeated use of Marot's name, Roger deduced that Louis had the ear of the town's revolutionary leader.

Most reasonably, Louis had disclaimed all knowledge. Roger had flashed a bright blue glance at him while Louis was talking to one of the clerks. A very young man to . . . No. There were little lines at the corners of the eyes and mouth that told a different story. A second part of the story was told by Louis's manner. There was no arrogance; he was pleasant and affable, even to the least and most pompous of the clerks. Clever, very clever, Roger had concluded. More information could be deduced from the attitude of the clerks. They feared Marot, but they liked Louis and did not fear him. Thus, Louis did not act the spy for Marot, at least not among the office personnel or not obviously. Now all Roger had to know was whether Louis was a faithful dog, a true worshipper of his leader, or a clever, ambitious devil.

By the next afternoon when Roger returned, he found his problem had been solved by a direct application to Marot. An honest tradesman was always welcome in Saulieu, he was told. He need only pay the same *taille* as any other artisan and he could set up quarters anywhere he liked. Roger paid with thanks, offering an assignat. It was accepted, but with a frown that showed how little faith the people had in their own government's currency. Roger smiled to himself. He had a better use for his gold and silver than paying French taxes—and that way, he hoped, was approaching at that very moment. Roger smiled at Louis, who had just come into the room, and asked if he would have a drink with him.

Louis was clever, but Roger was much cleverer, with years of experience in reading and outwitting men long

used to the high-level chicanery called "legal practice." As
Louis had played Jean-Paul, Roger now played Louis. He
was not afraid Louis would detect this, because he was offering just what Louis wanted in just the way Louis expected it to be offered—hedged around with safeguards to
prevent Louis from betraying Roger. The safeguards,
Roger assumed, were necessary; however, the main reason
Roger insisted so strongly on them was to convince Louis
that *he* was the one who was safe, the one with the upper
hand, that it was Roger who felt insecure.

Nonetheless, Roger was not completely successful. He
still believed that he might be able to free de Conyers, but
after the briefest conversation it was immediately clear that
he would not be able to induce Louis to allow Henry and
his daughter—Roger learned at once that Marie and the
young son were dead—to escape. Louis had ambitions beyond simple greed, and he was wise enough to know Saulieu was the only place these were likely to be fulfilled.
However, in veiled terms he indicated that there were ways
an escape could be "arranged" that could not be traced to
him.

That very night, well and ostentatiously armed, Roger
went to a wineshop in a section of the town that should
have been unknown to an honest artisan. His tailor would
have been appalled at the set of his coat, which was badly
distorted by the weight of gold rouleaux in one inner
pocket and a fine Lorenzoni pistol in the other. A second
pistol could be seen projecting from the top of Roger's right
boot, and a serviceable rapier, with a worn grip that spoke
silently of considerable use, hung at his hip.

Fortunately, he did not need the armament nor to drink
much of the execrable wine served. He was joined almost
as soon as he seated himself by an elderly man, decently
dressed—in which he differed drastically from everyone in
the place except Roger—but with the hardest eyes Roger
had ever seen. For a moment, Roger wondered whether
what he planned to accomplish was worth the agony he
might let loose on Saulieu. Were the lives of Henry de Conyers and his daughter of greater value than the others that
might be lost? Roger knew that once the plan was set in
motion there would be no way to stop it.

He had little time to worry. The man who faced him had

no fears about betrayal. Had the authorities the power to
take him, it would have been done long ago. He had his
own methods for ensuring his safety. He did not need to
deal in circumlocutions, therefore, and came to the point as
soon as he had made certain of Roger's identity.

"Louis le Bébé says you want a mob to break into the
Hôtel de Ville. That will be costly, very, very costly."

"That was not what I said, *patron*," Roger rejoined. He
had been told it was unhealthy to ask the name of the man
with whom he was to deal and that he should call him
patron, that is, "boss." "What I said," Roger continued,
"was that I wanted Henry de Conyers and his daughter.
The mob was Louis's idea. And I do not see why it should
be expensive. It should not cost much to incite a few
rabble-rousers to preach violence."

The old man smiled a grim acknowledgment. "No, likely
I would not even need to pay those—but I do not want too
much violence in this town. Besides, there must be a rabble
to be roused. People do not suddenly take it into their
heads to rush through the streets at night. And in this
town, we cannot begin in advance to whip up the temper of
a mob. Marot would not stand for it. He is no believer in
freedom of speech. There has been unrest already, and the
civil guard was called out at once to quell it. If you are to
gain your purpose, there must be no sign ahead of time."

Roger considered, his face expressionless. He was certainly willing to pay if the *patron* could keep the violence
to a minimum. Besides, what he said was true. There
would be enough room for bargaining without contesting
the obvious. "There is another part to it," he said. "I want
the prisoners, and I want them outside the gate. I do not
care about the mob. If it can be done without any disturbance, that will please me just as well. When we come to a
price, I will pay the whole whether one man or a hundred
is involved."

The hard eyes stared at Roger, personal greed struggling
with foreknowledge. Finally the *patron* shook his head, but
he smiled again, this time with a certain respect for a clever
opponent-partner.

"Very well, the prisoners free of the Hôtel de Ville and
outside the gates. It would be easy enough to do without
the mob, but I must live in this town. Marot would sur-

round this whole quarter and burn us out if a thief unlocked the prison and a bribe found a way through the
gates."

Roger shrugged. "Suit yourself, but remember that I am
a stranger here without resources. What I have, I have. If
we can come to terms—good. If not, I have no way of
finding more money. I am an agent, doing a job, nothing
more."

"Ah." There was an expression of satisfaction on the
seamed and hardened face. The cold eyes flicked from the
pistol to the well-worn sword. It made sense now, and the
patron knew where he stood, which made him comfortable.
He had been concerned that he was dealing with some
high-born idiot who would have all kinds of scruples. However, everyone knew Monsieur de Conyers was a nobleman
in his own land. It was most reasonable that his family
should send an agent. Doubtless the man would strike as
good a bargain as he could get, hoping to keep whatever
was left for himself. But it was also true that there was a
limit to the money. For a moment the eyes fixed on Roger
went even colder.

Roger could feel a trickle of icy perspiration down his
back and hoped similar beads were not standing so boldly
on his face that they could be seen. Still, he managed to
shake his head and smile coldly.

"I am not a fool," he said softly. "The pistol in my
pocket is aimed at your belly under the table, *patron*. And
the money is not at my lodgings. It is not even in the
town." This was a flat lie, of course. The money was where
it had always been, under a clever false floor beneath the
seat of the carriage. Roger, however, was quite accustomed
to lying in a good cause. "You will get it quicker and easier
by doing your part honestly."

The hard eyes blinked. The tense moment passed. A
price was named. Roger shook his head, although he felt
considerable relief. He had brought a good sum of money,
but he had been considering simple bribery, not insurrection. The price named was beyond his ability to pay, but
not very much beyond it. They began to bargain in earnest.
In this Roger was somewhat less successful than he hoped.
The price came down a little, but not nearly as much as he
expected.

"If you do not have that much," the *patron* said at last,

plainly impatient, "I am wasting my time and you are wasting yours. I will not do it for less."

"I have it," Roger said, "but just. I must also get these people to England. We must eat and sleep."

"That is not my problem. There are ways to eat without money. Surely *un des coureurs de rue Bow* can arrange that."

Roger stared blankly and then began to laugh. It had taken him a moment to connect the French phrase with the Bow Street Runners, an organization devoted to restoring lost property, finding missing persons, and trapping criminals—for a price. He did not know whether to be insulted or flattered. The Runners were not, in general, of high repute. The men employed were usually little better than the criminals they dealt with. On the other hand, some of them were hard, clever men, and it was plain that the reputation of the organization was better abroad than in England. There had been a challenge rather than a sneer in the remark about living without money.

The laugh, of course, was unwise because it finished the bargaining. Probably it did not matter; the *patron* did not sound as if he were open to more bargaining anyway. Roger was concerned at how little money he would have, but he had his stock of guns. Once they were away from Saulieu, he could sell what he had. He turned his attention to the arrangements for delivering Henry and his daughter and paying the fee agreed upon. When the matter was settled, Roger suggested, with a smile in the direction of the gun he carried, that his companion escort him to a safer quarter of the town.

"Do you think I will take this matter in hand on your word alone?" the old man asked, his face getting harder and uglier. "What is this, a joke?"

"No, I had forgotten." That was the truth, although Roger did not expect to be believed. No matter, the "excuse" was in character for the role he was playing. He pulled the rouleaux of gold from his pocket and slid them across the table.

The rolls of coins were weighed in the *patron*'s hand briefly. "More," he said.

"Not a sou," Roger replied. He stretched out his hand toward the coins he had passed over. "Give them back, and we are quits. I will not bargain with you further, and in any case I did not bring any more. You will have the people in your hands. When I receive them in good condition, you will be paid. And I do not want more than the two men we agreed on to acccompany them. If more come to the appointed place, I will not be there, and you will never find the money."

"And if I bring out your people and come with only two men, what is to stop you from shooting us or handing over gilded lead? I want more."

Roger stood up. He was sweating again, and it took an effort to keep the hand that was showing steady. However, the bulge in his pocket made by his hand on his pistol was very apparent. "I am in business, and not the business of murder," he said angrily, wondering what he could say that would convince this man. "It is in my interest to get de Conyers back safe, because I will be richly paid if I return with him. Moreover, it is not my money. I do not care whether I pay it to you or return it. But once the money *is* paid, it is my neck that is in danger. I must have either the people or the gold in order to go back to England—and I have a family there. I will take no chances on this. I can explain losing what I gave you. I could not explain losing more. This, or nothing."

"You did not tell me you would be paid again when you had the people safe," the *patron* grumbled.

"It is no business of yours how I am paid," Roger said sharply to hide his relief.

The truth was that he had never thought of the subject, because of course there was no question of his being paid for anything he was doing now. However, the *patron* seemed to find all the problems that had been troubling him solved by the idea of future payment and promptly agreed to see Roger safely out of the area. It was only later, when he was having a brandy by the fire in his own room, that Roger understood and began to laugh. The *patron* believed he had driven so hard a bargain that Roger would have to cheat in order to make a profit. Roger had smothered his initial burst of laughter, and now he chuckled softly. This business was going to be a dead loss financially, even if Stour wished to repay the expenses. Still, Roger would not have missed it for the world. He could not remember having been so completely terrified as he had been while bargaining with the *patron* since his older brothers had told him ghost stories and then left him alone in the dark when he was four. There was nothing like a bout of knee-knocking, cold-sweat fear to make one appreciate the luxury of a good brandy and cheerful fire.

Then Roger frowned. He had forgotten one thing—one essential thing. How would he know the man and woman who were brought to him really came from the Hôtel de Ville and actually were Henry and Leonie de Conyers?

CHAPTER 5

By the end of the week, Leonie and her father had specu-
lated themselves into total, hopeless confusion. No matter
what Leonie did, she could neither get Louis into the cell
nor get herself out. Still, the food continued to be excellent
and real luxuries had appeared—a half-bottle of wine, a
small cheese, a packet of raisins. Henry believed that there
was going to be an insurrection that would overthrow Jean-
Paul Marot and return his friends to power. Louis must
have heard rumors about it, he told Leonie, and was now
trying to get on the good side of his prisoners.

That was not possible, Leonie argued. She did not give
her father very strong reasons to support her assertion because she did not wish to expose her knowledge of Louis's
character, but she had reasons. Louis might want to get rid
of Marot, but he certainly would not want the officials
Marot had overthrown back in power. No, rather than
that, Louis would warn Marot of the danger. The most logical reason for Louis's refusal to take Leonie out in his
usual way or even to talk to her was that he was under
suspicion. But that notion was directly contradicted by the
sudden excellent quality of the food. Nothing could explain
the food.

The tension was growing unbearable, and Leonie decided that she would have some answer that evening. As
she had become more insistent, Louis had become more
cautious. Now he did not even permit his hand inside the
door. He pushed the bowl and bread in halfway and then
began to release them. If Leonie did not grab them, the
food would spill on the floor. Louis was not taking the
chance of having his hand or wrist grabbed by a frantic
woman.

Leonie had cursed herself as soon as she realized what
Louis feared. She had not even thought of doing that, dolt

that she was. However, there are more ways than one of accomplishing any purpose. Leonie did not consider reaching out to grab Louis because she knew he was not at all beyond slamming the door on her arm and breaking it. Instead, she gathered some of the rotten straw they used as beds and bound it around one of her feet, about as wide as the food bowl. When Louis opened the door, she would thrust her protected foot through it and ask what was wrong.

Henry had wanted to grab the door, wrench it open, and attack Louis, but Leonie pointed out it would never work. She was not strong enough to pull the door open, nor was she strong enough to hold Louis. If papa did succeed in getting the door open, he would be in the wrong position. It was not late enough when Louis brought their food. There were still people in the building. Louis would only need to run up the stairs, close the door up there, and call for help. That would finish any chance of escape for them. On the other hand, if she blocked the door open with no sign of violence, Louis might come in or come closer to push her out of the way. Then they could grab him.

Only desperation induced Leonie to suggest such a scheme. She did not have much hope that it would work, but she did not think it could do much harm. Louis could hardly be more cautious than he was right now, no matter what they did. And it should be safe because the good food and delicacies suggested that no retribution would be taken. In any case, all Leonie's carefully laid plans went to waste. As the door opened, before she could thrust her foot into it, Louis whispered, "*Préparez-vous! Cette nuit! Votre père aussi!*"

While Leonie stood paralyzed with surprise, the bowl was pushed at her, followed by the bread and then— wonder of wonders—two hard sausages. Leonie nearly spilled the stew down her dress while she clutched the sausages to her breast. A hard sausage . . . "*Votre père aussi!*" . . . Hard sausage was the concentrated food the poor often carried on a journey. It was quite resistant to spoilage, only growing harder and more spicy with age. It could only mean one thing—escape.

"What did he say?" Henry asked eagerly.

"He said," Leonie repeated in English, "be ready. To-night. Your father, also—oh, Papa, perhaps you were right, at least partly. Perhaps there will be an attempt to free us. Look at this!" She thrust the sausage at Henry. "It can only be meant to sustain us while we hide. Papa—do you think? . . ."

"I do not know what to think," Henry said slowly. "I could have believed in a revolt against that monster Marot and being freed by my friends when he was finished. But Leonie, they are not—not adventurous or daring men, and most of them are considerably older than I. Can you see Maître Foucalt arranging an escape? Child, I fear—I fear this may be a trap."

Leonie swallowed hard. It must be so. This must be the excuse that Louis and Marot were arranging, so that she and her father could be condemned to death and executed. She looked down at the sausage in her hand and nearly threw it from her. That was just the clever kind of thing Louis would do to convince them. Leonie began to shake.

"No, Leonie," Henry said, taking her in his arms. "Do not be frightened. Think. In order to accuse us of escaping, they must let us seem to escape. Since we are forewarned, we will still manage to get away. Do not fear. Only be ready to seize an opportunity."

For Roger, who sat down to his dinner at about the same time, it had been a particularly quiet day. He had been briskly active on the three preceding days, inspecting premises that might be thought suitable to setting up a gunsmith's shop and going to Maître Foucalt's house on the pretense of consulting with him about rents and leases. At least, that was what the innkeeper assumed they talked about, because Roger was loud in his praise of Maître Foucalt's knowledge on these subjects. There could be no doubt either that Roger was a skilled gunsmith. Several men brought weapons to be repaired. After politely asking the innkeeper for permission to conduct business on his premises, Roger did a very creditable job, improvising very cleverly when he did not have the correct part for one gun.

The previous evening, as he came back from Maître Foucalt's house, where final arrangements had been made for insurance against treachery by the *patron*, Roger became aware that he was being watched. He was quite familiar with the sensation; several times Solange had taken it into her head that he had a regular mistress among the upper-class ladies and had determined to find out who it was. She did not care, of course, except that she hoped to be able to hurt Roger by embarrassing or making trouble for his mistress by exposing her.

In the past, Roger had been furious and disgusted. This time he was delighted. Either the *patron* was hoping he would go and collect his gold from wherever he had left it, or he was watching for the danger of betrayal. Whichever was true, the watcher was proof that the *patron* intended to get the rest of the money. Since there was no chance that Roger would betray the whereabouts of the gold, it was a sure bet that the raid on the Hôtel de Ville would take place.

Not wishing to rouse suspicion of any kind at the last minute, Roger stayed quietly at the inn all the next day. He spent some time writing a letter to his father, detailing what he had done and warning Sir Joseph not to worry if he did not hear from him again for a little while. He and the de Conyerses might need to hide until the worst of the fury over their escape had passed. He left it to Sir Joseph, he added, whether to show Philip the letter or not. He enclosed this letter in a cover addressed to Pierre Restoir. He would give it to Maître Foucalt's clerk, who was coming to "borrow" his horse and carriage. The clerk was to drive the vehicle out of town, conceal it at a nearby farm until after dark, and then drive back and wait near the western gate after dark. Henry and his daughter were to be brought there by the *patron* and his men, who would then follow Roger in another carriage to the place where the gold was "hidden."

The carriage was "borrowed" exactly on time, as Roger was called to dinner. He found himself as shaken and excited by this preliminary move as he had been when he discovered the smugglers in the cove. It was very difficult indeed to do calm justice to the meal set before him, but he managed. He had contrived to get food down without strangling on it and with a calm and indifferent expression while Solange was berating him at the top of her lungs at a dinner party. To eat while his heart was pounding with pleasurable excitement instead of sick rage and shame was not nearly so difficult.

Later, in the early evening, he engaged in his usual desultory conversation with the other customers of the inn. A traveler who bought wine had come on his way south. He began to regale the company with an eyewitness account of the massacre of the king's Swiss guard and the deposition of Louix XVI. This was apparently not news to the others in the inn, although they listened avidly to the details; but Roger, who had left England on the twelfth of August, had not heard it previously. The events had taken place, he realized, on the tenth, and the information had not come to England before he departed. Why he had not heard of it while he traveled south, he could only guess. Either the small towns he stopped at had not yet received word of the events, or the people there had been afraid to talk in front of a stranger.

A lawyer has considerable practice in maintaining an impassive expression, but Roger felt sick with horror. He was no fanatical upholder of monarchy, but he realized this had to be only a first step along a more desperate and ultimately bloody path. England had tried deposing kings; one had finally been executed and the other escaped that fate only by fleeing the country before he was taken. Deposed kings were not conducive to political peace. Even from France, James II had caused much trouble and several bloody battles. How much more trouble, how many more insurrections Louis XVI would cause—even if he did not encourage counterrevolution (which was scarcely believable)—was obvious. There would be no peace in France until Louis was either dead or restored.

"You look troubled, monsieur," one of the men who frequented the inn remarked. "Do you pity the king?"

"I pity myself," Roger said quickly, annoyed with himself for betraying more of his thoughts than he intended. "I am afraid there will be more violence and that it will spread to the countryside. I am an artisan, not an adventurer. I do not wish to be involved in these things."

As he spoke, Roger suddenly realized that his involuntary expression of distress and the excuse he used to cover it had been most fortunate. He began to express himself more and more freely on his disapprobation of violence. He had left Cambrai, he complained, because of the threat of war. Yes, business was good for a gunsmith so close to the Belgian border, but dead men could not enjoy profits. Then he began to wonder aloud whether there was any place in France that would be safe.

"If you are so frightened," the man who had asked why

he was troubled remarked disdainfully, "perhaps you had better go back to England."

Roger first looked at him as if he had turned green; then, slowly, he allowed his expression to change. "I had never thought of it," he exclaimed. "What a fool a man can be! One grows into a habit, a certain way of thinking, and it takes someone outside oneself to point out the obvious. Monsieur, you have done me a great service. Let me buy you a drink. Indeed, you are right! That is just what I will do. I will go back to England where I will be safe."

The result of this announcement was really comical. Roger had considerable difficulty in keeping himself from laughing, instead painting an expression of uncomprehending hurt on his face. The man to whom he had offered the drink refused it curtly. The rest of the company withdrew from him. Even the innkeeper, who had been very pleasant to so well-paying and uncomplaining a customer, grew very cold. Roger made one or two feeble attempts to rejoin the company, who now combined to shun a self-confessed "coward," and then he began to show signs of growing angry. At last, after seeming to seek to buy his way back into favor by offering to treat the whole group, and being refused, Roger stalked stormily over to the innkeeper.

"It seems that my custom is not appreciated here any more," he said angrily. "Very well. I can take a hint." He drew forth his purse. "I would leave tonight, only that I was fool enough to lend my horse and carriage to one of your fellow townsmen. Tell me what I owe. I will not trouble you even for breakfast."

In private the innkeeper would probably have changed his tune and tried to pacify so good a customer, but the eyes of the rest of the group were on him. He comforted himself with the consideration that Roger was about to move into a shop of his own in a few days anyway, and he coldly stated the charge. Roger paid and stamped angrily out, smothering his laughter until he was safely in his own room. Even then he laughed softly. It would not do to have the company guess how they had been used.

Perhaps the device would not save Roger from being associated with the raid on the Hôtel de Ville, but it might. After the sentiments he had announced that evening, no one would be in the least surprised at his disappearance after a mob attack on the center of town government. Since he had paid his bill, the innkeeper would not complain or seek for him. It might even be possible, if it was necessary, for Roger to return openly to Saulieu. He need only avoid the inn and its environs. That is, Roger amended his thoughts with a new spurt of excitement, it would be possible if no one noticed him among the "mob."

The next few hours were a terrible strain on Roger's nerves. It was necessary for him to seem to have gone to bed. He doused his light and sat still in the dark until the last of the company at the inn was gone and the innkeeper had locked up for the night. Another hour passed while Roger waited for the innkeeper and his wife and servants to clean up and go to bed. Then, boots in hand, he crept down the stairs, trying to remember everything Pierre had taught him about entering and leaving premises. He kept as close to the wall as possible as he went down the stairs, to prevent them from creaking, and, after he slipped through the window of the private parlor, he pulled it shut and wedged the two halves of the window together. It was not that Roger was worried about the inn being robbed. This night every thief would probably have something better to do. However, Roger did not want the window to bang open and wake the innkeeper. He would prefer if his absence was not noticed until the morning.

The wineshops in the disreputable neighborhood where Roger had made his arrangements with the *patron* naturally did not shut their doors and cork their bottles as early as the type of establishment patronized by hard-working tradesmen who had to wake early. In fact, all the wineshops were packed to the doors, and free-spending agents of the *patron* were making rounds through the crowds buying drinks and urging the drinkers to stay. They did not need much urging, because they had congregated in response to hints that had flown from mouth to mouth all through the day that something "good" was "on the fire."

While Roger was sitting in the dark, counting the long minutes as they dragged past, speakers appeared in the wineshops. Each of them complained bitterly of the results of the "revolution" in France and, particularly, in Saulieu.

"Are we not 'people' also?" the agitators cried. "Think of the promises made to the 'people.' Have we benefited in any way from these promises? No! I do not complain that we are still hunted and reviled—although we were promised that all men would be equal. But I say to you that we are worse off than before Jean-Paul Marot took this town into his power, and if he rules here much longer we will all starve. He has taken the wealth and power from those who had it, that is true. But what has happened to this wealth? Why, an honest thief cannot keep flesh upon his bones. There is nothing left to steal. The rich are poor; the tradesmen are poor. Only the town is rich."

Laughter and cheers hailed these speeches. The various agitators all used the same theme and all used the same reasoning. The *patron* did not want any blood thirst. He wanted no citizens torn apart, no heads mounted on pikes. The backlash from such a spate of violence would do him and his "employees" more harm than good. The *patron* had a double purpose: first, to fulfill his bargain with Roger and collect his fee; second, to discredit Jean-Paul Marot even further in the eyes of the townspeople.

Louis was not physically the son of the *patron,* but he was a son in spirit. If the young thief's plans worked out, the *patron* would enter into a liaison with the new town leader that would benefit both greatly. Those who did not pay their "dues" to the *patron* would be hunted and prosecuted and punished by the law itself. The gendarmes of the town would be the *patron*'s enforcers. On the other hand, if a particular crime caused a greater than usual outcry, the *patron* could and would furnish a "criminal" to be punished—even, possibly, the criminal who had committed the crime—so that the townspeople would feel secure in the efficacy of their leader at keeping them safe from crime.

Thus, the agitators did not attempt to awaken any real bitterness in those they addressed. They concentrated on inspiring them to raid the town treasury and take back "what was theirs." There was, in fact, a considerable sum in the strongboxes kept in the Hôtel de Ville, Louis had informed the *patron.* Marot had been collecting the money for such worthy purposes as founding a hospital for the poor and supporting Saulieu's home for foundlings as well as for purchasing better muskets for the civil guard. To some extent Louis approved of the last purpose, but in his opinion the first two were completely ridiculous. The money would be far more useful in his and the *patron*'s hands.

By midnight one group had been whipped up enough to pour out of the wineshop—half laughing, half drunk— roaring, "To the Hôtel de Ville! We will take what has been promised to us." The movement was totally contagious. From one wineshop to another the crowd rushed, gathering strength and purpose with each influx of men and women. Perhaps those who first rushed out into the dark were partly in jest, but their intention was firmed as the others joined and cheered them on.

Soon the crowd had filled the narrow crooked lanes of the lower town and began to rush up toward the wider streets and central square of the Hôtel de Ville. The *patron*'s men ran the flanks, encouraging those who wondered whether the plunder of a private home would not pay better—while the civil guard and gendarmes were busy at the Hôtel de Ville.

Somewhere along the way, a dark-garbed figure, face smeared with dirt out of which glinted two bright blue eyes, joined the moving mass. Roger was deeply impressed with the *patron*'s efficiency and joined in the cries and cheers with a good will. He had been concerned that the idea of looting rather than of looting a specific place might disperse the mob into parties that would commit outrages all over the town and not achieve the primary objective. This did not seem to be the case, however, although Roger's growing confidence in the *patron*'s management did not diminish the vigor with which he shouted, "The Hôtel de Ville! The Hôtel de Ville!"

It was marvelous to be able to shout, to push forward in the crowd. It was a release after the years of strict propriety, of the sober and stuffy behavior required of a responsible barrister. The past few days of growing tension had added to the seething under Roger's calm exterior. He yelled with a will, releasing just a little of his volcanic emotions.

By the time they reached the Hôtel de Ville, Roger was well up among the ringleaders. He was quite sure the *patron* would not expose himself to danger by being in the crowd, and the *patron* was the only man who could recognize him that was likely to be in this mob. There was a small chance that someone else who had been at the wineshop would recognize him, but Roger doubted it. It had been dark and the rest of the drinkers had stayed respectfully well away from the *patron* while he talked business. Besides, if he was a new member of the *patron*'s group, there was good reason for him to be in the mob without any particular association with the prisoners. It would be safe enough, Roger judged.

Safe or not, he was determined to be right there when Henry de Conyers and his daughter were released from the cellar. He was taking no chances that Louis and/or the *patron* would foist two "ringers" on him and then demand ransom for the genuine pair.

Roger had a few moments of renewed anxiety when the mob reached the large, brassbound doors of the Hôtel de Ville. The men and women were largely the dregs of the town—petty criminals, whores, hangers-on of all types. To them the Hôtel de Ville had an aura of awesomeness; it was the place to which they were dragged to hear what punishment would be inflicted for the crimes they had committed. There was, therefore, a hesitation. Roger prepared to leap forward and fling himself at the door to break the pause before the entire crowd thought better of what it was doing and slunk away. He had, however, underestimated the *patron*. Before he could, most unnecessarily, draw attention to himself, one of the agitators seized upon a sturdy bench set near the doors.

"Here," he cried, laughing. "Here is your key of entry."

Half a dozen men, with Roger among them, leaped forward to swing the improvised battering ram with a will. It did not seem to Roger that those huge doors would even be shaken by so puny a ram, but he was wrong again. For all their imposing height and large, ornate locks, the doors of the Hôtel de Ville were not meant for defense. The building was not the old donjon of the town; that had been abandoned more than a hundred years before because of its dark, damp discomfort. When this building had been constructed, no one considered needing to resist such an outrage as was now taking place. With the very first blow the doors shivered; with the next the lock groaned in the wood. Three more lusty swings and the brass tore its way free.

The doors were yanked open and the crowd poured in. Torches sprang alight. In a corner of his mind Roger again complimented the *patron*. Everything had been planned, and planned very well. Mostly, however, Roger was wondering how he was going to find Henry and his daughter. A desperate visual sweep of the area, just before it was filled to overflowing with the mob, showed him a small quiet figure standing in a plain undecorated doorway to the far right of the entry. The man who had offered the bench as a "key" now let out a whoop of triumph and called to the mob to wrest open the ornate doors to the offices.

"In one we will find what we seek," he assured them. "And, remember, it is to be shared among us all. We are brothers and sisters in misfortune."

He harangued for a few moments longer, the crowd pausing to listen to him, but Roger paid no more attention. His watchfulness was rewarded. Two men had very quietly detached themselves and were moving toward the silent figure nearly hidden in the shadow of the doorway. As quickly as possible Roger inched his way in that direction also. He was in time to see that the figure in the doorway was Louis—a strangely disfigured Louis. His hair and face were splotched with blood and his garments were torn, his shirt nearly in shreds.

There was no time to wonder about such signs of violence when no violence had taken place. Roger saw Louis hand one of the men a set of keys and melt away from the doorway into deeper shadow. The door was unlocked and the men went down a steep, unfinished flight of stairs. Roger followed quietly, not too closely, his hand on the pistol set at half-cock in his pocket. Once well down the stairs, one of the men paused to light the torch he carried. Roger stopped abruptly where he was and flattened himself against the wall, afraid of being revealed in the light; but neither man looked back.

They moved forward from the base of the stairs. Roger came down only a step or two farther. He found that if he crouched and peered down the stairs he could see what was happening. Farther along was another door with a heavy lock. One man was struggling with it and finally got it open. Roger could not hear the click of the latch because of the noise behind him, but he heard a girl's light voice, high with fear, cry, "Papa!"

"Courage, Leonie, courage," a man's deeper voice came.

Roger's heart jumped and began to pound even harder. The man had spoken English! This must be de Conyers. That there should be two Englishmen imprisoned in a town like Saulieu was virtually impossible.

"Come quickly!" one of the *patron*'s men urged. "Quickly! Quickly!"

"Remember what I told you, Leonie," Henry said firmly but still in English. "We are forewarned."

The man in the cell door stepped back, the other raised the torch a little higher to provide better light. Roger saw a man—gaunt, bearded, clothed in filthy rags. Immediately behind him came the girl, one hand stretched to touch her father as if she feared to be separated from him. She was a little less ragged, a little cleaner, so that Roger could make out her features clearly—and the face held him riveted for a long moment before he remembered how dangerous it would be for all of them for him to be caught. He backed hastily up the stairs, just before the man with the torch came into sight.

Beautiful! No, not really beautiful, Roger contradicted himself as he drew back farther into the shadows where Louis had disappeared. Not really beautiful, but . . . What am I thinking, Roger snarled to himself. I will not be caught by a pretty face again. Besides, she must be young enough to be my daughter. And then, just as the *patron*'s man emerged from the doorway to the cellar, the tocsin began to clamor from the belfry. Roger gasped a curse, and the crowd, which had been cheerfully engaged in looting the building, froze silent for a moment.

In the next moment a new and more urgent bedlam broke loose. Snatching at anything of value, the mob began to rush for the doors. The alarm bell would bring the civil guard. What had been an amusing adventure with a chance for loot had taken on the aspect of real danger. If the mob had been inspired by a desire for justice or revenge or political purpose, they might have stood their ground, barricaded the doors, and demanded to parlay. Since no such high ideas had animated them—only a desire to steal— they thought only of escaping.

To Roger, cursing luridly under his breath, the meaning of Louis's disheveled appearance was suddenly apparent. The little devil was saving his hide. Roger was far angrier with *himself* than with Louis. It should have been obvious from the beginning that Louis would need some defense. He was the night watch. If he did not intend to leave Saulieu forever, he needed a *good* excuse for not sounding the warning before the mob reached the Hôtel de Ville. Roger

could not guess what that excuse would be, but no doubt
Louis's bloodied and tattered condition would lend verisimilitude to what might otherwise be an unconvincing story.

Those thoughts flicked across Roger's brain only briefly.
The one really important aspect of what Louis had done, as
far as Roger was concerned, was how it would affect getting Leonie safely away. It did not occur to Roger at the
moment that it was Henry he had come to rescue or that it
was remarkable her name should come first into his mind.

He had looked away from the doorway for just an instant after the tocsin rang and the crowd reacted to the
warning. Now Roger's eyes swung back just in time to see
the *patron*'s man pitch forward as Henry pushed him violently from behind. Simultaneously the light in the stairwell
went out and a crash came as Leonie turned and shoved
the man behind her down the stairs. Meanwhile, Henry
had kicked his victim in the head hard enough to stun him
and turned to help his daughter. She needed no assistance
but bounded up the remaining stairs and slammed the door
behind her.

Shock at the mass of men and women struggling in the
exit was mirrored on both faces, but Leonie grasped her
father's hand and pulled him strongly toward the struggling
figures. "Let us mix with the crowd," she called. "It will be
harder to find us."

"No," Roger shouted. "Wait!"

But he was too late and could only force his way forward, keeping as close as possible. He had one advantage
at least. Although Leonie and her father were as dirty and
ragged as everyone else, Henry de Conyers's gray-blond
hair and Leonie's honey-gold mane gave him a way of following their progress in the generally dark-haired mob. He
pressed hard toward them, but did not attempt to call out
again. For one thing, he doubted he would be heard over
the shrieks and imprecations all around them; for another,
he did not wish to call out in English for fear of calling
attention to them.

Actually, it was not as difficult as it seemed it would be
to get right behind Henry and Leonie because, for a little
while, all forward movement in the crowd had stopped.
The panic and desire for escape had worked in their usual
fashion, turning the mob into a mindless mass that pushed
and shoved, jamming itself even more firmly together, until

so tight a plug of entangled people had formed that the doorway was completely blocked. Adding to the problem were those who had been caught behind the half-open doors and were pushing wildly at them in an effort to get to the opening.

Finally the pressure built up to such a degree that those in the opening were catapulted forward. The men in the center were flung down the stairs, a woman on the extreme side had one arm torn from her body because her shoulder had been pressed against the frame of the door. Screaming horribly, she staggered a few steps and also fell down the stairs, causing those who were pushed through after her to stumble and fall atop her. Another ten or fifteen forced their way out, trampling the fallen and injured before the crush formed a second plug. This broke somewhat more quickly, there being fewer pressing forward and thus less entanglement. So, by fits and starts, the mob that had broken into the Hôtel de Ville was breaking out of it.

Henry, Leonie, and Roger were near the back of the group. They were thus in considerably less danger of being knocked down and trampled, but by the time they reached the street, the civil guard was running from its quarters firing indiscriminately into the crowd. It was quite apparent there would be no attempt to round up the mob, nor was the firing intended to disperse them—they were dispersing as fast as they could already. The orders of the men must have been to kill as many as they could, presumably as a lesson to any other group that wished to protest. Roger leapt forward, seizing Leonie by the arm and interposing his body between the advancing civil guard and the girl.

First she uttered a shriek and then launched a vicious blow at Roger, which he barely managed to duck.

Henry swung around, his fists raised.

"For God's sake, de Conyers," Roger bellowed in English, "run! Don't fight me. I'm trying to help."

Whether Henry or Leonie really heard or understood what he said, Roger couldn't guess. The danger from the civil guard was now so apparent that it was obvious unless they got away into one of the side streets they would be killed. Both men pushed Leonie and urged her to run, Roger managing to steer them toward the west rather than the south where most of the crowd was headed. Leonie hardly needed their encouragement. The explosions of the muskets and the screams of fear and pain lent wings to her feet.

Just short of a dark alley, Henry de Conyers paused and exclaimed. Roger turned toward him, but he was already moving forward on his daughter's heels again. They traversed that alley and turned into another with the sounds of firing and anguish dimming behind them. Halfway down the second lane, however, Henry de Conyers faltered again, calling "Leonie." She stopped and turned, just in time to see Roger catch her father to prevent him from falling to the ground.

"Monster!" she shrieked, coming at Roger with hands curved into claws.

"No!" Henry gasped.

Simultaneously Roger said, "Miss de Conyers, I did your father no harm."

"Go ahead, Leonie," Henry cried. "Go ahead, my love. I am hit. I cannot keep up."

"I will help you, Papa. I will not leave you."

Roger would have liked to examine Henry and find out how badly he was hurt, but a new spate of shots and shrieks, sounding closer, warned that that might finish them all. Instead, he drew Henry's arm over his shoulder. Leonie seized Henry's other arm, and they ran forward again. For a while, Henry was able to keep to his feet with their support. However, by the time they reached the avenue leading to the western gate in the wall, he was nearly helpless. Roger took more and more of Henry's weight, but he could not support him completely with the grip he had. Soon Henry's feet were dragging limply behind them, and Leonie was staggering under the burden.

At least all sound of pursuit had died away. The mob instinctively headed for its accustomed hideouts in the thieves' quarter in the south of the town. The moon was half full and the stars bright. In their faint light, Roger could just make out Leonie's blanched face with its fear-dilated eyes. In the shelter of a shop doorway he stopped.

"My name is Roger St. Eyre, Miss de Conyers," he said quickly. "I beg you to trust me. I do not have time to present my credentials, but I have come from England to this country only for the purpose of finding your father."

"You had better help him now," Leonie whispered, too frozen with terror to cry.

Roger let Henry down gently. His breath drew in sharply when he looked at him. In the moonlight the whole right side of Henry's body was black and glistening with blood.

CHAPTER 6

Roger tore off his coat and then his shirt. Meanwhile, Leonie shook herself out of her paralysis of terror and began to pull off the rags that clothed her father. She uttered a low, choked cry as she saw the wound, still pulsing blood. Roger ripped a sleeve from his shirt and wadded it against the hole in Henry's back.

"You will have to hold that," he said to Leonie, "while I tear up the shirt."

He hoped his firmness would encourage her to help him, but he feared she would fall over in a faint. She did utter a little choked wail and begin to sob, but her hand came out steadily to press the already bloodsoaked pad against the wound. Henry did not stir. Roger suspected he was already deeply unconscious. He could not bear to look up and meet Leonie's eyes. He knew Henry could not live. There was nothing Roger could do to stop the bleeding, and he was certain from the way the blood was flowing that some important organ had been damaged. Nonetheless, he bound strips of his shirt together and then wound them as tightly as he could around Henry. Even as he tied the knots, the strips were soaked through with blood.

Desperately, Roger racked his brains for a way to tell Leonie that her father was dying when, to his surprise, Henry's eyes fluttered open.

"Go, Leonie." It was only a thread of a whisper, but there was real authority and force in it. "I am dying. Do not let me die knowing I have killed you also. Go."

"Monsieur St. Eyre will help you, Papa," Leonie sobbed. "We will all get away."

"St. Eyre?" Henry's eyes moved to Roger.

"Yes. I have come from England." Roger said nothing of the reason. Henry did not need the additional grief of hearing at this moment that his brothers were dead. "Do not worry about your daughter, sir. I swear I will get her safely home."

Tears of relief swam in Henry's eyes. No one outside his own family could possibly know the name of his father's neighbor and closest friend. This was no trick and no trap. He managed almost to smile and made one single effort to utter his thanks—to Roger, to God, to anyone—but he had not the strength, and his eyes closed for the last time. Roger glanced at Leonie, expecting that her attention would be on her father and hoping to read in her face whether or not she realized that Henry could not possibly live. To his surprise she was looking at him, but the utter desolation of her expression answered Roger's question. Leonie knew.

"I have a carriage waiting," Roger said. "The gate is about a quarter of a mile down this avenue. I will carry your father. I—I do not think he will—will feel any pain."

The wide eyes, black in the dim light, stared at him and then past him. Roger prayed that the girl would not faint or begin to scream. Tears began to trickle down her face, but she gave no other sign of weakness except that, gently, very gently, she patted her father's face.

"He does not wish to live," she whispered. "He always wanted to die, so he could be with mama. He only tried to live because he felt it wrong to leave me unprotected." Then she brought the focus of her eyes back to Roger. "How will we get out the gate? Is there something I can do to help?"

They made a plan, as soon as Roger discovered that Leonie was not afraid to hold and fire his pistol—but it was not necessary. As soon as Roger appeared, the guard nodded and turned his back. Roger darted back into the shadows and lifted Henry again. Although he had some experience with wounds, he had none with death; still, something in the feel of the body told him that life was gone. This was not the time, however, to stop and make sure. Staggering slightly under his burden, with Leonie close on his heels, he made for the small door to the side of the larger entry. Just as they reached it, Leonie darted ahead and swung it open. As soon as Roger was through, she pulled it shut behind them.

Roger paused, gasping with effort. He had come in from the north of the town and did not know this area at all.

The road was unmistakable, wider and more traveled than
the way he had come. It was paler in the moonlight than
the grass edging it—and it was empty. A combination of
rage and helplessness flooded him. Even if Henry was
dead, they could not leave him. Yet how could they escape
burdened with a corpse? It would be impossible. . . .

Before the thought could be completed, Leonie tugged at
his arm. "There are *two* carriages," she whispered tensely.

Roger turned his head to follow Leonie's apprehensive
gaze. Alongside the town wall was a narrow lane. There,
his carriage stood and some yards behind it, another, far
more shiny and elegant.

"The first carriage is mine," Roger said very low. "The
man in it should be Maître Foucalt's clerk—do you know
him?"

"I have seen him."

"Good." He switched to English. "He may have a gun.
Do not be afraid. Do you remember how I told you to cock
and fire the pistol I gave you?"

"Yes."

Leonie's whisper was thinner, but it did not tremble.
Roger could not see her because Henry's body blocked his
vision. He took a breath and again prayed the girl would
hold steady.

"If anyone gets out of the *second* carriage, tell him to
stop or you will fire. If he does not stop—shoot! Can you?"

"Yes."

"All right. Walk a little behind me, just enough to the
side so that you can see."

Probably the precautions were not necessary. Roger realized that the complications of demanding ransom were almost certainly too great to make it worthwhile to the *patron*. The real danger would come later after Roger had
handed over the money. It was possible that Louis or the
patron would wish to buy favor by killing them all or by
killing Roger and handing Leonie back. Roger wished
mainly to discourage any such idea by exhibiting that he
was ready for any surprise.

They reached the carriage without incident, and it was
indeed Foucalt's clerk that got down. He uttered an exclamation of distress when he saw Henry, but was sensible
enough to help Roger get the body into the carriage. As he
helped lift it, Leonie stood with the pistol in both hands,

leveled and ready. Just as he propped Henry's body against the side, Roger heard her call, "Stop! I will shoot!"

He was out beside her in a moment, a second pistol in his hand. A man he did not know stood in the road, but the *patron's* voice called from the carriage, "Where are my men, honest businessman?"

"I do not know," Roger replied, knowing the *patron* cared nothing for the men and having not the slightest desire to explain what had happened. "But I have no intention of cheating you. I told you before, I am not a fool."

"You are armed to repel an army," the *patron* remarked, but the worst of the deadly softness was gone from his voice, replaced by an amused respect.

"Yes, and we will remain so armed. There are other muskets in the carriage, all loaded. You must have discovered that I am also a gunsmith. However, I mean no threat. I only wish to ensure my own safety."

"You have ensured it. Now, let us go to this cache of yours."

"Get in the carriage, Leonie," Roger said, forgetting the formality of "Miss de Conyers" in the stress of the moment. She obeyed quickly. "Now your man, if you please, *patron.*"

There was a low chuckle, acknowledgment of another move stymied, but the *patron* gave the order and the man returned to the carriage. Roger thought feverishly. He had no cache and had planned to hand over the gold right here and then drive away. Now that scarcely seemed like a good idea. If the escape had already been discovered, searchers would surely rush to each gate. It was most unwise to be so close. Still, Roger had not the faintest idea of where to go. He jumped up into the driver's seat. Leonie was in the back. It was very silent there. Did she knew her father was dead?

"Where are you going, monsieur?" the clerk whispered from beside him, and then, even more softly, "Do you know Monsieur de Conyers is dead?"

Roger nodded to the second question. As he did, he realized he might have an answer to the first. "The farm," he whispered in return, "can I leave you there?"

"That is very kind," the clerk said, but with a nervous glance over his shoulder, "but . . ."

He did not want the *patron* to know the farm. Roger bit

his lip. "Is there a lane, a bit of wood, anywhere that we can stop for a little while? I cannot be rid of those who follow until I give them what was promised."

"Ah, yes. Give me the reins."

Released from the need to drive, Roger turned back toward Leonie, but he could see nothing. Inside the carriage there was no light at all. However, the moon struck full on his face, showing the sorrow and anxiety he felt. After a moment, a tired, broken whisper came. "I know."

"I am so sorry," Roger said softly.

"I am only afraid," Leonie replied. "I have no right to be sorry. It is what he wanted."

"Don't be afraid," Roger comforted. "I will keep you safe. I promised your father, and I will."

There was nothing more to say. Roger wished Leonie did not have to sit beside her father's corpse, but there was nothing he could do about it. He racked his brains for new words of comfort without results. After another moment, Leonie said softly, "I am all right. Don't worry so."

It was the strangest thing, but even as she said the words, hoping only to ease the distress on the face of this stranger who had so miraculously appeared, Leonie realized she had spoken the truth. She was grieved about her father but knew her grief was selfish. He had not wished to live. The memories he carried were too bitter, the wounds in his soul too deep. He could never have found peace. Safety and comfort would have been a far more terrible punishment to him than imprisonment or death. He blamed himself for his wife's and daughter's despoilment, for his wife's and son's deaths. How could he have lived with such a burden?

For *his* sake, Leonie knew she should be glad. She had seen the joy of release in her father's eyes when Monsieur St. Eyre promised to care for her. She should be glad that papa had gone so quickly, with so little suffering. But it was dreadful to be alone, all alone in the whole world. A sob choked her, and then another.

"Don't cry, Leonie. My poor child, don't. Here, come change places with me," Roger said urgently. "It isn't right for you to have to sit—"

"I am not afraid of papa," Leonie managed to say. "I am afraid to be all alone. . . ."

Before Roger could answer, the clerk pulled the horse

sharply right into a dark, narrow lane. Roger gave a distracted glance into the dark and then said, "Stop as soon as you like," but the clerk drove on for another five minutes.

After he stopped, it was only a moment's work to pull up the floorboard and release the catch to the seemingly solid underside of the seat. Leonie had to move aside, but Roger was able to pull out the two small chests and close the panel again without disturbing Henry's body. Then Roger got down and asked the clerk to hand down the chests. The second carriage had just pulled up behind them. Roger dragged the strongboxes forward and then retreated to the side of his own carriage, but he made no attempt to get in. Behind him the long nose of a musket pointed outward at the man who descended from the *patron*'s carriage. He came forward, his eyes flicking so nervously between the muzzle of the musket and the pistol in Roger's hand that he tripped over the chests and nearly fell. From the closed carriage, the *patron*'s voice came.

"It is most unfortunate you are so suspicious." The tone implied that great gain would accrue to Roger if he would come and have a private talk.

In spite of tension and distress, Roger could not help smiling. It must be nearly impossible for the *patron* to understand how to deal with someone who had what he wanted and wanted no more. The smile died as Roger remembered that Henry was dead. Well, there was nothing the *patron* could offer him that would cure that.

"You may think so," Roger replied, "but I assure you that from your point of view as well as mine, it is not. I desire no trouble, only to leave here in peace and safety. Please count the money and go. I swear to you I have nothing more. You have left me with about five francs and my stock in trade."

Whether Roger had at last convinced the man he was stripped clean or whether he realized Roger was not going to make a mistake, the *patron* said no more. The chests were lifted into the carriage; a light came on inside. After a little time the horse was induced to back slowly until a wider spot in the lane permitted the driver to turn the carriage. Slowly the sound of the horse's hooves and the creak of the wheels died away. Roger allowed his pistol to drop and leaned back against the side of the carriage, breathing deeply. It seemed to him that it was the first time he had breathed since he had gone down the cellar steps in the Hôtel de Ville.

He turned to thank Foucalt's clerk for backing him up so cleverly, and his eyes fell on Leonie's strained face. The muzzle of the musket wavered. "My poor child," he exclaimed, taking the gun from her hands, "where is—"

"Gone through the trees to the road to make sure they do not wait for us. He will wait until their carriage is out of sight," she interrupted. "Monsieur St. Eyre, do you really think they will let us go?"

"I hope so," Roger sighed. "I would have allowed him to search the carriage, but even that would not have convinced him, I fear. Greedy men cannot or will not believe there is no more."

There was a pause. Roger strained his ears, but there was no sound except the ordinary noises of a late summer's night in the woods. Leonie looked at his clear-cut features and wondered whether all Englishmen were so good-looking. Papa was—her thought checked and she corrected herself—had been handsomer than all the other men she knew. Papa was dead, and she was alone. She had better keep her mind on essentials.

"Monsieur St. Eyre," she said anxiously, "now that we have a few moments to talk, I wish to thank you for making my father's last moments so happy. It was very generous of you. However—however—I understand that—that it might be—inconvenient. . . . I mean—"

"Inconvenient! Leonie! Oh, I beg your pardon, Mademoiselle de Conyers, I did not mean to be familiar."

Grief and fear notwithstanding, Leonie had to laugh. Only an Englishman would think of apologizing for informality at such a moment. "Please, Monsieur St. Eyre, do call me Leonie," she said.

"Perhaps I should," he mused. "We must travel together. Yes, of course. Could you bring yourself to call me Roger?"

"Travel together?" Leonie's voice trembled. "Do you mean? . . . Was it true what you said to papa? Not only to comfort him?"

"Indeed it was true, Leonie. I came to France with the single purpose of finding your father and helping him bring his family home, if he needed and would accept my help."

"My uncle sent you?" Leonie cried.

"My God," Roger muttered. "Oh, my poor child, I have more bad news for you. No, let it wait. You have enough to bear—"

"Tell me," Leonie insisted, her voice rising, so that Roger realized that uncertainty and doubt would be worse for her than fact. "Has my uncle changed his mind? Will he not receive us—me?"

"Not receive you? He would have done so with all his heart. He is dead, Leonie. I am sorry."

"Uncle William is dead?" Her lips quivered. She had never met her Uncle William, but they had corresponded, and he had sent her a present once that had been very dear to her. Leonie wrenched her mind away from that. It was all past, all dead, even the little dog, most likely. She must think of practical things now. "I am glad papa did not need to know. But then, Uncle Joseph—do you think he will not want me because he has his own children?"

"God in heaven, no! He is dead also, Leonie, and his whole family."

Her eyes widened. "I do not believe you," she whispered raggedly, at last on the verge of hysteria. "For some reason you are trying to drive me mad. It is not possible! It is not possible that every person to whom I could belong is gone! Why are you here? What are you trying to do?"

Roger caught her hands and held them. "Child, child, I am here to protect you. What an idiot I am! I shouldn't have told you. I swear you will be safe with me—as safe as I can make you."

Roger's effort at comfort was somewhat misdirected. Leonie did not fear him in a personal way. Nonetheless, the strong yet gentle grasp of his hands and his obvious distress steadied her. Her fears were general; one, which she had voiced already, was of the unknown. If her uncles had not sent St. Eyre to help her father, how and why had he come? Just now anything unknown had an air of mystery and menace. Her second fear was more formed and more poignant.

"Where am I to go? What am I to do?" Leonie cried.

"I beg you not to be frightened," Roger soothed. "First—as soon as I can—I will take you to my father's house. You will be safe there. Lady Margaret is the kindest woman. Then, when you are a little recovered from this dreadful experience, you will decide what you wish to do."

Leonie pulled back, and Roger released her hands. She put one waveringly to her head. "You mean you will still take me to England? But I do not understand. If my uncles are dead," she choked back a sob, "how will I live? I do not wish to be a beggar, a charge on strangers. I suppose— I suppose I could teach French. Does—"

"No, no, do not be silly. You will be no charge on anyone," Roger assured her. "I do not know exactly how the entail is arranged, but I am sure the bulk of the property will come to you as heir general. Indeed, Leonie, you will be a very, very wealthy young woman."

"What?" Leonie gasped. "What can you mean? Papa was not rich. Some money came from England, I know, but it was not—"

"That is true. Your father was the youngest son, and the estate settled upon him was not large. That will come to you in its entirety, I am sure, but you will also have nearly all of your Uncle William's and Uncle Joseph's property— no, not Joseph's unless—" Roger cut that off.

He was an idiot, he thought. How could he maunder on about the legal problems involved if Joseph's small daughters were not found? Leonie was staring at him, openmouthed. Then she swallowed and dropped her eyes. Had the answer to her second fear also answered the first? Leonie remembered her father and mother making jest of the "proprieties" of England, of the fact that an unmarried woman alone with a man would lose her "reputation" and be forced to marry him. Could he—Roger—have come to marry an heiress? No, how silly! When he left England he must have believed that mama and François were still alive. She would not have been an heiress under those circumstances. She raised her eyes again.

"I still do not understand. How did you come here? How did you happen to be in the crowd that attacked the Hôtel de Ville? How did you happen to be in Saulieu on this particular day? How—"

Roger cleared his throat. "I am afraid, Leonie, that I am—am in some sense guilty of your father's death. It was I who arranged the attack on the Hôtel de Ville—that is, the money I gave that man in the other carriage was for arranging it for me. I cannot tell you how grieved I am that this happened. I will never forgive myself for not having foreseen that Louis would sound the tocsin. I will always blame myself for—"

Leonie reached out and grasped Roger's wrist. "For not being God and having foreknowledge? Do not say it! Do not think it! I told you papa made himself live because he knew it was his duty to protect me, but he was—was dead inside already because he also blamed himself for—for many things only God could have foreseen." Leonie had almost said "for my mother and me being raped," but that was none of St. Eyre's business.

She was about to assure him again that death had been what her father craved, when the clerk returned from down the road. He had seen the *patron*'s carriage turn back toward Saulieu without hesitation. Then he waited until he could not hear the horse or wheels any longer. He could not, of course, swear that they had not stopped and waited farther down the road, but there was no way of being sure about that. He advised turning the horse, going back to the road, and, if the *patron*'s carriage was not in sight, going on their way.

"I—you have somewhere to go?" he asked uncomfortably. Plainly his conscience told him he should invite them to the farm his relative owned, but he was afraid they would either not be welcome or would be discovered there.

Roger hesitated. This had all taken much longer than he expected. He was very much afraid that search parties would be out looking for them very soon. He knew nothing of the area. If the clerk thought the farm would be dangerous, then . . .

"Yes, we have someplace to go," Leonie said firmly, cutting into Roger's worried thoughts. "Only tell us what will be best for you."

"That is easy, just leave me here," the clerk said with relief. "There is a path a little farther down this lane that will take me where I want to go. I wish I could have done more, but . . ."

Roger assured him that he understood, and Leonie echoed his thanks and gratitude. After a brief hesitation, the young man melted away in the shadows.

"I hope you meant what you said," Roger remarked, turning to Leonie. "I have not the faintest notion of where we are, let alone where to go. I am sorry to be so . . ."

He was very like her father, always feeling responsible

for everything, Leonie thought, as she interrupted to assure Roger she knew where to go and instructed him to turn away from the town when they came to the main road. Roger did not do that directly. He paused to descend from the carriage and reconnoiter. The woods certainly seemed empty, and listening did not contradict the evidence of his eyes. When he returned to the carriage, Leonie was in the front seat.

"I laid papa down," she said with only a small tremor in her voice, "so that he would not fall. I thought I had better sit here to direct you. I could not see very well from there, and the back lane to the château is rather overgrown."

"The château!" Roger exclaimed. "But Leonie—"

"I know it is most likely a ruin," she said, "but we must go there. There is nowhere else to go, and we can hide in the cellars. Papa told me how to find the deep passages. Also, he said there is money there, in a secret room, but—"

Roger choked back the protest that the château would be one of the first places searchers would come. It was clear from what Leonie said that she knew it. Also, Henry de Conyers must be buried. Roger hoped that the château, like many great houses in England, would have its own mausoleum or area of consecrated ground. What he would do for a coffin, he had no idea. It offended him and would hurt Leonie simply to cast her father into a shallow, hastily dug grave. He pushed the new problem away; his mind was reeling between fatigue and anxiety, and he did his best to blank it completely and give his whole attention to directing the horse. The moon was very low in the sky now, and the light was worse.

Beside him, Leonie leaned forward tensely, her eyes on the left of the road. After a few minutes she said, "There, that is the road to Thoisy la Bec. Turn there."

"Must we go through the village?" Roger asked. "It would be better if no one knew a carriage came this way, and so late at night the sound will surely wake someone."

"The road does pass through," Leonie replied, and then, "Wait, we can go round through the fields. The haying carts go through. Yes, there are gates. Turn on the road and then keep to the right."

Roger drove for a few minutes, slowing the horse to a walk as Leonie put a hand on his arm, but she shook her head. Another long minute passed. Roger could feel her hand tremble. "You are cold," he said. "Hold the rein a minute. I will give you my coat."

"You will be naked," Leonie murmured.

"I beg your pardon," Roger said coldly, appalled at forgetting he was wearing no shirt and furious at the picayune nicety that would worry about a bare chest at such a time. "I did not mean to offend you."

Again a laugh was drawn from Leonie. "Dear Monsieur St. Eyre—no, I am to call you Roger—I am not offended. If you give me your coat, you will be even colder than I. That was all I meant."

Her answer made Roger ashamed of himself. "Don't worry about that. It is not really cold, and I am larger and warmer than you. Just take the reins."

In fact, he was already feeling chilled because he was so tired, but he was also very worried about Leonie. Her fortitude seemed incredible. He expected any small additional pressure or shock to break her. He knew, too, that feeling cold intensified fear and loneliness. But Leonie did not reach for the reins; she shook her head.

"I am not cold, only nervous and frightened. I am used to being cold. I—oh, I did not miss it. There, turn right."

Roger directed the horse into a break in the tall grass that bordered the road. Before he could speak, Leonie jumped down and opened the gate. Roger drove through. She closed the gate, and Roger reached down a hand to help her back into the carriage. It was the first time he was conscious of touching her, although he may have done so before, and a shock of desire passed through him.

"Follow the track," Leonie urged, far too intent on their rough path to notice that Roger had held her hand just a little longer than was really necessary.

He did not answer but gripped the reins until his knuckles went white, wondering if he was going mad. Was this a time to feel such an urge? And how could he be such an idiot as even to think of such a thing in connection with this girl! She was little more than a child and was completely dependent on him. Fortunately, although the track was no more than two deep ruts, the ruts fitted the carriage wheels quite well, and they negotiated it safely, emerging on the road well west of the village. Again Leonie watched the left side of the road, unconsciously pressing against

Roger in her need to see. Roger was just about to suggest
that they change places when she pointed again.

"There." She sighed with relief. "I thought it was closer,
but I am sure that is—yes, there are the old gates that papa
never had repaired." Her voice failed and she began to
sob softly, hopelessly.

Now he would have to touch her again. Roger passed
the reins to his left hand and put his right over Leonie's
shoulders. He could feel his arm tremble with the effort he
was making to prevent the embrace from becoming more
insistent than an offer of comfort should be. He should
speak too, Roger knew, but he could force no voice past his
suddenly dry throat. They drove very slowly up the wind-
ing lane, which was pitch dark: the horse feeling its way a
foot at a time, Leonie locked in her misery of recollection,
Roger fighting himself.

Suddenly, ahead, there was a lighter patch. With a low
oath Roger pulled the horse to a stop. "Leonie, hush. I
must go and look to be sure no one is lying in wait at the
house. My dear, I am sorry to be so cruel to you. You have
much to weep for, I know, but try not to weep now."

He did not know whether his plea would overset her and
drive her to hysteria and he was prepared to muffle her
cries by force if he had to; but the sobs choked off and a
trembling hand took the reins. Roger made his way toward
the lighter area and saw, within it, the dark bulk of a large
house. There was no sign of life—no light, no movement.
Roger crept forward, crouching and sliding from one
shadow to another. Eventually he reached the house; he
could see that the doors had been wrenched from their
hinges and the hall loomed black and empty.

Nothing. Desolation. Ruin. Roger stared around, wondering whether he should permit Leonie to come here. She
had said she expected the house to be a ruin, but when she
saw it . . . Roger swallowed. The sky was already lightening with a predawn luminescence. The horse was tired.
There was nowhere else to go. They could not abandon
Henry's body as if it were a piece of dross. Shaking himself
as though to cast off a pall, Roger began to make his way
cautiously around the house.

No one was lying in wait. Roger had one fright when he
heard a scrabbling sound near the kitchen quarters and
something mottled pale and dark flashed away into the

shadows. After he had swallowed the heart that leaped into his mouth, he told himself it was just a rat and moved toward the stables. Those, too, were quiet, and Roger saw with relief that they had not been emptied completely. The horses were gone, of course, but those who looted the house had no use for a gentleman's carriages. What could be used had been ripped out of them, and they had been slashed and shattered—senseless destruction to relieve centuries of repression and hatred—but the remnants were still in the carriage house. Roger was reasonably certain he could conceal his own shabby vehicle among the broken ruins.

Alone in the carriage, Leonie stared around at the narrow lane that had been almost as familiar to her as the house itself. How often had she ridden down it astride La Belle, her pretty mare. Where was La Belle? She shuddered, pressing a hand against her mouth to silence the whimpers of grief and loss and terror. Broken! Overgrown! Ruined! Her whole life was like the lane, like the house she could not see—but she could sense the silence, the desolation. If she were dead . . .

That thought brought her up sharp. She was not dead. She did not wish to die. Her life was not a ruin! Monsieur St. Eyre had told her she was not destitute. Lonely and frightened—yes, Leonie acknowledged she was lonely and frightened. She wished mama and papa and François were alive—but she could not bring them back. Either she must give up and lie down and die, or she must put her grief behind her and look ahead to the new life she must make. Monsieur St. Eyre—no, Roger. Leonie lingered on the name, the pain of unshed tears in her throat easing. She was not alone.

Slowly, while Roger searched for hidden spies and traps, Leonie came to terms with what had happened. She felt a little guilty at not grieving more, but she knew that it was because there was little grief left in her. When mama had died, she had grieved full measure and overflowing. There was not much reason to grieve for papa now. His pain was over. He was at peace. If only she could bury him with mama. . . . He had wanted that so much.

A flicker of movement on the road made her gasp, but Roger's voice came softly almost at once. "It is I, Leonie." He came closer and looked up at her for a long moment.

"There is no one here yet, but . . . The house—it's—it's like a ravished woman."

Infinitesimally Leonie stiffened, but the pain and revulsion in Roger's face were very soothing to the hurt he did not even know she bore. Two things were clear to her. Roger was very sensitive, and he did not think it amusing—as was not infrequent with men—to force a woman. The conviction sent a flow of warm comfort through Leonie. She had not been consciously afraid of Roger, and she did not fear coupling. Nonetheless, the violence of the past hours had wakened an inner awareness of her helplessness and dependence, of her inability to resist. The dark and fear had sparked some subconscious comparison with the night she and her family had been seized amid violence. Rape, pain, and shame had followed. Somehow, deep inside, she had expected the same culmination.

"I am so sorry," Roger continued, getting into the carriage. "It hurt me to see such beauty despoiled, and I know it will be worse for you who loved the house. I wish—"

"Thank you for warning me," Leonie said as his voice faded helplessly, "but I knew. There is nowhere else to go and—and if I cannot bury papa by mama, which is what he wished, at least he can be here where her spirit lives."

Roger patted the small, cold hands before he took the reins from them. It was a relief that Leonie recognized the need to inter Henry, but Roger shuddered at the problems. Where was he to find tools with which to dig a decent grave? It was nearly morning. He did not think he could manage to do it that night; and, if he did, would not a new grave be noticed? It would not be safe to stay long after Henry was buried, but the horse could not really go much farther.

The lane led around to the back of the house and the stables. Roger stopped by the back door. Again there was a flicker of movement low to the ground. He glanced nervously at Leonie, hoping she had not noticed. Most women were terrified by rats. No, she had not seen the animal, and this time it had fled out of the house. Roger's heart contracted at her pain. Warning was one thing; seeing another. Her eyes were staring wide, her cheeks wet.

"I am glad papa is dead," she whispered. "I am glad."

CHAPTER 7

Somehow the things necessary for concealment were done. Roger pushed the carriage in among the wrecks and strewed it with straw, then leaned a broken wheel so that it concealed the perfectly sound wheel behind it. Meanwhile, Leonie took the horse away to hide it in the maze. There was a small sheltered area in the center of the maze. No one could see the center, and the tall hedges would muffle any sounds the horse made. It could not find its way out, and no one would attempt to thread the maze's overgrown paths. There was plenty of grass and even a small decorative pool at which the animal could drink.

Roger could have kissed the ground Leonie walked on for her marvelous self-control, for the way she put aside her grief and horror to be of practical assistance. He was also grateful that she went away. There was no way that Henry's body could be handled with dignity and decency. It would have been dreadfully painful for Leonie to see Roger haul her father's corpse around like an old sack of wheat, yet there was nothing else he could do. This way, by the time Leonie returned, Roger had been able to lay the body straight on a counter in the scullery. In the faint gray light of coming dawn, he was even able to find and pull down a window drape, too spoiled by fire and water to make it desirable as loot, to cover Henry.

Later, between them they managed to carry the body down into the cellar and place it where it was not likely to be discovered, since neither movement nor breath could betray its presence. Last, Leonie showed Roger the wine cask, warped and empty, that marked the entrance to the hidden tunnels. The sun was up now, and some light filtered through a distant window, at least enough to see. When one knew the secret, it was childishly simple. An iron hook lifted away from a support, and the cask swung

aside. Once they were behind it, a pull drew it back into
position and the hook, affixed between a hasp on the back
of the cask and a staple on the wall, held it rigidly.

Inside, however, it was black with a blackness no night
can produce. There was a silence. Roger clung to the hook
he had just fastened, sweating with panic, totally disoriented. Beside him there was a faint whimper that somehow expressed the blind, abject animal terror Roger himself felt. His grip on the hook tightened until the metal cut
painfully into his hand.

"Leonie!"

The word echoed and reverberated, producing a ghastly
image of endless black space behind them. Roger groped
wildly with his free hand, needing desperately to touch
something that would make the space finite. Fortunately,
before her courage or his own broke, his hand fell upon
Leonie's arm, and he drew her tight against him. She was
shaking so violently her body fluttered against his like that
of a captured bird, but she was silent now. Pity routed
panic.

"It's all right, Leonie," Roger murmured, keeping his
voice low but not whispering. The soft tone did not start
the hollow echo, and the ability to control his voice gave
Roger confidence. Still gripping the hook he pulled himself toward it until his shoulder touched the bulge of the
cask. Then he turned so that his whole back rested against
it, pulling Leonie with him. The solidity reoriented him. He
was no longer lost in the dark. He let go of the hook and
put both arms around the trembling girl

"What a fool I am," he murmured, "to shut us in here
without light. Just hold on to me. I will open it again. We
can search for candles and water. There won't be any food,
but if you are very hungry, I think I could walk back to the
village and buy some."

"Food?" The whisper hissed away into the long dark,
and Leonie, whose trembling had quieted, began to shudder again.

"Just speak low," Roger encouraged, "then the sound
does not come back. There must be a turn or a door after a
long corridor. That is what makes the echo."

Another silence followed, too long for a natural pause, so
that Roger was just about to speak comfortingly again. He
was interrupted by a soft giggle, and although he made no

sound, he thought lurid obscenities. This was not the place he would have chosen to deal with a woman in hysterics. Nonetheless, he really could not be angry, considering what the poor girl had been through and considering that he had almost succumbed himself. Before he could take appropriate measures, however, Leonie spoke.

"You are just like papa," she said, still chuckling softly, and Roger realized that the giggle had been honest amusement, not incipient hysteria. "Whenever I was frightened of things like the dark, papa would give me a long explanation of what caused the fright. I used to feel so angry. There I was with my heart pounding, feeling as if I would die, and he was telling me about the curvature of the earth or the way light is reflected. But it always worked. By the time he was finished, I wasn't frightened anymore."

Roger did not reply. He should have felt glad his device had worked so well, relieved that Leonie was so calm. All he felt was a bitter shock of disappointment. She thought of him as a father! Well, why should she not? He was nearly old enough to be her father. He could think of nothing to say and merely relaxed his grip on her, but she did not seem to notice any awkwardness in his silence.

"I have food," her voice continued.

She was still so close, because she had not stepped away when Roger released her, that he could feel her fumbling in her skirt. The movement stimulated highly inappropriate images in Roger's mind; he would have backed away, except that he was already pressed against the cask. A protest rose in his throat, but it was checked again when the fumbling stopped. Leonie's hand touched his bare chest. Roger stiffened, but the hand moved to his arm, down to find his hand, and a round, slick object was pressed into his palm.

"Sausage," Leonie said, her voice light with laughter. "I have another also. Louis gave them to me—ah, if I ever see him again, I must apologize for thinking ill of him. He did help to release us. . . ." Her voice faltered, and the happiness died out of it as she remembered what else Louis had done and that her father was not part of "us" anymore.

"Yes." Roger had found his voice again. He pushed the sausage back into Leonie's hand. "I am glad you have food. I am sure I can get water from the pump in the scullery. I think we will have to spend the day in hiding here, which is just as well because we both need sleep. Mean-

while, look around the cellar and see if you can find a
candle and, even more important, flint and tinder."

Roger turned, careful to keep his contact with the cask
so that he would not become disoriented again, and un-
hooked the catch. The cask swung out without difficulty,
and they emerged into what seemed to them brightness.
Roger made for the stairs, Leonie for what had been the
most frequently used portion of the wine cellar, where she
hoped to find candle stumps. As he went, Roger looked
around the floor and eventually spotted an old jug. The top
was broken off, but the body seemed sound. If he could
find nothing better above, it would do to hold water.

The full morning light that flooded through the scullery
windows showed all too clearly that Roger had been fortunate to find the partly unbroken jug. On the main floor
there was nothing usable remaining. Probably waves of
looters had swept over the château periodically, each group
taking less and less valuable objects until there was nothing at all worth taking. Then, in spite or wanton rage,
whatever could not be taken had been broken and battered.
Roger exclaimed with irritation. Even the handle had been
wrenched from the pump.

A brief investigation solved the problem. One form of
destruction made up for another. A splintered chair provided a stick with a crooked end that Roger was able to fit
into the pump to replace the handle. He worked it as vigorously as he could, hoping the mechanism had not been
damaged and the pump would not need priming. Fortunately, Henry de Conyers had installed the best of everything for the convenience of his servants, and the water
soon spurted. Roger rinsed the jug as thoroughly as he
could, then set it under the spout and pumped it full. As he
did this his gaze wandered out through the windows.

Midstroke, his hand froze on the handle he was working.
Men were on the lawn that stretched down from the front
of the house. Unaccustomed to being the object of a hunt,
Roger had forgotten to keep watching for pursuers. Breath
held, he watched and listened, but the movements he could
see were unhurried, deliberate. There was no sign that any
searchers had yet reached the house itself. They were only
now spreading out to surround the château and the out-
buildings.

Roger snatched the wooden rod from the pump. Clutching the slopping jug in one hand, the stick in the other, he fled to the cellar steps. Just before he went down, he paused to listen, but all was silent. He let out the breath he had been holding and eased his way down the steps. At the foot of the stairs, he had to stop. His eyes had adjusted to the light on the upper floor, and he was temporarily blind in the semidark of the cellar. Pausing briefly for his eyes to adjust, he strained his ears. Still nothing. He moved forward cautiously, feeling his way, still half-blind, wondering how he would find Leonie. He did not even know the full extent of the cellars, because she had led him directly to the keg that concealed the tunnel. Again he held his breath and listened. Nothing.

"Leonie, hide," he called softly. "There are men—"

He cut off abruptly. Footsteps. Should he set down the jug and go up, try to brazen out his presence in the house? How the devil could he explain the blood on his hands and coat? His lack of a shirt? Before he could think further, his hand was seized and he could have laughed at himself. The footsteps led him swiftly, and he did not pull away, even though by then he could see fairly well. Another moment and they were safely behind the cask, the hook firmly in place.

This time the dark held no terrors for them. They were both too relieved to have reached their haven undiscovered and too aware of their great danger to be troubled by imaginary fears. Reality was probably already seeking through the house and barns. Would the men find the carriage? The horse? Henry's body? Any of those discoveries might well doom them. Roger did not fear their hiding place would be discovered, unless some former servant already knew of the tunnels. But if any sign of their presence were found and Marot's men set themselves to watch the house and grounds for any length of time, he and Leonie could be trapped inside the tunnel until they starved or died of thirst.

Thought of food and drink woke in Roger a sense of his need of both. He had not eaten or had a drink since dinner the previous day. And Leonie was probably in even greater need. "Are you thirsty?" he asked softly. "I have water, but be careful. The mouth of the jug is broken. Also . . ." He did not wish to frighten her, but he had to warn her. "We may be trapped in here for some time because—"

"I know," she interrupted, her voice quite cheerful. "Even if they do not find us, they may leave watchers in the house to wait for us." She chuckled. "You do not need to worry about me. It will be a long time before they can starve me out. I know how to starve. Still, we have not come to that state yet. We should not gobble all we have, but I cannot believe they will stay more than two days or three. It is stupid to go hungry before it is necessary."

Roger considered that, trying to be sure it was not his stomach that was agreeing with Leonie rather than his head. Finally he decided she was right. It was better to eat a little now than to face the long hours hungry and thirsty.

"The only thing is," Leonie went on before he could answer, "I could not find any flint. I have two candles—but no way to light them."

"It does not matter," Roger said, "for now we can manage by feel."

He did not mind the dark at all now. All he could think of was that Leonie was the most incredible girl. Henry de Conyers's daughter must have been delicately raised, yet nothing seemed to break her spirit. She had endured violence, fatigue, fear, grief—and she had not been unaware of her bereavement or danger—yet she could laugh, even in the face of more pain and peril. A memory of Solange, spoiled and whining in the midst of the greatest indulgence and luxury, made Roger wince. How could he have been fooled by that exquisite doll-like beauty? Solange had never pretended to be other than she was. Roger could distinctly remember calling the discontented thrust of her lips an adorable, delicious pout.

But was Leonie even worse? She needed him now, so she was sweet and brave. When she was rich and safe, would she turn hard and contemptuous? It was stupid to keep whetting his appetite for what he could not have. "We had better sit down," he said. "Don't let go of me or move away. I have to slide down slowly or I'll spill this water."

In a way the darkness was now a blessing. They lost each other, found each other. Leonie nearly poked out Roger's eyes when she offered the sausage; Roger first could not find his clasp knife and then could not open it. Between amusement and exasperation at their clumsiness, they soon shook off the dreadful sensation of being blind, helpless, and hunted animals. They did not forget their danger. Even when they burst into laughter, they muffled the sound as well as they could. Nonetheless, they did laugh, at last clinging together with Leonie's face nuzzled into Roger's breast and his face buried in her hair.

Both realized the intimacy of their position simultaneously. Roger's arms froze; Leonie's laughter checked. For a few heartbeats they were still, Roger fighting the desire to tighten his grip and use his mouth for a purpose other than laughter, Leonie torn by a strange dichotomy. She had the strongest impulse to slide her hands under Roger's coat and caress his bare body; at the same time she could not bear the thought that Roger would use her as Louis had. If Roger demanded payment from her body for his protection, in what way was he better than Louis? Yet, when his arms dropped away from her and proved he was a better man, she could have wept aloud with disappointment.

"Have you had enough to eat, Leonie?" Roger asked, sounding as if someone had him by the throat. Leonie nodded. He could not see her but felt the movement against his shoulder. "I think we had better try to sleep then," he went on. "I wish it were not so cold, but if you take my coat—"

"Don't be ridiculous. You will freeze. I am wearing more than you are already."

To silence him—because she *was* cold and wanted very much to be warm—Leonie pulled her rags as closely as she could around her and lay down. Beside her she could feel Roger sliding himself flat. It would be warmer, Leonie thought, if she could lie against him as she used to lie against papa—but she did not dare suggest it, and Roger was careful not to touch her. A wave of misery flooded over Leonie, and she uttered a small sob in spite of her efforts to be silent.

"Don't," Roger murmured, turning toward her. "God in heaven, I wish there was some comfort I could offer you."

His hand touched her tentatively, and Leonie could bear her cold and her sense of aloneness no longer. She moved so that she was pressed against him, shivering and sobbing. Roger clutched her close, half horrified and half delighted. He tried without releasing her to take off his coat, but she guessed what he was doing and would not let him. However, while it was open, her hands slid under it. Sensing a reasonable compromise, Roger pulled the coat around her as far as it would go. Leonie's back was still exposed, but her arms were now warmed by Roger's body. Unthinking, craving only the comfort his warmth offered, Leonie pressed her legs against Roger's.

For a little while, as warmth and a sense of security diffused through her, Leonie sobbed harder than ever. Roger patted her back and murmured soothingly, just as he had done for his son when Philip was little and frightened. His sense of Leonie's femininity was temporarily submerged in his pity and concern for her. Slowly, however, the sobs diminished to an infrequent shuddering sigh and Leonie lay relaxed, her head on Roger's shoulder. Her breathing softened and slowed. Warmed by her body and by his satisfaction in having calmed her, Roger drifted asleep also.

Some time later he was wakened by Leonie's movement. Still asleep, she was trying to snuggle tighter against him. Fuddled and sleep-dazed, Roger responded automatically to the feel of a body against his by kissing her face. He wondered muzzily as his lips touched Leonie's dirt-streaked skin why the bed was so hard and cold, then recognized he was not in a bed. Could he have been so drunk as to pick up a Covent Garden nun and lie with her right in the street? A shock of revulsion startled him really awake, and he remembered where he was and why. In sleep, his hands had relaxed their hold on his coat and Leonie. She was merely seeking warmth.

Unfortunately, Roger's body did not catch up with his mind. What with staying at his father's house and his trip to France, it had been longer than usual since he had visited his regular pleasure haunt. Still unaware, Leonie pressed her leg between his thighs. Instinct responded as if she had offered him a deliberate sexual provocation. Desperately he tried to swing his hips back, away from her. The movement was sudden. Leonie jerked awake.

"What is wrong?" she whispered, still pushing forward toward the source of warmth. Then her breath caught and she froze. Her movement had pressed Roger's swollen manhood into her groin.

He jerked himself away from her and sat up, pulling his coat off and flinging it down on her. Leonie lay perfectly still, terrified and thrilled. There was a stirring in her body, a response to Roger's arousal that she had never felt before and did not recognize for what it was now. She felt him shift and bit back a whimper, not knowing whether it was a sound of protest or desire, but he moved farther away so that there was no longer any contact between them.

"I am very sorry," he muttered, his voice choked. "Please try to forgive me. I know you are offended, but, I—I had no intention of insulting you, Leonie. Men—sometimes a man's body . . ." How the hell did one explain such a thing to a girl like Leonie? Roger's voice died.

"I am not insulted," Leonie faltered. She could hear him breathing, deep intakes of air followed by pauses. "I am sorry too," she added softly. "I should not have—have leaned against you. I am not so ignorant as that. It was—I was asleep and cold."

"It is not your fault," Roger said stiffly. "I just hope you are not going to be afraid of me. If there was someone I could leave you with, I would not—"

"No!" Leonie cried aloud, seized by such a sense of loss and desolation at the idea of separation from Roger that she forgot the need for silence.

Instinctively Roger reached out and placed a hand over her lips. "Hush," he murmured tensely.

Both held their breaths as Leonie's cry rolled and echoed back and forth in the tunnel, reverberating hollowly until all semblance to a human voice was gone. They heard nothing more. There were many feet of packed earth and thick old beams between the tunnels and the rooms of the house above them. However, farther along, beyond the turn that sent the echo back to them, a narrow airshaft reached up through earth and floors into one of the chimneys of the château. From the hearths connected with that chimney issued a series of fading, unearthly moans, pulsing into silence as the echoes of Leonie's cry died.

In two different rooms of the château, men started nervously and peered around. Even though it was full daylight, the ruin and desolation were having an effect. Hatred emanated from the charred walls and shattered remnants of furniture. Those who had destroyed had hated, and the ruins reflected that hatred back. The men glanced around once again and left the rooms to join their fellows and ask whether they, too, had heard—something.

Had only one man heard the sound, the others would have laughed him into silence, but they were searching in pairs so that the two escapees would not be able to overwhelm one man. The four men passionately supported each other, unconsciously increasing one another's sense of horror until they all began to look around nervously.

"It was the wind in the chimney," Marot snarled furiously. "I can tell you there is nothing and no one in this house, or de Conyers and his bitch daughter are hiding here and deliberately trying to frighten you."

"What wind? There is no wind," one of the men said angrily.

"Then it was a bird or a loose stone," Marot snapped back viciously. "We must find de Conyers. Do you want him running to his friends in Paris and bringing the army down on us? He and Lafayette were bosom friends. Go back and search, I say."

Somewhat sullenly the men went back to their task. They had already been through the barns and stables and two top floors of the house, looking into every cupboard, turning over every heap of rubbish and rags, while others stood guard at the doors and the foot of the stairways so that the quarry could not escape. Most of them had lost their enthusiasm and began to murmur that de Conyers would not have been such a fool as to return to this house, which he must realize would be one of the first places searched. More likely he was hiding in the town itself—the gate guards all swore no one had been past them—or if they were lying, de Conyers must be well away on the road to Dijon or Paris already.

Marot alone knew a good reason for de Conyers to return. There had been money in the strongroom, money and jewels. He had got that information out of de Conyers's solicitor in Saulieu while questioning him in an effort to discover something discreditable about his enemy. Naturally that ill-gotten money, wrung from the sweat of the people, had been quietly taken and put to better use, but since de Conyers could not have known that his solicitor had given away the secret, he would believe the money was still there and he would return. However, this was not a reason Marot could afford to give his men. He knew them now; most of them thought money and jewels wrested from the oppressors should go into their own pockets. They did not consider the public need. If they found out about de Conyers's cache, they would demand a share, thinking Marot had kept the money for himself.

* * *

For a long time after she cried out, Leonie and Roger were still as death, listening. At last Roger lifted his hand from Leonie's lips. She uttered a tiny sob. "I am sorry," she whispered.

"I do not think anyone can hear anything," Roger replied, trying to keep his teeth from chattering. The shock had added to his chill. "But it is only reasonable to take care."

"Yes, I know, but . . . Monsieur St. Eyre—please—I— I am not so innocent as you think me. Please, I would rather be with you. Even—" Leonie barely stopped herself from saying, *even if you wish to make me your whore.* Somehow she realized that to say that would be a greater insult to Roger than to herself. "Even if there were someone else who would take me, I would rather go to England with you. . . ."

Her voice drifted away, a pathetically lonely sound. Roger clenched his fists to keep himself from drawing her back into his arms. Not so innocent as he thought—poor child, what could she mean? And then the realization of what she meant nearly choked him.

"Leonie! Do you mean you were . . . The men who took you prisoner misused you?"

"Yes."

The one word, thin, less than a whisper, cut Roger like a knife. "Oh God, oh God," he breathed, "you must want to kill me. I would never . . . Child . . ."

"I am not a child," Leonie said firmly, "and I certainly do not want to kill you. Why should I blame you for the bestiality of other men?"

It had been bitterly hard to get out that "yes," but Leonie was now relieved and delighted with the turn the conversation had taken. It had occurred to her that she would never need to confess her relationship with Louis. There was something ugly in that—the trade of flesh for benefit—even though the benefit had not been her own. There was nothing she could have done about Marot's assault, though. The only unfortunate thing was that Leonie knew some men set a very high price on virginity, and it was very likely, from the horror in Roger's voice, that he was one of them. Realizing how much he was beginning to mean to her, desolation touched her again.

Roger had not responded immediately to Leonie. He was not sure whether he was more surprised by her seeming generosity of spirit or suspicious because she could be dispassionate about such a subject. Senselessly he repeated his apology, again trying to assure her that no matter how unruly his body, he would never force a woman, particularly one under his protection. He was not, he said with indignation, apologizing for even thinking of such an abomination, only for an uncontrollable physical reaction that might have frightened Leonie.

"Indeed, I believe you," Leonie murmured. "I have said over and over that I was not frightened or angry." There was a little pause and Leonie sat up also, regretfully pulling off Roger's coat and pushing it back to him. "You cannot sit there for hours and hours uncovered. You will be ill from the cold."

It was impossible to contest that. Roger was shaking with chill. However, if he took the coat, Leonie would suffer. They needed each other's warmth, but the thought of taking Leonie back into his arms brought an immediate response. Why could the girl not be an ugly, whining burden, Roger thought petulantly. Then an idea dawned. If he put the coat on backward and Leonie lay against his back, she would be reasonably warm and his reactions would not be apparent.

Hesitantly, Roger made his suggestion. He did not know whether he was more pleased or shocked at her prompt acceptance. It was nice to have proof that she trusted him, but should she have? Perhaps she had not found his behavior offensive, had in fact found it pleasant? No, Roger told himself. This is not a lightskirt or a fancy piece, but a decently raised girl. Nonetheless, when he pulled on his coat and lay down and Leonie cuddled close beside him, Roger found himself fighting a losing battle against images of Leonie that were not in the least decent.

Leonie had slid one arm against his back and the other around his chest and buried her face in his nape. Roger closed his eyes and swallowed, struggling to keep his breathing steady. He could not understand why he should be so tormented by desire. His sexual appetite was strong but not indiscriminate, and this girl had done nothing to provoke him. Her grip on him was not more than necessary to hold them together, yet his flesh burned where she touched him, sending thrills down his chest and back that provided a near-intolerable stimulation.

It was worse than the misery of his early marriage, when he had desired Solange with an intensity that amounted to physical torture. She had often refused him so that he was frustrated—and in those early years he had been too much a romantic fool to pacify himself with whores—but he had at least been able to go away. Now he could do nothing but endure, with Leonie's body pressed against him in a constant, false simulation of willingness. He could not even ease himself with small movements. Each time he shifted his body, Leonie murmured and pressed herself even more tightly against him. She was, he thought, already asleep, but even that idea did not calm him. He ached to turn and hold her, to kiss her and caress her, but she was a gentlewoman. He could not use her like a drab, and he was resolved there would be no more gentlewomen in his life—no more dainty flowers that distilled a poisoned perfume.

In fact, Leonie was not asleep. Her clinging was as much to ease a restlessness in her body that she really did not understand as to keep warm. Well-experienced in the sexual act, Leonie was totally unacquainted with desire. She was aware that she wanted Roger to do to her what Louis had done, but she did not know why she wanted it or what would result. She did not recognize the physical symptoms of passion and pressed herself against Roger to satisfy a need for contact, not realizing she wanted more.

Several times Leonie thought of doing to Roger some of the things Louis had taught her. That would almost certainly cause Roger to satisfy her desire—but how could she explain knowing such things? Leonie was well aware that Roger had no contempt for her at present, even though her maidenhead had been wrested from her. His embarrassment, his fear of frightening her, his apologies showed that he considered her pure in mind, if not in body, and worthy of respect. To behave like a whore and invite his lust would certainly alter that attitude.

Fortunately, long-lasting frustration is almost as exhausting as satisfaction. When added to the physical exertions of the preceding night and the tension and grief endured, extreme fatigue was the natural result. Although the minutes seemed long to Leonie and Roger, they were really very few. The time passed, tiredness conquered desire, and both slept.

CHAPTER 8

Marot kept his men at their searching until every possible spot in the house had been examined. There was no repetition of the weird sound, but the thin, drawn-out howling of a miserable dog, which drifted through the broken doors and windows, somehow made the desolation of the ruined château eerie—particularly when the sun was covered by clouds and it began to rain. Therefore, it was not surprising that, in spite of Marot's prodding, the examination made of the dim, cold cellars was less minute. All obvious hiding places were investigated, but the men were far more cursory in delving into heaps of broken rubbish and rags so that Henry's body escaped detection.

Forced to concede that his prey was not in the house, Marot was still not satisfied. He ordered two men to remain and watch—and met opposition. Grumbling and resentful, those designated to watch wondered aloud why such an intense effort should be made to recapture de Conyers. He was ruined and powerless—let him go; he was no danger to them. Furious, Marot fell back on threats and imprecations. Anyone who wished to try strength with him could face the civil guard. Naturally, that ended the argument for the time being. Those assigned to stay at the house sullenly watched the others depart, but remained where they had been ordered.

As the day stretched to evening, however, the dog began to howl again, and the dark bulk of the house behind them—one guarding the front and one the rear—grew more and more menacing. At last the man at the front door cursed that Marot was mad; de Conyers would never come to the château now. Convinced by his own reasoning, he marched firmly around to the back and stated this to his comrade. He found instant agreement and support. The other man even suggested they could watch far better from the gatekeeper's cottage at the foot of the long front drive south of the house. It had been looted too, but it was much smaller—and de Conyers had never lived there. Before darkness had really settled over the countryside, Marot's unenthusiastic henchmen were comfortably settled in the empty gatekeeper's cottage with a cheerful fire of broken furniture warming their hearts as well as their bodies.

In the cellar, Roger had wakened periodically because of being cold and cramped. Leonie, more accustomed to sleeping under such conditions, slept soundly. At first Roger was afraid to move much for fear he would wake Leonie, and each wakening was a renewal of hell. He would lie still as long as he could, but then he would have to move to ease his cramp, and Leonie would move also, following his warmth. That would start him off again, precipitating him into a desire that could have no satisfaction. The third time, Roger could endure no more. He inched out of Leonie's arms, slipped out of his coat, and covered her with it. After listening with his ear pressed against the cask for a while, he eased it open.

The cellar was quite bright to his eyes, so it was not late enough for any real activity. However, after listening intently and hearing nothing, Roger took off his boots and crept carefully to where Henry's body had been hidden. He sighed softly with relief when he saw it was undisturbed. His next act was to find a distant corner and relieve his full bladder. Again Roger listened without result. Then, foot by foot, he crept to the stairs and up them. Judging by the light, it might be evening, but Roger saw the wet spots the rain had left and decided it was probably late afternoon. Holding his breath, he crept along the corridor, to the servants' stairs. Ears and eyes strained to the uttermost after each step told him there was no one moving in the house. Praying he was not deceived, Roger turned right past the stairs and eased himself into what had been the breakfast room. His goal was the formal salon where he had found the drape used to wrap Henry's body. There had been another drape hanging in that room, and Roger was going to get it. The cloth was heavy and would serve admirably as a blanket for Leonie. Even at the cost of his life, Roger was not going to endure again the unsatisfiable stimulation Leonie's embrace gave him.

The adventure did not cost Roger's life, but it was a near

thing. He managed to get the hanging down without noise and was retracing his steps—a trifle incautiously, because he had examined the grounds through the window of the salon and had seen no one. Just as he was about to step into the front hall, which was a shorter route, a creak of wood froze him. Roger did not leap for shelter; he did not breathe or blink his eyes. Still as a hunted hare, which escapes detection by immobility, he waited. The wood creaked again, and a heel scuffed the stone steps of the porch; another scuff, but the doorsill did not creak nor was the step onto the wooden hall floor; another step.

Roger's breath trickled out, and he shifted the hanging to his left arm so that his sword hand was free. Simultaneously he realized he could not afford to attack whoever was on the porch. There was no guarantee the man was alone. Roger had heard the phrase "minutes like hours." He had thought the minutes long while he fought his own body in Leonie's arms, but he now learned that fear and regret can draw time much longer. Fool that he was! To provide himself with comfort, he had probably thrown away everything, including his life and Leonie's. There was plenty of time for Roger to contemplate his own weakness and idiocy, to taste the bitter bile of fear and shame.

Finally, Roger realized it could not be merely the stretching of time. Several minutes had gone by, more than long enough for the man to have come in if he was going to come in. Softly, slowly, scarcely breathing, Roger backed toward the end of the room from which he had come. He faded out of the salon, silently offering prayers of thanksgiving. The unlit corridor to the back of the house was far safer, but Roger did not make another mistake. He crept along close to the wall and eventually came safely down the stairs and into the black haven behind the cask.

It was then the work of minutes to put on his coat again and wrap the drape around Leonie. To his pleasure, he found the hanging long enough to serve as a cover for him also, even when he was far enough away not to touch her. He was somewhat discouraged by the evidence that watchers had been left, even though Henry's body had not been discovered. Perhaps they had found the horse or recognized that the carriage did not belong in de Conyers's stable. He tried to guess how long the men would stay, but he soon concluded that such speculations were useless. After a while he came to the not very brilliant conclusion that he would simply have to investigate periodically, but he was warm now and he was sure there were hours before dark. He slipped into a doze again.

The idea of investigating was still in his mind when he woke, and he muttered a soft curse because he had no idea how much time had passed or how to judge the further passage of time.

"Are you awake?"

The soft murmur made Roger turn his head. "Yes. Have you been awake long?"

"I have no idea," Leonie replied, a smile in her voice. "I think not very long, but I haven't been thinking about time."

Leonie had been awakened by an urgent need to relieve herself. This she had accomplished without waking Roger, by feeling her way along the wall until it turned. Then, having felt her way back, she slipped carefully under the covers Roger had provided, drifting into a soft, pleasurable half-dream, comforted by the warmth of her covering and by Roger's steady breathing beside her.

"How in the world did you find a blanket?" she asked.

"I have been up into the house." Roger told her the rest of it, and at first Leonie could think of nothing that would help. After a moment, however, she exclaimed that it must be near evening or even night already, because she was quite hungry.

Roger laughed shortly. "That is not much of a guide. I was starving when I woke, and it was barely dinnertime then. Neither of us has had anything to eat, really, since yesterday."

"Yes, and it is reasonable for you to be hungry. You are accustomed to eating breakfast and perhaps even a luncheon, as well as a supper at night after dinner; but I am not—not for many months. We were only fed once a day, and I have grown accustomed to much less food than you are used to eating."

Roger stared through the dark. He could not see Leonie's face, but the voice . . . Again he was finding it hard to believe his ears. She sounded so good-humored; it was as if she were delighted that her deprivation had led to something that could help them. "My dear," he urged, his heart wrung with the thought of her suffering, "eat some more of the sausage."

She laughed. "But that would spoil everything. I must wait until I am really hungry, until I begin to have images of food in my mind. Then it will be time for us to try again and see if it is night."

"No!" Roger managed not to shout, remembering the way sound acted in the tunnel, but the depth of his revulsion at the idea of using Leonie's suffering to increase his safety rang through the controlled tone.

"What is wrong?" Leonie asked, stretching her hand to seek him in the dark.

"Do you think I would let you go hungry so that I could know the time?"

"But—"

It had always been assumed that Leonie would help and protect—and yield her convenience—to the other members of her family. She had never resented it because no unkindness was meant or practiced. It was a simple and natural outgrowth of the situation. Leonie was the elder child by many years, and naturally protected and cared for her younger brother; yet François was the *male* child, the heir to the lands and name, and his preferences came before hers.

When their world had been turned upside down, Leonie had, little by little, become the leader, the strong and responsible member of the family. Papa had been destroyed by what happened that first night. Mama had remained strong, but only for long enough to support Leonie over the shock and terror that had crumbled her world. When François fell sick, all mama's attention had been centered on him. She had accepted the little comforts Leonie had brought for him without question. Then mama had also sickened. Leonie had struggled to save them all, never thinking of assuaging her own hunger with the tidbits she "stole" from Louis. She was so accustomed to the acceptance of her sacrifices that she was startled and even a little angered by Roger's rejection.

"There are no 'buts' for such a thing," Roger said harshly. "I am trying to protect you, not torture you more."

That statement, of course, wiped away Leonie's brief anger and filled her with a warmth mixed with gentle amusement, so that when Roger pushed a substantial piece of sausage into her hand, she took it without argument.

"Eat," he insisted, "and do not tell me you are accustomed to doing without. I cannot bear it. I will get out of this house and get more food for you, even if I have to kill that guard."

Leonie giggled, although her eyes were full of tears of gratitude. "Don't be so silly," she murmured. "A full stomach is not worth a man's life, and more especially, it is not worth the danger you would face. Besides, we have enough food for now."

Nonetheless, she did eat what Roger had given her because she realized it was the only thing that would relieve his anxiety. She was quite right. As he heard her chew and swallow, Roger calmed down. The violence of his reaction surprised him in afterthought. Of course he would be distressed at the idea of any gentlewoman suffering hunger and would help if he could, but the sensation of hysteria with which he had urged food on Leonie was excessive. Most likely it was because he was hungry, he told himself cynically, not wishing to investigate the feeling that if he lost Leonie he would have lost everything. After all, it was ridiculous. He did not "have" Leonie.

"There is no need to judge by our stomachs anyway," Roger said suddenly, shaking his head over his own slowness at seeing an obvious fact. "All I need do is open the cask a little. Our eyes are so used to the dark that the slightest bit of light in the cellar will seem bright to us. When I went out, it was like day to me and the light above blinded me for a while."

They did just that and it worked perfectly. The first time Roger slipped the hook from its hasps there was still a dim grayness, and he pushed the cask shut again. Actually, they could have come out then, because the men Marot had left on guard had already retreated to the gatekeeper's lodge. However, the second time the cellar was nearly as dark as the tunnel. Roger tried to convince Leonie to remain in safety while he reconnoitered, but she would not, and, indeed, she was as silent and steady as he.

It took them nearly an hour of watching, hiding, and listening, but at last they were convinced that the house was empty and there was no one in the immediate vicinity. Possibly men might be hiding in the shadowed area of trees that edged the lawns. Roger went to investigate, and this time Leonie did not argue when he forbade her to come. In the house she could have been of help if Roger was attacked. She could have struck an enemy with a broken piece of furniture or thrown rubbish in his face. In the open she would only increase Roger's peril.

However, there was no peril to increase, although twice Roger had been startled by a mottled shadow that seemed to approach him and then skitter away. It must be a rat, Roger told himself, but it was very odd behavior for a rat. More important, as far as Roger had penetrated it, the park was empty. It was not reasonable that watchers would be farther away, because the house would not be visible to them. Roger returned and gently broke the subject of their next duty: to bury Henry. There was a brief silence, Leonie's face quivering on the verge of tears in the light of the rising moon. Then she sighed.

"Yes, but—but how?"

"I will manage. There are broken shafts and other things I can use for tools in the stable. What I need to know, Leonie, is where? I am sorry, but I do not think I would be able to take him to the churchyard. I—"

"There is no need. We have our own family place. It is nearby also. For state funerals, the carriages went down the drive and along the main road—"

She was interrupted by Roger's groan, which he turned into a cough. "That means the horse and carriage," he sighed. "Well—"

"No, no," Leonie hastened to assure him. "There is a path west of the house. You cannot see it because the maze is in the way, but mama used it often because it was a pleasant walk and she liked to tend the graves. There is a small chapel there. We could lay papa there while you"— her voice broke but she steadied it—"while you make everything ready for him."

"My dear, my poor child," Roger said gently, "would you consider saying farewell to your papa here in the house? I will do this as quickly as I can and then we will leave. I only wish to spare you pain, Leonie, but I do not know what would hurt you least. If you would stay here and pray for your papa while I lay him to rest, perhaps your memories would be less painful."

Leonie considered that, but after a moment she shook

her head resolutely. "I would have to go with you. The path branches. You might miss the way." She sighed again. "I must go so far back to find pleasant memories. . . ."

"But my dear, I have no—I am so sorry—I have no way to—to provide—dignity."

Leonie lifted her face to his. Tears leaked slowly from her eyes and tracked down through the dirt on her face. "It does not matter," she whispered. "Papa was a good man—truly good. His dignity is in himself, not in an ebony box with a satin lining, or mutes to carry it, or black plumes nodding on horses."

Unable to do anything else for her, Roger took Leonie into his arms. "You are right, and I assure you that I will feel true reverence for his body, even if I cannot always handle it just as I would wish."

It was, of course, impossible to handle Henry with dignity. The corpse was still in rigor and had to be carried between them, stiff as a board. Fortunately, they had laid it decently flat and were able to carry it wrapped in the hanging; however, Roger was prevented from bringing along such poor tools as he had hoped to find. As he laid Henry down in the tiny chapel and turned to start back to scrape up what he could, Leonie commented that everything here was untouched.

"And if they did not come into the chapel, perhaps they did not steal the tools from the shed behind. They were kept there for the gardeners who tended the graves and planted bushes and trees here."

Owing either to neglect or to superstition, no one had disturbed the chapel, and the key to the shed was in the little cupboard where it had always been kept. Roger sighed with relief as he opened it and found everything he needed. He had been much concerned that, in addition to the lack of a coffin, the lack of proper tools would not permit him to dig a deep enough grave to protect Henry's body from scavengers. The mattock and spade he took assured him that he would at least be able to provide that decency.

In the small graveyard, the first things Roger saw were two relatively new grave mounds, one larger than the other. Stooping, he made out the lettering on the temporary wooden markers: Marie Victoire Leonie de Conyers and François Henri Guillaume de Conyers. Good God!

Would Leonie be racked anew to find her mother and brother buried here? Roger could only assume that the bodies had been passed on to some friends to save the "state" the cost of burial. Briefly he considered trying to hide the fact by digging Henry's grave elsewhere, but then he reconsidered. Aside from the fact that, wherever he dug, Leonie might well notice the new graves, he also felt that when she recovered from the first shock it would probably be a comfort to her to know her family was all together. He began to dig beside Marie's grave.

In spite of blistered hands and an aching back from such unaccustomed work, it did not take Roger very long. The ground had already been softened by the previous burials and the afternoon's rain. When Roger had a neat trench, he returned to the chapel to find Leonie sitting quietly beside her father's body. He told her what he had found as gently as possible and was relieved to see a sad pleasure on her face.

"I am so glad," she sighed. "Papa wanted so much to be with mama. Now I do not need to grieve that I could not even do that much for him. They will be together and I will not worry about them. They were always happy together."

She did not cry when they carried Henry to the grave, even though they were both badly startled by a sudden reappearance of the scuttling black and white animal. It darted at them and, when Leonie jumped and cried out, rushed away. Leonie had almost dropped her father's feet, but she did not look down as she tightened her grip on the cloth; she stared after the creature, which had disappeared again into the shadows cast by the cypresses that bordered the graveyard. Even after they had lowered the body into the grave, she did not weep, only murmuring, "Good-bye, Papa, good-bye," but when Roger lifted the first shovelful of earth, she covered her face.

Roger laid down the spade and embraced her carefully. "Go back now, Leonie," he said. "Please go back to the house—or into the chapel."

Before she could answer, a long, thin, heartrending howl came from the cypresses. Leonie jumped and Roger clutched her tighter. She shuddered in his grip, then braced her body and nodded.

"Stay in the chapel if you are frightened," Roger urged.

"Frightened? No. I was only startled. The dog—it is silly

to say one recognizes a dog's voice—but that sounded so like my spaniel. She must be dead also, poor thing, she was so useless, so small and frail. No one would have taken her because she could not work."

Leonie shuddered again. The dog was still howling. Then she eased herself out of Roger's arms and began to walk back toward the house. Roger turned toward where the sound had come from, but he could see no flicker of black and white. The moon was almost down too, and he had better hurry and finish burying Henry.

Jean-Paul Marot had enjoyed his dinner far less than Leonie had enjoyed her piece of sausage. She sat on the ground in the cold and dark, but her heart was warm and full of hope. Jean-Paul had achieved all the warmth and light and elegancies that he had ever dreamed of in his present surroundings, but his heart was cold and dark. Somehow, the more his desires were satisfied, the emptier he became. For a long time after his victory, he had almost forgotten Henry de Conyers and his family, but there had been a burning, bitter renewal of his first satisfaction— when he had soiled the wife and daughter—when the news of the son's and wife's deaths was brought to him. Little by little de Conyers would be stripped of everything. He would end where Marot had started. Somehow, de Conyers was Marot's symbol: As Henry descended from power to nothing, Jean-Paul rose from nothing to power.

When he had been wakened by the sound of the tocsin and had been told why it rang, Marot was angry but he never associated the mob with Henry de Conyers. Marot had given the orders to shoot to kill because he did not believe in revolution—at least, not against himself. Besides, the town would never miss the type of people that caused that riot. After the mob had been driven away, Marot had gone to the Hôtel de Ville to assess the damage. He had listened without doubt to Louis's tale of the timid knock at the side door, the respectable-looking man who had a story of an emergency. Louis would not let him in, of course. He had stepped out, locked the door to protect the building and while he was so engaged, he had been seized, beaten, knocked unconscious, and bound. As soon as he could free himself, he had given warning.

Louis's disheveled and bloodied appearance gave mute

testimony in his favor, and Jean-Paul accepted the lies and turned his attention to the ruin in the offices, to the loss of the special funds to ease the lot of the foundlings and the poor. Most of the night was spent in inventorying the damage and setting the buildings to rights, tasks in which Louis busied himself assiduously—so assiduously that it was reasonable he should not think of prisoners in whom he would not be expected to have had any special interest. It was nearly morning before Marot himself noticed that the cellar door was still closed while all the others had been burst open. At first that satisfied him, but later he wondered why that door alone had not been opened.

The question led immediately to the discovery of de Conyers's escape. Marot exploded into violence bordering on hysteria. All other activity was abandoned while search parties were organized for the town and the gate guards were questioned. At the gates no one had seen anything or heard anything. The disturbance in the center of the town had not reached them. In particular the guards of the southwest gate were questioned, and they swore on their souls, on the souls of their parents, children, and wives, that they had not opened the gate for anyone—man, woman, dog, or cat. This was true; Leonie had opened the small door beside the gate herself.

Nonetheless, Marot was convinced that de Conyers had gone back to the château. His conviction rested on a number of rational reasons—the money in the strongroom for one—but most forceful was the totally irrational conviction that if de Conyers reached the château, somehow power would be restored to him. Thus, Marot himself went with the men who searched the château to be sure, very sure, absolutely sure that de Conyers had not found his way there nor would be able to do so later.

Discovery that the house was empty had not had the effect Marot hoped for. The more carefully he searched, the stronger grew the conviction that de Conyers *was* there, watching him, laughing at him. The growing reluctance of the men to continue the search and to remain on guard to catch de Conyers when he came reinforced the irrational fear that somehow de Conyers was taking over, ordering the men to go away, convincing them that he was harmless—while he gathered his forces to destroy them all.

Only the glances the men cast at Marot—glances that

grew more and more doubtful—gave Jean-Paul the strength to see this fear as irrational and prevent him from voicing it. However, when he was alone, it returned and grew. It was peculiar that no one else seemed to sense de Conyers's presence, Marot mused, except to obey the commands he was giving. Perhaps there was some special affinity between himself and de Conyers. This chance thought took hold and grew in Marot's mind until, by the time dark fell, he had reached a new conclusion: De Conyers could not be found because the other men were there. The question of who would hold the power in Saulieu must be settled only between himself and de Conyers.

As soon as he came to this conclusion, Marot was utterly convinced by it. What was more, he suddenly understood why all his achievements had brought him no satisfaction— had left him empty. It was because de Conyers still held the power. Even as a helpless prisoner, the right had been his. . . . No! Not the right! That was de Conyers's voice speaking in his mind. The evil influence . . . that was it! The evil influence that de Conyers wielded would exist as long as he did. Jean-Paul realized that his long dissatisfaction was his own fault. He had been thinking of himself, of the sweetness of revenge. What he should have done was have de Conyers killed. That would have cleaned the evil out of Saulieu—washed it away with blood, as the *Ami du Peuple* recommended.

Of course, the fact that de Conyers was alive had encouraged resistance. His evil fed the evil in the hearts of those who opposed the good Jean-Paul wished to do. When de Conyers's evil was gone, it would draw with it or weaken all the other evil. But Marot understood that through his error de Conyers's evil had been allowed to grow strong. That was how de Conyers had deceived the men who searched. He alone was able to resist, and it was his personal duty to return to the château and kill de Conyers. Then he would be free and Saulieu would be free.

There was no difficulty for Marot. True, the groom he ordered to saddle a horse for him looked rather oddly at him and the guard at the gate did also, but no one dared say anything. Later they talked about how strange he had looked, about how he had muttered to himself about evil forces in possession, and their tale was of considerable help to Louis. However, no impediment was placed in Marot's way, and he rode away sure of himself and his purpose.

Because he knew with perfect certainty that de Conyers was in the château and that the confrontation between them was ordained, he was neither surprised nor angered by the fact that his men had taken shelter in the gatehouse. He did not stop to reprimand them. What was the use? Either de Conyers or fate had arranged everything. Thus it was not the men's fault that they had abandoned their posts. That was a necessary part of Marot's struggle against the evil living in de Conyers. Calm in the conviction that good was stronger than evil and that he must triumph, Marot rode around the house and put his horse into one of the empty stalls in the stable. Then he went to the house.

"I am here alone," he called into the black emptiness. "Come and see if you can bend me to your will."

No answer, not even an echo. His voice rolled into the empty, ruined house and seemed to be absorbed. Jean-Paul felt a leap of joy. Good *was* more powerful than evil. Even though he was alone, de Conyers was afraid to come out and confront him. But their meeting was ordained. Thus, Jean-Paul was sure de Conyers could no longer hide from him. He began another systematic search of the house.

By the time he was finished, the moon was very low in the sky and Marot's conviction was beginning to waver. Deep inside grew a little sick fear that he was mad, that he had made up everything—de Conyers's power, his evil, his presence in the château. There was no way he could believe that de Conyers was in the house, but there was no way he could accept that sickness inside. He crushed it down, standing in the entryway, staring back into the house. Very well, if de Conyers was not inside, he was outside. Marot turned and, like a blessed assurance to wash away his ugly fear, he saw a figure in the moonlight just rounding the dark hedges of the maze and heading toward the back of the house.

Stifling a cry of joy, Marot ran quickly through the house to the kitchens. As he went, it occurred to him that what he did was stupid. De Conyers might turn aside, go back to the woods, run and hide. He pushed that idea away. It was not possible. The meeting and his victory were ordained. That conviction sustained Marot when he came to the back door and saw no one. Although he knew he should remain inside the house, where his enemy could not see him and he would have the advantage of surprise, there was enough suspicion of his own sanity under Marot's reiterated conviction of ordained fate to make it impossible to do that. Strangling his fears, he hurried along the path behind the house toward the clump of trees that shaded the stables.

The howling of the dog had disturbed Leonie more than she admitted. She had spoken the truth to Roger; she was not afraid. However, the voice of the little dog, a small, seemingly frail creature sent to her by her uncle all the way from England as a gift, brought back her whole easy, happy life before the revolution. The dog—named Fifi because it was the silliest, most useless name Leonie could think of—epitomized the old life—full of grace, intelligence that was rarely tested, love, and beauty. Fifi was a King Charles spaniel, exquisitely beautiful, with long, silky black and white fur, but she weighed no more than four kilos. As a puppy she had fitted into Leonie's hand.

Leonie remembered her practical mother, accustomed to hunting dogs and work dogs, staring at the tiny creature with amused bewilderment. But in the end they had all come to love Fifi. She was affectionate and very, very clever. She could be taught anything—to do tricks, play games, carry messages. Many times Leonie remembered her mother speaking with exasperation about Fifi's size. Such a clever dog could have been extremely useful if it were larger, Marie said. It was a shame to breed such silly creatures. Still, it was Leonie's pet and Marie did not deprive her daughter of any reasonable pleasure—not even such a foolish one.

Dead too, Leonie thought, tears rising to her eyes so that she was half-blind. Although Fifi's body was far sturdier than one would expect from so small an animal, it was inconceivable that the little bitch could survive alone. She had been hand-fed, cosseted, since the day she was born. Even if no one had killed her on purpose—because she was a symbol of the hated aristocracy—Fifi could neither hunt nor forage for herself, Leonie thought. But it was odd, very odd, that the howl had been so much like hers and the black and white mottling on the animal that had run out of the woods . . . No, I will not think about anything so silly, Leonie decided, and she kept her eyes resolutely on the path directly in front of her, not permitting herself to look hopefully for another flash of black and white so that she could call, "Fifi, Fifi," and again hope to hold that soft, wriggling bundle of joy.

Thus, Leonie did not see the shadow slipping along the trees, past the side of the stable. She was too fixed in her self-discipline to hear the indrawn breath and low curse Marot uttered when he realized the figure was that of a woman, not of Henry de Conyers. In the next moment he saw, in the low moonlight, that the woman's hair was pale; yet the stride was that of a young woman, not the stiff totter of a gray-haired crone. Blond hair was a rarity in Saulieu. Marot's heart leaped with joy. The only woman in the area he knew to have pale hair was de Conyers's whelp. If she was here, so was her father!

As Marot reached this conclusion, Leonie drew abreast of him. He shoved the pistol he had been carrying back in his pocket, let her take a step or two more, jumped out and seized her from behind, one arm going around her throat and the other around her waist.

CHAPTER 9

As soon as Leonie was a few steps clear of the grave, Roger turned his attention to filling it as quickly as he could. Reverence for the dead was a good thing, but care for the living was more essential. Roger was quite sure that if Henry de Conyers knew what was happening he would be far more anxious to be sure his daughter was protected than to have himself covered with earth with slow dignity. Fortunately, Roger thought as he threw and pushed earth into the grave, Leonie was walking very slowly. He should be able to catch up with her before she reached the house.

He had, in fact, just thrown the last shovelful of earth on top of the mound when Leonie reached the edge of the maze. With a sigh of relief, he put the spade and mattock back in the shed, closed the door, and hurried around the chapel into the alley between the trees that led back to the house. He was more than halfway down it when he heard a single choked shriek. Before his mind had clearly comprehended what it meant, Roger was running desperately along the path. His body reacted to the signal of danger, although he had not yet thought of what to do when he arrived.

Indeed, his mind was still frantically asking *where? where?* when a fusillade of shrill barking drew him instinctively to the left toward the back of the house. In seconds he saw Leonie struggling in the grip of a man. Without thinking of the pistols he carried, Roger launched himself forward again, but before he could reach Leonie's attacker, a small black and white animal charged from the trees beyond the stables, leaped high, and seized the man by the leg above the boot. Marot uttered a bellow of rage and pain and kicked out, but the gesture did not free him. Jaws locked, Fifi hung on as grimly as any bulldog, her turned-up snout permitting her to cling rather than leap and slash in the usual canine attack.

Marot roared again as his own jerk tore the flesh of his leg, since Fifi's jaws would not yield. Unthinking, reacting only to his own pain, he released his hold on Leonie to strike at the dog. Instantly Leonie twisted away, hitting Marot as she went, and simultaneously Roger struck him in a wild, flying leap. Both men crashed to the ground, Roger on top, while the violent shock tore Fifi loose from her hold.

Spitting out flesh and cloth, Fifi rolled to her feet, growling, ready to attack again. She was brought up short by the beloved voice that went with the beloved scent of the goddess.

"No!" Leonie shrieked. "No, Fifi. Come!"

If Leonie had know that Fifi could well distinguish between Roger and Jean-Paul and would attack only Jean-Paul because his was the scent that her goddess had cried out against, she might have risked losing that precious remnant of her old life to help Roger. She feared, however, that the tiny bitch would attack the wrong man and lose her own little life while bringing disaster on them all. Besides, what help could little Fifi be? For a full minute after her instinctive order to the dog, Leonie stood gasping and trembling. She had not seen the man who seized her, but he had asked her one question—where her father was—and she knew that voice. Never, never, would she forget the voice that taunted her father while despoiling her. In the single minute after her escape from his clutches, shock was submerged by hatred, and hatred by fear as Leonie saw Roger being forced back and over by Marot.

No! If she died for it, Marot would not hurt another person she loved. Leonie ran to the stable, grabbed a heavy spoke torn from a carriage wheel, and rushed back. In the few moments she had been gone, the tide of battle had turned. Roger's initial advantage, owing to surprise and the force with which he had hit Marot, had not lasted long. Roger was no weakling, but he had had nearly nothing to eat for two days and he was tired already from burying Henry. Besides, Marot, convinced he was fighting the Devil himself in the person of Henry de Conyers, had the inhuman strength of the insane.

After his initial cries of pain when Fifi seized him, Marot

had fought in silence, grabbing Roger by the throat and twisting. First Roger had struck at him, but Marot ignored one blow that split his lips like an overripe tomato and another that opened a bleeding gash below his eye. All his attention was on his own two hands, which were closing the air from Roger's throat, and his legs, which were lifting his left side so that Roger was toppling off him to the right.

Aware that his blows were useless, Roger tried to force his hands between Marot's arms to break the grip on his throat. At the same time he tried to brace himself on his right knee to maintain his superior position. But somehow, he could not seem to feel the ground, and his arms were soft and as limp as scalded celery stalks. Vaguely he noted through the roaring in his ears and the bursting sensation in his chest that the moon must have set very suddenly, because it was growing as dark as in the tunnel. Then he could feel himself falling, but was he falling into the dark inside himself or onto the ground?

As Leonie approached, Marot was just coming upright above Roger, his hands still tight on Roger's throat. His face—with the blood black in the little moonlight that remained, the eyes glittering in insane triumph—was a grotesque mask. Roger's hands clung to Marot's wrists, but they were slowly opening as the last of his consciousness left him; his mouth gaped wide in a futile effort to find breath.

"No!" Leonie snarled softly, and she swung the spoke at Marot's head.

The power of that blow was far beyond Leonie's ordinary strength. She was beside herself with hate for the murderer of every good thing in her life. In fact, she was so blind with rage that she missed her aim. The spoke caught Marot at the base of the skull, and it snapped the neck, crushed the bone, and tore the soft spinal cord right in two. Marot's head snapped back into an impossible position, the mouth gaping open but upside down in a seeming surprise that was more ludicrous than dreadful. The convulsion of his death throes tore Marot's hands from Roger's throat, and his body fell away, off Roger, jerking and contracting in senseless spasm.

Leonie was spared the horror of that, owing to her total concentration on Roger. Just as Marot released him, his hands had fallen limply. For one instant Leonie thought she had been too late, but then she heard the breath rattle into his abused throat and knelt beside him. Fifi approached, circling Marot's now-still corpse, growling and then whimpering and curvetting her body, tail half between her legs, half wagging, hoping this time to be recognized. So many people, who in the past had always petted her and fed her, had driven her away with kicks and blows, that Fifi had feared to approach even this most familiar, most beloved scent.

Roger was breathing in deep, painful gasps, which reassured Leonie enough to permit her to turn her head from him to the dog. "Hush, Fifi," she whispered, "hush. Come here."

The whimpering stilled. Fifi knew what "hush" meant. Trembling, crouching close to the ground, the spaniel approached and achieved heaven. A gentle hand patted her head, gathered her close. Fifi, silent as she had been ordered, vibrated with joy.

Holding the little bitch close, with Roger beginning to stir, Leonie was suddenly, senselessly happy. An enormous burden seemed to have lifted from her soul. She could have laughed aloud for joy. She had not forgotten that her family was all gone, but Marot, he who had destroyed them, was dead also—a debt paid in full! Without realizing she was doing it, Leonie closed the ledger that recorded her bitterness and hate. She was well aware that her troubles were not over, that hunger and cold and danger were still to be endured, but with Roger beside her, and a big pot of gold at the end of the rainbow, she was no longer afraid.

"Run. Hide."

The cracked whisper drew Leonie's eyes to Roger. Sense had returned to him, and he was trying to lift himself away from her so that she could escape to safety.

"There is no one to run from," Leonie assured him softly, helping him to sit up. "He only cried out twice, and that was a long time ago. If others were with him and had heard, they would have come already, but there has not been a sound." She looked down, released the little dog. "Who hides, Fifi? Who hides?"

That was a familiar command. Leonie and François had often played a form of hide and seek with the little dog, one holding her while the other hid. She would then search out the concealed one. Later the game had been expanded to warn Leonie of unwelcome visitors. In the year or two preceding the disruption of her life, Leonie had been plagued by suitors who were not to her taste, and Fifi had been taught to warn Leonie when one of them was about. Delighted at the renewal of a familiar task, Fifi darted away.

Roger opened his mouth to protest, to ask where the attacker had gone and why he had not finished killing him, but only a croak came out. Upright now, he had seen the dark form only a foot away. Leonie drew her eyes from the shadows where Fifi had disappeared and saw where Roger was looking.

"Who?" he got out over the pain of his bruised larynx.

"Marot," Leonie replied. "That was Marot, the man who . . ." Her voice wavered but then grew firm. "Who raped me in front of my father. I killed him."

Roger croaked again—which was about all he would have been able to do even if he had not nearly been choked to death. He did not know which shocked him more, what had been done to Leonie or what she had been able to do. Nor did he know whether he was appalled by the relative calm of her voice or proud of it. Roger knew women of every type—really stupid, helpless, fluttering creatures who became paralyzed with fear when asked to do the simplest things without the support of their menfolk; women who pretended helplessness to trap men but whose minds were as hard and cruel as a steel trap; fine women with brains and strength and courage, like his stepmother and Lady Alice—but all those women had been lapped in luxury and care. Roger had never dreamed a woman could endure terror, physical deprivation, the loss of all those she loved and leaned on and still remain sane—not to mention calm and capable of reacting as Leonie did.

He stared at her and she looked back quietly, then questioningly as she recognized his astonished bewilderment. "What is it?" she asked.

"Are—are you all right?" Roger croaked.

"Yes. Oh, yes," Leonie began, and then she realized there was more to Roger's question than a need for reassurance that she had not been physically hurt. "Oh, yes," she repeated. "It's all over now. I will still miss mama and papa and François, but they can rest in peace. And now I am free to go to England and build a new life."

Painfully, Roger got to his feet. His knees were still wobbly, and Leonie pulled his arm over her shoulder. From the side of the house, a black and white streak sprang forward, growling.

"No!" Leonie commanded. "Here, Fifi. Come here." The dog obeyed. "This is Roger," she said. "Friend, Fifi. Roger, friend." To Roger she said, "It is my little dog. I do not know how she survived, but she is here. She bit Marot so he had to let me go."

The bitch had stopped stock-still at Leonie's command, the growls dying away. Roger knelt shakily on one knee and extended a hand slowly. Fifi sniffed the fingers, found a strange male odor—not the scent that had made the goddess cry out with fear—and, mixed with the male scent, that of the beloved. Tentatively, the tail lifted a little, gave a timid, halfhearted wag. Roger reached gently upward, softly caressed the head, stroked the long ears. Up came the tail, wagging furiously as the body twisted sideways. Fifi wanted to love everyone. Far more than hunger and cold, she had suffered from loneliness, from the loss of objects on which to lavish her boundless affection.

Roger gave her another pat, slightly rougher, and whispered, "Good girl. Good Fifi."

Even through the roughness his bruised larynx gave to his voice, Leonie could hear the distaste with which Roger pronounced the name, and she laughed softly and explained how poor Fifi had come to be called something so ridiculous. Had Roger been able to speak, he would have indignantly pointed out the uses of the King Charles spaniel, a breed with which he was quite familiar, but the pain in his throat warned him that he had better save his efforts for something more practical. Their luck had been phenomenal so far; they had better not push it farther.

Originally he had hoped to be able to get his horse and carriage and leave immediately after laying Henry to rest, but that was not possible. He doubted he would have the strength to move the debris with which he had loaded his carriage or to drag it out of the stable. He was barely able to keep to his feet. Besides, they needed time to look in the strong room and hide Marot's body. If they could have left at once, they could have let it lie where it was; if they had to remain, it would be most unwise to betray the fact that someone had killed Marot on the château grounds.

Roger could have wept with weariness and weakness and
pain. His hands were blistered raw and his shoulders ached
from wielding pick and shovel; his throat was on fire and
he was bruised from the fight with Marot; hunger gnawed
at him and drained his energy. There was nothing he
wanted so much as to lie down for a while, but he did not
dare stop and rest for fear he would be unable to continue
at all. He stared at Marot helplessly, trying to gather the
energy to lift the body to his shoulders so that he could
conceal it.

"What is wrong?" Leonie asked anxiously. She could not
see the expression on Roger's face because the moon had
set and it was too dark, but she could sense his tension.

"Have to hide him," Roger mumbled and staggered forward a step.

"You cannot carry him yourself," Leonie said. Roger
shrugged angrily. "Wait," she urged. "I can bring a plank
or a wheel from the stable and we can carry him between
us on that."

Before Roger could insist that he would manage on his
own out of pure shame and stubbornness, Leonie had darted
away into the stable. There she paused momentarily, surprised by the increased dark because she had forgotten that
the moon had set. In the stillness she heard the stamp and
shuffle of a stalled horse. Uttering only a tiny squeak of
delight and laughter at herself—after all, how would Marot
have come to the château if not on a horse—she ran into
the aisle between the horse stalls. In another minute she
was out, leading the animal.

Roger's relief at not needing to carry Marot was so great
that his aches and pains diminished and a good part of his
energy returned. The problem of what to do with Marot
was completely solved. He could ride the horse down the
back lane to the road, tie the corpse to the saddle, head the
horse back toward Saulieu, and give it a good whack. Even
if the animal did not return all the way to the town where
its stable was—which it might well do—it would go far
enough from the château to eliminate all suspicion that
Marot had met his death there. Roger did not try to explain all this to Leonie, merely signaled her to hold the
horse while he hefted Marot onto it and then mounted himself.

"Hide," he urged as he turned the horse to the back lane.

Leonie nodded and smiled. Fifi, standing right by her ankle, wagged her tail furiously. Her world was coming right. The bad scent was being taken away. Roger, seeing the wildly agitated tail because its white patches picked up what little light there was, suddenly felt much easier about leaving Leonie alone. The little dog could do virtually nothing to protect her mistress but she could warn her of danger, and Roger did not push away the feeling of comfort.

It took nearly half an hour to walk the horse to the back gate, which made it a very long walk back to the château. Roger simply could not make it without resting for a while, and he was so tired that he fell asleep. That turned out to be most fortunate. The sun rose before he reached his goal and showed him an orchard, its trees laden with fruit. Most of it was not ripe, but some apples more precocious than their fellows lay on the ground. All the delight and pleasurable excitement Roger had felt at the beginning of this venture returned in a rush. It was like a sign that "Someone" was on their side. Chuckling with relief, Roger climbed the low wall, grabbed a ripe apple, and ate it. Then he loaded his pockets with more ripe fruit while he ate another and still another. Feeling like a completely new man, he climbed back over the wall and set out boldly for the château.

The blood from Henry's wound had long ago dried to indeterminate brown smears. His coat and breeches were torn and filthy, as were his once elegant boots. Those might give him away if anyone knew enough about boots in this rural and unsophisticated area to judge their quality, but that did not worry Roger. If he met anyone, he would be a vagabond. Ruefully he rubbed a hand over his three-day beard and grinned. He might be questioned as a suspicious character, but certainly not one who could be involved in Saulieu's troubles. And if the questioning grew too forceful . . . He patted the pistols that lay over the apples in his pockets.

Roger was almost disappointed when no one stopped him. The château was as desolate and deserted as when they had first arrived. Roger did not know of the men who had spent the night in the gatehouse, but even they were gone. They had wakened in the dawn and hurried back to their assigned posts at back and front doors. There they had waited, hungry and thirsty, for their replacements to come or for orders to return. As the sun rose higher, so had their rage and resentment when no relief had come. Finally, fury overmatched fear of Marot. About fifteen minutes before Roger reached the house, they had left it to return to Saulieu and complain of the treatment they had received.

Completely unopposed, Roger made his way to the cellar. Before he even reached the cask, Leonie had rushed out to grab him and sob with relief.

"You were gone so long," she gasped. "I feel as if I've been waiting forever, Roger! What happened to you?"

"Nothing," Roger assured her, patting her consolingly and explaining what had delayed him. "Here," he added with a broad smile, "have an apple. Have half a dozen apples. The house and grounds are empty—and I am full." Then he frowned. "Did you know that? You shouldn't have rushed out like that. What if it had been someone else?"

"Had to be you," Leonie mumbled around her mouthful of apple, while Roger bit off pieces of another to feed the little dog. "Fifi was wagging her tail. She wouldn't do that for a stranger. Oh, what a lovely breakfast!"

"She's a friendly little thing," Roger said doubtfully. "Are you sure she wouldn't just be glad to see anyone at all?"

"Not Fifi. Oh, she's friendly enough, but we couldn't have her cavorting around with the laborers or running into their houses. She has been trained not to approach anyone—or permit anyone to approach her—until she is introduced and told 'friend.' Are you sure the house is empty?"

"No," Roger answered, tensing. "I didn't search it or even go to the front. It just felt empty. Have you a reason to think someone is hiding?"

"I'm not sure. Some time ago, Fifi got up and listened. I was sure you were coming then—that's why I was so worried—and she acted nervous and restless until just a little while ago. But no one came down here."

Roger gnawed his lips for a second. He wanted to be away from this place. Apples were wonderful, but they both needed more substantial food, and Leonie—the cellar was dim, but now that he was not completely distracted by other more urgent needs he could see that she was dressed in filthy rags—needed clothing. Still, if Fifi sensed a presence, her instincts were far more reliable than Roger's own. It was stupid to take chances. Besides, Roger realized, although he felt much better he really could use a couple of hours' sleep.

Leonie was quite agreeable. She had not been doing anything physical while Roger rid them of Marot's body, but she had been too worried and frightened to sleep or really benefit much from the inactivity. In fact, they both fell asleep almost as soon as they lay down—showing clearly that Roger's decision to wait had been wise—without even a renewal of the sexual tensions that had tortured them earlier. They both had been more tired than they realized.

In the late afternoon Roger wakened with an urgent need to relieve his bowels and bladder. Cursing softly, he extricated himself from the portion of the hanging Leonie had thrown over him and opened the cask. Fifi sat up brightly. The dog showed no sign of wariness now, so Roger stepped out. Perkily, tail waving high, Fifi came with him and darted up the stairs without hesitation. Roger was not quite so incautious. In spite of Leonie's faith in the little bitch and the evidence of his own eyes about her caution in approaching them, he knew that dogs had infinite, if sometimes mistaken, faith in their human companions. Fifi's confidence might merely reflect her expectation that he would protect her from any danger that threatened.

He was somewhat reassured by the way Fifi paused at the top of the steps to sniff before she trotted out into the corridor, and his confidence was increased when he found that, indeed, the house was empty. A "Who comes, Fifi? Who comes?" sent the dog scampering around the house to return with tail waving—the sign that all was clear, Leonie had told Roger. A scuttling run, tail between legs, was the signal for Leonie to hide because someone *was* coming. It was safe—Roger hoped—and he went out to the jakes. Even if Fifi were wrong, there was not much danger for him. It was natural for a vagabond to seek shelter in a derelict house. That excuse would still be valid.

No excuse was necessary. House and grounds were empty, except for themselves. Roger made his way through the debris in the stable and extracted his traveling bag from the carriage. Then with a sigh of pleasure he blocked the drain in the scullery sink, pumped it full of water, washed himself free of the accumulated filth of days, and, finally, shaved. He would have preferred hot water and a shorter beard, but feeling clean and decent was worth the chill and scraping. Clothes were another and more serious problem. He had a clean shirt, but in full daylight the marks on his coat were, to his eyes, too unmistakably blood stains. He was just about to sponge the coat when Fifi leaped to her feet. The pistol Roger had taken from his coat pocket was leveled before he saw the dog's wildly wagging tail.

From the doorway came Leonie's low laugh. "Oh, Roger, no!"

"No what?"

"There is not a person who would take you for anything except an English gentleman." Leonie reproved him with laughing eyes.

Roger could feel the color flood into his face. With the words came recognition of what he had done. He had combed his hair, put on a cravat, in general done what he could to his appearance to make him acceptable to a gentlewoman. Although he had not allowed the idea to come into his mind, he was really getting himself ready to court a woman.

"I will be much more the thing when I have cleared the carriage and harnessed the horse," Roger said repressively, but his blush had betrayed him and Leonie only laughed.

"You had better at least take off the cravat," she said, and then, relenting, "but I am very glad to see you dressed. I had no idea how handsome you are."

For reply, Roger ripped off the cravat and stalked out of the house to the stable. He did not remain angry long, being fair-minded enough to see that what he had done *was* funny. Moreover, there was nothing in Leonie's manner to indicate that she had realized he had been trying to impress her and was laughing at him. She seemed to think he had merely been absentminded and acted by habit. As he pulled broken planks and old rotten straw off and away from the carriage, Roger remembered that Leonie had complimented his looks.

It had been a long time, a very long time, since Roger had considered how his appearance would affect a woman. He had been a reasonably confident youth, but Solange had ripped that confidence to shreds after their marriage. The fact that many women had praised him since then had not changed Roger's bitterness. Those women had been paid— some real whores, others established mistresses, but all living on his purse at the mercy of his goodwill. Roger had not for a moment taken anything they had said seriously. What could they say when starvation was the wage of honesty?

The remark Leonie had made was quite different—or was there an ulterior motive there? It was true that Leonie might feel beholden to him—Roger did not think that she should, because he had mixed himself into this business quite voluntarily and certainly without any request from her or her father. Nonetheless, why should she comment on his being handsome unless she really did think he was? There was no need for her to say anything at all, or at least anything more than *You look nice* or some similar noncommittal remark.

By the time Roger had the carriage cleared, he was again dusty and mussed but in an excellent mood. As a precaution he left the carriage at the door of the stable—he did not think it wise to stand it out in the yard—and turned to go for the horse. Midway to the maze, he stopped. He would as likely lose himself in the maze as not. Leonie would have to get the horse. At the door of the kitchen, however, he stopped again, all thought of the horse flying out of his head. Leonie had been cleaning his coat and looked up at his step. She had, however, cleaned herself first, and the result was far more startling than Roger's transformation.

"Beautiful!" Roger breathed before he thought. "You are so very beautiful." And then, as he remembered what her experience of men had been and that she might consider his appreciation a threat, he added, "I beg your pardon," stiffly.

There was no fear in the warm chuckle that came from Leonie. "It is not polite to take back a compliment by apologizing for it."

"That was not what I meant at all," Roger snapped, striding forward and then stopping abruptly when he realized he had intended to take her in his arms.

He cleared his throat, telling himself sternly that the girl was *not* beautiful, that every one of his mistresses had been far prettier. Leonie's skin, not pale by nature, had been bleached to sallowness by long incarceration. Her face was pinched by semistarvation so that the features were too large for it—a wide, mobile mouth, a straight, strong nose, and big eyes of a color that would have been hazel except that they lacked any touch of green. The hair was magnificent. Even Roger's attempt to discipline his unruly emotions by looking for every fault could discover nothing to criticize in that honey-gold mane, just fluffing and curling after its recent washing. But it was not the hair that wrenched his heart and, even in these unromantic surroundings, sent a wave of warmth through his loins. There was something in the face, completely unrelated to its features, that made it surpassingly beautiful to him.

"We had better see about that strong room," Roger said abruptly. "I have the carriage cleared. As soon as you get the horse and I hitch it, we will be ready to leave."

Truthfully, Roger did not really believe there was anything in the strong room. He doubted it was a secret from the servants. Even if Henry had been careful in his use of it, previous owners may not have been equally cautious, and servants were often almost as hereditary as property itself. That is, servants often married other servants in the household and their children became servants in turn. Mostly, long-term servants were honest in large matters, although they might take a little food or candles or worn clothing for themselves or their families. Some were even devoted, especially those who had been with a family for many years. In such a case the strong room might have been emptied to "save" its contents for the master.

Although Leonie handed Roger his coat and started for the library at once, she had as little confidence as he that her father's dream would come true. She had little difficulty in finding the latch, but the door concealed behind the molding opened only an inch or two and then resisted. Roger stepped forward to apply greater pressure. He pushed sharply, then staggered back with an exclamation of disgust. Although he had not succeeded in opening the door all the way, the odor that had hit him betrayed what he would find.

"Go away, Leonie," he said sharply, but the words were all but drowned in Fifi's howl.

"Hush!" Leonie ordered, but she was staring with dilated

eyes at Roger. She backed a few steps, then stood again. "Someone is . . . was in there!" she whispered.

"Yes," Roger muttered, controlling his urge to retch with an effort.

Doubtless there was some air vent into the room, but it could not have been large and the putrefaction of the corpse had been slowed. Thus, even after months, the stench was sickening.

"Don't—" Leonie began, but Roger cut her off with a gesture.

"Go away," he said again. "Go get the horse and bring it to the stables. I don't think there's anything in here, but I'd better look."

Leonie shuddered and fled. For her it was the end of any desire, present or future, to live in the château of her birth. The memories of her youth would become sweet when her immediate grief was past, but the château itself had become repulsive, a place of decay and blackened ruin, filled with a miasma of fear and death. All she wanted was to be away, to be rid of the place and the country, to begin anew.

Roger thrust at the door grimly, breathing as little as possible. He did not enter far, just enough to see that the money boxes were broken open. He was backing out when his eyes fell on several packets of papers bound in tapes. They might be nothing, but they might hold Leonie's claim to these lands—if France ever returned to quiet again. With clenched jaws he entered, scooped up the papers, and turned to go. What he saw made him gag and then bring up the remains of the apples in his stomach. He had disarranged the body in moving the door; nonetheless, it was clear that the man had not been killed. He had been locked in alive, to claw the door—from which the latch had been deliberately broken—and scream for help and die of thirst and starvation.

Terrified, Roger leaped for the half-open door. Outside he leaned against the wall, shaking, trying to rid himself of the vision of being accidentally shut in to die. A sharp bark broke him free of horror, and he bent to scoop Fifi into his arms and bury his face in her fur. He was a fool. Leonie would have known where he was. Obviously she had sent the little dog to get him. Still, it was with an enormous sense of relief that he set down Fifi, who had been licking his face ecstatically, threw the papers he was carrying into his traveling bag, and went out toward the stable where Leonie waited. His spirits were rising again. The worst was over. All they had to do now was get out of France.

CHAPTER 10

The next day, when Roger had a chance to count what money he had left, getting out of France did not seem quite so simple. They had traveled long after the light faded, stopping only at midnight where two cart tracks met outside of Semur-en-Auxois. In Roger's opinion they were still far too close to Saulieu, but they could not make good time on the country tracks they had traveled in the dark. This fact, plus Roger's realization that such behavior was far more suspicious than traveling openly by day, decided him. They drew behind a hedge and made a camp of sorts. That would be innocent enough. They would claim to be strangers to the area and, as such, could not be expected to know that there was a town a few kilometers farther on.

Wrapped in Roger's cloak and leaning comfortably against a wheel of the carriage, Leonie smiled happily. "Then we are to become respectable? Ah, what a disappointment. I had thought we would pretend to be tinkers." She looked up at the star-spangled sky. "It is very pleasant, this camping out."

Roger laughed. "Yes, when the weather is warm and dry, but I fear it won't hold much longer." He had some experience of cold, wet nights huddled against a pony's side waiting for word from Pierre. "It is also very pleasant to sleep in a bed, and I, to speak the truth, will find it a welcome change."

"A bed? What's that?" Leonie teased.

Once again Roger was amazed at her lightheartedness, her ability to accept physical privation. The cheerfulness was infinitely touching. It made him all the more determined that she should suffer no more.

"Tomorrow night you will sleep in a bed," he said, "even if I must shoot an innkeeper to obtain one for you."

"I was only joking." Leonie was rather startled by the intensity of Roger's response. "I really don't care where I sleep—and I'm afraid you will *have* to shoot an innkeeper before he will let me in."

Although the tone was still light, Roger could see that Leonie had sensed his suppressed violence and was troubled. "Probably," he replied, smiling at her and making sure his voice was easy, "but I think it would be easier and cause less disturbance if I got you some decent clothes instead."

For a long moment Leonie was silent, struggling with herself. She had not believed that the desire to be cleanly and becomingly clothed could be so strong. Over the bitter months in prison, she had learned what was truly essential, and certainly pretty dresses were not. Still, she had to bite her lips to keep herself from crying out, "*Oh, yes!*"

"Money," she forced herself to say calmly. "You told me you had not enough money. Should you—should you waste what you have on clothing for me?"

"It will be no waste," Roger assured her. "It is the only way we can travel safely. If word is sent out from Saulieu that you and your father have escaped, we must not match the description in any way. Now I do not look anything like your father, but you are blond, and that is not common. However, if you are dressed as a respectable tradesman's daughter, with your hair covered by a local headdress, I don't believe anyone would look at us twice."

"*Tradesman's daughter!*" Leonie exclaimed. "They will look at you several times more than twice if you are planning to claim to be my father."

"Well, we don't look much alike," Roger agreed, "but it is sometimes so. I don't look anything like *my* father—"

"Don't be so silly," Leonie giggled. "I'm not talking about looks. When would you have sired me? At ten?"

"I am more than ten years older than you," Roger said stiffly.

"But not nearly old enough to have sired me *respectably*," Leonie pointed out, laughing harder. "It may have happened," she continued merrily, ignoring Roger's affronted expression, "but only if you married my mother under the gun. *Respectable* tradesmen do not marry in their early teens."

Unable to help himself, Roger burst out laughing too.

"You are shocking me," he protested—and it was half true. The young daughters of his friends and relatives either truly did not know or, more likely, pretended not to know where newborn humans came from.

"Am I?" Leonie asked uncertainly. "I'm sorry. I will watch my tongue more carefully, but papa and mama—"

"No, of course not," Roger responded hastily, and then corrected himself. "I mean, you are not shocking *me*, but you will have to be careful what you say." He grinned at her. "*Respectable* tradespeople do not have the loose manners of the decadent aristocracy, you know."

Leonie smiled back, but her eyes remained serious. "It would not do, jesting aside, to try to pass me as your daughter. I do not *look* young or act young."

For one moment Roger was shocked silent. The simple statement was true—Leonie's eyes had seen too much for youth, and the pinching of hunger had added ten years to her face—but it also explained Roger's own reaction to her. Part of the distaste he felt for his desire was the thought of craving congress with a child. He was innocent of that, he now realized. However young Leonie was in years, she looked and acted like a woman, not a girl.

"My sister, then," he agreed.

"No." Leonie's instant negative was instinctive and forceful, out before she really had a reason for it.

"Now what's wrong with that?" Roger asked, beginning to feel a little annoyed.

By the time he had finished his question, Leonie understood why she had protested so vigorously. She did not want Roger to think of her as a sister—not for a moment. Such a thought can take hold in a man's mind and make any other kind of relationship abhorrent. It was clear enough that Roger did not presently feel either brotherly or fatherly—Leonie had a clear memory of what had happened to him in the tunnel—and she wanted to keep it that way. However, she could not give Roger such a reason.

"It will mean two chambers, and if you are going to buy clothes for me—which I admit I want very, very much . . . Oh, Roger, I can bear wearing these filthy rags if I *must*, but if I have a choice between decent clothes and sleeping in a field, I would *gladly* sleep in the field. Have you money enough to pay for two rooms as well as for clothes?"

"Probably not," Roger admitted slowly. "Perhaps I could sell a gun. . . ."

But he did not want to do that. It would mean seeking a buyer, drawing attention to the fact that he had a store of weapons, drawing attention also to himself and Leonie by making inquiries. What news Roger had heard before the riot had implied a deepening of the chaos in France.

"No," Leonie protested again, thinking along the same lines. "It is bad enough that you will have to buy clothes for me. A man buying women's clothing will be remembered. To sell something also will mark us too much."

"Then what the devil am I to do? I'd—"

"Just say I am your wife." Leonie could see objections rising to Roger's tongue and hurried on before he could make them. "Please. It is not only the money, Roger. Even if you had money enough, I would prefer that you said I was your wife. I—I am afraid to be apart from you. If I should somehow give myself away and be suspected as an escaping aristocrat, I do not want to be alone in a room where I might be seized before you could come to help me."

"Good God!" Roger exclaimed. "I never thought of that at all. You're right. How could I be so stupid? Of course I'll say you are my wife, and you must talk as little as possible so that your lack of *patois* will not betray you."

Leonie's lowered eyes did not betray the satisfaction she felt. She had not really been untruthful, only exaggerated a little what was a vague anxiety. Thus she had successfully diverted Roger's mind from what he felt to be an impropriety to what he felt was a real danger. Leave it alone now, she told herself; let it seem like his own decision. However, she was at a loss for a new topic that would be related but not belabor the point. Fortunately, Roger solved that problem by pulling out his purse and a second, folded leather wallet in which he had assignats. He laid those aside, saying to Leonie that he dared not try to cash those in a small town because the denominations were too high.

"They use them all the time in Paris," Leonie remarked.

"But we are not going to Paris. My friend, Pierre, who will take us to England, lives in Brittany. We must . . ."

Roger's voice faded as he looked from the few coins in his purse to the assignats. It would not be out of their way to go through Paris. On the other hand it might be very dangerous. Would it be less dangerous to set up as a gunsmith somewhere to make some money? Leonie, meanwhile, had also been thinking about Paris. She had seen dreadful things there, but they had not touched her and she had no specific fear of the city. Suddenly she recalled that her father had brought them all to Lord Gower's house for protection once when the quarter in which they were living was threatened with disruption.

"But you are English," she exclaimed. "Couldn't you get help from Lord Gower? Would he not at least—" A burst of laughter cut her off, and Leonie shrugged. "Is that so silly?" she asked, chagrined.

"I am silly, not you," Roger replied, chuckling. "Of all the classical asses, I am the stupidest and stubbornest. You have the right answer. The only reason I did not see it is that my mind was fixed into a rut. I came with Pierre, so I was going back with Pierre. But that is utter nonsense! Lord Gower will see us safe on a ship to England without the slightest difficulty. Well, now, that puts a different light on things altogether. There is money enough to get to Paris. We may not travel in luxury, but there will be comfort."

There was also enough for an extra comb and brush, two dresses, a shawl, and underthings. Roger chose one dress, the shawl, and a huge mobcap under which Leonie could stuff her hair, purchasing each item in a different shop as a "present" for his wife. In another town, Leonie purchased the other items, pretending shyness and stupidity so that she could point and mutter single words to hide her aristocratic accent. They heard along the way that the war was going very badly. The Prussian troops had crossed the border on August nineteenth and Longwy had been bombarded and had fallen on the twenty-third. Now Verdun was under serious attack. This news suited Roger quite well. They would pretend to be refugees from the war zone if there was any question raised when they tried to enter Paris.

What with the time taken for purchasing Leonie's new clothing in enough different places not to rouse suspicion, they did not get very far that first day. It was growing dark, and Roger was thinking of seeking shelter in a farmhouse when they were told by a traveler going in the oppo-

site direction that the town of Tonnerre was not far ahead.
The town was smaller than Saulieu, but large enough for
an inn where they had no trouble obtaining a room.

Partly because he had gone a little overboard on providing for Leonie—it was impossible for Roger not to urge her
to buy "just one more" when he saw the pathetic delight
with which she greeted the coarse and common dress and
shawl he had found—and partly to keep in character as a
small tradesman whose livelihood had been swallowed up
by war, Roger asked for a "cheap" room. It was, to his relief, commendably clean, but it was very tiny. Roger had
been thinking in terms of the rooms in which he had stayed
before when he agreed to the husband-and-wife arrangement. Those rooms had had a comfortable chair or a pad-
ded bench on which he expected to sleep. This had nothing
besides the bed and a rickety stand for the pitcher and
washing basin.

Inwardly Roger groaned, but he resigned himself to another night on the floor. They fed Fifi and left her with
their bags, after which they went down and had a good
meal—the second that day, for they had stopped at a ham-
let and obtained large bowls of thick onion soup and loaves
of fresh bread around midday. Roger could not help noticing how lovely Leonie looked. The new dress might be of
coarse material, but Roger had an eye for color and had
chosen a soft, clear blue that brought out the gold light of
her eyes. He also was a most excellent judge of size. Wives
buy their own clothing, but whores, and even kept women,
tend to put forth their best efforts when surprised by a gift
of a pretty gown. Thus, Leonie's new dress fitted admirably. The sun and fresh air had given her a little color, and
freedom from grief and anxiety had erased the lines of tension that had marked her face. Roger was uncomfortable
already, thinking of the night in that cramped chamber,
and Leonie was innocently making things worse. According
to their plan, she pretended to be shy, sitting as close as
possible beside him and ducking her head to his shoulder
when spoken to.

Good food and reduced fatigue added to the problem.
Recovery from the stress he had endured stimulated Roger;
physically he felt fine—too fine. At last he suggested that
they go upstairs. His original intention had been to leave
Leonie there and come down to the taproom again, but in

the empty corridor he remembered her plea not to be left alone. Although he was nearly certain no one was in the least suspicious of them, he did not think his assumption would be of much comfort to Leonie. He could not even say that he would hear Fifi barking an alarm, for it was very noisy in the taproom. There was nothing he could do but stay.

As soon as the door closed, Leonie flung off her cap and shook down her hair. "Thank heavens you came up. If I had to act the shrinking violet for another minute, I would have done something desperate. It does not suit me at all." It was too much like the part she had played for Louis, and Leonie was through with that.

"You do it very well," Roger said at random.

He felt horribly awkward, unsure of what to do. They had been alone in the tunnel, but there was something suggestive about being alone in a bedroom. Just as he started to sit down on the bed Leonie yelped, "No!" and Roger jerked upright, only to see her snatch her cap out from under Fifi, who had decided its voluminous body and flounces would make a good cushion to sleep on. Roger felt a little less foolish when he realized Leonie had not noticed his reaction, but he walked to the small window and stared out of it. Leonie was laughing and scolding Fifi playfully.

"She has very good taste," Leonie said to Roger after ordering the little dog to lie down on the floor under the bed. "I think that cap would make a good dog bed too."

"You look much better without it," Roger agreed stiffly, still looking out of the window. "I chose it to cover your hair, not to improve your appearance."

Leonie looked at his rigid back in surprise. Until now, Roger had always responded to her teasing with laughter. He enjoyed a joke, even against himself. She had noticed that he had been very quiet all through dinner, but she had assumed that was caution.

"I did not mean to criticize your choice," she said softly. "I was only joking. Don't be angry."

"I'm not angry," Roger snapped, appalled at his tone as the words emerged.

"You don't sound very happy," Leonie responded evenly. "If I have done something to annoy you, I wish you would tell me because I am truly unaware of it. I am very sensible of how much you have done for me, and very truly do not wish to anger you in any way."

"I'm *not* angry," Roger repeated even more furiously, then took a breath. "Sorry," he said shortly but no longer so sharply, "I am not angry at you, Leonie. It is nothing to do with you."

"That cannot be true," Leonie pointed out soberly. "Anything that has happened or will happen here has to do with me. If it were not for my family, you would not be here. Surely," she added, striving for lightness, "you did not suddenly remember that you neglected to snuff the candles in your home and have burned down your house in England. And even that would have to do with me, you know, because if you had not come away in such a hurry to rescue me, you would not have forgotten to snuff the candles."

She did not achieve her purpose of making Roger laugh. He did not answer, only leaned forward to press his forehead against the windowpane. Everything she did and said made her more desirable. She was the sweetest and most gallant woman he had ever come across, and he could no longer believe her sweetness was a pretense. But that goodness and the abuse she had suffered made any approach to her unthinkable. He thought wildly that there must be a whore in the town, that if he could ease himself possibly he could stop hurting Leonie by his peculiar and inexplicable behavior. Then he realized he could not do that. There was no money to be wasted on such a purpose. Besides, how could he find a woman? What would be thought if a man with a young and beautiful wife went out to seek a whore? Roger groaned aloud.

"What *is* wrong?" Leonie begged, coming up behind him and laying a hand on his shoulder.

"Don't touch me!" Roger snarled.

Slowly Leonie backed away. She was again in the grip of the dichotomy that had seized her in the tunnel. She wanted Roger, but could neither offer herself nor endure the thought that he might ask her to give herself. He felt her hand drop away and heard the reluctant steps on the uncarpeted floor. He did not know that it was unwillingness to obey him that made her move so slowly. To Roger the slow, hesitating withdrawal seemed like that of a wild creature, caught at the edge of the woods, which edges away a step at a time so that its movements will not incite the stalking hunter to act before a last, swift leap can take it safe into shelter.

Roger turned around. "I'm sorry to have frightened you," he said harshly, then shrugged. "I'll go out. I can say we quarreled if someone asks. I'll sit out on the stairs until the bar closes and then sleep on a bench in the taproom. No one will be able to seize you. I will watch."

"No!" Leonie got out. "I am not afraid of you. I have told you so again and again. I—I am only trying to think what is best to do."

"I could give you the money and the horse and carriage," he snapped bitterly.

"Don't be ridiculous," Leonie snapped back. "How could it be better for you to be abandoned here penniless and for me to be all alone too?"

"It couldn't. That's why I didn't suggest it. And since we cannot separate, you must just try to forgive me and put up with my bad temper."

"And you? What must you put up with?"

Roger looked at her, somewhat startled. The voice was harder than he had ever heard from Leonie, but her expression was not that of a coquette. She looked anxious and concerned. He dropped his eyes. It was not really safe for him to look at her too long.

"You need not worry about me," he said grimly. "One thing I know how to endure is wanting what I cannot have."

There was a little silence. Leonie half turned away. "There is no real reason for you to endure it," she whispered at last. "I have nothing to lose and—and I would not—would not resist you."

"Leonie!" Roger exclaimed. He was appalled at what he had said, at the sick self-pity, the insidious demand of such a statement. Leonie misinterpreted the recoil in his voice. Color flamed into her face and she turned back to him abruptly, her eyes flying defiantly to his. However, the contempt she feared was not there, only an expression of wonder.

"You are the sweetest, most generous—" He laughed. "But don't—I beg you, don't make such offers. I *could* not. You know I couldn't take such advantage of you."

Leonie did not know whether she wanted to weep with

gratitude or slap Roger's face with frustration. He had turned back to look out the window again. Now what was she to do, Leonie wondered? Such nobility was marvelous, but it was also placing her in a dreadful position. Leonie knew what she wanted but she could not formulate the terms upon which she wanted it.

"There arises a question of sleeping," Leonie pointed out.

"In the bed for you, on the floor for me," Roger replied promptly without changing his position.

"It's not fair," Leonie cried.

Roger could not help laughing. Strangely, he was suffering less since Leonie had offered herself to him—although not in body. There matters were worse, and his steady stare out the window resulted as much from a nervous fear that even his coat would not hide his condition as from the need to avoid looking at Leonie, who was causing the condition. He ached with need physically, but he did not feel ashamed and miserable as he used to when Solange refused him. He could laugh.

"In a way it is fair," he replied. "I know this morning I said I would prefer to sleep in a bed, but at least I remember what it is like. You claim to have forgotten even that."

"You know I was only joking," Leonie protested.

"Yes, well—" Roger laughed again. "You wish to be kind, but I assure you I will sleep sounder and quieter on the floor than in that bed with you in it also."

Leonie was silent. She knew which emotion predominated now. She wanted to wring Roger's neck. There was no sense in offering to sleep on the floor instead of him. He would only laugh at her some more.

"I suppose I had better go to bed, then," she said at last. "We will want to be up and away early."

"Shall I go out while you make ready?"

That was the ultimate in stupid questions, Roger thought, the minute he had asked it. And when Leonie promptly replied that it was not necessary, he silently ground his teeth. What else could she say, after she had assured him she was not afraid of him? And what was wrong with him? Surely over those bitter years with Solange he had learned the techniques that reduced longing and frustration to a minimum. Why the devil had he not simply said he *would* go out, instead of phrasing it as a question. Now he had to listen to her movements, hear the whisper of cloth as her dress and shift were removed, the two soft taps that marked her shoes being set on the floor. And each step baring her body was vivid in his mind's eye while he stared blindly into the darkness outside the window.

Without intending provocation, Leonie was slower about undressing than she might have been because her mind was busy. Obviously there was no need to worry about Roger demanding payment from her for his services. That question had been settled in Leonie's mind for all time. She had offered, and he had refused—making it clear that he understood what was being offered. Now only the other side of the problem remained. If Roger would not take her—thus leaving her blameless—how was she to get him without making herself seem a strumpet?

Sighing, Leonie slid under the blankets. Roger heard the creak of the bed and clenched his jaw. After a moment, Leonie said softly, "I forgot to snuff the candle."

Without replying, Roger doused the light. In the dark he removed his coat and shoes, took his cloak from where it lay across the traveling bag, and moved toward the window.

"Take one of the pillows," Leonie urged, a catch in her voice.

As he took the bolster she held out to him, their hands touched and a wave of urgent need surged through Leonie. His fingers seemed to cling, but maybe she only wanted to believe that. Suddenly she was afraid that if she did not get him to make love to her that night, a pattern of resistance would be set. Also, Leonie realized, no matter how kind Roger was, he would not willingly inflict suffering on himself. Doubtless as soon as they got to Lord Gower, he would leave her in the English ambassador's care and get away where she could not tempt him. She heard him lying down as far from the bed as he could get. A rush of loneliness made her sob.

"What's wrong, Leonie?"

"I don't know," she wept. "I can't bear that you should be on the floor."

"I don't mind," Roger said after a pause. "Truly, it's—it's better for me."

Leonie only sobbed harder. His voice sounded calm

now, as if he were already sinking into acceptance of the
situation, making headway in destroying the craving he felt
for her. He would leave her when he believed she was in
safe hands without even any regret. Perhaps he would be
ashamed of what he had felt. He might avoid her when she
was in England. She might never see him again.

"I am so alone," she whimpered.

"It's all right, Leonie. Don't cry. Don't be frightened. I'll
go out. Bolt the door behind me. You will be perfectly
safe."

"No!" Leonie cried. "You don't understand."

How could the man be so blind, Leonie wondered. Why
did he keep insisting she was afraid of him when she told
him over and over that she was not? Then, quite suddenly,
the answer came to her. It was because of what Marot and
the others had done! Roger thought she was afraid all men,
any man, would hurt her the same way. Yes, of course, he
had said what amounted to that in the tunnel that first
night.

But that was ridiculous. She had—but Roger did not
know about Louis. And she *had* been afraid at first when
Louis said he wanted her. She had been in a cold sweat,
shaking with terror, fighting herself to endure him for the
sake of her mother and brother. Only Louis had not hurt
her, and as time passed, she grew quite accustomed and
indifferent. But Roger did not know that either. All at once
a solution to her dilemma came to Leonie. She choked,
strangling a laugh at birth, and heard Roger sit up.

"No, I don't understand," he said tensely. "Leonie, I
can't bear to hear you cry. If you could tell me what you
need, I'll try—"

"I need you."

"What?"

"I'm not afraid of you," Leonie whispered. "I don't know
why, but I'm not. Perhaps it's because in the tunnel you
didn't hurt me. But when I lay down in this bed meant for
two and I thought of sharing it with a man . . . I am
alone. I will be alone all my life unless you help me."

"Child, I'll do anything to help you, *anything*. Just—"

"I am not a child," Leonie wailed. "I am a woman, and I
will never know what it is to be a woman because I *am*
afraid."

Roger had gotten to his feet and taken an uncertain step

toward the bed. He halted abruptly when Leonie said she was afraid.

"I am afraid also," he whispered huskily. "I am afraid to leave you alone in your misery and afraid to do you more hurt still."

"I am not afraid of you," Leonie urged. "Teach me not to be afraid of *that*. Teach me, Roger. Help me."

He moved quickly then, but only to kneel beside the bed and take her in his arms. "I'm likely to be a very poor teacher," he said painfully. "I only taught my wife to hate me."

Leonie gasped. She had known it was likely that Roger was married, but the confirmation of her fear still hurt. The slight stiffening of her body had an instant effect on Roger, who loosened his grip. Loss washed over Leonie, and physical need reinforced it so that she protested, "No, don't let me go. Will your wife—"

"She's dead."

There was something odd in Roger's voice, but Leonie could not think about that. She had heard what she wanted to hear—Roger was a free man—and her growing desire swept away all other considerations. "See," she murmured, putting her arms around Roger's neck, "I'm not afraid. I'm not cold or shaking. Come into bed with me?"

He hesitated, then moved so that he could sit beside her without pulling completely free of her arms. "Are you sure?"

Somewhere in the back of his mind, Roger knew quite well that what he was doing was not only outrageous but stupid. He felt that it was Leonie's generosity that was driving her to make a sacrifice of her body. She was too young for him and too rich. He should never have admitted his need to her because it was the kind of need that grew with satisfaction. He was only making more grief for himself. But the desire for her was coursing through his body with his blood like a fire. And there was just barely enough possibility that what she said was true. If it was true and he refused her, that would be the ultimate cruelty.

"Yes, I am very sure," she murmured. "I am not afraid of you, and I need you."

He got up then and began slowly to remove his shirt and then his breeches and stockings, pausing periodically to give Leonie a chance to tell him to stop and go away. She was

watching him; he could make out the gleam of her eyes in
the moonlight that came from the uncurtained window, although the light did not fall directly on the bed. However,
he could not see her expression and did not know whether
she was frozen with terror and horror or simply curious.
He would have been much suprised and greatly flattered if
he had recognized that what Leonie felt was avidity and
impatience.

By the time Roger had unfastened his underdrawers and
shoved them off over his hips, Leonie could have shrieked
at him to hurry. Fortunately for Roger's sense of propriety,
which was very strong, she was so afraid that he would
think ill of her, that she did not make a sound. He had
turned his back while he removed his underwear, then took
a breath and turned around, half-expecting that Leonie
would scream with fear. She did make a slightly choked
sound—Louis was a small fellow and Roger was very well
endowed—but she put out her hand and caught his before
he could even wonder about it.

He yielded to her pull, bending over her to touch her
mouth gently with his. Leonie's lips were pursed to kiss,
like a baby's, sealing into Roger's mind a conviction of her
innocence. This, indeed, was no pretense on her part.
Louis had never bothered to kiss her, and her mouth knew
only the gentle salutations of father, mother, and brother.
But Roger's mouth was different; it was hard and hot and
did not withdraw. Her lips flattened under his and parted
slightly. His free hand touched her hair, stroked her throat,
a single finger tickling gently below and behind her ear.
Leonie sighed; her grip on Roger's wrist relaxed, and her
hand ran caressingly up his arm. Slowly, not releasing her
mouth, he eased down beside her.

Strangely, after the agony of frustration he had suffered,
Roger was in no hurry now. His desire remained, but he
was so intent on Leonie that it was held in abeyance; it
responded only to her. When her hand crept slowly up his
arm and around his neck, Roger's kiss grew more intense.
His tongue touched her parted lips, slipped between her
teeth. His hand slid from her neck to her breast. Leonie
gasped. Roger paused, but the arm around his neck
clutched him tighter, and he stroked her breast, gently,
gently sliding his palm over the erect nipple.

Leonie bucked against him, an awkward, involuntary

movement. She had moved smoothly under Louis's thrusting, as she had been taught, matching her rhythm to his, but she felt nothing much. This was different, a response to a personal need. Nor did Roger need to worry this time whether the motion was fear or passion. Leonie's other arm had gone around him and was tightening convulsively. Now Roger was faced with the problem of getting the blanket off Leonie or getting himself under it. He had thought briefly of it when he lay down, but had not wanted to place his naked body against hers immediately. Because he feared that if he broke the mood Leonie's fears would overwhelm her and he would lose her, he continued his caresses.

For a time Leonie managed to keep still, except for clutching Roger to her, but it was becoming harder and harder. She began to whimper and try to grasp him with her legs. The blanket frustrated her. Feeling her movement, Roger released her lips.

"Are you sure?" he whispered.

"Yes, yes!" Leonie cried softly.

Swiftly he slipped from the bed, pulled off the cover, and let himself down upon her. He knew he should have given her one more chance to change her mind, but he knew also that it would be beyond his ability to let her go now. He must believe she was willing; he feared he would take her by force if she were not. Still, he had not forgotten Leonie nor the reason she had given for this union. He did not thrust deep and hard, seeking a quick satisfaction, which was all he had craved for years. Slowly, lingeringly, he made her his until the drive of Leonie's own body pushed him quicker, harder, and brought them to a culmination that wrung groans of joy from both.

CHAPTER 11

They did not leave early in the morning. By the time the sunlight struck their uncurtained window, it was already past eight. Roger groaned when the ray fell across his face and tried to bury his head in Leonie's shoulder. Leonie, however, started awake. It had been many months since she had wakened into sunlight. She cried out fearfully, thinking at first that she was in Louis's room and they would be found out. Roger jerked awake at her voice.

"It's all right, Leonie," he soothed. "I won't hurt you."

His voice brought everything back into focus for her, and she caught at him to keep him from leaving the bed. "Not hurt me!" she teased. "Liar! You nearly killed me."

"But Leonie," Roger exclaimed in a horrified voice, still fuzzy with sleep and thinking the quiver of laughter was fear, "you said—"

"Wake up!" Leonie chuckled. "When you do not know a compliment from a complaint, you must still be asleep."

He searched her face with troubled eyes, wondering whether it was again her kindness that was speaking, trying to mask a real shrinking in a jest.

There was nothing in Leonie's clear eyes or sweet smile that could resolve his dilemma, but after a moment she began to look concerned and a little puzzled. She must not, she told herself, joke with Roger about lovemaking. He seemed to regard the matter with great seriousness, almost with fear. Leonie restrained a sigh. She would have to be careful, very careful not to act too free.

"I have never had a compliment before—only a multitude of complaints," Roger said slowly.

That was not strictly true, of course. Many women had told him he was a good lover, but he discounted that. Since he paid for their services, what could they say? Leonie, however, took his statement at face value and blushed with pleasure. She assumed that he had made a special effort for her—which was true enough—or that she had inspired him to a more than usually virile performance. Both alternatives were flattering.

"I would gladly give you more proof of my sincerity," she said, "but it is late, I fear. Fifi must be let out, and we must be on our way or we will never arrive."

"Of course." Roger had reached toward her tentatively, but he turned the movement into a stretch, swung out of the bed and, concealing himself as much as possible, began to dress.

Fifi, hearing voices and movement, was out from under the bed, prancing about the door, her tail whipping the air. Roger recognized the little bitch's need and gave Leonie credit for her tenderness to all creatures, large and small. He only wished he knew whether the dog's need was a welcome excuse to her or a duty she acknowledged with regret. She had seemed to respond with enthusiasm each time they had coupled.

Perhaps, however, that was why she was making an excuse. Unaccustomed to sharing his bed, except when he was with a whore, Roger had wakened several times at her touch and had caressed her instinctively. By the time he was awake enough to remember the true situation, he had also been sufficiently aroused to wish to continue, and Leonie had seemed as eager as he. That was also why they had slept so late and why his legs felt like overcooked noodles. Fifi frisked ahead of him as he returned from the jakes. She had obviously finished her more serious duties also and was ready to return to her mistress.

I will have to explain, Roger thought, *that I am not usually so exigent.* His unhappy marriage told him no decent woman could enjoy having her rest broken four times in a night, yet Leonie had seemed equally eager each time. Old hurts twisted in his mind, raising unjust suspicions. Could she think she had to pay this price or be abandoned? But if it had not been pretense, it would be offensive to Leonie if he *now* said he would not share her bed. *I will make a full explanation and then let her choose,* Roger said to himself firmly. However, when he reached the room, Leonie was dressed and waiting for him, exclaiming that she was starving.

Plainly this was no time for lengthy and involved expla-

nations about the results of sexual frustration and how satisfaction diminished activity. Roger merely agreed that he
was very hungry also—at which Leonie blushed, making
Roger tongue-tied because of the implication about what
had caused their mutual appetite. Moreover, the public
room of an inn is not the place for discussion of intimate
subjects, and later Roger found that Leonie was not willing
to meet his eyes. Even when they got into the carriage and
were private, she was much less talkative than usual and
gave him no opening.

Leonie was too busy with her own thoughts to notice
Roger's uneasy glances. She was wrapped in a mixture of
intense joy and poignant regret. The nearly subconscious
craving for sexual satisfaction awakened but never fulfilled
by Louis had driven her to tempt Roger into her bed. However, Leonie had not really known what to expect. To hear
others speak of the pleasure of love, of which Leonie's
friends had told her, even to see the results of it as she had
seen Louis's enjoyment, is a far cry from tasting it oneself.
The explosion of release that Roger had brought her was
far beyond her expectation. Still better, the fact that the
excitement and delight had been renewed with equal or
greater intensity several times promised a whole future
of thrilling delight.

It was for the future that Leonie felt regret. After Roger
left, she had used the chamber pot, washed, and dressed
slowly, reliving the experience of the past night and Roger's
every word and gesture. During that delightful process it
had dawned upon her that Roger's statement about her
compliment had to be a polite lie. It was a convention that
a gentleman did not blab of his *amours*—a convention
probably more frequently violated than kept by most "gentlemen." However, Leonie believed that Roger was a *real*
gentleman; he would never think of implicating any woman
by ever admitting there had been one.

It was not so much that Leonie was jealous of Roger's
past—although she was—as that she was jealous in advance of future rivals. It seemed to her that only an excep-
tionally skilled lover could have produced the effect Roger
had upon her and doubtless so skilled a lover must have
had very full and diverse experiences. Then the unpleasant
notion that it might be hard for any woman to hold him for
long occurred to Leonie. She could not believe Roger

would be deliberately cruel. Perhaps his past mistresses had been like the women she knew who spoke so cynically of their lovers. No one was hurt in parting in such affairs because no one had felt anything to begin with, except a desire for novelty and excitement.

However, Leonie already felt a great deal and realized she would feel more the longer she and Roger were together. Having fixed her affections, it was unlikely that she would cease to love. If he knew it, Roger would not cast her aside—not even if he were bored to death with her. Leonie understood that, but she did not think she could bear to hold him by pity.

Through a long, silent day of steady travel, broken only by stops to rest the horse and let Fifi run, Leonie and Roger both worked on their own problems. Neither made any decision or developed any plan of action. For Leonie, of course, the matter was not critical. All she could resolve was that, under the guise of innocent experiment, she would "rediscover" the things Louis had taught her and she had invented. Tried one at a time, they should keep Roger interested for a while.

Roger's mental exercises bore even less fruit. He was reduced to telling himself that he would ask Leonie outright what she wanted him to do. However, it was full dark before they finally stopped in the town of Sens, and all personal considerations were temporarily pushed out of their minds. The advance of the Prussian troops and the fall of Longwy on August twenty-third seemed to have reduced the government (such as it was) in Paris to complete, demented hysteria.

A young renegade priest was at the inn, his tongue loosened by wine and the sympathetic attitude in the town. On the twenty-sixth, he recounted to a breathless audience, among whom were Roger and Leonie, the legislative assembly had voted that all priests who did not take the oath to obey the assembly and abjure the instructions of the pope were to leave France or to be transported to a penal colony. That was not all, he went on. There was a strong movement in the assembly to execute out of hand all the prisoners now in the Abbaye prison.

"In God's name, why?" Roger asked before he could stop himself.

He received a contemptuous, monitory glance. "Because

they are traitors to the revolution, and they will kill the wives and children of those who go to defend Paris against the Prussians."

Roger swallowed and held his tongue, even forcing himself to nod seeming agreement after Leonie squeezed his arm warningly. There was nothing he could do for the prisoners in Paris, and Leonie was his responsibility. He could not endanger her by engaging in a political argument.

"But if they are in prison already—" someone else began.

"They have relatives and dependents who can incite or pay others to begin a counterrevolution," another man growled, scowling at the one who had implied prisoners are harmless. "Marat says in *Ami du Peuple* that we must cleanse the state with blood."

Roger thought sickly that blood was not very cleansing, but he said nothing, only drew Leonie, who had shuddered, closer to him.

"Oh," the young priest said proudly, "the assembly will take care of that. There is a proposal to take the families of all the *émigrés* prisoner and hold them hostage."

There was more to follow. Rule by law had been virtually overthrown. A deputy who had protested that the imprisonment of innocent women and children was an evil thing was answered by another that "To combat the enemies of the country, all ways are good." Still another—the priest remembered his name, Jean de Bry—proposed the formation of a corps of volunteer tyrannicides, whose purpose would be to assassinate all the foreign sovereigns leagued against France. Later, a decree was passed that punished with death any citizen who, in a besieged place, should speak of "surrender" and the utter destruction of Longwy was decided. When the city was restored to the power of Paris, it should be razed to the ground and its inhabitants be deprived of all civil rights forever.

At this, most of Roger's horror dissipated. It was utterly and completely ridiculous and self-defeating. He cast his eyes up to heaven, and said sardonically to Leonie, "The most practical and humanitarian idea I have heard in a long time. Just the thing to inspire loyalty."

It was not, however, a matter for jest. As soon as their retreat would not cause unfavorable notice, Roger led Leonie up to the room they had been given. Here they discussed the news in lowered voices, debating the subject of whether, considering the situation, it was wise to go to Paris. The major advantage was that Paris was so large a city and in such turmoil, already filled with strangers and refugees, that they would never be noticed. In almost any other place, they were marked as outsiders and, therefore, suspicious persons. Also, England had not yet thrown in her lot with Austria and Prussia. Roger had asked the priest, who admitted he did not know for certain but believed the newspapers that circulated so widely would have announced so drastic a political event.

In the end they decided to go on. There had been much violent debate, but no actual violence. In addition, from the general talk in the inn, Roger had determined that the smaller cities were following Paris's lead. If the hysteria grew worse and all strangers were to be seized and interrogated—which was not impossible, as spies from Austria and Prussia were suspected everywhere—they would be far more vulnerable in a town where everyone knew everyone else than in Paris. Nor would they need to be exposed to the dangers of the city for long. Once past the gates, where the worst danger would lie as they actually entered the city, they could go directly to Lord Gower's residence. There they should be safe from anything except a general insurrection, such as that which had broken into the Tuileries to seize the king.

"But if you will be afraid, Leonie," Roger said finally, "perhaps I could—"

She walked into his arms. "If we are together, I will not be afraid. Come to bed now. We cannot plan until we know how matters really are. It is not impossible that that stupid little priest was exaggerating everything to make himself more important."

That settled Roger's personal problem temporarily. Obviously it would be ridiculous to ask Leonie whether he should join her after she had invited him. And he found, when they were in bed, that she turned toward him quite naturally, offering her lips as if it were an old custom. In one way, Roger felt as if it were. There was no embarrassment, no strain, no sick expectation of a sharp *Well, if you must, hurry and be done.* In another way, it was all new and thrillingly exciting, as if he had never touched any woman ever before. His knowledge of her past ill-treatment made great care necessary. It was like having a virgin each time—an eager and willing one, but still a tender creature who must not be alarmed.

One other problem was also settled that night. Sated, both slept without stirring until the morning noises of the inn woke them soon after dawn. Roger was greatly relieved. Somehow it did not seem so bad to take advantage of Leonie's generosity if he did not take *too* great advantage. Just now, when their situation might turn dangerous at any moment, she needed him to comfort her, Roger told himself. He was doing her more good than harm. Once they reached Lord Gower, it would be different. There could be no questions of sharing a room then or of being afraid of seizure. Then their liaison would end quite naturally without any need to say anything.

The depression that gripped Roger when he came to that conclusion was intense. He began to discuss again whether they should turn aside from Paris; however, when Leonie said cheerfully that she was ready to do anything he thought best, he realized what he was planning. To satisfy his own desire for her, he was thinking of dragging her all across France under the most dangerous and even degrading conditions. Furious at himself, he reversed his arguments and made for Paris by the most direct route. In fact, he would have pressed on right into the night, except that Leonie reminded him Paris had reverted to an earlier age and, unlike London, was closing its gates and setting guards at them.

Roger did not need much convincing. They stopped for the night outside Pringy, about fifty kilometers from Paris, obtaining a bed and dinner in a farmhouse. The people were not willing to talk about what went on in the city. Roger could not guess whether they were merely taciturn or were frightened, and he was too cautious to press them further than a general question as to the latest news. He and Leonie did not make love that night; the bed they shared was in a large room where the farmer's old father and aunt also slept.

Surprisingly, it was a wonderful experience, full of peace and joy. Roger was able to hold Leonie in his arms and feel her pliant body against his almost without desire, with only the memories of the rich tumult of passion to add warmth to the embrace. She clung to him, not speaking of fear, although each knew that it was possible this was their last night together. Still, there was no need in either for more than the embrace, the gentle touch of lips. It was solace and comfort enough; both found in it the courage to face the peril of the next day.

At first it seemed as if all their qualms had been imaginary. The questions at the gate were cursory. No one asked for identification or where Roger and Leonie came from. Instead, Roger was asked whether he was afraid of the Prussians. To this he replied quite truthfully that he was not in the least afraid of them. Would he fight to defend his country against them, he was next asked. By all means, he replied, barely restraining a smile. It was not likely, he said to Leonie, after they drove away, that England and Prussia would come to blows, but he would certainly fight for England any time he was called on to do so. Leonie laughed, a bit more than the joke deserved, giddy with relief.

Because they were concerned exclusively with their own affairs, neither Roger nor Leonie stopped to think that the closing of the gates might not be to prevent people from entering the city but to keep them from leaving it. This only became clear after they met with their first shock of disappointment. The entry to Lord Gower's residence was locked. This was not much of a surprise, considering the events of the past year. Roger rang the bell with a will until, finally the caretaker came down.

"Begone," he said crossly. "There is no one here. Lord Gower has returned to England."

"Returned! When?" Roger asked.

"He left five days ago. There is no one here except myself and my wife."

"Good God!" Roger exclaimed. "But who is here to attend to the affairs of Englishmen?"

"No one, I say." The caretaker turned away.

Roger rattled the gate ferociously. "Wait," he ordered with a cold authority that stopped the caretaker in his tracks. "Where is Mr. Lindsay, the chargé d'affaires?"

"In Versailles—if he has not left also—but I think he has" was the sullen reply.

Roger went back to where Leonie waited in the carriage with the strangest mixture of feelings. He had been so relieved when they passed the gate that he had for the mo-

ment forgotten he would lose Leonie when they reached
Lord Gower. As he rang the bell, that realization had made
his heart sink painfully. To hear Lord Gower was gone,
which should have brought him near despair, had quite the
opposite effect. Instead of worrying about the danger they
would face, all Roger could think was that he would *not*
lose Leonie.

Leonie's emotions mirrored Roger's almost exactly, with
the exception that she had been wondering whether he
would be glad to be free of her to look for a fresher and
more interesting companion. Thus, when he said he had
bad news, and told it, he was rewarded with the sunniest of
smiles.

"Well, that is a sad disappointment," Leonie said
brightly, not looking disappointed at all. "What shall we do
next?"

"I suppose," Roger replied slowly, "that we had better
cross the city and take the road to Versailles. If Lindsay is
about to leave, we can go with him. I doubt there will be
any trouble about it—I know him fairly well. However, if
he has left already . . ."

The sparkle of Leonie's eyes had dimmed. She had
thought that with Lord Gower gone Roger would be bound
to her until they found another way to leave France—and
leaving the country had definitely fallen very low on her
list of priorities. First and foremost among those was keeping her hold on Roger. Leonie was more interested in
avoiding Lindsay, whoever he was, than in catching him if
that meant Roger's responsibility for her would end.

"If he has already left, we could go on toward Brittany,
if we had money. Roger, would it be safe, do you think, to
try to obtain coin for those assignats you have? Do you
know anyone who might do that?"

"I do," Roger answered much more cheerfully. Leonie's
obvious indifference to Lord Gower's departure improved
the situation enormously. Then he reconsidered, frowning.
"Well—I used to know people in Paris. God knows if the
poor devils are still free, or even alive, and whether, if they
are, they still have the resources to help me. There is another problem. If Lord Gower left under a cloud—that is,
if England is about to declare war—it may not be wise to
identify myself as an Englishman."

"I wonder if we could pick up a newspaper?" Leonie suggested.

That was a practical move that could hold no danger, but it probably was not wise to drive a horse and carriage, even so shabby a vehicle as Roger had, all over town. Leonie suggested a stable not far from where they were, which she remembered from her earlier stay in Paris with her family, and they set out on foot for one of the political centers. It was one Leonie's father had told her was republican but not violent about it. They expected a hive of activity, with people coming and going, where no one would notice another couple who came in to talk and read the papers and notices. However, to their surprise, they found the place strangely silent and deserted. The few men there looked at Roger with suspicious surprise when, for something to say, he asked for Citizen Brissot.

"How do you not know that he is at the Salle de Ménage? There is a most important meeting of the assembly," one said.

"I have only come to the city today," Roger replied. "I thought I might be useful in these perilous times. I am a gunsmith, but I do not know to whom to offer my services."

His voice was perfectly calm and his face nearly expressionless, but Leonie, who was close beside him, saw a sheen of sweat on his temple, and his right hand was in his pocket where his pistol lay. She looked around for a movable object she could lift and throw to protect herself, but the bad moment passed.

"Ah," the spokesman said, "you will be very welcome. Do you have guns? We need muskets."

"I have a few, but not with me. One does not carry muskets around the streets. And mostly I have tools and parts for handguns."

"That is reasonable," the man agreed. "Where are you from?"

Roger knew better than to claim residence in the east. He would be suspected of fleeing the Prussians. "I am from Brittany," he replied, "but I am French."

"Ah." That was a sound of satisfaction. "I thought your accent was strange. You are a good citizen to come. Where are you staying?"

"I have not yet found a place. You see, my wife is with me."

The man peered past Roger. Leonie hung her head modestly, grateful for the voluminous ruffle of the cap that fell before her face. Feeling her tension, Fifi squirmed in her arms and growled softly.

"There is a café, not far." The man drew a sheet of paper toward him. "What are your names?"

"*Citoyen et Citoyenne* Saintaire," Roger replied. It had flashed through his mind to give a false name, but he only made his own into one word to avoid the chance it would sound too aristocratic divided. To abandon it completely seemed unnecessary and would subject him to the danger of failing to answer when he was spoken to. He could always change his name later, if it were necessary, since he had no papers of identification anyway.

"Here," the man said, handing Roger the torn sheet. "Tell the landlord at the Café Breton that Lefranc sent you, and he will take you in. Return here tonight. Citizen Brissot or perhaps Vergniaud or Gaudet will be here to speak with you."

Concealing his relief as well as he could, Roger drew Leonie out. They walked quickly in the direction pointed out to them before circling back toward the stable where the horse and carriage had been left.

"I don't like this, not at all," Roger said. "Everything is too quiet. It's as if people were holding their breaths. I think we should try to get out. God knows what we will do if Lindsay is gone, but I have the feeling that Paris will be a very unhealthy place soon."

Leonie could not object. She sincerely hoped that Lindsay *would* be gone, but she, too, felt the sense of waiting. They had the horse harnessed and then drove toward the western gate that led to Versailles. As they passed down the rue de Rivoli, Roger exclaimed. The brass plate of a lawyer he had dealt with for many years was still in place and, more importantly, still shone brightly with recent polishing. Roger pulled the horse to a halt.

"Fouché is still here," he said. "He is one of the men I know, and I do not believe he would betray me even if France and England are on the brink of war. Shall I take a chance, Leonie, or do you just wish to leave as quickly as possible?"

"Let us try," Leonie responded quickly. "Surely the few minutes it will take to see if he can help us will not be significant. And if he *can* give you money for the assignats, we will be much better off."

The street seemed quiet. Roger set Leonie in the back of the carriage where she would not be seen and left her a cocked pistol while he went in. He did not expect her to hit anything if she was forced to fire, but the shot would bring him to her rescue. A few minutes later he came out again, accompanied by a clerk who now took over the job of holding the horse.

"Come with me, Leonie," Roger said. "Fouché is here, and he will help us as much as he can, but I fear I have led you into a trap."

"What kind of trap?"

"No one is to be allowed out of Paris. That is why it was so easy to come in. They do not care even if spies come in since they will not be able to get out again."

Leonie absorbed that as they walked up the stairs. "But it cannot be for long, Roger," she said finally. "It is quite mad. Trade will come to a standstill. People will starve. Sooner or later they must allow the people to move."

"Certainly, in fact—" Roger stopped speaking as he opened the door for her. Maître Fouché rose from his chair, and Roger said, "Maître Fouché, let me present you to Lady Leonie de Conyers, daughter of the Earl of Stour. She has been living in France for some time, but in view of the situation here her people asked me to fetch her home. Unfortunately, I was not quite quick enough, and we have had some difficulties. I was just telling her that we seem to be trapped in Paris."

"An honor, my lady," Fouché said.

He did not inquire, Leonie noticed, why she had remained so long or where she came from. Clearly he realized she was an aristocrat on the run. Whether he was powerless to help and felt that ignorance of the true situation would be a protection for her or whether he simply did not wish to become entangled in something dangerous to himself, Leonie could not guess. She made the proper replies to his conventional remarks and then reintroduced the subject she had started.

Fouché smiled at her. "You are quite right, my lady, but you have not understood. It is not so much that *no one* will be permitted to leave—although even that may be true for a few days. To get out will require special permission, a passport signed by a special officer of the Commune of Paris. I have heard some very disquieting rumors. We—er—have 'friends' who sit in the gallery of the assembly, listen to the debates, and bring us news."

"At the Girondist headquarters I was told there was a crucial debate going on right now," Roger said.

"Yes, Danton—" Fouché looked around as if to be sure he was far enough from the open windows and then lowered his voice until Roger and Leonie had to lean forward to hear. "That monster—that traitor to his own kind—is calling for the seizure of 'all traitors.' He means by that anyone who opposes him."

"Do you not think we should try to leave before the debate ends?" Roger asked.

"No! Merciful heavens, no! They will regard as suspicious anyone who tries to leave. They will think you are fleeing from the Prussians and question you most severely."

Roger laughed. "Probably we would be safer with the Prussians! Well, then," he added, sobering, "can you give me coin for these assignats? I know they are now worth virtually nothing, but I will repay the face value when I return to England. Whatever you can spare would be very helpful. If we have some money, we can stay in Paris for a few days and leave whenever—"

"I can give you money," Fouché interrupted, "but you will need papers or protection, and I cannot give you that. I wish I could. Indeed, I wish it most sincerely, Monsieur St. Eyre, and I hope you believe that it is not fear of danger for myself that prevents me. My name is valueless to you. Although I am not actually suspect—as far as I know—my connection with the past government . . ."

"Do not distress yourself," Roger said. "I think I know how to manage." He told Fouché how he had pretended to be a gunsmith to disguise his purpose in traveling in France, then described the conversation he had had with Lefranc at the Girondist headquarters and showed Fouché the note Lefranc had given him. "If I voluntarily bring in the muskets I brought to support my role as gunsmith and offer them for the defense of France, I can probably get one of the deputies to give me a 'certificate of residence' or whatever is necessary. All I ask of you is that you admit you have done some trifling business for a Citizen Saintaire —that is the name I will use—from Rennes, if you are asked. You need not say you know me. In fact, that would not do either of us any good."

"Yes, I see. That will establish that you did come from Brittany."

They decided quickly that the business would be the failure of a British gunmaker to provide replacements for some parts that had arrived damaged. Fouché was well known to have an influential British connection—which happened to be Roger himself—but that would be reason enough for a person from Rennes to employ Fouché rather than a lawyer of his own city. Then he gave Roger a substantial sum of money.

"One last thing," Roger said. "I have a horse and carriage. Do you think it would be safe for me to keep them?"

"Safe? It is not safe to breathe these days," Fouché said bitterly. "I will keep them for you, if you like."

He told Roger where to leave the equipage after he had settled and how to reclaim it when he wanted it. They took leave soon after and Roger drove directly to the Café Breton, where he and Leonie found, to their shocked surprise, that the owner was expecting them.

"I wondered what had happened to you," he said worriedly. "Citizen Lefranc came more than an hour ago to ask for you. He said you wished to speak to Citizen Brissot, who had come in for a little while."

"I had to get my goods and tools," Roger replied.

"We were lost," Leonie added, realizing that a good deal more time had passed than was reasonable for fetching Roger's property. "We have been all over Paris, I swear, looking for this place."

"Ah," the landlord said, his face clearing, "it can happen so to a newcomer. This is your first trip to Paris?"

"Yes." Roger's voice was reluctant. The innkeeper smiled at him, thinking he did not wish to admit he was a 'rustic,' but Roger's anxieties were more practical. In fact, Paris was almost as familiar to him as London, and he was afraid he would expose his knowledge in some inappropriate way.

"You had better hurry," the innkeeper urged. "Perhaps

you will still catch Citizen Brissot. You may leave your
wife here. I will show her the room we have and help with
the luggage."

Roger got down from the carriage. "Leonie?" he said
questioningly, then turned to the landlord. "She is very
young," he told the man apologetically, "and she is afraid
to be alone in such a strange place."

His eyes searched the landlord's face and found nothing
there to distrust. The expression was open, kind, and cheerful. Leonie had been watching the man also, and now she
smiled at him and came down from the carriage. Still, she
clung to Roger's arm.

"Will you be long?" she whispered. "Can I not come
also?"

"It would be better for you to stay here," he said slowly,
trying to convey to her that it would be a form of protection for him. If he should not return, at least someone
would know where he had disappeared from and that he
had disappeared involuntarily. "Unpack the very small
black case first," he said to her.

After a blank, wide-eyed stare, Leonie nodded her head
sharply. She had remembered the small black case. It held
a pair of pistols, not so fine as those Roger carried constantly, but quite effective. He handed it to her and she
went into the café, where she asked for the jakes. In that
privacy she loaded the pistols as Roger had taught her on
their first day on the road and replaced them in the case. If
Roger did not come back in a reasonable time, she would
go and get him. It surprised Leonie that Roger should
make such a suggestion. Usually he was very protective,
trying to shield her from any danger or even inconvenience
and seeming surprised when she did not dissolve in the
rain. He was coming to see, she told herself, that she was
not a child but a responsible, grown woman.

Roger would have been far more surprised than
Leonie—and thoroughly horrified—if he had realized how
she had misinterpreted what he said. He had offered the
pistols as a consolation, so that she should not feel totally
defenseless when he left her alone. It never crossed his
mind that she would actually consider firing one, much less
that she would consider coming to his rescue.

Fortunately the ridiculous misunderstanding did not precipitate the disaster it could have if Leonie had become

frightened or impatient. Roger drove to the Girondist club and actually met Brissot coming out the door. The deputy looked harried and very worried, but he listened to Roger's brief tale. In fact, Brissot's distraction worked strongly to Roger's advantage in that he asked only the most cursory questions, and when Roger offered the muskets he had to "the cause of the war," Brissot went back into the building signaling Roger to follow him. He not only gave Roger a receipt for the guns but filled out an identification form and then another that gave Roger permission to reside in Paris and perform the "useful and necessary duties" of gunsmith. Then, thanking Roger for his patriotism, he rushed out to return to the assembly in which, Roger gathered from what he heard as he left the place, a momentous vote was about to be taken.

Later, after dinner that evening, Leonie and Roger discovered how close they had come to utter disaster and precisely what Fouché had meant when he said they needed protection. Before the light failed, a decree was posted ordering all citizens to shut up their business and go to their homes. The next day, and all following days until the order was rescinded, they were to wait at home for a Committee of Inspection, which was empowered to collect all muskets. That was the surface reason for the "domiciliary visits." However, the committee was also empowered to seize any "suspicious persons"—and this included any person not in his own dwelling. The simple fact of being a visitor in a friend's house was enough to make one suspect.

That night in bed Leonie snuggled comfortably into Roger's arms. She was completely content. For a week or two anyway, Roger would be hers, and by then, Lindsay would certainly be gone. That meant she and Roger could take a leisurely trip to Brittany. With any luck, they would be delayed until the weather was too bad to cross the Channel. Perhaps she could hold Roger until spring, and by then perhaps he would have become so accustomed to her that he would not seek another mistress.

"I think we will be safe," Roger said softly, assuming the cuddling was a seeking for reassurance.

"Oh, I am sure we will," Leonie replied lightly. "Just think of the way things have happened to us. It is as if there is some power guarding us from harm."

"It must be a pretty absentminded power," Roger replied

caustically. "It sort of forgot to get us to Paris in time to travel with Lord Gower—which would have removed the need for any further intervention."

"How do you know?" Leonie pointed out. "This is not a responsible government that acts according to protocol. Perhaps Lord Gower's word would not have been enough to protect me. I would not be surprised if his entourage was examined with particular care to prevent the escape of anyone 'guilty' of being an aristocrat. Anyway, I do not care," she said defiantly. "I do not think I would have liked to travel with Lord Gower as well as I like being with you."

"Leonie, does that mean . . ."

"It means anything you want it to mean," Leonie murmured.

"May I—you do not mind if I—"

"You do not listen to me," Leonie complained softly, kissing Roger's throat. "I tell you the same thing over and over, and you do not listen to me."

CHAPTER 12

Leonie's conviction that they would be safe was fulfilled, although as the twenty-ninth of August dragged slowly by tension did develop. Inspections were to begin at ten o'clock at night. The residents of the Café Breton were fortunate in that they were among the first to receive a visit from the commissioners, who arrived at dawn on the thirtieth. Among them, as if to confirm Leonie's belief that "Someone" was protecting them, was Lefranc, the man who had first spoken to Roger and recommended that he stay at the Café Breton. Well aware of the value of a "friend at court" Roger stepped forward at once to draw Lefranc's attention. Another of the commissioners threatened him with a raised baton.

"I beg your pardon," Roger said stiffly, shrugging. "I only wished to thank Citizen Lefranc for bringing me to the attention of Citizen Brissot and for recommending this place. We are very happy here—but if it is not permitted to be civil . . ."

"Ah, the gunsmith from Brittany," Lefranc said, turning to see what had caused the disturbance. "Have you found a place to set up business yet?"

"No, citizen. I have not had time to look. You remember we were ordered to stay within."

"Yes. Yes, that is true. Well, when this is over, come to the club. Perhaps I will hear of a good place. I will ask."

He nodded pleasantly to Roger's renewed thanks and said sharply to the other men that "those two," meaning Roger and Leonie, were good citizens and not "suspect." Roger's move had been judicious. The only other guest was dragged out, despite the landlord's protests and the production of identity papers. The young man, a wool salesman, should be serving his country, not making money, one of the commissioners growled. To love money better than

France was "suspect." No one argued terribly hard against the seizure, not even the man taken. They all thought it meant a few hours of inconvenience while a responsible person in authority straightened out the mistakes of the crude and ignorant commissioners. At worst they assumed it meant a few days' detention while the validity of the papers and business were established. Had anyone foreseen the events of the next few days, no one would have dismissed the matter so lightly.

For Roger and Leonie, however, the inspection had excellent results. The first was the establishment of their characters as "friends" of the Girondists. The second was a development of real rapport with the landlord and his wife and the proof that they could be trusted.

After the commissioners left, the landlord took Roger aside and said, "You are not Breton. Why did Lefranc say you were?"

Roger shrugged easily, but his right hand slipped down into his pocket. Could he trust this man? "He noticed my accent, and I did not wish to admit that I am English by birth. I *have* lived in Brittany and also in the Côte d'Or— my wife is from the Dijon area. In these times, one does not look for trouble."

"My name is Aunay," the landlord said, indicating a turn toward the development of a personal rather than a purely business relationship. "And I agree with you about trouble. You can count on me to say nothing. I knew you were not Breton because I am, yet you use phrases now and again that are from my country."

Roger mentally blessed his unconscious use of Pierre's phrases, then changed the subject slightly by saying it seemed to him too late to bother going to bed. Since they were all awake anyway, they decided to have a breakfast. Madame Aunay prepared the meal herself. She was a Parisian and not as trusting as her good-natured, provincial-born husband. She had noticed that neither Leonie nor Roger had any spare clothing to speak of. This cast grave suspicion on Roger's story that he had come deliberately to Paris with the intention of staying. However, having heard Roger's smooth response to her husband's questions, she felt she would have a better chance to get the truth from the younger, more innocent, and presumably more easily disconcerted Leonie. In this, she was gravely mistaken.

Leonie was no more likely than Roger to falter at a lie or lack for a clever explanation. What was more, unlike him, she enjoyed the game.

By the time Madame Aunay drew Leonie aside and the subject of the lack of clothing was specifically raised, Leonie had an inkling of what was troubling the woman and had her story pat. She turned her face away and uttered a sob. "Oh, I know I should not care," she said. "Roger promised that he would replace all as soon as he had the money, but—but it will not be the same."

"What do you mean?" Madame Aunay asked.

"Stolen—all was stolen. My whole trousseau! We were not supposed to marry until the spring, but when Roger said he would go to Paris, I—I could not bear to be parted from him." Leonie had looked at her interlocutor while she answered the question, but now she turned her face away again, as if she were blushing. "I did not think it wise that he should be alone in Paris. Who knows whom he might meet—women, perhaps."

Madame Aunay laughed and nodded. "That was very wise. You are quite right. Paris is full of women looking for a man with a good, safe trade. But I do not understand . . ."

"The chests of clothing, my sheets, my tablecloths—everything—was strapped on the back of the carriage. The guns had to be inside, you see, and Roger's tools. One day when we stopped for a meal—oh, it was terrible!" Leonie sobbed dramatically again. "Someone cut the straps and disappeared with all our goods. All we had left were the few things that had been in the traveling bag we had been using so that the trunks would not need to be taken down each night. I cried and cried."

Madame Aunay clucked sympathetically. She thought them fools for having left their possessions open to such easy theft, but she had a born Parisian's contempt for "rustics" and did not really find it surprising that those from the provinces should be so silly and trusting. If she did not watch what her own Gaston did, they would have been robbed and cheated many times. She was glad the explanation of the suspicious circumstance was so simple, for she was a good woman at heart, although experience had made her cautious. Now she was able to turn her attention to a far pleasanter subject—advice to a new bride.

Soon after, the landlord and his wife returned to their daily tasks, and Roger and Leonie had a chance to exchange information on what had been said. The morning reached toward noon, and still the drums did not rattle to mark the end of what amounted to house arrest for everyone except the commissioners of investigation. Roger and Leonie slept for a while, but their room was hot in the breathless afternoon and they soon came down again. Out of boredom they asked if they could help out with any small chores. This and that was found for them to do, which helped to pass the time and confirmed their hosts' good opinion of them.

There was no release until the night of August thirty-first. Naturally, after so much inactivity, everyone rushed into the streets as soon as word came that the investigation was over. Perfect strangers told one other who and how many had been taken from this house and that. At first it was all just exciting, very uplifting to feel that you had escaped. Gradually, however, both Roger and Leonie began to feel uncomfortable and went back to the quiet of their room.

"Add it up, Leonie," Roger said. "Altogether we spoke to about twenty householders and they gave us news of about seventy or eighty others of which they had heard. Even if only half what they told us was true, thousands of people must have been taken prisoner."

"What can it mean? Roger, there cannot be thousands of spies and traitors."

"No, but there can easily be thousands who would wish to see the monarchy restored. If the mobs who have terrorized everyone and pushed even the conservative deputies into more and more radical positions are sent off to fight the Prussians—although God knows what good they will be against disciplined soldiers—those deputies who have counted on the support of the mob may be in trouble."

"Then they will not do it. They will see France defeated before they relinquish their power," Leonie said bitterly.

"I don't think so. They may be fanatics and may even be dishonest fanatics, but they are not—even the dishonest ones—traitors in the sense that they wish to see the Prussians triumph. That is the one thing they *cannot* permit because it would result in the restoration of the monarchy."

"But thousands of people cannot be kept in prison for long. There is no way. . . ."

"No," Roger agreed, tight-lipped. "They must either let them go—and what would that accomplish, except to make the radicals even more hated and to demonstrate that they are a small, weak minority who can only succeed when hysteria drives the majority to bow to them—or they must . . . Nonsense! This business of night visitations and listening to unsubstantiated horror stories in the streets is making me take my own lurid imaginings as truth. You are probably right, Leonie. This was not a planned thing but a panic reaction. In a few days, particularly if the war news grows better, the prisoners will be released and the whole affair will blow over."

Unfortunately, the next day brought worse news from the front, not better. Verdun was besieged. Before that news came, there had been some protests against the arbitrary and violent behavior of the commissioners—some had used the opportunity to loot houses as well as to seize "suspicious" persons. The assembly called for the dissolution of the Commune of Paris, which had instigated the visitations. The commune struck back. Robespierre prepared an address justifying the actions of the commune and calling for the continued dominance of the only organization—he said—that represented the will of the people.

A mob was generated to support this address, but for the moment shame had conquered panic and the assembly stood firm. However, after the news came of the further Prussian advance, insanity seemed to supervene. Danton called openly for terrorization of the royalists; Vergniaud incited the mob to "dig the graves of our enemies"; then Danton was up again, crying, "Let everyone who refuses to serve in person or to give up his arms be punished with death!"

Roger brought the news of these increasingly incendiary speeches from the "club," which he visited periodically. Although the city was quiet, there was no peace in the quietness. Rather, an air of restrained hysteria, a kind of hushed panting that any moment could break into wild, clamorous action existed. Through the day there were rumors brought to the café by customers of new imprisonments. Leonie borrowed a needle and thread from Madame Aunay and sewed a belt with two deep pockets that she could wear un-

176 ROBERTA GELLIS

der her voluminous skirts to carry a pair of small, one-shot ladies' pistols. By splitting short sections o. the seams in the sides of her gowns, she devised a method of reaching the guns without having to lift her skirts.

Roger did not permit her to fire the weapons for fear of the noise, but Leonie practiced drawing and aiming until she was accustomed to the weight and the working of the mechanism. That night Roger did not ask Leonie's permission to make love. He seized on her hungrily, as if it might be his last opportunity, and she responded with near violence.

On September second, the dreaded sound of the tocsin came, and all the steeples and public buildings displayed the black flag of emergency. Roger did not go out for news because there was too much chance that a young, able-bodied man might be swept up and pressed into the army. The Café Breton, however, was on the Capucines, just a little way from the Jacobin Club. From the doorway it could be seen that there was considerable activity there in the late afternoon. Finally, Aunay, who was well-known to the members, went down to inquire.

He returned white-faced. "There has been a tragic accident," he told them. "Some priests who were at the *mairie* were seized by the Marseillais and carried off to the Abbaye prison. On the way those maniacs incited the crowd to murder them."

"Who are the Marseillais?" Leonie asked.

"You have not heard of them?" A mute headshake was enough. "They are a battalion," Aunay continued. "At least, that is what they call themselves. They came from the south and appeared in Paris near the beginning of the month. They took part in the storming of the Tuileries on the tenth, and everywhere they go they drag with them a cannon, ready loaded. They do not desire peace or freedom," Aunay said bitterly, his good-natured mouth drawn hard, "only blood."

Leonie shrank toward Roger, who put an arm about her comfortingly, cast a significant glance at Aunay, and said, "Well, they have had their blood now. I hope they will be content and allow the rest of us some peace."

But he said it only for Leonie. Aunay's face gave him the lie, and the fearful glances of the landlord's wife did nothing to improve the situation. Nor was the anxiety misplaced, although all was quiet for some hours. In the dusk a confused sound drifted to them over the river from the left bank. Had they not been already uneasy, they might not have noticed it at all or might only have wondered vaguely what it was. Even anxious as they were, Roger and Leonie might have missed the significance of the dull snarling that rose and fell sporadically as the wind shifted. Both had brief acquaintance with the sound of a mob, but only very close, where the high-pitched shrieks and yells dominated.

It was the renewed and increased tension of Aunay and his wife that alerted Roger. "What is it?" he asked.

"The *sans-culottes* are on the march again," Madame Aunay breathed. "Gaston, should we lock and shutter?"

"God knows," the landlord groaned. "They are far across the river. They may never come here. Let us pray for that."

"It is better to act first and pray later," Roger snapped. "If we will be safer with the doors locked, I will make up to you whatever custom you will lose by closing. My wife was once caught in a riot."

They looked at Leonie, who was very still but whose eyes were so wide that the whites showed all around the irises. Aunay shook his head.

"Believe me, I am not concerned with my custom but with all our safety. If I am open and they come and I serve them, that may suit their humor and they will pass on. If I lock up, they might pass by, but it is much more likely that they will break in and drag us all out. We will have become enemies by trying to save ourselves."

"I see." Roger looked at Leonie, but she seemed no worse. He could not send her away, yet there were things he needed to know. "How likely is it that they will come here?"

Aunay shrugged. "God knows that too. In the past, the clubs here—the Jacobins and the Feuillants—were friends of the mob and its attention was directed elsewhere. But this business is not the doing of the clubs. Those in the Hôtel de Ville—the commune—Marat, Danton, who are of the Cordeliers Club—they lead, if anyone leads. Then, too, if they should take it into their heads to 'appeal' to the assembly . . ."

"That is only a few streets away," Leonie breathed.

Suddenly, Madame Aunay began to weep. "Our whole lives are in this place," she cried. "We are too old to begin again."

Leonie's breath shuddered in incipient hysteria. Roger glanced from her to the stricken, white-faced landlord.

"Then let us not sit here like a group of dummies and wait to be destroyed. Aunay, have you a cellar?"

"It is no place to hide in," the landlord disclaimed, shaking his head.

Leonie whimpered. She had had enough of cellars.

"I do not wish to hide in it," Roger snapped. "But I think you should put all the brandy and all the good wine there and also as much of the furniture as will fit. The less there is for them to get drunk on and for them to break up, the less chance there will be for damage to be done. If you think we can get away with it, we should fill the empty spaces on the shelves with bottles of watered wine and well-diluted brandy. That will also reduce the chances of drunkenness."

"You have a head, Saintaire. You have a head," the landlord cried, color coming back into his face.

Madame Aunay wiped her eyes. "Yes, Gaston," she exclaimed, "and do you put on the clothes you clean in and a dirty, torn apron—and I will also. Yes, yes, and I will dress Madame Saintaire as a barmaid, and you, m'sieu, can be our porter. Come, quick, let us get to work."

They changed clothes first, Roger thinking amusedly that the use of *citoyen* and *citoyenne* was a thin veneer. At the first stress the old forms came back. The change of appearance to make them seem of the same class as the rioters was most important; lives were the greatest essential to be saved. Then Roger's tools and parts and spare pistols were secreted in the darkest corner of the cellar. Enough havoc was wrought with clubs and knives. No one wanted to see guns in the hands of the mob.

The fine brandies and other "strong waters" followed, the landlord masking them with a layer of empty bottles. The remainder of the empties he brought up, and Leonie and Madame Aunay began to fill them, as Roger had suggested, with watered wine. Then the best glass and china were carried down, and, finally, extra benches and tables that made the café a comfortable, cozy place were piled so as to hide, as best as possible, the most valuable wines and liquors.

It might save the Aunays some losses, Roger thought, as he grunted with the effort of maneuvering a long, heavy table around a corner to set it in front of the cellar door, but far more important to him was that color had come back to Leonie's face and the look of helpless terror was gone from it. That had been his intention from the beginning, and he had succeeded. He had broken the feeling that there was nothing to do but wait for disaster to strike. Activity was necessary in time of stress to stem panic.

They were so busy that they did not hear the noise of the mob fade. That was just as well, for it would have given them a totally false sense of security. Having massacred the two dozen people they had taken at the *mairie*, the agitators had begun to cry, *To the Carmelites*! where the non-juring priests who were to be "transported" were being held. It was the noise of this further massacre that took place in the previously sacred sanctuary that those in the Café Breton had heard faintly. But that had not sated the mob.

"It is not enough! We must purge the prisons of all who would slay your wives and your children while you are marching against the enemy," the leaders cried. "Back to the Abbaye!"

Most followed, but there were those who were afraid and desired the sanction of the assembly or who did not wish the assembly to escape being smeared with as much blood as the Commune of Paris would be. They rushed across the bridge and across the Place Louis XV—where the statue that had been cast down had already been hauled away to melt into cannon—to demand that the deputies lead them.

"The people," the commissioners sent by the commune told the assembly, "wish to break open the doors of the prisons."

The assembly had not the courage to keep out the commissioners, but the guards did manage to divert the crowd that had followed them. This relatively small mob surged through the streets near the Salle de Ménage bellowing the words of the new anthem called La Marseillaise.

Madame Aunay froze. "They are upon us," she cried.

"So? We are ready," Aunay answered.

He was no coward, and with a plan of action laid out for

him, he had taken heart. Roger glanced at Leonie, but
there was nothing to worry about there either. She had removed her cap and darkened her hair with oil. The work in
the cellar had darkened it still further with dust and cob-
webs, and her face and hands were smeared. She looked a
proper slattern physically, and in her eyes was the hard
light and angry calm they had held when she announced *I
killed him* over Marot's corpse.

The cellar door was closed. There was nothing they
could do to hide it, but a table loaded with mugs and bottles had been drawn across it to give the impression that
the door led nowhere and was not in use. The noise of
shouting and singing grew louder. Aunay went to stand in
the doorway as if curiosity had drawn him there. Sometimes, he had heard, the mob could be turned by a jest or
the offer of a gift. Madame Aunay cried out for him to
come away, but he told her curtly to be still.

"If we can hand out those watered bottles and keep them
from coming in, we will have lost little and gained credit as
supporters of the people," he said grimly.

It was an excellent idea and it might well work. Nonetheless, there was a dangerous side to it. Those who were
"friendly" to the mob might be expected to join it, Roger
thought. If they were asked to do so, Aunay and his wife
might reasonably protest that they had to remain in the
café, but it would be more dangerous for Roger and Leonie
to refuse than to go along. They could always slip away
after a time. The shouts and roared snatches of song were
coming closer. Roger gave Leonie one last kiss and warned
her what might happen.

"What if we should be separated?" she asked, fear flick-
ering in her eyes again.

Roger had not thought of that. He almost sent her up to
their room to hide, but if the mob should come in and find
her there and should be in a nasty humor, worse might
befall her than she had suffered at Marot's hands. Suddenly
Roger remembered a long coil of thin rope behind the
counter. He pulled it out and tied it around Leonie's waist,
wrapping it round and round her like a thick, awkward
belt.

"If we should be dragged out," he said, "I will tie the
other end to my arm. Act like an idiot. I will use that as an
excuse or think of another."

He might have said more, but a voice from the outside called angrily, "What are you doing here? Do you not know the enemies of France must be slaughtered before they slaughter us?"

"I am here to serve the friends of France," Aunay shouted. "Wife, bring me a drink for my friend here."

Shaking, but with a smile pasted on her face, Madame Aunay carried forward the cheapest of the tin mugs half-filled with wine. It was accepted with a cheer. No more was said about joining the crowd, but other hands were thrust forward. Aunay stood at the door, seemingly the better to hand out the drinks more quickly, but his position was also effective in blocking the entryway. Roger began to hope that they would yet escape anything worse than the depletion of the landlord's stock of ordinary wine and cheap mugs. Leonie filled cups at the bar, and Roger and Madame Aunay ran back and forth carrying them.

Soon, however, the drinking vessels were gone. Aunay began to hand out the bottles of watered wine. The crowd was good-humored now, laughing and singing, passing the bottles from one to another; however, the bottles were disappearing very quickly, and at the first refusal, the temper of the mob might easily change.

"No more than a dozen bottles left," Madame Aunay hissed into her husband's ear as she handed him two more.

From his position, Aunay could see that a few more people had crowded the street. He hoped it meant that this was just a splinter group broken off from the main body. In any case, he had to get them moving again. "Where are the enemies of France?" he cried. "You are refreshed. Let us go and destroy the enemies of France."

"The enemies! The enemies!"

The cry went through from mouth to mouth. There had not been enough drink to inebriate them, but it took little to inflame their minds.

"We have drunk wine," a voice bellowed. "Now let us drink blood!"

There was a surge of movement toward the corner of the avenue, which would take the mob back to the Salle de Ménage where the assembly sat. Aunay turned slightly in the doorway to look at his wife, who was proffering two more bottles.

"You have served us," another voice cried. "Now come serve your country."

The landlord's arm was seized and he was dragged out into the mob. Madame Aunay shrieked and dropped the bottles to reach for her husband. A man grabbed her outstretched hand and pulled her out also. Roger had started forward to help the landlord and his wife, but two men and a woman burst through the doorway. The woman took hold of Roger's arm. Leonie rushed from behind the counter, eluded the grasp of the two men, and seized Roger's other arm. Behind them, the two men surged forward.

After the first minutes of acute anxiety, Roger and Leonie realized there had been nothing threatening about their seizure. The men and women around them, although filthy and ragged and wild as beasts, wished them no harm. Indeed, Roger and Leonie looked little better than their present companions and were taken to be members of the same ill-treated and oppressed group. Those who had dragged them out only wished them to share the pleasure of easing the years of helpless hatred that cruelty had bred in them. They thought they were giving Roger and Leonie a rare treat—a gift of release and revenge that they had been too afraid to take on their own.

As they were pulled and pushed along, they were separated from the woman and the two men who had drawn them into the crowd. Roger managed to unwind the coil of rope from Leonie's waist and tie it firmly around his left wrist. One man behind them noticed and pushed his way forward.

"What do you do?" he snarled. "Is she of the *émigrés*?"

"No," Roger shouted back, forcing a laugh. "She is my woman, but she is a little simple." He touched his temple in the time-honored gesture indicating an affliction of the brain. "If she is drawn away or lost, she will never find her way home."

The moment passed, the questioner being pushed elsewhere by the tide of people. Roger drew Leonie to him and held her, concealing the rope as well as he could. In spite of the danger that the question asked of him exposed, he was unwilling to take the chance that Leonie would be dragged away. Several times he tried to edge toward a street opening and escape, but it was impossible. Either they were hurried along too fast, or, just as Roger prepared to dart into the darkness, a new group came rushing out of the alley to join them. The crowd was growing larger and tighter-packed in the street.

From time to time Roger glanced at Leonie. It was dark now and he could not read her eyes, but her body moved freely against his, giving no indication of the stiffness of terror, and, when she realized he was looking at her, she smiled at him. He took it for gallantry, for a sign of her remarkable courage. In a way, he was right; Leonie did have courage, but at this moment she was not aware that she needed it. She had realized as soon as Roger did that unless they met some other mob that intended to stop the one of which they were a part, they were in no danger.

In an odd way, Leonie was even enjoying herself. Although Aunay had said the mob desired blood, she was not thinking of that. From behind the counter of the café, she had not heard the shouts about slaughtering the enemy or drinking blood. Thus, she strode along, merely uplifted by the excitement of the crowd around her, secure in the circle of Roger's arm and in the knowledge that even if the press of people should push them apart, the rope would prevent total separation. Her fear of the mob had been that its animosity would be directed against her. Now that fear was gone, and she had not yet considered what would happen next.

"Where are we going?" she yelled into Roger's ear under the cover of the noise.

"I wish I knew," he bellowed back. "We're on the rue de Rivoli now, heading east. There is the Tuileries, but they have been sacked already."

The wandering route of the crowd had confused Roger. They had set out toward the Salle de Ménage but then had veered away, come almost to the bridge that took one to the Versailles road, and then veered away again to travel eastward. Hopes that the marching was aimless and the crowd would simply disperse after a while alternated with fear that some small incident would suddenly enrage them and they would go on a rampage of senseless looting and burning. This fear made him begin to work his way toward the edge of the group again, hoping he could turn off into a side street.

Achievement of his first objective ruined nearly all hope of achieving the second. Free of the roar and jostle on all

sides, Roger became aware that the march was not nearly
so haphazard as he had thought. Before he could make the
mistake of trying to slip off and thus identify himself as
someone not in sympathy with the mob, he recognized
"flankers" who prodded and encouraged along those who
seemed to be tiring or losing interest. Moreover, he could
now make out the individual cries from those in the lead,
which the body of the mob had only answered with hoarse
roars of approval. "To the Abbaye!" was the cry.

The Abbaye . . . Roger had heard the name before,
and recently, but he could not place it at the moment, wondering—as they came to the once beautiful, now tattered
gardens of the Tuileries—whether it could be a meeting
place. In the gardens he tried to escape again when the
mob spread and the pressure of moving men and women
diminished.

"This way!"

"To the Abbaye!"

"Over the bridge!"

"The traitors will not escape us!"

Each cry was another voice; each shift of direction
seemed to be blocked by a different body or pair of reaching arms. The last voice, however, struck horror into Roger's soul. Had they not already been on the bridge—the
Pont Royal, it used to be called—Roger would have taken
his chances at breaking free because he now knew what the
Abbaye was and what the mob's purpose there would be.
The Abbaye was a prison, and the mob was set on turning
the wild speeches of the radicals into fact. They were going
to try to murder the prisoners taken in the domiciliary visitations.

When they came off the bridge, Roger made a determined effort to escape. He swung Leonie around and
pushed sideways. This, however, permitted a tattered scare-
crow of a man, whose only whole piece of clothing was the
red cap of the revolution, to seize Leonie by the arm so
violently that he tore her free of Roger's hold. She
screamed with shock and revulsion and pushed at the tat-
terdemalion and he staggered away, but the damage was
done. Others were shoved between Leonie and Roger. The
rope around her waist prevented them from being really
separated, but Roger could no longer control the direction
in which Leonie moved. She tried to stop so that he could

come up to her, but that nearly precipitated a real disaster.

The mob was gaining momentum, the whole mass moving forward more nearly at a run than at a march now, and Leonie's hesitation only resulted in two collisions with people close behind. The first she twisted away from, jerking the rope that Roger had been gathering up out of his hand so that only the fact that it was tied to his wrist prevented his losing her entirely. The second collision all but knocked her from her feet. Leonie shrieked again, this time with fear, realizing what would happen to her if she fell. She made no further effort to go against the tide. Sooner or later, she told herself, they had to stop and then Roger could reach her. Roger had come to the same conclusion almost simultaneously and gave up any notion of pulling back on the rope. Resistless, both were swept along.

Then the pace slackened, and quite suddenly Leonie was pushed into a nearly solid mass of people. This time she was in no danger of falling or being trampled; it was impossible to fall. She put a hand on the rope behind her and tried to wriggle backward, but that too was impossible. Inexorably, she was pushed ahead into the filthy back of the person in front of her. The pressure grew, forcing her face into the stained, odorous rags until Leonie thought she would smother. Desperately, to keep breath in her body, she slid sideways into the indentation of space where the shoulder of one person pressed against the shoulder of another. And still the pressure behind her grew as more and more people came from the streets to join the mob.

The shoulders Leonie had been pressed against parted slightly, parted more. Leonie pushed back, seeing what was about to happen, but she was unable to prevent it. Like an olive pit pressed between thumb and forefinger she was squeezed between the two shoulders and propelled forward into another tattered, smelly back. This time she resisted as long as she could, turning only her head so that her nose would not actually be enveloped by the rags that clothed the body in front of her. She knew Roger would be trying to work his way along the rope to reach her.

It was the feel of the rope, painful as it was, dragging at her body this way and that as people pressed against it, that kept Leonie from panic. In spite of the real dangers she recognized, she did not feel alone or helpless. Still, she could not avoid being pushed sideways again, and again forward, and she began to fear that the rope would snap or be torn from her waist or from Roger's wrist. The immediate concerns of breathing and hoping that Roger would be able to reach her kept Leonie from realizing that the noise of the crowd was increasing as she was pressed forward and that, mingled with the roars and yells of excitement, were screams of terror and pain. It was thus not until nearly an hour later—an hour of being slowly and involuntarily squeezed through one opening and then another, a process that was producing a ponderous type of circulation within the mob—that Leonie found out what was happening.

She had been pushed forward once again, but this time there was no one in front of her to stop her progress. She plunged ahead, to be brought up hard against the baton of a man who, she realized later, must be concerned with controlling the mob. At the moment, Leonie realized nothing but the pain of the bump and the force with which the man thrust her back. She gasped and staggered and would have fallen, except that the packing was not so tight at this point in the crowd because the line could bend, and Roger burst out after her and caught her in his arms.

Not realizing who held her, Leonie shrieked. Then, as she turned her head to see who had grabbed her, her eyes swept past the man who had pushed her back and over the entrance to the building a few yards away. Another scream was torn from her, and then another, before she was turned forcibly around and her cries were muffled in Roger's breast.

The steps of the building were wide and deep, and they were gleaming wet and red with blood—the sections of staircase that could be seen in front of the great doors. The rest, to either side, were obscured by bodies, some of which still twitched as the life blood, streaming from gashes made by pikes and sabers, drained away. As Roger watched for some minutes, too horrified to turn his eyes away, a woman came voluntarily, even eagerly, out through the doors. The crowd roared. She paused in surprise. Simultaneously, a saber slashed her, cutting through neck and shoulder, and a pike was thrust into her chest just below her breasts. She did not have time to scream but fell forward as the pike was pulled out. A third man darted forward from the side and dragged the body onto a heap already lying there.

Roger fought back his desire to retch, suddenly aware that he was being poked at with a hard object. It was one of the agents of the commune who was shouting angrily, desiring to know why Leonie was screaming and hiding her face. It was fortunate that Roger did not dare release her. Had his hands been free, he might have acted before he thought and flung himself at the butchers of the bloody shambles. As it was, he was too aware of the need to get Leonie away to permit his outrage to rule him.

"Does she pity these traitors who would murder her and her children if we did not deal with them first?" the agent of the commune demanded.

"She knows nothing about such things," Roger roared, realizing that to say what he really thought would result in Leonie's body as well as his own joining the heap. He lifted his left arm, showing the rope and then pointed to its terminus on Leonie's waist. "She is simple," he bellowed. "She is only afraid. She does not understand."

"Are you simple too, to bring such a one here?"

"I could not help it," Roger replied. "I could not leave her in the café alone when I was drawn out by the crowd. But it would be best if I could take her away from here."

Leonie had fallen silent. She had recognized Roger's voice when she drew breath to scream again, and she had choked back the cry. The agent of the commune looked around, but the street was clogged with people in all directions.

"It may be best, but it may also be impossible," he growled. Then he gestured with his head toward the left. "Go that way. When the cart comes to take away the bodies, you can get through behind it."

The idea was not pleasant, but Roger was now so desperate that he would have accepted a far more unpleasant method—any method, in fact—that would get him and Leonie away. Dragging her with him, he began to work his way along the front of the mob, dodging blows and ignoring curses as he blocked first one and then another person's view. Soon the mad bellow of the crowd increased again. Roger turned his face away and shielded Leonie's also. There was nothing he could do. The protest could cost his life and Leonie's and would still not save a single victim.

The third time the eager peal of blood-lust rose, Roger was almost up against the wall of the building only ten meters or so from the cross street where the carts would enter. He began to avert his head again from the horror he could not prevent when the ululation of the mob changed. A young man in the remnants of a uniform had dodged the pike thrust aimed at him, spun away from the saber cut, and leaped onto the pile of bodies on the steps. From there, another leap carried him halfway down, right in Roger's direction. Just behind him two pike-wielders struggled over the corpses and in front of him the agents of the Commune of Paris converged, raising their batons.

There was a limit to what Roger could endure, and he thrust Leonie away to the side. A single glimpse at the young face showed fury, not fear, and the ex-officer's arms were raised to defend himself rather than hopelessly to ward off the coming death blows.

"Stop!" Roger shouted. "This is no traitor or enemy. I know this man. He is from my own town, an honest man, and pressed against his will into the Capet's service. People," he cried, turning around, "this is a mistake! Will you see one of your own slaughtered?"

The agents of the commune turned, batons raised, toward Róger. Another leap carried the young man between two of them, almost into Roger's arms. Roaring, the mob surged forward.

CHAPTER 13

What had seemed the first step toward a painful, bloody end was actually a move of rescue. Instead of tearing them apart, the surge of the mob enveloped Roger, Leonie, and the erstwhile victim. The agents of the commune and the pike-wielders fell back before the wave of movement, recognizing by the laughter and cheers that there had been a new verdict handed down, far more powerful and binding than that of the revolutionary tribunal that had originally tried this case. "The people" who an instant before would have cheered at his death were now, with the wild irrationality of a mob, cheering the prisoner's escape.

To thwart that many-headed monster was death. The batons of the agents of the commune were only a mark of their office, no defense against the mob. Even the pikes and sabers of those paid to butcher the prisoners would have little effect if the mob disapproved of what was happening. To both groups it meant little that one victim was spared. They shrugged and laughed and turned away. Encircled by their "rescuers," Roger embraced the young man with one arm and Leonie with the other and grinned as broadly as he could force his lips apart.

The three clung together, weak from reaction, all wondering how they would be able to get away before the mood of the mob changed again. Questions—not angry, merely interested and congratulatory—were already being called. No one was yet suspicious, but Roger could not answer *any* question. No matter what town he claimed for his origin, it was not impossible that someone in the crowd near them would know that he did not speak the proper *patois*. Moreover, the instant the young man was forced to open his mouth, it would be plain to all that he and Roger could not be countrymen.

The near miraculous rescue and the fact that she could

no longer see the shambles of the steps restored Leonie to rationality. She had heard enough people comment on Roger's accent on the trip to Paris so that she understood the problem at once. Her difficulty, of course, was almost as bad. Not only the Côte d'Or was in her speech but also the mark of the aristocracy. Still, she should be able to say one single word without betraying herself.

"*Ami*," she cried, as if she had been shocked and had only just realized whom Roger held in his other arm. Then she twisted past Roger and hung herself on the young soldier's neck, kissing his cheeks. "Your name?" she hissed into his ear.

"Journiac de St. Méard," he hissed back.

"Journiac!" Leonie cried. "*Cher* Journiac."

Those about them beamed, and then, mercifully, the front ranks bellowed as another victim came through the door. In the instant, Roger, Leonie, and Journiac were forgotten. As those around them pushed in front to see better, they were able—both men pressed together to shield Leonie—to move back a little way. Another effort, which permitted those farther back to move into the space they left and, therefore, come closer to the bloody acts taking place, gained another decimeter or two.

How long it took, none of them could remember. Every move, which drew curses from those they pushed or tread upon, was a fearful chance. At any moment someone might ask why they were moving back rather than forward where "the traitors" were receiving their "just deserts." Any moment someone might suddenly take it into his head that they—or Journiac—were "escaping." When they finally pushed their way through the stragglers on the periphery, Leonie and Journiac were near fainting and Roger, although he managed to drag them along, was not much better off. He got them around another corner and then sank gasping into a doorway.

"Thank you. Thank you," the young man whispered, shaking like a leaf now that he was safe. "Why? Why did you do it? I have never seen you before in my life."

The accent was refined, the voice steadying already. Roger took another deep breath and sat with his head on his knees, numbly thanking God that he and Leonie were still alive. He made no answer. What could he say? There was no *rational* reason for what he had done.

"It is a habit with him," Leonie replied, giddy with relief, her voice trembling between terror and laughter. "I did not know him either, but he came and plucked *me* out of a riot and saved my life also—and now we are married."

Journiac looked utterly blank, as well he might. He then noticed the rope around Leonie's waist and bit his lip. Very likely they were both mad and had acted without any reason—but what was he to do now? Mad or not, they had saved his life. Could he simply walk away and abandon them, perhaps leaving them in their madness to be hurt or killed? Yet, if he stayed, what could he do for them?

At this point in the poor bewildered man's thoughts, Roger lifted his head. "Forgive my wife," he said. "She is nearly hysterical. Naturally I do not make a habit of saving people in the middle of riots."

"How many riots have you been in that you can say it is not a habit?" Leonie interjected mischievously. "You have done it in the only two you have been in—as far as I know."

"Leonie!" Roger protested. "Do you want Monsieur de St. Méard to think we are insane?"

"Oh, he thinks so already," Leonie laughed. "He has been looking at the way you have me leashed. I am afraid he does not think that it is just the thing for a wife to wear when taking an evening stroll on the boulevard with her husband."

"You are not Marseillais!" Journiac exclaimed as Leonie's accent finally penetrated from his ear to his brain.

"No," Roger agreed, and explained briefly how they had been caught up in the mob. "Have you someplace to go?" he asked finally. "I don't think it is too wise to be out in the streets."

"Yes, of course—" Journiac started, and then broke off abruptly. "Perhaps I had better not go back. I do not know whether it would be wise to go to my friends."

"Come with us," Roger said. "I know the Aunays have another bed, because there was another guest. They are good people. They will let you stay the night—what is left of it. Tomorrow will be soon enough to think what to do."

Although Roger did not untie Leonie for fear they should come across and be swept up into another mob, they reached the Café Breton without further incident. All along the Capucines they gathered up discarded drinking

mugs, Leonie making a sack from the front of her skirt.
The café door was open, as it had been left when they had
been hustled out, but the place did not seem to have been
much damaged. One table and two benches were broken,
others overturned, and the few bottles of watered wine that
had remained were gone, a few smashed on the floor. However, the table that had been drawn across the cellar door
was still in place, Roger noted with relief. There was no
sign of the Aunays.

They were all exhausted, yet they knew that sleep was
out of the question. Leonie first ran up to their room and
found Fifi safe, asleep under the bed, which she had
learned was her place. She brought the little dog down and
then went back into the kitchen. That had been invaded
also, but not completely stripped. She found bread and
cheese, not fresh but still edible. Roger and Journiac meanwhile had set the room to rights, and Journiac had explained how he had come to be in prison. There were so
many reasons—or no reasons—for a gentleman to be imprisoned these days that she was not even curious.

When she rejoined the men, Roger was saying, "I could
not believe it. Why did you all walk out of there, right into
the hands of those butchers, as if you were going to freedom?"

"We thought we were," Journiac replied bitterly. "At
least, most of them thought that, or that they were to be
transferred to another prison. The reason I am alive—in
addition to your courage and generosity, Monsieur Saintaire—is that I had been near a window when a deputation
came from the assembly to stop those maniacs from mur-
dering us."

"This was not ordered by the assembly?" Leonie asked.

"No!" Journiac exclaimed. "How could you think so?
They are not bloodthirsty murderers. That is, only Marat
and Danton, and, perhaps, Robespierre—well, perhaps the
whole group from the Cordeliers Club. I know it is not the
assembly's will. Deputy Dessaulx and Deputy Bazaire came
and tried to reason with the crowd, but they were driven
away."

"It is worse than I thought," Roger muttered. "It is bad
enough when a government orders its citizens to be slaughtered to achieve some purpose, but this—this is real an-

archy. A bad law can be changed, but when there is *no* law . . ."

"Then each man must fend for himself," Journaic said.

Roger shook his head but did not reply. Pierre's anarchist ideas and behavior within the confines of a stable society were somewhat amusing. To contemplate the results of each man fending for himself when all control had broken down . . . Roger saw again the heaps of bodies, the blood running down the steps, and shuddered.

"But if it was not the assembly, who judged you? Why did you think you were being released?" Leonie asked curiously.

She had not Roger's well-trained, legalistic horror of anarchy or the lack of a clear legal right and wrong. Her world had collapsed and fallen apart long before. She had come to terms with a society gone mad and agreed wholeheartedly with Journiac. Leonie was not beyond being horrified by suffering and death, but when they were over she shook them off. She had suffered so much herself, had lost so much, that to dwell on such things could lead to a total breakdown of her own mind and will. Her stability was now Roger. This last episode—starting with his suggestions to the Aunays and ending with Journiac's rescue and their own present relative safety—had reinforced the conviction she already had that Roger could do anything.

"Who judged us I cannot say, except that two were renegade priests—their tonsured hair was still growing in—and one other was apparently a shoemaker. They called themselves a revolutionary tribunal. As for why the prisoners thought they were to be released—that was the verdict the tribunal handed down. '*Release Citizen So-and-so.*' For some, who were obviously guilty of some crime, they said 'La Force' or 'La Châtelet' which implied the prisoners were to be transferred to another prison. There seemed to be nothing to fear."

He paused, and his eyes grew distant with remembered horror. "Most of us *knew* we were not traitors, *knew* we had done no wrong," he continued. "That we might be snatched up among others by mistake—that was frightening but within reason. But that we should be killed after no more than a minute or two of questioning—without witnesses or counsel . . . Even the king did not do that. It was inconceivable! It was easier to believe that such a tribunal had indeed been convened to release all those obviously innocent and remand for real trial before proper judges those who might be guilty."

"What made you suspicious?"

"Mostly that the deputies had not been allowed to speak more than a few words. I was not really suspicious of the tribunal. What I thought was that they either did not know or did not care that the mob outside was ugly. I was thinking of running and dodging, of how to escape the mob, so when I heard that roar . . . Thank you again, m'sieu, and you also madame."

Roger gestured away the thanks, frowning over his own unhappy thoughts. There was, however, a gleam of hope in them. If total anarchy came to the city, the watch at the gates might well fail. Perhaps he and Leonie could escape.

This, however, was not the case, Roger found the next day. The Aunays had returned soon after dawn. In their joy at finding the café virtually intact—even many of the cheap mugs back in place—they made nothing of Roger having invited a guest without their approval. They would have consented to his remaining, but Journiac decided he would see if he could contact his friends secretly and left about midmorning. Soon after, Roger took a walk to the nearest gate. Here he asked anxiously for a mythical friend who was supposed to have come into the city a week before.

The guards were civil enough. There had been only three days when the gates were shut to entry, they informed him, so his friend should have come in without difficulty.

"But we have moved, and I am afraid my letter with my new direction did not get to him in time. Perhaps someone remembers him going out?"

The guard shook his head firmly. "Not out of this gate, unless he had a special pass. Those names are written on a register and the names of those who passed them out also."

"Ah, would it be possible for me to look for his name? I do not know whether to write to him again or begin to search the city for him."

"I will ask the captain."

They would not allow Roger to look at the register, which did not surprise him, but obligingly looked up the common name Roger offered as the name of his friend. It did not happen to be there, which was another disappointment; Roger would have liked to know who was able to sign passes out of the city. A greater disappointment, however, came when Roger asked how long it was likely that the restrictions on leaving would last. He put the question in positive terms—as being a benefit to him by giving him a greater chance to find his friend.

There was no suspicion in the guard's face, but he shrugged his shoulders. "Ask the Prussians. When they are driven back, we shall be free to come and go as we please."

Roger had to smile and did so, adding some platitude about how that would not be long because the revolutionary army would cut them to ribbons. He did not get back to the café until late afternoon, where he met more discomforting news that he had to greet as if it were the dearest wish of his heart. Lefranc had been in again—the helpful devil—with word that he had heard of excellent premises where Roger could set up business.

"Shall we go and look, Roger?" Leonie asked eagerly.

There was nothing else she could do, Roger knew, and they set out, Fifi frisking at their heels. When they were alone in the street, he told her what he had learned and said he was sorry.

"Sorry for what?" Leonie asked.

"I do not seem to be very good at keeping my promises to you. I said I would get you safely to England. Instead, we seem to be trapped here where God alone knows what will happen next."

Leonie looked at him for a moment and then smiled. "But the truth is that I don't mind a bit. I am even looking forward to setting up a business. Will you let me help serve in the shop, Roger?"

"Serve in the shop?" he said in a horrified voice. "The heiress of Stour serve in a shop?"

"But what will I do?" Leonie asked reasonably. "I will go demented if I must sit in one small room all day. After all, you will be serving in a shop."

"A man is in a different situation," Roger replied reprovingly. "Your reputation, if someone—" As he said it, he realized how ridiculous it was and began to laugh. "Habits die hard," he gasped. "Neither you nor I will have a shred of reputation left if *any* of this gets out. Of course you may serve in the shop, my dear, if you wish to do so."

She hugged his arm in appreciation, and when they had

obtained the direction of the place from Lefranc and found it, she examined both shop and the rooms above with great interest. There was even a garden at the back. Roger allowed that the place would be suitable, particularly as it seemed to be furnished, but he was frowning and to Leonie's questions replied that he did not see how he could afford to pay the rent for a whole house. He could see Leonie was disappointed, and years of unhappy memories of the result of refusing a woman anything made him cold. Leonie, however, only shrugged.

"Oh, well, perhaps the Aunays will permit you to work in our chamber. We will manage somehow."

Roger had been about to say that what they needed to find was a way out of Paris, not a place for him to work, but he was so grateful that Leonie neither made a furious scene nor whined nor wept that instead he determined she *should* have what she wanted. If he had to, he would go to Fouché again. He said nothing to Leonie, however, not wishing that she should be disappointed again if he could not contrive to rent the place. Her slightly dejected appearance served a good purpose. Lefranc clucked his tongue after one look at her.

"It seems the place is not suitable to you, Saintaire?" he asked.

"It is suitable, but I am afraid you overestimate my resources, Citizen Lefranc. I cannot see how it would be possible for me to pay the rent on a whole house. It will take time to build up custom—no one knows me here in Paris."

"No, no." Lefranc waved such matters away. "We have no gunsmith in the Section, and wish to keep you here. If the club recommends you, you will have business enough. Also, the premises belong to the Section. The fool of a tailor who held them before was a conspiring royalist." He said the words as if he had been reporting that the tradesman murdered small children and drank their blood. "He will be executed and the property confiscated. I am sure Citizen Brissot would make a special arrangement for so ardent a patriot as you, who gave up his stock in trade for the good of the nation and came himself to serve her in her hour of peril."

"I would not like to accept special favors for what I did," Roger said stiffly.

It was very distasteful to him to benefit from the decep-

tions in which he had engaged. It was one thing to do and
say what was necessary to save Leonie's life and his own; it
was an entirely different thing to reap material benefit from
such lies. Roger did not stop to realize that such seemingly
noble behavior would only confirm Lefranc's mistaken conviction that he was a passionate republican, but that was
the effect his statement had. Lefranc again assured Roger
that all matters would be arranged to suit him, perhaps a
rental scaled upward so that he would have time to establish himself and the financial burden would match his income. Roger was about to protest again when Leonie
tugged at him.

"Roger," she said sharply, "don't be a fool. The place is
perfect. If you feel you owe the Section something, you can
always pay more than the rent when you can afford it.
Meanwhile, you can begin to work, and I am sure France
needs gunsmiths now."

After that there was nothing more Roger could say. He
agreed to terms with Lefranc and promised to return to
complete the formal arrangements the next day. However,
he was thoroughly angry with Leonie. He had intended to
get the shop, using his first statement as a bargaining point
but paying a fair rent. Leonie had not given him a chance.
Women either got their way or made a man pay for it, he
thought bitterly. When they were out of the premises,
Roger headed back toward the café but Leonie tugged at
his arm.

"I'm tired," he remarked coldly. "I've been walking all
day, down to the gate and—"

"We need not go far, but I want to talk in private,"
Leonie said. "You are angry. I'm sorry, but I couldn't let
you refuse the place after he said it belonged to a conspiring royalist."

Roger had been about to point out that he realized she
liked the house and she could have trusted him to try to
satisfy her, but her reason stopped him cold. "Conspiring
royalist? What has that to do with accepting a favor prof-
fered on the basis of a lie."

Now Leonie was confused. She could not imagine what
Roger was talking about, and she said so. When he had
clarified his thinking to her, she had a very difficult time
keeping herself from laughing. "I regret I did not think the
matter through," she said as gravely as she could. "All I

could see was that the man was imprisoned, tried, and will be executed in this Section and that, perhaps, in other places it would not be known. No doubt Lefranc believes you to be an ardent republican. He is sure that if the tailor's royalist friends—or, rather, those who knew he was a royalist but did not know him personally—came to the shop, you would report them. I was afraid that if you refused the place, Lefranc might find someone who really would . . . Have I said something wrong?"

Roger had stopped in his tracks and was staring at Leonie with his mouth slightly ajar. The ideas she had suggested had never crossed his mind. Now that Leonie had stated them, he had to agree that what she said was logical and might well be true. It made him feel much better.

The next day, Roger completed the formalities and paid the very reasonable rent for the first quarter. Remembering the events of the previous night had eliminated any twinges his conscience might have felt. Although he had little patience with the extravagance and stupidity of the king and his court, Roger was coming to hate and despise those who were presently in control of Paris. Thus, he was beginning to take considerable pleasure in the idea that he might be able to cheat them. What had sparked this intense feeling was hearing, through Aunay, that there had been a repeat at La Force prison of the massacre carried out at the Abbaye.

The first massacre might have been a result of confusion, lack of preparation, or powerlessness on the part of the government. Once the mob was on the move, it could be stopped only by force, and it was plain that the assembly did not trust the present army to carry out its orders. Thus, what had happened at Abbaye might have been unavoidable, at least in the sense of being unexpected. Young St. Méard had said a deputation from the assembly tried to stop the executions. However, the same excuse could not be given for what had happened at La Force. Whether or not the assembly had initiated the massacres did not matter. They had had a full day to prevent a similar event from taking place and had done nothing. If there was anything Roger could do to save someone from falling into their hands, he would be overjoyed to do it.

They moved the next day, carrying with them a generous supply of food from the larder of the café. Madame

Aunay had pressed this upon them, saying it was only a trifle compared with what Roger had saved them by his cleverness. Leonie accepted finally with the most heartfelt thanks she could muster. She should be grateful, she knew, but it had only just occurred to her that she had not the faintest idea what to do with the stuff. The closest she had ever come to cooking was slicing the sausage she and Roger had eaten in the tunnel or handing him the bread and cheese she had found in the café kitchen.

The most pressing problem, Roger said firmly, was setting up his stock and tools, using the counters, hooks, and other furnishings left by the tailor. He began to work at this with great energy, making himself too busy to answer Leonie's questions about helping him and becoming quite short with her. Leonie was surprised at first but then began to feel frightened and guilty. She had pushed Roger into setting up a business, but he was *not* a gunsmith. He was an English gentleman and, she guessed mistakenly, knew very little about the art. Now he was worried about betraying them by his ignorance.

It was too late for regret, she realized. The best she could do was keep out of his way until he got his worries under control. Then they could think of some way to conceal his lack of knowledge and training until they could escape. She lugged the traveling bag with their clothes up to the living quarters and, to submerge her own uneasiness, began to consider her duties. The first was easy enough. She stripped the bed and opened the window to air the room. After that she hung up their few garments. Then, searching produced sheets and pillowslips, which after some puzzling and trial attempts she got on the bed in a reasonable fashion. Finally, she came down again and went into the kitchen at the back.

Roger heard her, but did not lift his head from what he was doing. His frantic activity had, of course, nothing to do with acting the part of a gunsmith. It had occurred to him during the process of moving that there was no longer any reason for Leonie to share his bed. The house was, like most in Paris, tall and narrow with the shop on the ground floor and a kitchen built out in the back. On the floor above was the tailor's bedroom and dining parlor, but there was still another floor where the children and servants had slept. Roger knew quite well that he should choose one of the upper rooms as his own. That would be the proper thing to do. Nonetheless, he simply could not do it.

Conscience warred with desire; they were so even a match that all Roger could do was metaphorically stick his head in the sand and drive Leonie to make the choice without any influence or suggestion. When he had snapped at her until she trudged upstairs dragging the heavy cloak bag, he was flayed by guilt. If he had had a chance, he told himself, he had just spoiled it by implying he would be hell to live with. What was wrong with him that he could not make himself agreeable to the only two women he had ever wanted?

That thought started a new train of guilt—what right had he to want a girl like Leonie? She was half his age— literally—and ten times as rich—a great heiress. His scowl was so black, as he fastened a vise to the counter where cloth had been cut, that Leonie tiptoed past close to the wall. She knew she had been wrong, and she did not want to draw notice to herself. Aware of every move she made, almost of every breath she drew, Roger read the guilt in her manner but misinterpreted it. His heart sank sickeningly.

Again war raged in his mind. Desperation urged him to go and know the worst so that he could come to terms with the bitter knowledge and not make himself even more obnoxious. Cowardice whispered that he should wait. Perhaps shame at seeming ungrateful for his protection would make her change her mind when she saw he was unhappy. Appalled at the notion of such crude and disgusting blackmail, Roger promptly dropped what he was doing and ran up the stairs. He went all the way up first, but obviously Leonie had not been there at all. Suppressing the hope that rose so fast it nearly choked him, he came down to the main living floor. The parlor was empty. Biting his lip he walked through to the bedchamber. The first thing he saw was the empty traveling bag, the second was the neatly made bed. That was not final, he told himself to still his leaping heart. There was no reason why Leonie should make a bed for him. She was not a servant, after all. She might expect him to make his own bed. But Roger did not believe his own arguments, and when he saw their clothing hanging side by side in the wardrobe, he knew Leonie assumed they would share the room.

Perversely, conscience immediately gained the upper hand. Roger came down, passed through the shop, and came upon Leonie, staring bewildered at the crane with its hook and ratchet in the fireplace. "Leonie," he said more harshly than he intended, "there is no reason we should continue to sleep together. There are rooms—"

She whirled on him, her face flushing, which made her eyes bright as new-minted gold. To scold her for stupidity would be reasonable; however, it was cruel and spiteful, Leonie thought, to withdraw the comfort of his physical presence, to leave her alone to worry and regret what she had done. Angry as she was, Leonie would not plead, but she was not angry enough to want to do without Roger either. Nor was she going to let him have his own stupid way just because he had flown into a temper.

"Don't be stupid," she snapped. "I'm sorry to have put us in a dangerous situation, but it can't be improved by adding to duties for which I am totally untrained and unfitted. It's enough to make one bed and keep two rooms and this kitchen clean. I have no desire to add another bed and room to my burdens."

"Good God," Roger exclaimed. "I had never thought of it. It's not fitting for you to do such things, Leonie. I will have to find a servant for you."

"Are you mad?" Leonie cried, bitterly hurt at how far he was willing to go to free himself of her and suddenly wondering if the bad temper was only an excuse. Could he already want a different woman? "What would Lefranc think, after you said you were too poor to pay the rent, if he came here and found we had a servant? Not to mention that anyone who employs a servant is just begging to be spied upon and have everything done or said reported to the commissioners of the Section. Can we endure such examination?"

"No," Roger agreed. "No, we can't. But what is to be done, Leonie? You can't cook and scrub."

"If you can learn to be a gunsmith, I can learn to cook and scrub," Leonie said.

"You are an angel," Roger sighed, marveling at her sweetness and adaptability.

It was only a fit of temper, Leonie thought. *He is not yet really tired of me.* "You will not think me an angel when I have prepared a meal," she assured Roger. "It is far more likely to taste like a devil's brew than angel food. Tell me, do you know how this contraption works? I can see that it is to hang pots over the fire, but . . ."

"Yes, I can show you that," Roger replied. "Our cook was a motherly body and didn't mind if we 'helped' in the kitchen—so long as no big dinner was being prepared. I loved putting pots up and down the ratchet and turning the spit when I was a boy. But what to put in the pots—that's another matter."

Leonie allowed her eyes to wander from the fireplace to the packets of food and spices piled on the table. Madame Aunay naturally assumed that she had been trained by her mother to her duties as a wife. Had she a modicum of sense, she would have said her mother was a bad cook or had died young or some such tale when she explained the loss of her clothes. It would have been natural to confess all her troubles at once. She had missed a second opportunity when Roger announced they had taken the shop. Now it was too late. It would seem odd, Leonie feared, if she said she could not cook. Besides, bad cooking was one thing, total ignorance another.

"We will contrive," Roger was comforting her. "I can get food at a *cafetier*."

Leonie nodded, but in a dissatisfied way. It was ridiculous that a person who could read several languages and discourse on philosophical theories of government and science could not produce a simple stew.

"That would do for a few days," she replied, "but it would be expensive. Besides, unless you go a long way, they will soon know you have a 'wife' and begin to wonder. It will be best if there is nothing special to remark on about us." She frowned. "Roger, there are books on deportment, on how to build a house—on everything. Surely, there must be books on housewifery."

He burst out laughing. "My dear girl, you have the kind of courage that leads a forlorn hope. By all means, let us go out to dinner this afternoon—that will be nothing to remark upon, when we have been so busy moving and are tired—and we will search the bookstalls for a treatise for your edification."

"If you think I am brave," Leonie giggled, "wait until you have to taste what I have prepared."

CHAPTER 14

The book on housewifery and a second on cooking were found. All in all, Leonie discovered that a mind strong enough to grasp political theory, science, and languages could usually grasp instructions on cleaning and washing. Cookery was another matter. Sometimes her efforts were successful; sometimes all Roger's courage and her own were insufficient to cope with the disaster she produced. On such occasions, the *cafétier* and Leonie's sense of humor came to the rescue so that they did not starve.

The fact that the visits to the *cafetier* were relatively frequent soon did not matter from the point of expense. Citizen Lefranc had not forgotten his promise to his republican friend and recommended Roger's shop to everyone he knew who owned a gun. Since Roger was a good and a most unusually honest workman, those he served also sang his praises. Soon he was as busy as any tradesman could desire and was making—to his stunned amazement—a great deal of money. If he had not found such great difficulty in obtaining parts, he believed he would soon have become rich.

Although this situation tickled his pride and his fancy, Roger would greatly have preferred if Citizen Lefranc had minded his own business and been less helpful. The money he made was useless to him now because there was still no way out of Paris. The feeling against *émigrés* was hotter than ever, and each person who left the city was closely scrutinized. Those caught escaping were as good as dead. What was worse, Roger's popularity as a workman and Lefranc's good offices had made him known to a great many people. He received compliments on his patriotism from men he had never seen before.

It was thus impossible for Roger to ask for a pass to leave. What excuse could be offered by a patriot for wanting to leave a booming business when he had only been in Paris for a few weeks? After some months or a year, a man might say he wished to make a visit to relatives left behind or see to some property in the hands of an agent. A dying relative could be used as an excuse, but the commissioners who issued passes had grown very strict. They wanted to see the letter, know who had brought it, or examine the newsbearer if the information came by word of mouth.

Had Roger been desperate to leave, he might have searched harder for, and found, the means. Actually, his personal life—aside from twinges of his conscience when he saw Leonie down on the floor scrubbing or, with soot-smudged face, wrestling with her recalcitrant cooking pots—was so delightful that he hated the thought of disrupting it. For the first time in his life he was truly and completely happy in a woman's company. He had little fear of being rejected—not that Leonie did not sometimes refuse him; she did. But there was tenderness and regret in the refusal when she was too tired or had her flux. She was never cruel or contemptuous. Nor was there any chance that a particularly satisfactory lovemaking would be turned sordid and ugly by a coy demand for some financial reward.

Sometimes Roger wondered if Leonie would conceive. The thought brought him alternate flushes of joy and chills of horror. A child would bind them together irrevocably. There would be his perfect reason for marrying Leonie—and it would be sheer joy to have a child with her. Her boundless warmth and generosity proved she would make a perfect mother. Still, the danger of childbearing was something Roger dreaded for his pearl without price, and an infant would be a dreadful additional burden and danger if their situation became worse. Nonetheless, hope outweighed fear, and it was more than sexual disappointment Roger felt when Leonie refused him because her monthly flux had come.

Naturally enough, Leonie did not press Roger to find a method of escape. Had anyone told her, before Marot had destroyed her world, that she could be happy scrubbing floors and sheets, polishing furniture, and cooking, she would have thought that person demented. But she *was* happy. Not that she liked the crude, hard work of housekeeping; she did not. Nonetheless, there was a sense of satisfaction in it, a challenge fairly met and conquered as Roger met and conquered the challenges of the gunsmith's trade. In the small house Leonie could hear him at his work, humming sometimes when a job went well, cursing and grunting with effort when his tools were inadequate or something did not fit as it should. Some things Leonie did enjoy, among them dealing with customers in the shop when Roger was out or busy.

Even if Leonie had hated what she was forced to do— and she did not hate it, merely felt there were other things she could do better—she would have been happy. Roger showed no further signs of tiring of her. He had opportunities enough now if he wanted to seek pleasure or variety elsewhere, but Leonie did not think he did. He never went out alone, except when it was a matter of business and he could not find a trustworthy messenger or his own presence was necessary. Leonie knew the district well now and could judge how long it would take to go somewhere. Roger was always back before she expected. It was obvious that he hurried back as fast as he could when he did go out without her.

Thus, both were happy, and although they sometimes talked of escape, neither really wanted to leave. Within the satisfaction of each was a shadow, but not so dark a shadow as had lain there previously. Roger was beginning to hope that he might win Leonie. Solange had done him great damage, but, bitter as he was, he could not completely dismiss Leonie's response as all gratitude. A few times he had been on the verge of asking her to marry him. He had checked the impulse sternly, knowing it to be completely unfair. There were two big roadblocks.

The age difference was large, but it was common enough for twenty years to separate marital partners without unhappiness. His stepmother was more than twenty years his father's junior, and no one could doubt Lady Margaret's satisfaction with her husband. Unfortunately, Roger could not lean too hard on that happy example. Lady Margaret had been a widow, a mature woman in her thirties, when his father had courted her. Leonie was an inexperienced girl, under twenty. He could not take advantage of her innocence. He must give her a chance to enjoy the courtship of the many gentlemen who would flock to her. She was also the heiress of Stour, fitted by birth and wealth to a far more exalted social position than the youngest son of a baronet.

Every time Roger thought of that, he found a new excuse not to seek an escape from Paris. Leonie had a very similar feeling. She, too, was beginning to hope she could keep Roger. It was true she did not expect to marry him. She believed that if he had wanted marriage, there was nothing to stop him from suggesting it. However, his efforts to please her in every way, his praise and caresses, clearly indicated that he was not bored or losing interest. Leonie had not yet needed to employ any of the devices she knew for stimulating a lover. Roger was eager enough without. In fact, his techniques had such an effect on her that it was only before and after they made love that she could think of it.

Actually, the only reason that the subject of escaping Paris came up was that the political climate seemed to be growing more and more extreme. After the panic and massacres inspired by the fall of Verdun, relative quiet settled on the city. Although the signs of the breakdown of authority were everywhere—gangs roamed the streets at night assaulting passersby and looting houses while the agents of the commune stood by and even joined them—no large-scale violence took place. In this period, Roger and Leonie made a quiet visit to Fouché so that Roger could leave letters to his father and son with him to be transmitted if and when it would be safe to do so. The letters said little—nothing that could cause any trouble to Fouché or his messenger if they were opened—only that Roger was well and safe and had Henry's (he did not further identify de Conyers) daughter with him.

Fouché assured him that if he were able to get the letters to England he would and, if they went with a messenger from his firm, that the man would be instructed to take the letters personally and give Sir Joseph a reassuring account of Roger's actual circumstances. As he was seeing Roger and Leonie to the door, a man entered. Fouché smiled a welcome, greeting the newcomer as "cousin." His words drowned Leonie's slight gasp and Roger's good manners were sufficient to conceal a start of surprise, because the young man Fouché addressed as Joseph was an albino. On a later visit to Fouché, they learned that the cousin—also a Fouché—was the deputy from the town of Nantes to the

National Convention, which was about to convene in a few days to replace the useless assembly, by now held in contempt by all.

"You can imagine," Fouché said, "how very happy I was when he came here and claimed cousinship. Thank God I was able to ask him to live with us. He is clever—you would never guess it from his looks, but he is the most astute man with whom I have ever dealt. For the first time," again Fouché lowered his voice and looked around to guard against eavesdroppers, "since everything went mad, I feel a sense of security. Joseph will warn me of trouble, I am sure."

"I'm pleased that things are going better for you," Roger said politely, not much interested although Joseph's physical oddity had, of course, made him memorable.

"Perhaps to your benefit also," Fouché said with a smile. "I told Joseph the story we agreed upon, except that I said we had done considerable business together and had become—through letters—friendly. I have a feeling about that young man. He is no visionary. If he establishes influence for himself, he may be able to help you. We shall see."

"Thank you very much," Roger replied sincerely. Fouché was no fool, as Roger had known for years. If he said his cousin Joseph might be a good man to know in the future, he was very likely right.

"Meanwhile," Fouché went on, "I have more immediate good news for you. Your letters went off three days ago. I suppose that is what you came about."

"No, although I'm glad to hear it. My father would have begun to expect me to return 'any day.' At his age I don't like to have him worried. What I came for, however, is to return part of the money you gave me for those assignats—which I know were near worthless. I'm in a good way of trade now." Roger laughed heartily. "In fact, if I must remain here much longer, I will end a rich man."

Fouché did not wish to take the money. He did not need it and knew Roger and his family would be good for it. If he should need to flee to England himself . . . In the end, he said he would be Roger's banker for it and return it at any time if Roger should find he needed money. Then he nodded.

"Actually, that will work out quite well," he said. "There is no reason why I should not be your man of business.

You would naturally come to me if we had done business before. It will be an excellent excuse for you to come here."

Roger agreed heartily, and it was through Fouché that he and Leonie learned what was really happening. The first news was good. Charles François Dumouriez had been sent to take charge of the army that faced the Prussians. A republican himself, he understood the troops he led. They were a mixture of volunteers, National Guard, and old army regulars, and they could not be expected to obey blindly or respond to the same discipline as the armies of the past. He changed both tactics and the way orders were given and, on September twentieth, his army met the Prussians at Valmy and threw them back.

A vast sense of relief swept the city. As a happy coincidence, the newly convened National Convention began its operation at noon on September twenty-first publishing the news of this victory as its first duty. In a reaction to new hope and horror of what had been done, the Commune of Paris was abolished. However, the final efficacy of this move was very doubtful, Roger said to Leonie when they were at home and considering the news.

"Since all the worst radicals, even that diseased monster Marat, have been elected to the convention, I do not see that much has been accomplished in curbing the commune. It will merely operate from a new base."

The truth of his words became apparent soon enough. By October sixteenth the question of the king's fate had been raised and Bourbotte, a deputy from Auxerre, had called for the deaths of the whole royal family. Most of the deputies drew back, temporizing, but on November sixth Valazé made a report on papers found in a secret safe in the Tuileries and accused Louis XVI of treason. He called for a trial of the deposed monarch. There were a few who protested, but Valazé's report had inflamed many and the Jacobins seized their chance. The Girondists, always split into violent factions, were still uncertain of which way they wanted to jump and played for time. They compromised on setting a date for debate on the matter.

On the fifteenth of November the subject was open for discussion. The aim of the Jacobins was to avoid any trial and pass a sentence of death without public discussion or pleading; however, they could not push the convention that far. Too many voices were raised in support of mercy.

Thomas Paine, who had left the newly born nation of the United States because it was not sufficiently republican, offered an impassioned plea in favor of banishment rather than death, as did a number of others. Finally, the Jacobin faction was forced to accept a trial.

Leonie had been attending to the bulletins concerning this discussion with close attention and was overjoyed when she heard this. She was surprised, then hurt, when Roger did not respond in any way to her attempts to discuss the matter but continued to eat his dinner—one of Leonie's successes—with his eyes fixed on his plate.

"Perhaps the subject is not very interesting to you because you are English," she said rather sharply.

At first Roger seemed to pay no attention to this remark either. He was aware of how strongly Leonie felt and was reluctant to say what he must. In a way, he had hoped the Jacobins would succeed in their purpose. The end, he knew, would be the same, and if the Jacobins had their way, the agony would be short, no one would be deluded by false hopes or by the pretense of legality. Roger raised his eyes at last. The surface hurt Leonie felt at his seeming indifference had not extinguished the hopeful expectation underneath. He could not permit her to cling to that. Roger knew personally that, under certain circumstances, hope was the greatest of all evils rather than the single good that had been packed into Pandora's box to be let loose on humankind.

"It has nothing to do with being English," he said. "Englishmen are men like any others. It is only that—Leonie, I am sorry, but this trial can have only one conclusion. Perhaps I see that more clearly because I am English."

"What do you mean?"

"A deposed king cannot be allowed to live."

"Why?" Leonie cried. "God knows, I have little enough love for Louis. He is stupid, and he permitted an extravagance that had already ruined the country to continue, even to increase. He stood in the way of every reasonable reform that was suggested. No one except a lunatic could believe that he should be allowed to rule this nation absolutely. But it was wrong to depose him—"

"You have said it," Roger interrupted. "The constitution your father helped to write was a reasonable compromise. If only there had been time enough. . . . But it is no help to talk of might-have-beens. Once Louis was deposed, his death warrant was signed."

"I cannot believe that! They have not condemned him. There is to be a trial. Roger, you *know* the king is not really guilty of all those silly things. They say he shed the blood of Frenchmen. It is ridiculous! If he had not been so anxious to *avoid* bloodshed, he would not be where he is. If he had ordered the Swiss and the loyal troops to fire on the mob, probably they would have run away."

"Yes. That is another reason he must die." Roger sighed. "Think, Leonie. If the king is innocent, then those who deposed him must be guilty of a crime. Can the republic admit that it had no right to depose and imprison Louis— whether or not he is innocent?"

"But the deputies agreed to a trial. The majority of the convention voted for it. Many spoke against death and suggested banishment. They could say he was guilty of conspiring with the *émigrés* to restore the absolute monarchy—"

"That is treason," Roger pointed out.

"Oh, nonsense," Leonie protested. "If someone took away something I always believed was mine, would it be wrong for me to try to get it back?"

"In law, yes. Even morally, if it had been explained very carefully that it was not yours and why it was not yours. . . ." Then Roger shook his head. "No, it does not matter. Even if he had not conspired, even if he had done his very best at all times to act in accordance with the constitution, it would not matter. Once he was deposed only two choices remain: Give him back his throne—or kill him."

Leonie was neither weak nor silly, but she had abundant evidence that Roger always knew what he was talking about. Tears rose in her eyes. She did not give a thought to the first possibility. After what had been done and said, it was out of the question. Louis was a kind and merciful king, but even he could not overlook the insults and disrespect with which he had been treated. No one in the government could afford to consider restoration.

"But why death?" Leonie asked. "So many have spoken for banishment. If he were sent away and made to swear he would not return. . . ."

"You must know Louis's character and realize he would never give such an oath. He would rather die than—"

"He permitted himself to be deposed," Leonie interrupted.

"My dear, he could do nothing to prevent that, except what we have already said—he was either too weak or unwilling to do—but he never agreed to it either. Anyway, I tell you, it does not matter. Even those who spoke for banishment will vote for death when the vote is taken. Leonie, at this point I would vote for death myself—if I had a modicum of common sense, which I begin to fear I have not."

He pushed his chair back impatiently and began to stride around the small room. Leonie watched him, the horror she had felt at his saying he would vote for death fading as she saw his agitation and recalled the final part of his sentence.

"There is nothing I can do!" he burst out.

"No, of course not!" Leonie cried, also jumping to her feet. She had forgotten in her absorption in the fate of a person she felt was being ground to bits between the millstones of an inexorable force, that Roger, like her father, always felt responsible for things that happened.

"And even if I could, I know I *should* not," he went on, not seeming to have heard her. "It is one man, one life. Is it right to preserve that one life when thousands and thousands would die because of it? I don't know. When is justice wrong? Is it a thing that can be measured in terms of cost, like a bushel of corn?"

"What are you talking about?" Leonie caught at Roger and stopped his pacing.

"A deposed king must not live," Roger repeated. "Charles I was executed—that was wrong, an injustice, although he was a foolish man—but his death ended the civil war in England and the country was at peace. Perhaps it was not such a peace as many could have wished for, but the bloodletting was ended. Then James II fled the country and was deposed. That saved the nation the blood of one stupid man and brought us instead a torrent of blood—the Boyne, and Culloden, and the massacre at Glencoe, not to mention the many little hopeless risings and the heads on Traitor's Gate. As long as the deposed king lives—or his acknowledged heirs—there are those who will try to restore him."

Leonie put her hand to her mouth.

"Think about it," Roger urged, "and do not be so quick to call 'monsters' all those who vote for death. Some are monsters—Marat, Danton, perhaps that 'incorruptible' block of ice Robespierre—but most are only men, torn apart between what they know is just, their fears for themselves and their own families, and their knowledge of what is good for the country. When the last two agree on an answer and overshadow the first so greatly, does that make a man who accepts the answer a monster?"

Shivering, Leonie pressed herself into Roger's arms, and he held her and kissed her. "I am sorry to kill your hope," he whispered against her hair, "but it will hurt you less if you understand."

That was true. As the weeks passed and Leonie saw the moves, like a stylized dance of death, she grew to accept what Roger had said. On December eleventh Louis was arraigned, on the nineteenth he and his lawyers had finished examining the documents to be used as evidence against him. Sometime during that period he said to Lamoignon de Malesherbes, an old friend and ex-minister who had petitioned to help defend him, "They will put me to death: I am certain of it. For all that, let us engage in the trial as if I were about to gain. I shall gain really, because justice will be paid to my memory."

This statement and others made their way mysteriously from Louis's closely guarded prison and aroused considerable sympathy for him. Nonetheless, Leonie was not seduced into hope again, and on December twenty-sixth the trial was held. A few, moved by the logic of the defense and the quiet dignity of the king, forgot practicalities. A deputy called Languinais even pointed out that the tribunal that had boldly declared itself the author of the event of August tenth, which had resulted in Louis's deposition, could not, in reason, also be his "impartial" judge, and cried in fury that he would rather die himself than condemn to death, by a violation of all legal forms, the most detestable tyrant.

However, these voices were drowned in the more vocal radical outpourings of St. Just and Robespierre. St. Just cried passionately, "To pardon the tyrant is to pardon the tyranny." But it was Robespierre's cold, quiet, unemotional voice that really drowned resistance to the judgment against Louis. "So far as I am concerned," he had said, "I abhor the punishment of death of which your laws are so profuse, and I ask for its abolition. . . . I have for Louis neither love nor hatred. I only hate his crimes and therefore pronounce with regret the fatal truth: Louis must die because the country must live."

Voting on the verdict began on January sixteenth and on the seventeenth the sentence of death was announced. A movement for reprieve was voted on and rejected on January nineteenth with a much greater majority than the original vote.

When they had that news, Leonie said to Roger, "You were right—although you are too generous, I think. The more they thought about it, the more they realized it would not be practical to let him live. Only I think what turned the tables was their fear for themselves, not for the nation." She shivered. "Roger, can we escape from here? I want to go to England."

"England isn't any better," he soothed, hugging her to him. "We did it too, although that was a long time ago. Still, it isn't likely to happen again. Poor old George is just as stupid as Louis, but everyone knows he's mad, and Prinny—he's too clever and too weak-kneed to cause any real trouble."

Nonetheless, Roger went to see Fouché the very next day. He agreed with Leonie, in spite of some reluctance, that it was time to get out of France. There were aspects of the situation that he had not mentioned to her because he did not wish her to be frightened. Roger was reasonably sure that Louis's execution would cause a reaction in other nations that would result in an intensification of the war. On that front, things had been going well. There had been another French victory, at Jemappes, which had driven the Prussians off French soil completely. It seemed to Roger the best opportunity to leave Paris. There was no war panic, he had been in the city four months and might reasonably wish to visit his home for a few days. There would be, he hoped, a period of quiet before the king was executed during which he might obtain a pass.

In this hope he was disappointed. "There is no time," Fouché replied. "Joseph told me last night that the execution—murder, I should say—will be tomorrow. You will see the notices up when you walk home, I do not doubt."

"They are cleverer than I thought," Roger said with a

tinge of bitterness. "I would lay a high wager that Robespierre knows his Machiavelli by heart. If you wish to do a series of evil things, do them all together as quickly as possible. I am only surprised that he did not call for Marie Antoinette to be tried at the same time as the king."

Fouché changed color, and Roger gasped. "You cannot mean that he did! What grounds could there be?"

"She was never loved," Fouché replied, "and, truly, she was probably more guilty than Louis of the things of which he was accused. She was a strong—and generally a bad—influence on him. Anyway, the motion was not carried to the convention. It was something thrown out to see whether the idea would take. Let us hope it will never come to pass. She is powerless now. As to your problem, I do not know what to say."

"Do you think it would be wise simply to go? The barriers are not so carefully watched now. Since the Prussians were defeated, the patriotic fervor is somewhat dimmed. Times are hard, too—although God knows not for me—and if I used a golden key I think the lock might open easily."

"You might get out of Paris," Fouché said. "There is so much contempt for all authority. But the roads and the towns are all most carefully watched for *émigrés*. Besides, how would you get out of the country?"

"I have a friend in Brittany who has a ship and knows the English coast well," Roger replied.

"Ah," Fouché breathed, "I remember. In that case, come back tomorrow—" Suddenly Fouché shuddered. "No, not tomorrow. Come back the beginning of next week. I will ask Joseph. . . . But you know, my dear St. Eyre, it is not really reasonable for a man to abandon a thriving business and travel all that distance in the depths of winter to 'pay a visit' to relatives."

Roger sighed. "Yes, and we are likely to be held up by the weather from crossing the Channel too, which might put my friend in danger. Let it go then. I am certainly in no danger, and the lady I was sent to bring home is taken for my wife and not suspect. It would be foolish to bring attention to ourselves. However, give my compliments to your cousin and tell him I would be happy to serve him at any time."

The last was a polite nothing, spoken without much con-

sideration. Roger's mind was on the events of the following
day. He found the notices up, as Fouché had said, and read
them with horror. Louis was to be executed in the Place de
la Revolution—only a few streets from their house, which
sat in the shadow of St. Roche. He could do little for
Leonie except warn her and when the drums began to
sound—they had been ordered to beat continuously so that
no cries of mercy or support for the king nor signals for
rescue could be heard—take her in his arms to kiss and
comfort her.

The drums stopped once. Roger heard later that the king
had wanted to say a few words but had not been permitted
more than a single sentence lest his dignity and generosity
inflame the crowd. Leonie had shuddered and sighed with
relief that it was over, but before Roger could release her
the hideous rattling began again. The second time they
stopped, a salvo of cannon fire followed. Then Leonie had
wept.

"It is ridiculous," she sobbed. "I didn't know him. But it
is so *unfair*. He wasn't a bad person. He meant well. He
didn't deserve to die."

By the next day Leonie seemed recovered, but for Roger
the sound of those drums lingered in the house. Then, three
days later, he had been working a pressure-fitted piece into
place with quick, repeated taps of a hammer, which caused
another piece of metal sitting in a pewter dish to rattle.
When he was finished, he heard Leonie crying in the
kitchen. She apologized for her silliness after he rushed in
to ask what was wrong, but she was shuddering with horror, and Roger knew she heard the drums also. Then, the
day after that, a man came asking by name for the tailor
who had been accused of conspiring with the royalist party.
Roger said as blankly as he could that he knew no one by
that name. That did not silence his visitor, who explained.
Roger then said he still did not know the man and had no
idea what had happened to him.

"I will leave my name," the man said.

"For what?" Roger asked angrily.

"Oh, in case someone asks for Janine. You can say that I
was asking for him also."

"I am not a messenger," Roger growled, and the man
turned away.

Later, however, Roger found a card—enough in itself to

suggest aristocratic or bourgeois connections without the elegant printing it displayed. He showed it to Leonie.

"It is time for us to move," he said. "I do not know whether I am being tested by my republican 'friends' or by the royalists—although I am pretty sure it is the latter— but it is unhealthy either way."

"Yes," Leonie agreed with every sign of relief. "Oh, yes, Roger. I—I would like to move away from here."

All they needed was an excuse, and by the end of the week they had that, although Roger would have preferred a less harrowing one. Times, as Roger had said to Fouché, were very hard. There was no work; prices were very high; there was real suffering among the laboring classes. Moreover, the king's death, in a typical reversal of mob feeling, had not pleased the people. There had been considerable sympathy for Louis, which had been displayed in various ways, one of which was the cheering of any royalist sentiment in a play. The convention promptly closed the theaters, which did not please anyone much either.

Also, even among those who had approved Louis's death, there was dissatisfaction. They seemed to have expected some miraculous result—a solution to all the economic and social problems of the nation. Undisciplined mobs—smaller than those organized to depose the king on August tenth or initiate the massacres on September second, but also destructive—broke into the convention several times to demand or protest. On their way to obtain their "civil rights" they uncivilly assaulted and robbed whomever they met and often looted shops.

One of the first streets to be visited by these furies was the one that held Roger's shop. The mob broke into the baker's at the corner and beat the poor man severely— because the price of bread was too high. Roger had heard the noise as the small mob moved from the avenue into his street, but he was engaged in a delicate piece of repair and did not look up from his work. Leonie came from the kitchen, where the sound had been muted, and looked curiously out the door just in time to see the invasion of the baker. She uttered a muffled shriek, which brought Roger to his feet with an oath.

"Damn it, Leonie—"

"The *sans-culottes*," she gasped, "they are breaking into the bakery."

Roger said a word, fortunately in English, that later he could only hope Leonie did not understand, but he did not waste time in mouthing further obscenities. A quick glance told him it was too late to shutter his shop. He thrust Leonie back toward the area where sales stock and finished work lay.

"Load," he ordered. "Load every gun you can—don't forget the patches. I would like to murder them all, God knows, but—"

He broke off to call to the grocer, who held the shop next to the baker and who had just fled his premises with his wife and son on his heels and his infant daughter in his arms. The movement attracted the tail of the mob, those who could not fit into the bakery. A shout was raised and a few turned to pursue the grocer. Roger fired one pistol over the heads of the crowd. There was a hesitation, then a surge in his direction. He took careful aim and brought down the man closest on the grocer's heels.

From the door of the shop, another pistol barked. A second in the crowd fell. If Roger had not been scared nearly witless, he would have laughed, knowing that Leonie's success was pure accident. The grocer and his family had reached them. Roger pushed the man toward his shop as Leonie's other pistol went off. By the counter near the door, guns lay in a row. Roger snatched up two. The grocer dropped his small daughter into her mother's arms and grabbed up two more. Leonie began to load the guns that had been emptied. Had the mob been a large one, all in Roger's shop would have died. As it was, the defenders were driven back from the street into the shop itself. There the odds were somewhat in their favor because only one or two of the mob could enter the doorway at the same time. Even so, there were three dead and five wounded in the doorway before they convinced the rest of the mob that their street was too thorny a branch to grasp and break. Cursing and threatening, the mob retreated to find easier pickings.

Roger and the grocer ran to see what could be done for the baker. Leonie stood, pistol in hand, watching the heap of men in the doorway where groans and movement warned there might still be life enough to be dangerous. The grocer's wife tried to comfort her screaming children. In a few minutes, Roger returned, his face black with rage.

The other shopkeepers were out now, shuttering their
premises in case the mob should return. Then they came to
give what help they could.

Among them they separated the wounded from the dead.
Leonie and the other women bandaged the wounded while
Roger and the men carried the dead away. What they did
with them, Leonie never asked and Roger did not mention.
The wounded were eventually piled into the grocer's cart
and carried to the nearest hospital. Finally everyone went
to help the grocer and baker salvage what they could from
their ravaged shops.

That night the men came as a deputation to thank Roger
for his defense.

"You are very kind," he responded, "but I do not deserve any special thanks. I was saving myself. I am glad you
benefited also, but I must point out to you that we are in
equal or greater danger now. If anyone from that mob
complains to the convention or the Section, we may be accused of 'incivism'—and you know what comes of that."

"The guillotine!"

"Yes."

"What is to be done?"

"I am not sure," Roger replied to the frightened questions and exclamations, "but it seems to me that the safest
thing is for us to go all together tomorrow and complain
also. At least that way our side of the story will also be
heard and Citizens Chouar and Dillon can ask that their
shops be examined as evidence of the violence. Otherwise it
may be said that we fired upon harmless citizens marching
peacefully for a redress of their injuries."

A brief discussion ensued, but no one could think of anything else to suggest and it was decided to do as Roger
suggested. When they were gone, he said defensively to
Leonie, "It *is* the best thing to do, even if it will serve my
particular purpose also."

Leonie had been sitting with her hands in her lap, staring out the window. Mob violence always brought back the
horrors of her own experience and her losses. She turned
now to look into Roger's troubled eyes and smiled at him.
"Of course it is the best thing to do. Even if no one in that
crowd of animals should think of complaining, or be listened to if they did complain, everyone in the street knows
that *sans-culottes* were driven away from here. There is

bound to be talk—and God knows what distorted talk. Sooner or later someone will accuse someone else for private reasons—" Leonie shuddered. "Perhaps us. Women have remarked to me when I was buying food how many people come to our shop. Perhaps it is only curiosity, but times are bad. Curiosity can become envy."

"It's all right. Don't worry. Fouché is looking for a new place for us. We should be out of here in another week or so. The quarter ends with February, and I can give notice on the first of the month. I'll say you are frightened to be so near the meeting place of the convention because you think the mob will return, that you have been having nightmares."

"And so I would be," she said, getting up and going over to him, "if you weren't there. You're so warm and solid, Roger. I can't be afraid when you're beside me."

Roger stood up too and put his arms around her. He hoped she had not seen the pain in his face. It would be cruel to make her feel guilty over an innocent remark meant as a compliment, but it was a bitter lesson to him. Probably it was true that she did not find him repulsive, but it was clear enough that she did not love him either. He had been mistaken in thinking she was no longer afraid and welcomed his lovemaking for its own sake. Well, he was a fool to have thought of reaching the sun. At least he would have her as long as they were in France.

CHAPTER 15

Roger's plan for moving out of an area in which he and Leonie were too well-known, and which had become distasteful to them, worked moderately well. By the time he gave notice, the convention had been mobbed twice more. Fortunately, their street had not been invaded again, except by the noise and a few individual rioters, but it was reasonable that a young woman would be frightened and that a man who had no roots in the district might want to move. There was some resistance—gunsmiths were not so plentiful that a Section liked to lose one—but Roger pointed out that he was not leaving Paris, only moving to the rue de la Corderie, and he would be available.

The only serious drawback was that the papers permitting Roger to move and work in another district were now marked "within the environs of Paris." Roger asked with a slight show of indignation why such a restriction should be applied to him. It was not him alone, he was told. In these perilous times his trade was very necessary. All skilled artisans who could be of use to France in her time of peril must be available and where they could be reached in an emergency.

"What emergency? What peril?" Roger asked. "Are not the armies of France victorious? Have we suffered a defeat?"

"No, but England has sent home our ambassador heaped with insults and has decreed a day of mourning by the entire nation for that tyrant Louis. I believe the convention will declare war on them today or tomorrow, and likely on Holland also."

"I see," Roger murmured, his well-trained face giving no indication of his concern although the news was as bad as it possibly could be.

He said nothing more about the papers. The last thing he wanted was to raise any suspicion that he intended to leave Paris, particularly now that England and France would be at war. So far, the few people who had been aware that his accent was foreign had thought little of it. However, if an all-out attack should be launched at France, all foreigners might become suspect. Worse, all the northern coast would be watched and guarded with ten times the care shown in the past.

If he had been alone, Roger might have considered escaping from the city and making his way across country on foot, avoiding the roads, to find Pierre. That would mean sleeping in barns or in the open, living worse than a tinker, who at least had a wagon for shelter and a pot to cook in. To inflict such suffering on Leonie at this season of the year was impossible, particularly when there did not seem to be any acute danger. In the summer, if the situation grew worse, Roger knew he might have to reconsider his opinion. For now, it was best and safest to continue the pretense they had been living thus far.

Roger was not the only one hit hard by the announcement that France and England were at war. In the elegant breakfast room of his London house, Sir Joseph stared at the newspaper that had been laid beside his plate as if it had turned into a venomous serpent.

"What is it, my love?" Lady Margaret cried.

"France and England are at war."

"Oh, no! But I thought there was *not* to be a declaration of war. I thought—"

"We have not declared war," Sir Joseph interrupted. "France has."

"Those madmen!" Lady Margaret exclaimed. "Was it not sufficient to cut off their poor king's head? It may not have been much of a head, but he was certainly not guilty of anything beyond stupidity—and that has never yet been a capital offense."

"Perhaps it should be for kings," Sir Joseph remarked bitterly. "Louis's innocent stupidity has already cost the lives of many better men than he, and now thousands will die."

"But why did they declare war?"

"Because they oppose tyranny. They will free all mankind—whether they want to be freed or not—from the yoke of the tyrants."

Lady Margaret had very pretty, well-set blue eyes. They opened so wide in amazement at that response that one might have feared they would fall out. "Tyrants? Old George? Prinny? Oh, I would laugh myself sick if I weren't so worried about Roger. How will he get home, Joseph? Oh, dear! I shouldn't be adding to your worry, my love."

"Roger will manage, if any man can, but I won't pretend to you that it will be easy, especially burdened with Henry's child."

"A child? Is she a child? I thought—"

A wintry smile curved Sir Joseph's lips. "They are all children to me, Margaret, but actually she must be a young woman. However, all those 'gently reared' French girls are beautiful nincompoops. I only hope she does not betray them both by some stupidity—desiring service or acting the 'lady' at the wrong moment."

He thought back on the three letters he had received from Roger, searching his memory for a hint of whether Henry's daughter was likely to be the death of his son. The first letter had come, in devious ways, to a cheap alehouse near Kingsdown, which Sir Joseph strongly suspected was a smuggler's den, and from there by a groom who had ridden over to Stonar Magna. All that letter had said was that Henry's wife and son were dead and Roger had arranged to get Henry and his daughter out of prison. Roger had not said how, and Sir Joseph had assumed bribery. Now he wondered, because somehow Henry was gone and Sir Joseph could not believe that the man would abandon his daughter voluntarily.

The second letter had said even less than the first, but the clerk who had delivered it provided more information. It appeared that Roger and "mademoiselle" were well but trapped in Paris. They were safe and unsuspected, but because Roger's business was *nécessaire* he could not obtain a passport to leave. Sir Joseph had raised his brows at that. What business? Ah, naturally that was not Monsieur St. Eyre's normal profession. He was a gunsmith. Sir Joseph thought that funny? But he was a very good gunsmith, and Sir Joseph was not to be concerned, the clerk assured him. Maître Fouché would watch over Roger's safety.

The third letter had been no more explicit, except for

saying that Roger "intended" to remain in Paris for some time to come and that Sir Joseph should not expect him at any time soon. Sir Joseph realized, of course, that Roger's "intention" was far more a matter of necessity than volition, and the phrasing was chosen equally to spare his father worry and to deceive anyone who might open the letter. If it had served the second purpose, it had certainly *not* served the first. Sir Joseph had been inquiring about the situation in France, and what he had heard appalled him. He did not blame himself for allowing Roger to deceive him or allowing his son to go. Even if he should have known better than to believe Roger's glib explanations, there was nothing he could have done to prevent him from sticking his neck out. Nonetheless, he *was* worried.

"Is there nothing we can do to help?" Lady Margaret asked anxiously.

"I don't know," Sir Joseph said quietly.

He was not a man to give way to emotions, but Lady Margaret was not fooled by his outward calm. Roger was his favorite son. He loved all his children, admired and respected his heir, who was just the right type of person to inherit and manage the estate. In fact, Arthur was "squire" in all but name already. But Roger had a spark that tickled his father's sense of humor and made him particularly dear. Lady Margaret knew how her husband had grieved to see his son turn sullen and grim, lightless, under Solange's cruelty. And now, after Joseph had only just seen Roger coming to life again, to lose him even more finally would be bitter.

"Money," Lady Margaret said. "Joseph, money can buy anything if there is enough of it. Can't we somehow buy him a passport—forged if necessary. I—you can use my jointure. Somehow . . ."

"You are very good, my love," Sir Joseph said, raising her hand and kissing it. "If it were only a matter of money, I would have acted long ago—not by touching your jointure, of course. There is money enough. Do you think Arthur would object to anything I chose to do to rescue his brother?"

"But how do the *émigrés* get out? They escape. Why can't Roger escape? He isn't—isn't in particular danger, is he?"

"I hope not." Sir Joseph tried to be soothing, but his

voice shook a trifle. "It's more likely that he's afraid to take any risk with the girl—or she doesn't want to leave, and he won't leave her without protection."

"But surely he must have realized . . ." Lady Margaret's voice drifted away.

It did not matter what Roger realized. If Henry's daughter was as stupid and willful as Solange, Roger could have talked himself blue without accomplishing anything. And this was not a situation in which anything other than persuasion would be of use. Roger could drag Solange physically from the gaming tables. He could not drag Henry's daughter out of Paris because that would increase her danger. How could the girl be so stupid? She had been imprisoned already. Suddenly Lady Margaret realized what they were doing in their anxiety.

"Joseph, we aren't talking of Solange. Not all Frenchwomen are like her. Let's not hate the girl before we see her. Poor thing, she's all alone, her parents and brother dead, and she's been in prison. Perhaps she's ill."

"Yes. . . ."

"But what are they doing in Paris?" Lady Margaret asked, sitting more upright. "I never stopped to think of it before, but Roger must have known that Paris was the most dangerous place—"

"I can answer that easily enough," Sir Joseph replied. "Roger was taking the girl to Lord Gower. Obviously he would not travel alone with a young woman longer than necessary. He would wish to place her in Lady Gower's care."

Lady Margaret watched her husband's frowning face and did not say anything more. No answer was necessary to the explanation. She should have thought that out for herself. However, that was not what kept her quiet. It was clear from Joseph's expression that less than half his mind had been given to his answer. After a moment, his eyes focused on his wife again.

"Well, it can do no harm," he said suddenly.

"What can't?"

"The main reason I daren't buy a forged passport is that one doesn't know from one moment to the next who should have signed it. The government ministers are not only being shifted, which wouldn't be too bad, but are being accused of treason and *executed*. If Roger should be caught with a passport signed by the wrong minister, he might be executed out of hand also."

"Why?" Lady Margaret cried, her eyes widening. "That's insane! When you apply for a passport you don't necessarily condone the policies of the man who signs it. Usually you don't even know him!"

"Just now, my dear, the French are not operating on their famous logic. What I have been hearing from Gower would curdle your blood. Just believe me and don't ask for the details. I have thought of two ways to—well, I wouldn't say 'attack' the problem. It won't be as effective as that. More like nibbling away at its edges. However, it will be *something*."

"Oh, yes, anything—anything at all," Lady Margaret sighed. "I am so worried, and Philip—God in Heaven, it would about kill the child. Roger is all he has. That mother! Poor darling, he doesn't even have good memories to cling to. Can you tell me what you are going to do, Joseph, or would it be safer if I didn't know?"

"There isn't anything definite enough in my mind to 'know,' but there is a network of English spies in France. Some of those men aren't very trustworthy—they sell information both ways—which is why as long as the situation was not acute I didn't wish to use them. However, now . . . The other thing—Roger's first letter didn't come through Fouché. It came from a smuggler's den near Kingsdown. I wonder who brought it there?"

"You can't go asking such questions in a smuggler's place. They wouldn't answer you."

"No . . . but . . . I wonder how Roger traveled to France. His servants might know that. Perhaps his valet—no. Old Peters died, and Roger took on someone Solange urged on him—to make him more elegant." Sir Joseph snorted with contempt. One thing Roger had always been was elegant. "His groom—that's who I can ask. Shannon has been with him since he was a boy."

Lady Margaret was already ringing the little silver bell to summon a maid. The girl sent a footman, who ran off to bring a message to the stables. Nothing more could be done on that score until Shannon rode in from Dymchurch House, but Sir Joseph finished his breakfast with more appetite than he expected to have after his eyes had fallen on the newspaper. He was busy enough during that day and the next to prevent the time from dragging.

At Sir Joseph's request, Lord Gower invited certain people from the Foreign Office to speak to him, and they were most interested in the problem. Sir Joseph would have felt better if he had been more convinced that they wanted to get Roger out rather than that they wanted to use him while he was in Paris. Nonetheless, he felt a certain reassurance. They would certainly try to contact Roger—they had asked for a "token," and he had given them a pair of pistols Roger would recognize—and would spread the word about him only among men in whom they had absolute confidence. They would also certainly do whatever they could to help him if he were in serious trouble.

On the evening of the next day, Shannon was shown into Sir Joseph's study. He was a sturdy man of about fifty, with a normally placid countenance—anyone who had to keep up with Roger in his boyhood needed a calm disposition. Now his face was distorted with worry.

"Ain't nothing 'appened to Master Roger, 'as it?" he blurted out, his anxiety overruling the awe he felt for Sir Joseph.

"I hope not, Shannon, I hope not. However, I *am* worried about him. I don't know whether you have heard that France and England are now at war. I'm afraid that will make it impossible for Roger to return."

"Nosir, that it won't—at least, if 'e can find Monsoor Restoir it won't. 'E won't care about t' war. Anyways not so it would stop 'im from 'elping Master Roger."

"Restoir? Why does that name sound familiar to me? Restoir. . . ."

Shannon shifted his feet uneasily. He knew he was not supposed to speak about Pierre or his business. However, he could not believe that restriction included Sir Joseph or that it applied in a time of emergency. Still, the habit of silence was strong. However, Sir Joseph solved his dilemma.

"This Restoir is a smuggler," Sir Joseph said, alerted by Shannon's uneasiness. Then the name and the business clicked together in his mind taking him back twenty years. "My God, he must be the man who saved Roger's life that time. How, after all these years—"

"Oh, it ain't years. Oftentimes when Monsoor is over 'e stops for a crack with Master Roger. I brings up word, and

Master Roger rides out to a place they meet—now o' course Monsoor comes up to the 'ouse, since 'er ladyship," the man's lips twisted in remembered hatred, "is dead."

"All these years?" Sir Joseph murmured; then he frowned, and before he could stop himself—because he did not really want to know—he asked, "Was Roger in the smuggling too?" If he was, it was the fault of the French bitch, but Sir Joseph wished his son had come to him if he needed money instead of engaging in such an enterprise.

But Shannon laughed. "Nosir. It were just friendly like— at least these years. When 'e was younger—I didn't know or I would've stopped it—'e used to go out with Monsoor in the boat for *fun*. When I found out, I told 'im the shame 'e could bring on you, and 'e stopped. But they was friends—is still. Monsoor took 'im over when 'e went."

"So!"

Doubtless that was how the letter had come, too. Roger addressed it to Restoir and he brought it over. Well, thank God for that. Roger did have a safe way out of the country—if he could get to Restoir. The next logical thought Sir Joseph had was to wonder whether Restoir could be of any other help. Sometimes a smuggling network ran far and deep and reached into high places. Information and money could travel those underground ways.

"How good a friend is Restoir?" Sir Joseph asked quickly. "Think hard before you answer, Shannon. Would you risk Roger's life on the man's goodwill?"

"On his goodwill—yessir. 'E wouldn't do nothin' willin'ly to 'urt Master Roger, nor Master Roger to 'urt 'im. They'm friends for long and Monsoor, 'e—sometimes 'e says things like Master Roger was still a little boy and needed care took of 'im. The only thing . . ."

"Yes? This is important, Shannon. Say anything you know—anything."

"Well, sir, Monsoor—'e'm wild like. 'E'm clever too, but 'e'll take a chance. 'E got a laugh like a wild bird, and a wild eye too—like—you'll pardon me, sir—like Master Roger 'imself when—before 'er ladyship."

"You think he might lead Roger into danger?"

"Yessir, 'e would that, and Master Roger—these last few months before 'e left, beggin' pardon, sir, but 'e was like— like bilin' inside, bubblin' sort of. I begged 'im and begged 'im to take me. . . . Sir, I would've gone 'gainst 'is say, only 'e told me I'd be a danger to 'im, not 'avin' any frog language like."

"He was perfectly right, Shannon. It would have been very dangerous for Roger to have an English-speaking servant. You mustn't blame yourself, no matter what happens."

"Nosir." But the groom's face was twisted with misery, and he burst out, "It ain't no good to say it. I should've knocked 'im on the 'ead. I would've, too—only I knew it wouldn't do no good. 'E'd've only gone anyways—with a sore 'ead and without Monsoor. At least Monsoor knows frog ways and could tell Master Roger things."

Sir Joseph was touched. He knew the groom had been with Roger a long time, but he had not realized how attached the man was. "Don't worry too much," he soothed. "Roger has a good knowledge of French ways himself. You know he has been to France many times. I should have told you, but I didn't know you were worried. Roger is quite all right. We've had letters. I was only worried because of the war, you know, that he might not have a way to get home."

Shannon's face lightened. "Oh, no. If 'e can find Monsoor, 'e'll take 'im 'ome."

"Er—" Sir Joseph did not want to alarm Shannon again, but it was obvious to him that Roger's problem was that he could not reach Restoir. Perhaps, however, if the bond between Roger and the smuggler were close as Shannon thought, Restoir could reach Roger. Certainly it was worth a try. "It could be just as well—an insurance, as it were— to let Restoir know Roger is still in France," Sir Joseph went on. "He might not know that. Is there any way to reach the man?"

"Yessir. I could take a note to the Soft Berth—that's the alehouse where 'e stops to—well, I'm not supposed to say, but it's safe with you, sir, I'm sure—where 'e does business. But with this war—I dunno. It wouldn't be safe for 'im to come to town. I ain't sure, even, when 'e'll be back."

"Nor am I, and I certainly wouldn't want to put Roger's friend in danger. However, it could do no harm to leave a letter for the man. He can read? Oh, yes, you said Roger sends a note. Go down to the kitchen, Shannon, and get your supper. You can ride over to that alehouse tomorrow morning. Then, about once a week or so, ride up there and find out if he's come. If he hasn't, make sure they haven't thrown the letter away. Grease them in the fist each time—I'll give you some money—to be sure interest is kept up, and promise a golden boy if Restoir will leave a note behind to say he had my letter."

Shannon nodded eagerly. He could do that, he told Sir Joseph. Roger's horses needed exercise anyway, and it would give him something to look forward to. It might be many weeks, however, even months, before Pierre came again. He believed that, war or no war, the smuggler would come sooner or later. Sir Joseph nodded agreement. Prices of French wine would soar now that war was declared. Restoir would not miss out on that. If he could dodge the swift, sleek revenue cutters, he was not likely to be worried by a lumbering warship or two. Perhaps it was ridiculous to place any faith in that kind of person, but somehow the thought of the smuggler knowing Roger's problem was very soothing. Sir Joseph pulled a sheet from his writing desk and began to detail the whole story in careful French.

Roger had to tell Leonie about the war, but he said nothing of his fears, and she seemed quite content to remain in Paris now that they were well away from the meeting hall of the convention. Their new location had one major drawback. It was very near the Temple, where the royal family were held prisoners. During the September massacres the mob had invaded this area also, to taunt and terrify the king and queen, but Roger considered the matter and dismissed it. The king was dead, and the likelihood of any further demonstrations around the Temple was much reduced. No matter where one was, he thought, there would be something.

The house was not as pleasant as that near St. Roche. The rooms were meaner and there was no garden, so that Leonie was forced to walk with Fifi or let her run alone in the street. However, the little bitch was clever at avoiding horses and wheels and well trained. She would not permit anyone to approach her whom she did not already know as a "friend." This required a formal introduction with the specific use of that word. Fifi would run and hide even from customers who were often in the shop and whom she knew quite well.

Roger had hoped his move would reduce his business,

since there was no helpful Lefranc to recommend him in this area and he believed his past customers would not bother to come so far. In this he was quite wrong. They soon found their way to him, berating him for moving without giving them notice and making them go to the trouble of inquiring at the Section headquarters what had become of him. Worse, because it was a long walk they stopped in the local cafés to rest and drink, and often ended spreading the word of Roger's skill. Soon the commissioners of the Temple, who guarded the royal family, became his clients. Roger cursed his luck and tried to give the impression of having an irascible and taciturn nature so that he could speak as little as possible to conceal his accent.

Nonetheless, trouble started very soon after he and Leonie were settled. One of the commissioners, François Toulon, a passionate revolutionary who had played a conspicuous part in the deposition of the king on August tenth, came in with a pistol that was jamming. The shop had been empty, and Leonie was playing with Fifi in the kitchen, talking to her volubly. Toulon cocked an eye at Roger.

"Your wife speaks a fine French," he said.

"She was lady's maid to Marie de Conyers," Roger replied.

"She was fond of her mistress?"

Roger kept his eyes on the gun he was examining, pressing his hands down on the counter so that they would not be seen to tremble. "She was fond of eating," he growled. Then he shouted, "Leonie, be still!"

The chatter stopped at once, but Fifi, alarmed by the sudden undercurrent of tension and the odd tone of Roger's voice, dashed out into the shop to see what was wrong with her god that had upset her goddess. Toulon looked down at the dog and raised his brows. He was of good family himself, but from Gascony, where even the high nobility were poor as church mice. Nonetheless, he recognized the quality of the dog. Roger slid one hand under the counter where a loaded pistol lay ready.

"That is a noble little animal," Toulon remarked neutrally.

"Not any more," Roger growled. "It is a common bitch like any other, now that it lives with us."

Toulon laughed. "How right you are," he said in an odd voice. "Well, can you fix my gun?"

"Yes. It is no great matter, but I need my glass."

He was surprised when Toulon did not object. Most shops had a rear exit, and if Toulon intended to denounce him, he should not offer the chance to escape. Roger deduced that Toulon was not decided. He would take his chances, but Leonie must escape. He went into the kitchen and said softly to her, "Get your cloak, go out through the alley. Go to Fouché."

Leonie's eyes went wide, but she did not move. "No. Wherever you go, I go too."

"Idiot," Roger hissed, but he knew he would only make matters worse by delay, and he hurried back, carrying a magnifying lens through which he peered at the faulty mechanism, although he already knew quite well what was wrong with it.

A touch with the file, a tap with a tiny hammer, and the sliver of metal that had caused the jamming was smoothed. Roger loaded the pistol with a half-charge and a wad and presented it to Toulon, pointing wordlessly at a blank wall scarred by its frequent use as a testing ground. Toulon fired, reloaded himself, fired again. Then he smiled at Roger.

"What is the charge?"

Roger shrugged. "Two *sous*. You saw what I did. It was nothing."

Toulon stared fixedly at him. Roger stared back, scowling. It was not the expression of a man who wished to ingratiate himself either with a customer or with someone he feared, Toulon thought. Fifi was still standing near the door of the kitchen. She sensed the tension, but she had learned that the anxiety of her deities did not necessarily imply the presence of an enemy, and she did not growl or bristle, only watched for a signal. Toulon smiled again.

"You are an honest man. Another would have kept the gun for a week and charged for a replacement of the whole firing mechanism."

"Not me," Roger said.

"So I have heard. By the way, my name is François Toulon. I wished to see for myself an honest man. After all, Diogenes searched for one all his life without finding one."

With that he left. Roger sat for a moment with his head in his hands waiting for his heart to stop pounding. Then he went into the kitchen. Leonie was sitting at the table with a pillowslip she had been darning in front of her. Her eyes went past Roger toward the shop.

"He's gone," Roger said. "Why didn't you go when I bid you?"

"What if he had asked to see me? He knew I was here and then if I was suddenly gone, what would he think? That would surely have given us away."

"And what if he had men waiting to arrest us?" Roger countered furiously.

"Unless he is an idiot, there would have been men at the back also." Leonie lifted the pillowslip. Under it lay one of the pistols she always carried. "No one will arrest me," she said quietly.

"You cannot—" Roger began hotly, and then cut that off. There was little point in arguing what had not happened. They needed most urgently to decide what next to do. "He may have gone to summon men. You should—"

Leonie shook her head. "I think not."

"This is no time for thinking," Roger snarled. "In a few minutes, we may both be caught in a trap. Go to Fouché. Perhaps his cousin can help you. If we are both imprisoned, no one will even know what happened to us."

At that, Leonie looked startled. "You are right! I will go, but not to Fouché—not yet. Roger, I could not see this Toulon's face, but I could hear him well. I tell you, he is not thinking of denouncing us. It is something else he wants—money, perhaps."

"You may be right," Roger said a little more calmly. "I had the same feeling, but with the guillotine rising and falling so freely these days, it is no time to count on feelings."

"Yes, and no time to give people any reason to think we have anything to hide. I will go out the front door with my basket—to shop. You will come to the doorway to watch me—a fond husband. If I am taken, do not be foolish. *You* go to Fouché. If I am not, I will come back to see what has happened. Then I can go out again."

The look on Roger's face did not give Leonie any confidence that he would pay attention to her logical suggestions. Fortunately, there did not seem to be any reason to worry. No one paid the least attention to her, except for the chandler's wife, who called out to ask Leonie whether she was going to the produce market. Since Leonie did not

care where she went, she obligingly offered to bring back
anything her neighbor wanted and stood and chatted while
Roger sweated blood behind the door. Finally Leonie disappeared. Roger went back to his workbench, but his
hands were shaking too much for him to do anything except stare at the weapon he should be repairing.

Time passed, then more time. Eventually Roger picked
up the gun at which he had been staring and began to remove the barrel from the breech block. *Surely*, he thought,
*even if time is dragging because I'm scared nearly witless,
Toulon could easily have come back with men to arrest me
by now.* He tilted the barrel of the gun into the light and
squinted down the false ramrod where the powder was
stored. Cursing softly, he took a thin rod from the shelf
beneath the counter and poked gently at the clogged maga-
zine. "Idiot," he muttered, annoyed at the fool who could
afford so expensive a weapon and had not enough brains to
learn how to care for it. Soon he became absorbed in his
task and panic receded.

Leonie returned, changed to her next-to-best dress, and
went out again. "Came back from shopping. Going out to
visit," she said briefly, but she was also more relaxed. It
began to seem as if either Toulon had only been innocently
curious or her guess was right; that is, he did not intend to
denounce them but wanted to exert a little pressure before
starting open blackmail. Nothing further had happened by
late afternoon when Leonie returned again. Roger put
away his tools and came into the kitchen where she was
laying the plates for a belated dinner.

"Well, what do you think?" he asked. "Sometimes they
prefer to make arrests at night."

"I haven't changed my mind," Leonie replied. "It's
blackmail I heard in Toulon's voice, not death. However,
there isn't any sense in taking chances. We should go out.
It's a shame the theaters are closed. Oh, I know. Let's go to
the Café Breton."

They did so and had a very pleasant evening, staying late
even though that meant they would have to chance the
bands of thieves that roamed the streets. They were even
lucky there and came home safely to a neighborhood completely quiet. Quite clearly there had been no attempt to
arrest them, and Fifi's investigation of the area indicated
that no one was lying in wait for them at the front.

"We will see," Roger remarked, opening the door so that Fifi could carry out a similar investigation at the back.

Here it seemed their luck had run out. The little bitch hesitated on the doorstep, stiff, her head thrust forward. Roger's hand went into his pocket.

"I am not a thief," Toulon's voice came from the dark in the alley. He came forward into the faint light cast by the kitchen. "You are an Englishman," he went on, so softly that only Roger could hear. "Your head is forfeit the moment I speak. No, do not shoot me. My comrade Lepitre knows where I am and why."

"What do you want?" Roger asked. "If you intended to denounce me, you would have done so already."

"It is a little matter of treason," Toulon said, grinning as he pushed gently past Roger into the room, "for which you will be well rewarded. Since you will lose your head either way—if I denounce you or if you are caught for treason—it seems to me a practical man of business like yourself would prefer to take the chance and the reward."

Roger shooed Fifi out gently and closed the door. She would soon be back to indicate whether there were other men out there. He was aware that Leonie in the bedroom above could hear them now. If she came down and distracted Toulon. . . . He shook his head.

"If you think I am a spy from England and can give you information, you are sadly mistaken. I have been many years in France."

"I know that. I have English friends—which is why I caught the accent—but very few would recognize more than that you were not a Parisian, or not from any other particular place with which they were familiar."

That was probably the only good thing Solange had done for him—refusing to answer if he spoke to her in English and making fun of his French until in self-defense Roger had learned to speak nearly perfectly. That flicked through one part of his mind while the other part considered what Toulon said. If Toulon believed he did not know any secrets, what treason could he possibly commit against England? . . . No, stupid, Roger said to himself, the treason must be against France if he might lose his head for it. They hung men for treason in England.

"Then I do not understand you at all," Roger said.

"Let me ask you a question," Toulon remarked. "How did you feel about the execution of—of Capet."

There was no point in lying; one might as well be guillotined for a sheep as for a lamb. "I saw the political necessity but grieved for the man, who was innocent, I think, of ill intent."

"Just—" Toulon broke off as he heard the creak of the stair. He turned and gasped when he saw Leonie with her pistol held in both hands and leveled at him.

"Stand very still, m'sieu," she remarked quietly. "I am not afraid to fire. I have done so before."

"Put it down!" Toulon cried, but there was irritation rather than fear in his voice. He turned to Roger. "Saintaire, take it away from her. She is likely to kill you as me!"

Roger could not help smiling, for what Toulon said was quite true. However, his mind was racing. Toulon had no need to set traps for him concerning royalist sympathies. The question about Louis, then, had some other purpose. In fact, to ask it gave Roger a weapon against the questioner. It was not much of a weapon; Toulon was a commissioner, and Roger was in no position to accuse anyone of anything. Thus it might be useful to indicate to Toulon his goodwill. He shook his head at Toulon.

"Oh, no," he said. "A gunsmith's wife grows accustomed to guns. However, you said I was an honest man. I hope you are. I would like at least to hear what you have to say. Sit down on the stair, Leonie. I do not believe Commissioner Toulon intends us any harm."

As he said the words, Roger was convinced by them. He had been making the mistake of thinking in ordinary legal terms, of thinking that evidence was required to prove a case, in a situation where legality had been totally abandoned. If Toulon had wanted them imprisoned, or even dead, he had only to accuse them of incivism. He was a trusted arm of the revolution—no further evidence would be needed.

"I may bring you harm," Toulon said suddenly, with great earnestness, having been much moved by what Roger said, "but I swear it will not be by intention."

Roger nodded and gestured to a chair. "Please sit down, commissioner. Will you have a glass of wine?"

The dog whined and scratched at the door, and Roger went to let her in. She had not barked nor run back, and

her tail was high and waving. There were no strangers in
or near the alley so Toulon had come alone. In these days
a man did not walk alone in the streets at this hour of the
night unless he had a good reason. Then another bit of
evidence that Roger had *not* seen added a final affirmative
point. Toulon was not wearing the scarf that identified him
as a commissioner. Yet that scarf was a relatively sure protection against the gangs that roamed the city. So! Toulon
must be very eager to keep this visit a secret. Put all that
together with the question about Louis and one obtained an
interesting answer.

"Put your pistol away, Leonie," Roger said, "and bring
us some wine and join us. I am sure that Commissioner
Toulon's treason will be an honest one and bring no harm
to France."

Toulon's breath hissed in sharply. "You are right, of
course. Have you guessed?"

"Not what it is you want of me," Roger replied, "but
that it has to do with the royal family—that I have
guessed."

The wine slopped on the table as Leonie started with
surprise. Toulon looked at her.

"Did you hate Marie de Conyers when you were her servant?" he asked.

Leonie looked at him with startled eyes for a moment,
then remembered that Roger had excused her aristocratic
accent by saying she had been her mother's maid. "No,"
she breathed. "She was a good woman, kind to me."

"Did you know," Toulon went on, "that there are those
who say that the—that Marie Antoinette should meet the
same fate as her husband?"

To avoid spilling more of the wine, Leonie set the bottle
down. She clasped her hands to hide their shaking. Roger
pushed her gently into a seat and poured the three glasses
of wine himself, but no one reached for it.

"I had not heard it," he said untruthfully—where could
a simple tradesman hear such things? "But I am not surprised. She was always hated."

"And with reason," Toulon remarked. "She was extravagant. She had no understanding of the dreadful condition of
the country. Also, there is good cause to believe that she
urged Louis to resist all reform and drove him away from
the people who could have saved the monarchy."

Neither Roger nor Leonie knew what to say. They agreed with Toulon. How often had Leonie heard her father damn the queen for her pride and her resistance to Lafayette's advice. How often had Roger and his friends in England discussed the fact that the queen's influence was pushing Louis into the arms of ministers who only intensified the ills of France? But there was nothing treasonous in hating the queen—not to the current government. And Toulon's statement had been dispassionate. There was no hatred in voice or expression. His look was that of a man unavoidably mentioning an injury long forgiven.

"That is all true," he went on, "yet she is also a woman, a gentle, tender mother—and helpless. What you said about the—about Louis Capet was true. His death was a political necessity. If he lived, the republic could not. However, there can be no gain to the country in Marie's death. That would be an act of wanton cruelty. She has no power now and will not have ever again. She can never be a danger to the state."

Roger lifted his glass and drank, not realizing that his action might well be taken as a toast to Toulon's words until he saw the smile of relief on the man's face. Actually, Roger had only wanted to hide his eyes. Toulon was wrong about the fact that Marie Antoinette could not be dangerous. If the forces ranged against France won the war and seated the dauphin on the throne, Marie would again exert the same influence—or even a stronger one. The boy was only eight years old; he had been deprived of his father in a horrible way of which he was no doubt aware. On whom would he lean if not on the gentle, tender mother Toulon described. Perhaps for a time Prussia and England would choose a more stable regent, but Marie Antoinette would be teaching her son all the wrong things.

It was clear enough now where this talk was leading. Toulon must be involved in a plot to permit Marie Antoinette to escape. Roger could still not guess what his part was to be, but he was not thinking about that. He should, he knew, point out to Toulon that the queen could still be a formidable danger to France—and more formidable in exile, where her pleadings and promises might stimulate a more determined attack on France than was now being made. As long as Marie was a prisoner in France, she *was* powerless and no threat. As soon as she was free, she might be the cause of much suffering and loss of life—now and in the future.

As much as he abhorred what was going on in France, Roger believed that to break the revolution by war would be useless. The people had the bit between their teeth now. Conquest of the country and restoration of the monarchy by force could only breed more and bloodier insurrections. It would be necessary to quarter a huge army of occupation in France to put down these revolutions. Internally, Roger shuddered at the suffering that would cause, the hatred that would grow out of it.

Possibly Toulon would pay no attention; possibly he had thought of these matters already. But, just possibly, his pity for the queen had not permitted him to see the pitfalls her freedom would open. If he listened and abandoned the plot . . . Roger's hand clenched on the glass he was holding until his knuckles showed white. Fortunately, it was a thick, common drinking glass. He would have crushed the delicate, stemmed crystal out of which he drank at home. *If Toulon listens to me and abandons the plot and Marie Antoinette is executed, I will be her murderer,* Roger thought.

"What do you want of me?" he asked.

"Very little," Toulon said eagerly. "A refuge for a little time. A place where clothing may be changed, new disguises assumed. You will be in no danger. Even if the escape should be noticed—and we have taken good care that five hours at least will pass before anyone has reason for suspicion—there will be two commissioners standing in your shop talking to you. They will, of course, assist any men who come here, should the worst happen and a search be instituted."

"Oh please, Roger," Leonie pleaded with tears in her eyes, "help her. She has lost so much—her world is all broken. Her husband is dead. Don't be the one to take away her very life. Whatever she has done ill, she has paid for it already and—and I don't believe it was done in malice."

Roger nodded without delay, but not because his refusal would have any effect on the plot. There were many other places in the area that could serve briefly as a shelter. He might be able to take away Marie Antoinette's life, but not by refusing to receive her. That could only cost Leonie's life as well as his own. Obviously if they refused to help they would have to be silenced—disposed of, one way or another, both to protect Toulon and his fellow conspirators and to protect the plot. Their lives might be forfeit anyway, Roger knew, but to agree at once and without reservation was the safest path in a morass of quicksand. He smiled at Leonie. Her ingenuous pleading had probably done more to protect them than any reasoned action.

"I never intended to refuse," he said. "Commissioner Toulon is right. There is little risk in what he asks of us."

"Yes, and then you will be given passports and can go where you like."

Roger shrugged offhandedly to conceal his eagerness. "I will be glad to have them, but where to go is more than I know. I would as soon stay here—but you know me for English-born. How long before someone else hears it in my speech? And in England, if I could get there, they will call me a French spy."

Leonie blinked once at this wild fabrication, and then she understood. Roger dared not act as if the passport was important. Toulon might begin to wonder why a man settled in a good business should be so willing to throw it away. All at once, however, she saw another danger. Toulon should not know the true facts of their case. He should not know they wished to go to England. Why, then, did he offer *passports* as a reward—why not money? Because it *was* the thing Roger wanted most, he had missed the point. Toulon was not really offering a reward; he was ordering them to leave Paris, so that they could not betray him, or whoever had been in the plot and remained behind.

"I will be glad to go," she said quickly. "I am afraid to live in Paris any longer. Twice already we have been caught in riots. The next time we may not be so lucky. And even if you make more money here, the prices are so high. . . . Oh, Roger, you can work anywhere, and—and I have thought of a way we will be welcomed in England." Both men looked at her, and she laughed. "Commissioner Toulon remarked on my speech. Could we not pretend to be aristocratic *émigrés*?"

"So we could." Roger pretended to brighten.

"Very good." Toulon seemed to be satisfied. "What we plan is this—"

"No!" Roger interrupted. "I beg you, don't tell me. I am not a talkative man, but what I don't know can't slip from

my lips by accident or be torn out by torture. You need my
house. I need to know no more than that—neither when
nor why. From this night on either Leonie or I will be here
at all times. Whenever you need the house, it will be
ready."

Toulon seemed a trifle disconcerted by Roger's lack of
curiosity, and a little disappointed too. Nonetheless, he saw
the good sense in it and shortly took his leave. When he
was gone, Roger sat staring at the door, unmoving, while
Leonie put away the wine and washed up the glasses. She
was humming softly. Unaware of the political consequences
of freeing the queen, she felt none of Roger's complex guilt.
Nor did it occur to her that Toulon had been far too willing to impart information to a man he hardly knew.

Leonie was aware they were in danger. If the plot failed
and they were accused with the others, they would die.
However, she was far more absorbed in the positive possibilities than the negative ones. Her empathy with the political prisoners was, of course, complete. Leonie was not
thinking beyond the horror of her own incarceration and
the glee she felt in being able to help release those similar-
ly imprisoned. As for the danger—she smiled at Roger's
back as she closed the cupboard on the dry glasses—
Roger would not let anything happen to her.

CHAPTER 16

A week passed without giving Leonie any reason to worry or Roger any reason to stop worrying about the outcome of this venture. They knew they were being watched, although it was done discreetly enough so that their neighbors did not become suspicious of them. It seemed reasonable to Leonie that Toulon should take precautions, and she thought no more of it. It drove Roger near crazy because he was afraid that even an innocent delivery or customer coming in would precipitate disaster. Finally, after a miserable Sunday during which leisure gave Roger far too much time to think, a man came into the shop on Monday with an exquisite pocket pistol by Negroni that had its snaphaunce lock broken off. Roger winced at the damage done and began to shake his head.

"I am Commissioner Lepitre, President of the Committee on Passports," the man said.

For the moment, his mind being fully occupied with the damage to the gun, Roger did not remember that Toulon had mentioned Lepitre in connection with the plot. "I don't care if you are the Archangel Michael," he growled. "I cannot fix that gun. It must have a whole new lock mechanism, and I don't have one and I don't know where I can get one."

Fear flashed across Lepitre's face. "Didn't Commissioner Toulon have a pistol repaired here a few days ago?"

Then Roger stopped wondering how such damage could have happened. The gun was just an excuse. He touched it gently—another beautiful thing wantonly destroyed, and probably all for nothing. "Yes," he said, "that is true."

"Your name is Saintaire?" Lepitre asked, now nervous and seeking to be sure without committing himself by prodding Roger into an admisssion that Toulon had spoken of the plot to him.

"Yes," Roger replied impatiently. Then, fearing to be thought either uncooperative or loose-tongued, he temporized by adding, "Very much at your service and the service of your friends, commissioner."

Fortunately, he had hit the right note. Lepitre was far more cautious than Toulon and found Roger's carefulness reassuring. He leaned forward as if to examine the gun and said softly, "All the passports will be brought here at the same time. You and your wife will be expected to leave in the morning, immediately after the other party has gone." Then, much louder: "I am sure you can find some way to mend it. Keep the gun for a few days anyway. Perhaps someone will bring in a part."

After Lepitre was gone, the phrase he had used, *all the passports*, came back to haunt Roger. He could not put his finger on why it disturbed him. Certainly if there were passports for himself and Leonie and the queen and a companion or two, one could say "all." But Roger could not convince himself. He began to fear that the plan was not to save only Marie Antoinette but her children and Louis's sister as well. They would never succeed; he knew it—and the feeling of helplessness, which was worse than actively facing any danger, grew greater.

It was not even possible for him to hide this new development from Leonie because, a few nights later, Toulon again appeared at the back door, carrying a large box. He did not come in, just passed the box to Roger and told him to conceal what was in it. They had no cellar, and the attic under the roof was bare of accumulated odds and ends. Roger looked at the box.

"Where the hell does he think I can hide something this size!" he muttered furiously, not realizing that Leonie had heard the knock and was again on the stairs with a pistol in her hand.

"It can't be a single thing," she said, shoving the gun back under her skirt as she came down the stairs. "Open it, and we will see how to distribute what is in it."

They saw more than how to distribute the clothing—for that was what the box held. They saw the whole plot laid out. There were two suits of men's clothes of the style customarily worn by the commissioners who were in charge of the prisoners, and two of the special scarves that identified these men. Leonie grabbed those up at once and thrust them to the very bottom of the bag in which she kept the rags for cleaning. For a citizen who was not entitled to one of those scarves, to have one was treason and death. Beneath the suits there were two dresses of sober style and color but excellent cloth and cut—typical gowns of wealthy bourgeois wives. And below those were two different sets of clothes for a boy and girl—the soiled and worn garments that the children of a common laborer would wear and another set that matched in quality the women's dresses.

"Well, thank goodness it is nothing worse," Leonie said cheerfully. "I will just hang the dresses and suits with ours. I doubt anyone will notice that the sizes are wrong. The children's things I cannot put in the wardrobe, of course. They would be noticed. However, they are small. I think—"

"Leonie," Roger said tightly, "don't you understand what this means? Toulon is trying to get *all* of them out of the country."

"Of course," Leonie responded.

"What do you mean, 'of course,'" Roger snapped, his voice rising.

Leonie blinked at the fury of his tone, then shrugged. "Naturally the queen would not consent to go without her children and her sister by marriage. I would not go without my mother and father and brother. Marie Antoinette may be proud and foolish—but she is not a monster."

She was not thinking of her answer, however. She was thinking of the change in Roger's manner to her this past week. Ever since he had promised Toulon there would always be someone in the house and had begun to go out alone more, he had been different. He was always silent or angry now, and although he did not drop off to sleep immediately as he sometimes had done when he was physically very tired, neither did he offer the tentative touches or kisses with which he customarily initiated their lovemaking.

The only way Leonie could account for this change was that Roger had met another woman, who, being fresh, was more interesting to him. Until now she had not permitted herself to believe it, seeking other reasons for his withdrawal and sharpness. Grief and horror numbed her. He was tired of her, chafing under the pretense of marriage but far too good a man to abandon her. No wonder he was so eager to obtain a passport that he had made himself believe that only the queen was escaping. Of course it would be easier that way, but Leonie's generous heart had never conceived for a moment the notion that a woman would leave her children to save her own life.

To say the least, Roger's experience of spoiled women—and there could be no doubt that Marie had had every least whim satisfied from her infancy to her fall—gave him a different outlook from Leonie's. The children could not be in any real danger. Even the lunatics who were now in charge of the government would not think of harming them. In fact, they were a valuable form of insurance. As a last resort a puppet monarchy could be set up with the boy as king. The girl was a priceless trading piece, although Salic law forbade a woman to rule in France. Thus, Roger had assumed that Marie Antoinette would seize the chance to regain her own freedom.

"It would have been far better for us," he snarled, "had she been a little more sensible—even if that would make her a monster in your eyes."

Leonie's arms tightened on the clothing she held. She was crushed by Roger's anger, believing that he was not angry about anything she had done or said but annoyed by her very existence. She could only assume that anything she did or said would be hateful to him because he was so bored. It was typical of the breakdown of a love affair, she knew, that the parties grew irritable with each other, then quarreled wildly, then parted. For married couples, the beginning was the same, but because they could not part, the end was worse—hatred.

Although Roger read the fear in Leonie's expression accurately, he misinterpreted it completely. He was, of course, aware of having been short-tempered during the past week. His struggle to control the sense of doom that pervaded him had not been made any easier by Leonie's unnatural, cheery blindness to his mood and had resulted in snappish outbursts. He had not even been able to apologize to her, because when he tried, either rage or fear welled up in him so that he could only go out and walk and walk for hours until he had some control of himself. Now, seeing Leonie's blanched face, seeing how she clutched what she held to her, as one clings to anything in a moment of terror, Roger realized he had even failed to prevent infecting her with his fear.

Wildly he tried to think of anything to comfort her, any ray of hope. There was nothing—no gleam of an idea of how they could escape, no flicker of expectation that Toulon's plot could succeed. The plan to get the women and children out of the Temple, which Roger had guessed from seeing the clothing, might have had some chance of working. Apparently Lepitre, who controlled the official forms, would provide not only passports but passes to get the queen and Princess Elizabeth out dressed as commissioners. The children would be disguised as the children of some servant and removed separately. Presumably they would all come to Roger's house, change to inconspicuous clothing, and leave Paris.

It was there the idea fell apart. Obviously it was not possible to send a queen, a princess, and two royal children off to fend for themselves. Even if Marie Antoinette had been willing, the minute she opened her mouth she would give the game away. Not only was her accent unmistakable—strongly German even after all these years because no one had ever had the courage to correct her speech—but she would not have the faintest idea of how to ask for a meal or engage a room at an inn. That meant at least one man, perhaps more, as escort and protection.

The party was already too large for a small, inconspicuous carriage with one horse. It meant a large coach, four or six horses—in these times such a vehicle and its passengers would be minutely examined. They would be caught. However, it was not concern for the escaping prisoners that was turning Roger's bowels to water. Had he hoped that the escape plan would work, even as far as taking the queen's party on the road, he would not have feared for Leonie or himself. By the time they were apprehended, he and Leonie would be either safely away or safely hidden.

Roger's fear centered on Toulon himself. The man was honest, he was sure, and brave—to a fault. What he was not was careful, secretive, or sensible. On the very first day, when Toulon had just met him, he had wanted to tell all the details of the plan. Would he not tell others? Might he not even give hints away without even realizing? And Roger knew that he and Leonie would go down with Toulon. It was inevitable. If he blabbed about the plot itself, he would surely expose his accomplices. That would make Roger and Leonie vulnerable in many ways—as conspira-

tors, as the least well known and, therefore, the most likely
to be betrayers. . . . Because they were watched, they
could not escape; because they could not control Toulon,
they were doomed.

To die is bad enough. To live in fear is worse. Leonie
had enough of that, and Roger had been trying to spare her
any more. Now he had exposed it all. He opened his mouth
to say everything would be all right, that there was no need
to be afraid, but Leonie had turned away and rushed up
the stairs, the sound of a strangled sob drifting behind her.
There had to be a way to save her. She was only eighteen.
She had not even begun her life.

Think! Roger told himself. *You damn fool, stop worrying and* think. The mental articulation of the difference between worry and thought seemed to clear his mind like a
cool wind sweeping away fog. Of a sudden, it came to him.
As long as there was one woman in the house, the watchers
were unlikely to know whether that woman was Leonie.
He, of course, had to stay because his skill marked him.
No other man could take his place. Roger was sure that
some of the men who came into the shop came in only to
be sure he was still there. But Leonie could be saved.
Roger bounded up the stairs with the first smile in days
lightening his features.

"There is nothing to worry about," he exclaimed, bursting into the bedroom where Leonie was trying to cudgel
her brain into conceiving of a hiding place for the children's clothes, when all she could really think was Roger
no longer wanted her. "You do not have to stay here," he
went on with enthusiasm. "I will go tomorrow to see
Fouché, and he will arrange for a woman to change places
with you."

"What?" Leonie gasped. The one thing she had counted
on was that Roger would not part from her. As long as she
was with him, she believed she had some chance of reawak-
ening his interest in her.

"It will not be difficult," Roger went on, seeing in her
wide-eyed breathlessness hope rather than horror. "You
can meet her somewhere safe—Fouché's house or, well,
someplace—and change clothing with her. Then Fouché
will give you money and tell you where to live while she
will come here. Even if Toulon or Lepitre or one of the

men who are watching later realizes you are gone, it will not matter because—"

"No one will realize I am gone because I will be right here," Leonie spat, her eyes blazing.

The initial shock she felt had dissolved into rage. The one thing she had believed was that Roger was an honorable man. She knew honor had nothing to do with love or desire. The best man in the world might fall out of love or lose his desire for a particular woman, but he would not abandon her. When she first heard Roger say she should go, she could not believe her ears. Bored with her, even hating her, she could not believe he would simply throw her out and take his new light of love in her place.

His explanation had removed her incredulity. He was not simply casting her away. He was behaving—according to his code—in a perfectly honorable manner. He would provide her with money, with a place to live, even with protection. No doubt if she allowed him to finish his explanation, he would have pointed out that as long as they were confined to Paris, there was no need for them to be together. If Toulon's plot worked and the passport was provided, Roger would get her and take her to England, as he had promised, and place her in the proper hands there.

Leonie was so furious when she had thought this out that she would have tried to claw out his eyes if she had not realized that he probably did not know she felt differently than he did. She knew that in an attempt to keep Roger from becoming complacent she had never said she loved him, never initiated lovemaking—aside from that first time. She had done her best to arouse doubt in his mind to keep him interested. Apparently all she had succeeded in doing was to convince him she was indifferent.

The expression of amazement on Roger's face, the way he stammered, "But Leonie—" was proof to her that her deduction was correct. He did not know she cared for him. He assumed she was as bored with their relationship as he was. Perhaps there was still hope. If only she made the right moves, if only she could get a chance to display her skills as a temptress, perhaps she could win him back.

It would not do simply to cry out that she loved him. Even if he believed her, knowledge of her love would not spark his interest. He would be too good to drive her out if he knew, but rather than feeling love in return it was far

more likely that he would feel trapped. Love does not grow
out of being smothered in the musty miasma of unwanted
devotion. Nor would it do to begin to act like a whore.
That might waken a temporary interest, but it would end in
disaster. Roger would be sickened by the notion that she
had pretended innocence all these months. He would turn
away all the more swiftly when the faint, corrupt fascina-
tion of her devices lost power. Yet she had to make him
know she cared.

"You will be safe," Roger urged, following his first surprised protest, thinking that she feared separation from his
protection.

"And you will have a chance to indulge yourself with a
fresh piece of flesh, no doubt," Leonie snarled.

The words were no part of any plan on Leonie's part.
They were wrenched out of her by jealousy, which over-
came the knowledge that Roger was trying to give the comfort he believed she wanted. The effect, however, was a
revelation. Roger's mouth dropped open and his blue eyes
fairly bulged from his head. In an instant, Leonie saw a
way. A woman's jealousy was flattering to a man. No doubt
repeated scenes would be unwelcome, but one would make
clear enough her desire for him. He would almost certainly
respond, and that would give her both a chance and an
excuse to display the abilities she had hidden.

"What did you say?" he gasped.

"You heard me well enough," Leonie shrieked. "Lecher!
I am not enough for you. Perhaps I am too delicate. You
need a stronger, coarser flavor to stimulate your appetite."

"Leonie! I swear—"

"What do you swear? Liar! Lecher! You swore you
would bring me to England, but you cannot wait so long to
plow a new field."

Roger swallowed, opened his mouth, closed it after all
that came out was a protesting squawk. For a week he had
been on a treadmill of despair. His mind had been fixed
into its round of worry, unable to accept Leonie's fate and
equally unable to discover a way to avoid it. Even as he
rushed up the stairs to tell Leonie he had found a way to
save her, he had known there would be problems. What if
they could not find a woman to take Leonie's place? Was it
fair to endanger some innocent person? A dozen other objections had ranged through his mind while he described

the idea to Leonie. He had even expected she would object. Frightened as she was, her gallant spirit would resist leaving him when danger threatened.

Thus, he had not been really thrown off course by her initial refusal, only a little surprised at how angry she looked. He had been marshaling arguments to convince her it was best for both of them and to reassure her about their separation when her remark about a "fresh piece of flesh" had burst on him like a bombshell. The concept was so far from any thought of his own—so foreign to his insecure view of himself as a lover—that he had, for a moment, thought Leonie was angry because he had criticized her cooking and wanted someone else as a housekeeper.

It was that ridiculous idea that had wrenched his unbelieving "What did you say?" from him. However, when the word "lecher" made perfectly clear Leonie's meaning, he still did not believe his ears. It was simply inconceivable to Roger that any woman could be jealous of him. Even his kept women had never been jealous—which, although Roger did not think of it, was not surprising, because he only chose experienced partners with easygoing temperaments who knew exactly what the score was and had no emotional involvement with him. He had had quite enough emotionalism from Solange.

Leonie was delighted with the effect her attack had produced. One thing was sure, all preoccupation was gone from Roger's expression now. He was totally aware of her, totally concentrated on her—a thing she had not seen for a week. No wonder he had been bored; he had thought her a fool as well as an innocent. Well, it would do him no harm to learn otherwise.

"Did you think I wouldn't realize?" she hissed. "It didn't take you long to find another, did it? No sooner did you walk out alone for pleasure than your eyes began to roam—"

"No! How could you think such a thing? Leonie—"

"What am I supposed to think? You have made it clear enough. You could barely bring yourself to look at me this past week."

That, of course, was true, and Roger gaped again, unable to deny the fact and also unable to defend himself. He had been so afraid that Leonie would see his fear and be terrified herself that he had, indeed, avoided looking at her and speaking to her.

"There is no other woman," Roger asserted passionately.

"No?" Leonie drawled, eyes blazing and venom dripping from the word. "Are you telling me that you prefer boys? One or the other it must be, for you are so drained out that you could not even pretend an interest in coupling with *me* this past week."

"Leonie!" Roger gasped.

He was dizzy with conflicting emotions, but paramount among them was an uncertain and incredulous joy. She was jealous! Would a woman be jealous where she did not love? She was angry because he had not made love to her. But then, surely, it was because she took pleasure in it.

"Leonie!" She mimicked his shocked gasp bitterly. "Stupid Leonie, who would not even guess that her simple charms had lost their savor. Innocent Leonie, who could be wrapped like a package and left on Fouché's shelf until it was convenient to call for her and drop her off at another convenient spot in England. You want more spice in your meat? I will give you spice!"

Before Roger could reply, she had whirled away from him and discarded her dowdy, unflattering dress. Under it, her linen was very fine. Since it was not safe to display wealth outwardly, Leonie had spent a good part of the money Roger had given her on provocative undergarments. She had always known it would be necessary to restimulate his interest sooner or later and, particularly this past week, had been prepared. She swung back slowly, blushing furiously, which made her eyes glow like molten gold. One hand fingered the ribbon tie of her chemise.

"Do you like it quick or slow, Roger?"

In the past they had undressed either separately or in the dark. Roger thought he was sparing Leonie's modesty; Leonie was always afraid of seeming whorish. Now she had the most wonderful excuse. She knew that a woman driven by jealousy was capable of anything, even murder. Nothing she did would be really surprising to Roger nor make him suspicious of her past life. It was quite apparent to Leonie that he was not presently capable of thinking at all, but she was convinced that, even later when the shock and sexual excitement had passed, he would assume that jealousy had pushed her outside her normal behavior-pattern.

Leonie was not at all surprised when Roger did not answer her question. He swallowed and ran his tongue over his lips in an effort to ease a suddenly dry mouth. Leonie pulled the bow loose and shrugged her shoulders so that the lace straps slid down. She did not wear a corset; her breasts were high and firm and needed no support, her waist narrow enough to do without lacing. The soft silk of the chemise dropped from her breasts, catching provocatively on her erect nipples for a moment before it left her completely bare.

A strangled sound, mixed passion and protest, caught in Roger's throat. He should stop Leonie; he knew that. When her fury abated, she would be appalled at what she had done. However, it was quite impossible for him to speak or move. What she was doing was holding him like a mesmeric trance. It was a most peculiar sensation, as if he were divided into two men. In one, the mind operated, telling him that Leonie would be embarrassed, that he should stop her, that he had seen women strip provocatively before—many times—and had been mildly stimulated, mostly amused. The other man was a creature of pure sensation, trapped in the molten lava of desire, linked in some way to the woman so that each movement she made, each new sliver of skin exposed, produced a hot throbbing in him.

By the time Leonie was naked, Roger was finding the restrictions of his own clothes physically painful. He had once put his hand to his breeches buttons, but Leonie had said, "No," and he had let his hand drop. Now she approached him, put one hand behind his head to pull it down so that she could kiss him, and began to undo his buttons with the other hand. The first man, the man of mind, drowned in the hot lava of desire and was seared away. Roger grabbed at Leonie, became aware of his coarse work shirt, and broke their embrace to tear it off. Before he could grasp her again, she had slid down along his body, pulling his breeches and underpants off together. Playfully, she tickled the inner sides of his thighs with her tongue.

"Oh God," Roger moaned. "Oh God, oh God."

He grabbed for her head, eager for any caress that would both ease and increase the roaring pain/pleasure that filled him, but she twisted away. An agony of fear that she had been playing with him, enticing him so that she could re-

fuse him at the height of his need, made him bend and
seize her brutally. She struggled, increasing Roger's fear
of rejection, and he stopped her lips so that she could
neither scream nor deny him. Muffled sounds came from
Leonie's throat as she tried to tell him that she wanted to
take off his shoes, that he was not really undressed, but
he did not want to know what she was trying to say. He
pushed her backwards, keeping his lips fastened to hers,
intending to back her onto the bed.

To Roger's horror he found his feet bound, so that he
tipped forward instead of taking a step. Fortunately, the
room was very small. A hand flung out caught the edge of
the wardrobe, pushed them both upright. Blind with fury,
thinking that Leonie had somehow tied his legs together,
he lifted her and threw her on the bed, reaching down
simultaneously to rid himself of the entanglement. It was
no feat to push off his shoes and breeches, and the
knowledge of what had hampered him was so foolish that
he cooled a trifle. The added fact that Leonie had not
moved might have restored Roger's self-control, but then
she giggled.

Fearful of shocking or frightening his partner, whom he
knew had been sexually abused, Roger had been restrained
in his lovemaking in the past. He had been careful to stimulate her and to be sure that her passion was satisfied, but
he had also been careful to confine his kisses to those erog-
enous zones that were "decent"—her lips and ears, throat
and shoulders. His caresses, too, had been circumspect; he
had stroked her body and breasts, but carefully, avoiding
those intrusions he thought she might consider "dirty."

Leonie had been equally careful, striving to maintain the
appearance of innocence. She had clutched Roger to her
and returned his kisses, but she had kept her own hands
and mouth from those forms of stimulation that an inexperienced girl might be ignorant of or shy of using. She had
even moderated her own response to Roger's lovemaking.
Soft sighs and whimpers and little moans of delight had
been drawn from her, but she had set her teeth against the
loud, tremulous cries that had sometimes welled up in her,
not even realizing that the effort of self-control was damp-
ing the full flood of pleasure, so that her release as well as
her voice was muted.

The giggle Leonie uttered was a sound of sheer delight.

Roger's violence, his forgetting he had not finished undressing, were proof of his urgent need. There was no contempt in her, but Roger was too aware of awkwardness, of embarrassment, and heard contempt in the sound. Suddenly, all his restraints were broken.

"Laugh at me, will you?" he muttered. "I will make you howl like a bitch in heat!"

Moments before, he had been nearly crazy to satisfy his own need. That urgency retreated. Years before, Roger had learned to hold his passion leashed in his attempt to break through Solange's frigidity. Now he used that power again coupled with every technique he had learned or invented to conquer indifference. He sucked and licked, kissed and bit —and made good his threat. Leonie wailed with passion, fighting to draw him into her, convulsing in climax, only to have him withdraw and begin all over again—and again— until she began to weep with exhaustion. The tears peaked Roger's temporary insanity. He knew he had lost Leonie for good. Solange had hated him for less. Considering Leonie's background, he knew she would never look at him again. One last time he impaled her, driving like the madman he was until his body exploded. Then, shuddering with revulsion at what he had done, he rolled away. He would have left the bed, but she caught at him and held him.

"Oh, my," Leonie sighed, running the hand with which she had grasped him up his arm while she wiped away her tears with her other hand, "I must remember to make you angry and laugh at you again—but not too often."

Roger had frozen into stillness at the sound of her voice. It was only a thread of a whisper, and he had expected to hear the hiss of hate in it, so the words did not make sense. But there was no hate, and the light touch of her fingers on his arm held him motionless. They lay in silence for a few minutes while Leonie gathered strength to turn on her side and Roger mustered the courage to turn his head and look at her. She was smiling! Her hair was dark and wet with sweat, her lashes still shining with tears, but she was smiling.

"You never gave me a chance," she pouted playfully.

"What?"

"I was going to show you that you did not need to look

elsewhere for more lively entertainment—but you seem to have found out for yourself."

"What are you talking about?" Roger lifted himself on one elbow and winced at the marks he had made on Leonie's white skin. She had been smiling at him wistfully, but now her lips tightened.

"I am talking about your taste for trulls—and I wish you would do me the favor of according me a modicum of intelligence. When a man who has given every sign of contentment—good humor, eager hands and lips, loving looks—suddenly turns sour and turns his back in bed too, he has seen another woman he likes better."

"You are mad," Roger breathed. "There *is* no other woman. I am not that kind."

"No? I suppose you learned what you just showed me from a group of holy celibates! And no doubt you want to get me out of the house so that you can better practice religious austerities."

"I want you out of the house to save your life, you little fool!"

Roger bit his lip in chagrin at giving way to his temper and again exposing Leonie to fear, but she did not look frightened. From the yellow glare in her eyes, he realized that she did not believe him. He did not know whether to laugh or cry. Not only was Leonie jealous, but it was quite clear she did not object to the "religious austerities," only to his practicing them with someone else. And now that he had a woman who wanted him, he had to lose her.

"Leonie, there isn't anyone else. There never will be. I love you. I swear it." He spoke in English. It was impossible for Roger to speak of love in French. It was nearly impossible for him to speak the words at all, associated as they were with years of misery.

The shift in language brought conviction to Leonie. Somehow she was sure Roger would not lie in English. The light of rage in her eyes softened. "Then we will speak no more of my going away," she said, also in English. "And since you say you love me, I will also be discreet and ask no questions about where you learned to do such delightful things. After all, it is not really my affair what you did before we came together."

Roger was looking at her most oddly, with such intensity that it seemed as if he never expected to see her again. It occurred to her that if Roger had told the truth and his withdrawal was not because he was tired of her, something else must be seriously wrong. Nonetheless, at this moment it could not be important. A more compelling concern was absorbing her. It would not be possible if Roger really did love her to make a jealous scene every time they made love. Nor did she wish to return to her passive, innocent role. Also, it was true that, however sincere Roger was at this moment, variety was a spice that kept love strong. She touched his face.

"We will not talk about where you learned, but you will teach me—yes? It is not fair that you should know so much what will give me pleasure and I should know so little what to do for you."

"Sweet—" Roger began.

"Not so sweet," Leonie chuckled. "I wish to know for your sake—yes—but also for mine. You have too great an advantage this way."

Roger swallowed hard and took a deep breath. "I wish I could. I swear I would gladly give my whole life—religiously—to teaching you. But—tomorrow you must go. It is too dangerous for you to stay here."

He was deadly serious. It was not a desire for freedom but really fear for her. "Has someone recognized me?" Leonie asked, switching back to French.

"No, it is not that—" Roger stopped abruptly.

He could have kicked himself for missing such an opportunity. He would not have needed to explain everything, and Leonie would have had no reason to be afraid either for herself or for him. It was such pain, such joy, so mixed together with physical exhaustion that he could not sort reason from emotion or seize an idea when it was presented to him. Leonie, however, was not subject to the same confusion of mind and picked up his answer before he could cover it.

"Then why should it be more dangerous for me to stay here than for you?" she asked briskly.

"It is not that, my love." Roger's voice trembled a little on the last words. How often had they been spat back at him with insults and mockery.

"What is it?" Leonie murmured, reaching for him.

"Nothing, nothing now, only—it is hard for me to say 'I

love.' It seems to me that as soon as I dare say it, I lose what I love."

"You will not lose me," Leonie assured him; then, teasingly, "Not even when you wish you could."

"But I must. I told you. Tomorrow you must go."

"But I do not wish to go, and I will not."

Wearily, Roger tried to think of a rational explanation for a situation that would be dangerous for her but not for him. He supposed there must be many things that could produce such a result, but he could not think, only feel the wrenching loss, foretaste the misery of the empty bed. And the whole thing was made worse by the fact that Leonie cared for him. If he were accused with Toulon and guillotined, she would grieve. That was almost sweet enough to mask its bitterness, but more bitterness lay behind. If he died, Leonie would be without protection. Fouché would do what he could—perhaps.

"I am so tired, Leonie," Roger sighed. "Let us leave it for the morning."

CHAPTER 17

By morning Roger had regained his wits, but it was too late; Leonie had regained her strength. The preceding night, exhausted as she was, Roger might have played on her fears, on her memories, and convinced her to go into hiding. In the clear light of morning, well rested, and with buoyant spirits riding the crest of Roger's confession of love, no specious excuses could satisfy her. Roger had begun while they were dressing—he had started to withdraw to do that in his usual way, but Leonie had called him back. He tried first to convince her that he had not clearly understood her question the previous night, that someone had recognized her as an aristocrat. Leonie listened to him with her hands on her hips in unconscious imitation of the wife of the fishmonger next door when she was in an aggressive mood.

"Blather!" she exclaimed succinctly.

Roger barely restrained himself from taking her over his knee and spanking her. Here he was, preparing to tear out his heart to save her from harm, to protect her from fear and grief and guilt, and she dismissed what he was saying as "blather." "Very well," he snapped, "I did not wish you to feel guilty, but I must tell you plainly that one of the commissioners has conceived a desire for you. You must go away before he demands that you yield to him."

Leonie considered that. Roger's irritation lent it some verisimilitude, and she did not discount the power of these common, trumped-up officials. Such a fact would accord well, too, with Roger's behavior. She could understand that he might be both angry and jealous. Perhaps he thought she had encouraged the man, whoever it was. Two small doubts tickled her mind, however. She had not been much in the shop since they had moved, and she could not remember any man who had paid the slightest attention to her. Certainly no one had tried to engage her in conversation, and even these common clods would not try to obtain a woman by asking her husband for her. Also, she could not see the point in bringing another woman into the house to replace her. That last stuck in her craw.

"There is no need to have another woman here," Leonie said slowly. "In fact, if we are to tell a reasonable tale—such as I have gone to attend a sick relative—it would not be reasonable for you to have another woman in the house."

Roger could not say that the purpose of the other woman was to convince people that Leonie had *not* left. "Am I to starve and the house become a pigsty?" he countered.

"I will arrange with one of the women on the street to come and do for you," Leonie offered, then nodded. "Yes, and that will establish that I am coming back and that there is an innocent reason for my going. We must not frighten Toulon, you know. Yes, you can eat at an inn or get meals from a *cafetier*—and you can come to visit me and my 'sick relative.' That would only be natural." Her eyes laughed at him, hot and golden. "I would not wish to fall behind in my lessons before I even start. It will not be for long. In a few days, or at most a week or so, Toulon's escape must take place. Then—"

When Leonie provided so reasonable an answer to Roger's last proposal, he wondered for an instant if he could somehow make the exchange of women by force. Then her suggestion that he should visit her seized his mind. He rejected it as impossible, but loss stabbed him and he began to reconsider. Open visits to a "sick relative" were impossible. He would be followed and Leonie's hiding place discovered. However, if the exchange worked and Leonie was still thought to be in the house, he might pretend he was making a delivery to the place. While he tried to convince himself that it would not endanger Leonie, her remark about Toulon hit him with the force of a physical blow. Before he could control it, his face twisted. Leonie's voice cut off midsentence and she stared at him, her skin slowly crimsoning.

"No one wanted me," she said. "You think Toulon's plot will fail and that he, or others, will confess we are involved and we will be guillotined. You would have dragged some innocent person—"

"No. She would have known nothing, and—"

"You know innocence is no defense in these times. What were you thinking of?" Leonie asked furiously.

"That I love you," Roger said helplessly. "That I cannot bear you should be hurt or frightened. That your life—you are so young, Leonie, you have hardly lived at all—was too precious to lose."

"I cannot think why you should have such feelings about so depraved a person as myself," Leonie raged, "a person who would desert her lover at the first sign of danger, who would consent to the execution of a perfectly innocent and unknowing bystander in her stead. Not to mention a person who was such a fool as not to realize that once her protector was guillotined—"

Despite the seriousness of the situation, Roger began to laugh. "But obviously I didn't believe any of those things or I wouldn't have lied myself blue in the face trying to hide the true facts from you. No, Leonie, listen—"

"Not to any such nonsense. I do not wish to die, but I do not wish to live with such things on my soul either."

Roger recalled suddenly how Leonie had said, the night before, that she could have escaped from prison but would not leave her family behind, that if Marie Antoinette had consented to escape without her children and her sister-by-marriage she would be a monster. He stared at Leonie, biting his lips with anxiety.

"Very well," he said slowly, "I have one more idea."

"If it means being apart, I will not listen," Leonie warned.

"Only for a few hours—"

"No. I don't trust you. You wish to save me from myself."

"Leonie, be reasonable."

"I *am* reasonable. What will I do, alone in this city, without protection or papers of identification? How long can I survive?"

"Fouché—"

"He owes *me* nothing, not even friendship. Perhaps for your sake he would try to help me, but what if that should bring him into trouble? Besides, I have no one in the world except you, Roger. I—" She stopped suddenly and then went on, "I don't even know why you are so sure Toulon will fail."

Sighing, Roger told her, and Leonie was forced to nod in acknowledgment. She was not nearly as pessimistic as Roger, but she did realize there was a good chance that the plot would be exposed. Again, she was not certain that they would be involved, but that, too, was possible. To Leonie's mind, however, it was not a strong enough probability to make it worthwhile to flee, leaving behind Roger's valuable stock in trade and her own few, but therefore precious, things.

"If we were accused," she said slowly, "they would send three or four men to take us, would they not?"

"Or more," Roger replied grimly. "This involves the royal family, and they would not wish any sympathizers to escape."

"Then we will have warning," Leonie pointed out. "It is not often that more than one or two men would come together to have a gun worked on. And they will send men to the back door also—so we will know their purpose."

"Yes. Now you can see why—"

"Then we must leave the house another way," Leonie interrupted, not paying any attention to him. "If we—"

"Flew out the window like birds?" he asked bitterly, but even as he spoke he realized the remark was not foolish. The houses were all joined together, and they could escape over the roofs. What a fool he had been to be trapped in his own mind. Anything that threatened Leonie turned him so frantic that he seemed unable to think. Hopelessness gone, Roger could laugh at himself. The house did not have an existing way out to the roof, but that was all for the best. No one would suspect that they could get out that way.

That night he began the work and finished it the following night. It was a crude job, but it would let them out and that was all Roger cared about. If the roof leaked, well, that was too bad. Leonie, meanwhile, had prepared a strong sling into which Fifi could be fastened so that she could be carried. Everything else would have to be abandoned, of course. Leonie sighed, but not deeply. The clothes she had were better than the rags she wore in prison, but she had no great affection for them. When they got to England, she would show Roger that she was not naturally a dowdy person.

And then—nothing. For a week their tension was intense, and since Roger sat up a good part of every night expecting either the escapees or a group to arrest them, there were no "lessons" for Leonie. The next week, Leonie insisted on sharing the watch with him, because he was getting so tired that his work was suffering—and that would rouse suspicion. And still nothing happened. Another week dragged past—March was over.

"The attempt has fallen through," Roger said to Leonie, and she agreed, although there was no outcry, no outward sign of conflict among the commissioners.

The only confirmation Roger had of his guess was that Toulon and Lepitre did not come into his shop again and—more important—the men who had been watching Leonie and himself disappeared. He breathed more freely after that, but not for long. On April third Roger and Leonie went to Fouché's office to deposit a sum of money. Roger's account was now substantial enough so that Fouché could give special attention to so valuable a client without arousing the curiosity of his less-trusted employees. He passed along the news that his cousin was seriously worried about events. On April first the convention had passed a resolution repealing the inviolability of the deputies.

Roger's blue eyes blazed. "You cannot mean what I think I hear," he said. "Are you telling me that those—er—patriots—" The window was open and Roger had no intention of being overheard calling the members of the convention idiots, but the word stood large in his expression. "They have made themselves liable to prosecution for *political* acts?"

"That is so," Fouché agreed. "My cousin said," his eyes fixed Roger's with an intensity that belied his casual and approving tone, "that he, too, voted for the decree because men should be willing to support their opinions with their lives, and if their lives are not at stake, they will be inclined to make their decisions lightly."

"If," Leonie whispered in Roger's ear, "they do not become incapable of making any decision at all."

"I see the point," Roger remarked, his lips twisting wryly. "How noble-minded they are, to be sure!" He turned his head toward Leonie. "You are cold," he whispered.

On cue, she complained rather loudly, "Oh, do forgive me, but I am afraid my shawl is too thin. It is so strange. I was warm enough while walking outside, but now, sitting here, I am growing cold. Would it be possible, Citizen Fouché, to shut the window?"

That done, they were able to speak more plainly. "What the hell brought on this lunacy?" Roger asked.

"The army was defeated—very badly—at Neerwinden, and Dumouriez has gone over to the Austrians. So far, it is being kept a secret."

"I cannot believe that so good a general as Dumouriez—"

"Oh, he did not wish to go into Holland, but the convention forced him with some crazy order about liberating the people of the Netherlands."

"Since the people of Holland have been electing their rulers for some hundreds of years, and have fought the French viciously to maintain that privilege, it seems the wrong nation to attack," Roger remarked caustically.

Fouché shrugged. "I am a good Frenchman. I love my country," he sighed. "I approved of the doings of the Estates General with all my heart. I approved of the constitution with all my heart. Now . . . Monsieur St. Eyre, I am come to the point where I have begun to wonder whether France would be better conquered by foreigners than free."

"I cannot doubt that it would," Leonie snapped. "At least we would be rid of this government. A republic—that I do not like, but it is possible. It has worked among the Swiss and it seems to be working among the Americans. But it is not possible to have a republic governed by homicidal maniacs."

"Hush!" Roger protested. He agreed heartily with the sentiments, but it was not his place to say anything, being, as it were, a member of the enemy camp. "I am afraid I am concerned more with personal matters," he said apologetically. "It seems to me that the situation is growing worse, and I must make an effort to get Mademoiselle de Conyers to England if I can. Do you think it would be safe to approach your cousin with a request for a passport to Brittany? From there I can manage."

"I will mention to him that I have a client who wishes to

know whether it is safe to travel to Brittany and whom to approach for a passport, but Joseph will do nothing. He was a teacher of physics, you know, and he judges things by action and reaction. He says the pendulum has not reached its full swing, and there will be more violence. At the moment he will do nothing for anyone that could bring any attention to himself. Perhaps he will recommend someone who might be willing. . . ." Fouché's voice trailed away. It was obvious that he did not believe his cousin would even go so far as that for fear his name might be mentioned. Joseph was not a man to take a chance—not any chance at all.

On their way home, when they were sure no one could overhear, Roger and Leonie discussed the problem in lowered voices. This time Leonie was willing to go if they could find a way. Roger's avowal of love had given her confidence. She thought that when she was dressed and perfumed and bejeweled and freed by her "lessons"—which still had not started because the starvation imposed by anxiety had made both of them too eager for refinements— from the pose of an innocent young girl, she could hold her own. Englishwomen, she had heard, were cold and correct, propriety being necessary to obtain a husband in that country. But she was not interested in propriety or a husband as long as she could have Roger.

The problem was whom to approach. All the deputies knew that a dangerous crisis was coming. The creation of the Committee of Public Safety, which the Girondists hoped would be their club to combat the "Mountain"— that coterie of violent radicals including Danton, Marat, and Robespierre, who sat in the highest rows of the convention hall—was the first sign of how the wind would finally blow. Not a single member of that party, which appeared to hold a majority in the convention, was elected to the small, all-powerful body. The Girondists saw the handwriting on the wall but still struggled to save themselves. This meant that no one allied to them would wish to do anything that was not strictly routine. On the other hand, the Jacobins, who leaned toward the Mountain, were not yet secure in their power. They, too, were not likely to provide exit papers for a man and his wife who could not really prove their identity nor produce a valid reason for leaving Paris.

Needless to say, approach to the wrong person might cause instant incarceration followed shortly by death under the guillotine. It was not that life did not continue for ordinary citizens. Men did lose their papers of identity and obtain new ones, but those men could prove who they were by long-time friends and family. Roger and Leonie could not produce any evidence beyond their arrival in Paris at the end of August—and they were branded by their accents. Nor were they too eager to use the papers they had obtained on arrival. Brissot was surely one of the first who would fall with the Girondist party. Thus they continued from day to day, watching each move of the Girondists fail.

On May twenty-first the crisis broke. A well-organized mob invaded the Tuileries and besieged the Salle de Ménage where the convention met. Roger thanked God that he had moved in February, but he found that physical removal from the eye of a hurricane does not keep one from being swept into the fringes of the storm. On June first a gentleman of elegant dress entered the shop and laid one of a pair of English-made pocket pistols on the counter. Roger's breath caught, and he did not make any attempt to touch the gun, which was a beautiful one-of-a-kind creation of Knubley and Brown that Roger himself had purchased as a gift for his father.

"You recognize it, I see, Monsieur St. Eyre," the gentleman said softly.

"Is my father in France?" Roger asked.

"No, no. It was passed along to me only to identify me as someone trustworthy. Sir Joseph was well, residing in London for the Season, when he gave us that token. I am sure he has no intention of doing anything that might increase your difficulties or those of Mademoiselle de Conyers."

Roger's held breath sighed out, and he lifted his head. There was no need for any pretense with this man. He obviously knew all there was to know. "What can I do for you?" he asked.

"For me? Nothing. I am not in need of help. What are you willing to do for your country?"

That was a nasty question. The answer, obviously, should be *Anything I can*, but Roger was not really willing to do "anything." He felt an odd reluctance to take part in any action against France while he was accepted as a citizen and pretending to be one. As much as he disapproved of the present government, he did not feel England to be in any danger from it. And even though he knew France had declared war, not England, he felt her to be like a frightened puppy snarling defiance. It was more sensible to gentle a frightened animal into obedience; kicking it merely turned it vicious.

"I am ready to serve my country," Roger said slowly, "but my first responsibility is to Mademoiselle de Conyers. Frankly, I am not willing to do anything that might endanger her. Also, I cannot see what help I can be to you. I am not involved in the purchase or repair of military weapons—"

"I am aware of that," the gentleman interrupted. "What I wish to ask of you has no connection with military action—at least, no immediate connection with it. As you must have heard, the Mountain is planning to purge the convention of all its moderate members. I—and others, of course—when I say 'I' you must understand others than myself to be of the same opinion."

Roger nodded. No names would be named and Roger felt—as he had in Toulon's plot—that the less he knew, the better off he would be.

"I believe it too late to prevent the purge," the man continued, "but it may be possible to save the men themselves—or at least some of them."

"I will do anything I can to help you in that," Roger agreed immediately, "but what can I do?"

"Could you hide a man?"

"Not really," Roger replied, and then snapped his fingers. "Wait! If he is not too old and is reasonably agile—yes, I can. However, it will not be a comfortable hiding place, as it is completely exposed to the weather." He paused a moment and then added, "Do you want to know where?"

"No. The fewer who know the better. However, since I know your name, it is only fair that you should know mine. I am the Chevalier de Rocheville. I was once a colonel of the Grenadiers. My purpose is to see this nation under its rightful king again."

Roger did not groan aloud, because de Rocheville would not have understood. It would have been all very well that the chevalier should be a gallant gentleman who did not wish to have any advantage over Roger had they been playing tennis or even dueling in England. Here, where a whispered word might be carried on an errant breeze and cost a man his head, Roger would infinitely have preferred caution to gallantry. However, he reminded himself, it was only the gallant who involved themselves in lost causes. If he had any sense himself, he would have refused to have anything to do with de Rocheville. He was quite sure his father's gun had not been meant for the purpose to which it had been put.

Nonetheless, it was impossible to refuse, just as it had been impossible for Roger to point out to Toulon the danger in freeing Marie Antoinette. He could have no part in condemning those men, and to refuse to help was tantamount to approving their deaths. Sighing at his own foolishness, he even volunteered the use of his horse and carriage if anonymous transport were necessary. The offer was accepted with joy. He said nothing to Leonie that evening, clinging to the hope that the political crisis would ease, but she looked at him very peculiarly, and he was relatively sure she guessed he was hiding something. The next day, June second, all hope was gone. Twenty-seven Girondists were formally suspended and placed under house arrest. Roger confessed to Leonie that he had agreed to help them escape to safety if he could, and Leonie enthusiastically approved everything he had done.

"But where can they hide, Roger?" she asked.

"On the roof."

"The roof is peaked. It is not possible—"

"So is the next roof. A man—even two or three men— might lie down in the trough between the houses. At night they could climb over the roofs to the end of the street and get down with a rope, as we planned to do."

"Yes, of course, how clever. Fifi, be still. What are you barking at?"

The little dog hushed on command and Roger listened, but he heard no footsteps in the alley, which was what usually set her off. A moment later, however, there came a faint scratch on the door. He gestured at Leonie, and she snatched Fifi and ran up the stairs. Out of sight, she set down the dog with a further admonition to be silent and drew her pistol, which she half-cocked and concealed in a fold of her skirt.

There was no need for defense, however. Only two nervous, badly frightened men crept in when the door was opened. They were so tense, expecting pursuit any minute, that they would have gone to hide on the roof at once, but Roger objected. He pointed out that there was no sense in opening and closing the trapdoor and moving around in the attic and on the roof more than necessary. It was not likely, but it was not impossible that a neighbor would be in his own attic and wonder about the noise.

They stayed three days, never needing to go into hiding because, if there was a search, no one suspected Roger's house. It seemed to Roger that de Rocheville was no fool and no one might ever suspect. The refugees did not know his name, did not even know what part of the city they were in. They had been brought in a sealed carriage to the end of the alley and told which door to scratch at and to remove their boots so they would make no noise. The only problem that arose was how to get food for these extra mouths, since Leonie could not simply suddenly buy double quantities. Fortunately, most of the women in the neighborhood were aware of her inexperience as a cook. They were quite accustomed to seeing Roger rush out at dinner time to bring in food from a *cafetier*, even though his wife had bought food to cook in the morning. On the second day the fishmonger's wife called out teasingly to ask if Leonie had forgotten everything she knew.

"*Au contraire,*" Roger replied, laughing. "She is growing adventurous because what she knows she does so well."

That brought an answering laugh and an admonition for Roger to be patient. "She is clever, that little one. Now, when she is so beautiful, she learns. Later, when she is old and ugly, you will be tied to her by your stomach."

Roger smiled a mechanical acknowledgment and went on. Any reference to his future with Leonie dragged him into a maelstrom of conflicting emotions. Ever since Leonie had acknowledged her jealousy and her pleasure in his lovemaking, Roger had been on the verge of suggesting that they marry. It would not be impossible, although it would be dangerous. First, they were supposed to be man and wife already; second, for the marriage to be legal they would have to give their true names. Consideration had convinced Roger it was too dangerous and had raised the idea of asking her to promise to marry him as soon as they arrived in England.

This raised objections more painful than danger. Roger knew what would be hinted behind their backs and perhaps said openly to Leonie herself if he married her as soon as they arrived. Every mother of a son with encumbered estates, every fortune hunter in the country, would say that Roger had grabbed the heiress before she had a chance to choose for herself. It was not true, of course, but how could a man prove such a thing? Would Leonie begin to believe the stories? If she accepted him because she thought she cared for him but thought so only out of ignorance, because she had had no choice, marriage would not prevent her from falling in love with another man. Roger knew he could not bear that. If Leonie chose to marry someone else, he would survive. He could avoid her—even if it meant leaving the country—and live much as he had lived when Solange was alive. If she was his wife and turned cold or betrayed him . . . There was a well of violence in him, Roger knew, like a dry shaft filled with black powder. Solange had filled it, but it was Leonie who might set a match to the explosive and be destroyed by it.

There was the other side of the coin, of course. Sometimes Roger let himself think about that. If he brought Leonie to England and left her completely to herself, allowed her to go to balls and to be courted, and she still chose him, after the others had their chance, he would be sure. He tried not to think about it too often, tried not to permit himself to believe that dream would come true, but Leonie had said . . . It was when he believed, even a little, that it was not only youth and inexperience and gratitude that drew Leonie to him that Roger began to devise ways to escape from France. It was bitterly hard to taste her sweetness and to fear constantly that the sweetness hid the bitterness of parting. Better to know at once than to go on drugging himself with a love that might be only ignorance.

Unfortunately, at present there were no hopes of escape, there was only the constant danger of betrayal. Once again Roger tried to convince Leonie to leave him for a safer dwelling. Although their two "guests" had been collected without incident, as silently and mysteriously as they had

arrived, Roger guessed that they would not be the last. If it
had not been for the danger to Leonie, Roger would now
have been enjoying himself. He liked the spice of immediate peril, and he acknowledged that what de Rocheville
was doing was well worthwhile. In the provinces there was
enormous resentment of many of the acts of the convention. If the Girondists could rally those with moderate republican sympathies and come to terms with those with
royalist sympathies, the present group of bloody lunatics
might be overthrown.

This time Leonie did not laugh or lose her temper. "Oh,
no," she said passionately. "Do you think I don't know this
is France's last chance for peace and a good government? I
don't wish to live here anymore, Roger. There is too much
bitterness, too much hurt and heartbreak here for me. I
need a new life, completely new. I want to go to England
and find that new life, but this is the land where I was
born. My father and mother loved it. Papa knew when he
was elected to the Estates General that it might cost him
his life, yet he did not hesitate an instant."

"Enough lives that you love have been given, Leonie,"
Roger interrupted.

"And I am still alive," she said. "And you are telling me
to stand aside and watch you—you are all I have, Roger—
watch you risk your life too? Oh, no. If you can bring
yourself to abandon this last hope, I will escape with you
because you are all I have—but I will not do it willingly. I
am the last de Conyers. I owe my father's memory one last
attempt to save this country."

"I cannot bear to know that you are in danger," Roger
sighed.

"I cannot bear to know that *you* are in danger," Leonie
echoed. "But, Roger, this is more important. If the Mountain can be cast down, the constitution that papa helped to
write can be reestablished. A new assembly could be
elected, according to the constitution. The dauphin could
be king. Certainly he would cause no trouble by opposing
the will of the assembly."

"The queen might," Roger pointed out, "although I
think she would be far more careful about what she tried to
put in the boy's mouth than what she tried to put into her
husband's. She is not a stupid woman. Perhaps she has
learned."

"I doubt she could cause trouble. The Girondists would be looking for the slightest excuse to imprison her again or exile her. Oh, Roger, if it could only work, it would be best for us too."

"Yes," Roger agreed. "Once the monarchy was reestablished, the other nations would be willing to make peace—at least, I hope they would. That could occur only if no one decides to take advantage of the inevitable civil war—for there will be civil war, Leonie. The radicals will not give up without a bitter fight. If, as I say, Austria and Prussia and my own dear, generous government do not decide that the civil war will provide the right moment to dismember France—"

"They wouldn't!" Leonie exclaimed.

"They might. However, they will get short shrift. If there is a unified government that has the trust of the provinces, France will throw them off. The English government, I am sure, will come to terms as soon as they have their hands slapped. They really have very little taste for war; the commoners are businessmen and small landholders who don't like the taxes war brings or the interference with trade."

"So there will be peace and we can go to England—home to England."

Leonie's eyes rested on Roger. For the moment he was relaxed, although when she said "home" a look of longing crossed his face. It was odd, she thought, that she should call England home and feel a true desire to be there—a place she had never seen—yet she knew that anywhere Roger was would be her home. She turned away and busied herself with some unnecessary task at the stove to hide eyes suddenly full of tears.

Since Roger had spoken to Fouché about obtaining passports, Leonie had given considerable thought to living in England. She found she did want to live there, but she was less and less sure she could be content to have Roger only as a lover. He had a profession, a home, a son, a large family. How often would he be able to visit her? How much time would he dare spend when he did visit—a few hours? Leonie thought of the long empty days and nights. She had no friends or relatives. She would have to live alone, with a companion, perhaps, to give her countenance.

She tried to push those thoughts away, telling herself

that Roger would not abandon her. He said he loved her; he would find a way. Deep inside, a voice cried—*if he loves you, why doesn't he marry you*? She tried not to listen to that ugly voice, but it was hard to ignore it. And the day before, the fishmonger's wife had said something to her when she had come in to buy mussels that had wakened both a new hope and a new problem in her. The beginning had been innocent enough. The woman teased her about her cooking experiments that sent Roger to the *cafetier* for three days. Leonie had given a light answer to the effect that she was buying mussels to prevent that happening again.

"One cannot spoil mussels, after all," she said.

"Ah, but you do right," the woman replied. "Now is the time to tease him and be sharp and make him run errands and cook meals that cannot be eaten. Then, when you are heavy with child and ugly, you can bind him to you with sweetness of disposition and delicious food."

Somehow Leonie had managed a reply that did not betray her, but she was aghast. Not that she thought Roger would stray from a woman he loved because she was swollen and petulant with pregnancy. He was too tenderhearted for that. What had shocked Leonie was the realization that she was *not* pregnant. She had been living with Roger for over nine months and she had never missed her flux. She had not conceived of Louis either, but he had told her he would take care that she should not. Was Roger taking care also? Was that a sign he would not marry her under any circumstances?

Leonie did not doubt for a moment that Roger would marry her if she got with child. She was not a shop girl but a de Conyers, and there could not be any doubt, after all this time, that the child was his. For a moment, Leonie was suffused with delight at the thought. She would have Roger and his child also. Then reality intruded. It was reality that brought tears to her eyes. The fact was that she was *not* with child, and although she could not guess what he was doing to prevent it, Leonie was ignorant enough to believe that her inability to conceive was Roger's doing. *Ah well,* she told herself as her tears dried in the heat of the stove, *probably he is doing it for my sake.* It would increase their danger manyfold to have an infant or even for her to be swollen and unwieldy. *This is a dangerous game we are playing,* she thought. *Who knows whether we will get to England at all.*

The game was indeed dangerous, but either they were blessed with unusual good luck or de Rocheville was as clever and skillful as he was gallant. Roger came to believe the latter as the weeks passed and more and more men and women were funneled out of Paris. His house was only one of many that were used, he guessed, yet it was used with frequency. By the end of June, the people who passed through Roger's hands were obviously no longer deputies of the convention. Some may well have been English or Austrian spies—Roger did not ask because he didn't want to know—but many were simply people who needed to escape because they were threatened by imprisonment and death.

Once Roger said exasperatedly to de Rocheville that he was scarcely more secure than those he was helping to escape.

"Their need is more immediate," de Rocheville replied simply. "You will not be forgotten, I assure you. If you are in real peril, we will open the gates for you also." Then he frowned and cleared his throat. "If you wish to send Mademoiselle de Conyers . . ."

"I wish it with all my heart," Roger sighed—which was true and not true at the same time, of course. "But she will not go and swears that if I drug her or bind her she will escape and come back." That was absolutely true, for Roger had once in a fury threatened to do just that to Leonie.

"I thought it might be so," de Rocheville remarked, his face expressionless and his voice perfectly neutral.

"She believes she is serving her country," Roger grated.

Then de Rocheville smiled. "Ah, yes," he murmured, making Roger wish he had held his tongue. "Women have become quite passionate about politics, have they not?"

CHAPTER 18

Roger did not often protest against the "guests" de Roche-ville sent to his home. The haggard faces of the men who passed through his house, the women who trembled and wept in Leonie's arms, were sufficient evidence that they must continue to do whatever they could to help as long as they could. It would not be much longer, Roger feared. The hopes he and Leonie had discussed during the early days of June had died swiftly. Instead of joining forces with the royalists and coming to terms with them so that a uni-fied front could be presented against the radical foes, both royalist and Girondist allowed their differences to prevail. Revolution against the dictates of the government in Paris flared, but it was disorganized and sporadic.

The opposition, of course, inspired even greater violence and suppression. Anyone who had ever been heard to op-pose or even grieve over the massacres of September or the execution of the king—indeed, almost anyone who had been on speaking terms with a person who had expressed anti-Jacobin views—was regarded as a criminal. Also, the war was going very badly. The English had taken Dunkirk, and the Austrians the city of Valenciennes; Mainz had been handed over to the Prussians by treason; the Spanish invaded France at both ends of the Pyrenees.

This was particularly dangerous to Roger; if his accent were recognized as foreign—as Toulon had recognized it as English—he might be seized as a spy, even though there was no reason to suspect him. Then a weird act of vio-lence—the murder of the darling of the mobs, Marat—by a sweet, gentle-looking woman from Normandy complicated everything. The *sans-culottes* went wild, attacking and loot-ing anyone or anything they decided was "provincial." To Roger's and Leonie's sorrow, the Café Breton was de-stroyed and the Aunays murdered. Fortunately, before the

mob got around to Roger's area, they had been pacified by
the state funeral for Marat designed and presented by
Jacques Louis David. Marat's coffin was followed by young
girls dressed in white, by the whole of the convention—at
least, those who had not fled or been arrested—and by representatives of the Sections. Incense was sprinkled, revolutionary hymns were sung. Marat was changed by death
from a diseased, repulsive, murderous madman to a pure
martyr.

It was the death knell of all moderation in general and of
the Girondists in particular. By the end of July the rising
they had inspired in Normandy and that headed by royalists in Brittany were both defeated. Free of the fear that
their friends would storm Paris, the remains of the convention decreed that those Girondists who had not fled would
be subjected to a mass trial. To be certain of the result, a
law was passed that permitted the jury, after hearing evidence for three days, to declare that they were "sufficiently enlightened" and the judge could order the trial ended.
There were still people sympathetic to the Girondist point
of view, however. In addition, the demands of the war and
the battle against the rebellious provinces would call for
great sacrifices. Therefore, Robespierre, who was now one
of the dominant figures in the convention, decided to distract the people from the fate of the Girondists and the new
hardships that were about to be inflicted by a more appealing sideshow. In August it was announced that Marie Antoinette, the hated Austrian who had seduced the French
king into oppressing his people, would be tried for her
crimes. She had already been moved from the Temple and
was lodged in the Conciergerie prison.

To Roger's relief, Leonie did not react much to the announcement of the queen's imminent trial. She was sorry
for Marie Antoinette, who would certainly be convicted
and executed for crimes of which she was not guilty; however, the queen was not completely innocent either. There
could be no doubt that she had attempted to make her husband resist reform of any kind, had been dissipated and
frivolous. Her "crimes" were not such as should call for the
punishment she would receive, but Leonie was too aware of
the horrible deaths of truly innocent people like the Aunays
to be much moved by the queen's troubles. Every few days
the fugitives that passed through their house reminded her

that the same fate awaited those who had never had power or influence and who had been condemned without any real reason by the bloody Committee of Public Safety.

It was not only Roger and Leonie who were being pushed into an interest in refugees. When the royalist uprising in Brittany was defeated at the end of July, the convention sent commissioners to extirpate any further seeds of rebellion. Pierre Restoir had taken no part in the uprisings, for he had no greater affection for the king's government than for that of the "people." Neither had ever troubled him, for he had no love for show and lived quietly in a small Breton fishing village; the large profits he made from his illegal enterprises had been turned into gold pieces and hidden safely so that neither king nor people could rob *him* for the "good of the nation."

Pierre was annoyed when war was declared on England in February. The immediate reaction, he knew, would be to make everyone—even the men with whom he had done business for years—think of him as a "Frenchman" and possibly as a spy. Thus, from February 1793 through the end of July of that year, he confined his activities actually to fishing. What with the disruption in the country, food was scarce, and he was getting an excellent price for his fish.

The bloody terror inflicted on Brittany after the defeat of the royalists was something outside Pierre's normal experience. He was accustomed to injustices of government, to oppression, high taxation, even to a judicial murder now and again, but the wholesale imprisonment and slaughter taking place in Brittany added a new dimension to Pierre's conviction that all government was bad. He did not change that view, only came to the opinion that some governments were even worse than others. He was not inclined by this conclusion to attempt to establish a better government— Pierre did not think in such terms—but he was impelled to do whatever he could to disrupt and irritate the officers of the present detestable regime.

Just about the time that Roger was drawn into de Rocheville's schemes, Pierre began to smuggle again—only now his cargo was human. Most of the time, to his pleasure, he did quite as well financially from this enterprise as he did from carrying wine and lace. For one thing, the *émigrés* were so eager to leave that they provided Pierre more profit per hundredweight than an equal load of brandy. For another, the exhausted and terrified human freight he carried was *not* unwelcome to the authorities of England. For the first time in his life Pierre did not need to dodge naval and revenue vessels. Sometimes the refugees would be taken aboard English ships; sometimes he was escorted to the nearest port to discharge his passengers. This made his channel crossings short, swift, and sure and permitted him to make more frequent voyages.

However, other areas of France had developed an equal distaste for their present leaders. The idealism that had choked off Pierre's tax-free supply of liquor had waned sharply. By November 1793 word came through the old network that, if Pierre wanted it, a substantial cargo could be assembled. Pierre considered the fact that, in all probability, his old customers were bone dry by now, and the wine and brandy would fetch a handsome price. In addition, he had been wondering for some months how Roger's venture had turned out. It had been a long time, he thought, since he had seen his friend. Thus, in the first week of December, after his cargo was unloaded, he made his way quietly to the Soft Berth. His approach was cautious; he did not wish to be taken up as a French spy. However, his welcome by the landlord was hearty—if private—and he was given Sir Joseph's original letter plus a second one that had been written in September.

In the quiet of the landlord's own parlor, Pierre read them both. The first made him frown and whistle worriedly through his teeth. The second made him curse, luridly and obscenely. In it Sir Joseph reported that he had received further news of Roger by word of mouth. One of the *émigrés* had been personally known to Leonie, and Roger had taken the chance of sending a message to his father. Sir Joseph now knew the address of the shop in the rue de la Corderie, and he passed this along, together with the information that he was very much worried by the use to which the token he had given had been put. If anything, Pierre was even more worried than Sir Joseph because he did not discount, as Sir Joseph did, the horror stories told by the *émigrés*. Pierre had seen the commissioners of the Committee of Public Safety at work.

He did not communicate his fears to Roger's father in

the note he wrote to say he had received his letters, only assured him that he would do his best to obtain news and pass it back. However, he revolved the problem in his mind, came to the conclusion that Roger had gotten himself into real trouble, and decided he had better be dragged out of Paris as fast as possible. Pierre was unable to act on this resolution immediately. When he returned home, he found an urgent message awaiting him concerning a new boatload of refugees. As much as he wished to rescue Roger, it was impossible for Pierre to ignore the more acute and perilous situation of his prospective passengers— or the substantial sums they were offering for transportation.

Pierre made a quick trip although the weather was foul, and while he was battling the storm on his return voyage a brilliant idea occurred to him. Why shouldn't he sail right into Paris? Not in the *Bonne Lucie*, of course, but in a small fishing vessel that could navigate the Seine. If he had been fishing and was blown off course by a storm, it would be perfectly reasonable for him to unload his fish in Paris rather than have them go bad while he beat his way back to his usual home port. It would be much easier, Pierre thought, and quicker, too, to arrange Roger's escape by boat. There was no trouble obtaining a suitable ship, but Pierre had to spend three weeks fishing and selling fish before the right kind of storm blew him in the right direction.

Long before Pierre made his decision, Roger and Leonie had been in considerably more danger than either Sir Joseph or Pierre realized. Despite their lack of interest in the fate of the queen, they found themselves involved in her affairs again. On the night of August twenty-seventh Fifi again warned Roger and Leonie that someone was coming down the alley. It was already late, and they were preparing to go to sleep. Roger hurriedly bundled up the quilts they used as a bed and hid them while Leonie rushed upstairs to warn the guests already in the house. Roger waited tensely. Perhaps it was only a thief or someone who had a reason to visit secretly one of the other houses that backed on the alley. If not, it was trouble. De Rocheville had never before sent two groups of guests at the same time, and he always provided warning in advance when the guests would move on.

It was trouble, but not the kind Roger was braced for, not the kind Leonie waited for, pistol in hand, not the kind the trembling guests expected, crouched under the trapdoor, ready to climb out the moment they heard Roger's voice raised in the protesting cue words—"There is no one above but my wife, and she is in bed, asleep." It was, instead, de Rocheville, tense with excitement, talking softly as he pulled his boots back on.

"I will move the people tomorrow," he said, "and there will be no one else until the night of September second. You will have only one guest that night, a lady—a great lady."

On hearing the soft voices, Leonie had peeped down the stairs. Now she came all the way down and her eyes met Roger's over de Rocheville's head. "It is a long way from the Conciergerie to this house," she said.

"That is no problem. She will be accompanied by Michonis, who is a well-known officer of the gendarmerie, and two gendarmes—myself and Baron Friedrich von Trenk. He—"

"Michonis is a commissioner of the commune," Roger interrupted. "Is it wise—"

"This is not the first time he has tried to help the queen," de Rocheville replied. "He was in that business with Toulon."

"Yes, and that was betrayed," Roger said sourly.

"It was not betrayed. In any case, not by Michonis. It was abandoned because Simon became suspicious. He is the man," de Rocheville's lips twisted in angry distaste, "an illiterate shoemaker—and a bad one at that—who is now president of the Temple, and believe it or not, he has sole charge of the queen."

"Why did Simon become suspicious?" Roger persisted.

A faint unease passed across de Rocheville's face. "I am not sure," he conceded, "perhaps some careless expressions . . . But certainly there was no deliberate betrayal. The fact that Toulon and Lepitre are alive is proof of that."

That might be true, but Toulon and Lepitre were men with powerful connections in the Jacobin group. An attack on them might have been considered an attack on their whole party. Also, conditions now were far worse than they had been then. Watch committees had been established to certify the loyalty and background of every person. Roger and Leonie had barely managed to pass the investigation. Fortunately, the shopkeepers near his previous residence, whom he had helped protect from the mob, had been willing to swear that the statements Roger made about himself and his wife were true. They had no way of knowing, and, of course, the statements were a mass of fabrications, but they remembered what Roger had saved them from and were grateful. Roger and Leonie had cleared the next hurdle also. When general conscription was ordered in August, they were afraid he would be shipped off to the front to repair weapons. This time his services to the commissioners stood him in good stead. Roger had been allowed to remain in Paris, but his private business was severely curtailed; now he serviced the guns of the gendarmerie.

The latter was another problem. These days the gendarmes were in and out of his shop constantly. They came singly and also in groups. "I have no way of knowing," Roger pointed out to de Rocheville, "whether a group of men is coming to have guns worked on or to search my house. Is the queen capable of climbing onto the roof and lying in the hot sun or in the rain? Do you want to take this chance with so great a lady?"

"She will not be with you more than the one night. Mademoiselle Fouché—"

"Who?" Roger gasped.

"Mademoiselle Fouché," de Rocheville repeated with a smile. "Yes, the daughter of your friend. How did you think I learned of you? Monsieur Fouché is—never mind that, but his daughter has for a long time visited the priests and nuns who are imprisoned in the Conciergerie to bring them what comforts she can. She has managed to see the queen. On September third, Mademoiselle Fouché will come here escorted by a gentleman—me—to pay a visit to your wife. Thank God it is summer and she can wear a large hat and carry a parasol. She will change clothes with her majesty, who will leave after a suitable half-hour visit. During the afternoon, Mademoiselle de Conyers should make several trips to shop or visit, alternating her use of the front and rear doors to come and go. One of the trips, Mademoiselle Fouché will go out instead. No one will remember how many times Mademoiselle de Conyers came and went. Obviously, if she is at home, she must have returned each time."

Leonie nodded. "That will work, except—I have heard the queen's hair is white now. Be sure there is a wig to match Mademoiselle Fouché's hair color and one for Mademoiselle Fouché to match mine."

A broad smile illuminated de Rocheville's face. "Thank you, mademoiselle. That was one thing we had not thought of. You also have a large hat, I hope?"

"Yes, one moment and I will fetch it so that you may get another to match. It is very common."

She ran up to get her hat, and Roger shook his head at de Rocheville. "I wish I were as sure you will be able to free madame as Leonie is that this exchange of women will work."

"It shouldn't be difficult," de Rocheville said. "Most of the people who have come here have been taken from the prisons. The jailers are such drunken, depraved animals that a few coins will buy a prisoner out."

"But the queen is not 'any' prisoner."

"Then the coins will have to be gold," de Rocheville said cynically.

"There must be gendarmes specially ordered to guard the queen," Roger insisted.

"Michonis is an officer of the gendarmerie," de Rocheville countered. "He will be sure that there is no trouble with the men who are supposed to guard her. And the chief jailer will give no trouble—although he pretends he only obeys Michonis in everything."

Leonie had come back with the hat, and de Rocheville lowered his eyes to it and began to study it with, Roger felt, more intensity than it deserved. He felt decidedly uneasy, for all the assurances he had been given, but he could not bring himself to refuse. This time his cooperation really was necessary. It was not likely that Mademoiselle Fouché, who could come to visit Leonie without raising suspicion, was also acquainted with others in de Rocheville's escape route. He said nothing, watching de Rocheville hand the hat back to Leonie and begin to pull on his boots.

"I will go with the queen," de Rocheville said, his eyes fixed on what he was doing, "so you will not see me again on this business we have been doing together. Someone, however, will come. You will know him by your father's gun."

Roger closed the door after him and went wearily to get

the makeshift bed from where he had hidden it. Leonie watched him, then said softly from behind him, "You think this will fail."

"Yes."

"Why?" There was no protest in the question. Leonie, too, had sensed something in de Rocheville's manner.

Roger shook his head. "I suppose because it seems so easy. Madame will just walk out of the prison. Well, others have done so. . . . Yet . . ."

"He does not really believe it," Leonie said. "He said he would not see you again—but if he comes with the queen, he *will*. That was a slip, wasn't it? Does he expect to be betrayed?"

"No. He would not have involved us if he thought that. I don't believe we are in any special danger, Leonie. No matter what happens to de Rocheville, he will not drag anyone down with him. Perhaps he just wants it too much or—I have heard Michonis is a great one for a jest—perhaps he thinks his tongue will slip."

"I am sorry for the queen," Leonie sighed.

It did not occur to her that Roger could be wrong, and indeed, he was not. On the night of September second they waited—and waited in vain. At twelve they doused their lights and sat together in the dark. At three Leonie went slowly up to bed. The guard changed at midnight. No matter which set of guards was supposed to have been bribed, it was now long past the time it would have taken to come to their house from the prison, even on foot. On September fifth Roger heard from a customer that Michonis had been arrested for complicity in a plot to free the "widow Capet."

He kept his eyes on the gun he was working on to free a jammed lock-mechanism. "All by himself?" he asked caustically. His voice gave no indication of any interest deeper than a relish in gossip.

"The chief jailer will be removed, and the gendarmes who took the bribes will be shortened by a head, but Michonis says there was no plot. He insists it was a joke, a mistake, a misunderstanding. . . . You know the kinds of things they say."

Roger asked another question or two, but idly, as if he had little interest. He was relieved that de Rocheville seemed not to have been implicated. He expected, indeed, to see him or to have another group of guests arrive any day, but this did not happen nor did anyone else bearing his father's gun come to see him. He could only assume it was because the whole situation was growing steadily worse and worse.

Life in Paris had become a nightmare even to the people who had nothing to hide. Shops closed early, which was reasonable because it was illegal to carry a package after dark, so that it was pointless to buy anything after the sun set. In fact, only the direst need could bring a person out in the streets at night. To be caught on even the most innocent errand by a night patrol generally meant imprisonment—which led in short order to execution, regardless of whether or not a crime had been committed. Not that barricading oneself in the house was of much use. It was quite usual for a night patrol to burst in and examine everyone in the household. To entertain a guest was equivalent to engaging in a conspiracy.

Because Roger serviced the guns of the officials and gendarmes in the area, he was well-known to them and—unless there was some good reason—it was unlikely that his house would be invaded. Still, the atmosphere was horrifying. Ten, then twenty, then more were guillotined each day. Again and again Roger thanked God for Leonie's courage. It was marvelous to him, not so much because she showed fortitude in the face of danger but because she was cheerful, almost merry, going about her daily tasks and laughing as often and as easily as ever. It was more marvelous because it was not gallows humor, either. Leonie made no jokes about "sneezing into a basket."

Had Roger known the source of Leonie's placid good humor, he would have been appalled. She did have courage and would have faced even certain death without hysterics. But Leonie did not even think of death or imprisonment. She was so convinced that Roger would find a way out if danger became imminent that she was able to stay alert to any sign of suspicion or odd behavior without any real fear. To her mind the worst that could happen was deprivation and discomfort. Perhaps they would have to flee and go hungry and hide in the dark. Naturally, she would rather continue to live in relative comfort, but she was not afraid of running and hiding.

She saw that Roger was worried and put up with his occasional sharpness without impatience. It never occurred to her that he was personally afraid—in which she would have been reasonably correct, considering a slip on either of their parts would get them guillotined, and he had no more wish to die than any other healthy young man in love. However, Leonie did not think in terms of the guillotine; she blithely assumed that Roger was distressed because he did not want her to "suffer." She never forgot how he had reacted to the idea that she should go hungry or the way he insisted she must sleep alone in the bed at the inn. Although that had annoyed her at the time because she did not *wish* to sleep alone, she did not forget how grateful she would have been for Roger's self-denial if she had not already loved him. Her heart swelled with tenderness at his foolish concern for her, but she said nothing. It was useless to tell him she would not mind what he called "suffering," that to her it would be no more than an irritating inconvenience. That would make him feel even worse.

Thus, both faced the future in happy ignorance of the other's real thoughts. Fortunately, revelation was not forced upon them. If Michonis had known of them, he went to the guillotine without ever implicating anyone, reiterating that no treason had been intended. Roger could not guess what had happened to de Rocheville. Perhaps he had escaped from the city. All Roger knew was that he heard no more of him and, more important, no more of any further attempts to rescue Marie Antoinette. Her trial began on October twelfth; on the fifteenth she was declared guilty of a number of fanciful crimes, the most disgusting of which was that she had taught her son immoral practices; on the sixteenth, at 12:15 P.M., Marie Antoinette was executed.

If the trial and execution of the queen were meant as a diversion, it failed. Nothing could divert the people of Paris from a situation that grew steadily worse. In September the royalists had given the port of Toulon to the British. Immediately after this, government by terror was publicly declared to be the "business" of the convention. On September seventeenth the Law of Suspected Persons, drafted largely by Robespierre, permitted—or rather encouraged— the immediate arrest of persons whose conduct, associations, talk, or writings showed them to be "enemies of liberty." In addition, all persons who did not have a certificate of citizenship or who could not prove they had "carried out their obligations as citizens"—whatever that meant—were subject to immediate imprisonment.

Safety for Roger and Leonie hung on the thin thread of the goodwill of the commissioners who were his customers and the fact that most of the gendarmes in the Section knew him well. The commissioners themselves were not much safer than the ordinary citizens. They watched each other constantly, wondering whether they should accuse their friends before their friends accused them. Among the bloodiest of the supporters of Robespierre in his concept of government by terror were Joseph Fouché and Pierre Gaspard Chaumette.

Joseph Fouché had been sent to Lyons by the convention when the royalist forces there had been defeated, and he had made a sanguinary example of the city. In future the provincial cities would know better than to object to the dictates of the convention. Chaumette had performed a similar duty elsewhere, but Roger knew of him because he was in charge of the commissioners of the Temple, where the dauphin was still imprisoned. The other commissioners spoke about Chaumette sometimes—with glances over their shoulders that betrayed what they thought of him. Still, Roger was not disturbed when Chaumette first came into the shop. Times being what they were, Roger assumed he came to buy a gun, and that was indeed what he asked for.

Roger showed him what he had with easy apologies because it was very little. His main business was repair, he pointed out. It was almost impossible to buy guns now or even the parts from which to manufacture them, and he had nothing for sale except the few pieces confiscated by gendarmes or other officials from persons accused of various crimes. To his surprise, Chaumette did not leave after he had rejected the few weapons Roger had for sale. Instead he looked at Roger measuringly and said, "You are of excellent repute both as a workman and as a citizen, Saintaire."

"Thank you," Roger replied briefly, turning away to lock the unwanted pistols into a cupboard.

"I have heard of you from a common friend, Citizen Fouché."

"He does what little business I need done," Roger agreed, reluctantly turning back again to face Chaumette.

He was worried now. Chaumette was a known and avowed atheist; he could have nothing in common with Fouché, whose daughter devotedly assisted the nuns and priests who had been imprisoned for refusing to set the state above the Church in their loyalties and who had offered herself as a substitute for the queen in the escape plot. It was true that Fouché himself made no parade of his sympathies and that probably Mademoiselle Fouché kept her activities as quiet as possible, particularly since Joseph Fouché was also strongly atheist. That thought clicked in Roger's mind, and he put it together with the expression of mild surprise on Chaumette's face and smiled.

"Oh, you must mean Joseph Fouché. I was thinking of Jean-Baptiste Fouché *avocat*."

"Yes, Citizen Fouché's cousin. I know him also. Joseph lodges with him."

"Yes, I have had the honor of meeting Citizen Joseph Fouché once or twice."

"So he said. He also said you had a horse and carriage. Is this true?"

"Yes," Roger replied.

He leaned forward a little, as if he wanted to speak softly while he explained why he happened to have such an equipage, but his real purpose was to level a pistol at Chaumette's belly under the counter. The ball would be only slightly impeded by the thin wood of the back of the counter, and its impact should double Chaumette up, giving Roger time to shoot him in the head with the other pistol. It was convenient, he thought grimly, that the sound of shots was a frequent, everyday occurrence in his shop and would not bring curious neighbors. The only dangers were that Chaumette's screams when the first bullet hit him might be heard, and that someone might remember he had entered Roger's shop and not emerged.

"I am glad to hear it," Chaumette remarked with every sign of relief on his face, referring to Roger's excuses for not selling the rig—an act that might easily be construed as a hint of a desire to leave Paris and thus treason, punishable by death. "The necessary severities of the government are making good citizens like yourself needlessly nervous."

There was, of course, no answer Roger could make to so palpably untrue a remark. The severities of the government were *designed* to make everyone so nervous as to be paralyzed. However, the statement, coupled with Chaumette's expression, did keep Roger from pulling the trigger—a forbearance he was to regret bitterly in the future.

"I have heard also," Chaumette continued, "that you lived for some time in Brittany and had some acquaintance with the fishermen there, those who carry cargo other than fish when it is convenient."

Roger gaped at him. How in the world could Chaumette have heard that? He did not ever remember saying anything about Pierre to Joseph Fouché. Then he realized that his friend Fouché—Joseph's cousin—must have heard about Pierre from the clients "on the run" whom Roger had arranged to have smuggled out of the country. Pierre brought them across, but it was through Fouché that Roger had sent them money to live on. Doubtless one or more foolishly had mentioned the smuggler's vessel on which he had traveled and Fouché—somehow—had passed this information to his cousin, who had passed it to Chaumette.

After his experiment with terror in Lyons, Joseph Fouché had made a mental note that such excesses might result in a backward swing of the pendulum. The whole concept of revolution and republicanism might become abhorrent, inducing a longing for the "good old days" of the monarchy.

Naturally, a real reestablishment of the monarchy would be tantamount to suicide for those who had voted for the death of Louis XVI—and Joseph had so voted—unless . . . Unless the nine-year-old dauphin could be developed into a monarch who was a fervent republican, convinced of the guilt of his father and mother and willing to be a puppet on the throne to save the revolution. This idea came together with the need for a new direction for the revolution to travel in case the conflict between Danton and Robespierre disrupted the government.

As the days passed, Joseph could see a conflict approaching nearer and nearer. While Robespierre urged a greater and greater intensification of "the Terror," pressing for more arrests and more executions, Camille Desmoulins, Danton's friend, had turned about-face and was urging clemency. In the third issue of the *Vieux Cordelier* he wrote: "Do you really think that these helpless women, these old men, these poor laggards of the Revolution whom you have shut up are dangerous?"

It caused Joseph considerable anxiety to think that copies of this publication on December fifteenth were snatched up by an avid public the instant they appeared. The entire edition was sold out in hours. It was not he who commented on this fact, however, but Chaumette, whom he met in the café devoted to those pushing the cause of atheism and superiority of the state. It was also Chaumette who hinted that, perhaps, Robespierre was going too far and who remarked somewhat later, as if at random, that he had been to the Temple to see "the boy Capet."

"Is he well?" Joseph had asked blandly.

It was an innocent question, implying nothing more than polite interest in what his companion had said, but after replying in the affirmative, Chaumette added, "And under Simon's care, the child is growing to love the revolution better than his own mother and father. Simon is a good warden. He and his wife are really fond of the boy and bring him all kinds of toys and treat him with kindness. This cannot be pretended. The child recognizes it and he, in turn, will do almost anything to please Simon."

"I am very happy to hear this," Joseph remarked, with a spark of genuine interest and enthusiasm in his pale eyes.

"Yes, I think it of great importance that the boy be kept in good health and that he be instructed in the revolutionary faith. I have taken good care that he should be completely separated from those who might vitiate his mind or weaken his republican principles and that no harm should come to him."

Again Joseph agreed, with rather more heartiness than his usual tepid approval—and not long after that he mentioned, quite casually, that his cousin did business with a Citizen Saintaire, a gunsmith who lived near the Temple. The man, who owned a horse and carriage stabled by his cousin, had lived in Brittany and was well acquainted with the fishermen—who sometimes carried other cargo—of that place.

Roger's name was already familiar to Chaumette. He had been mentioned more than once by the gendarmes who guarded the Temple and by those commissioners who carried pistols. Joseph's comment merely remained an odd fact in Chaumette's mind for a day or two—a coincidence that Joseph Fouché's cousin should do business with the gunsmith that lived only one short street from the Temple. Five days later, however, a new edition of the *Vieux Cordelier*, of which far more copies were printed, was snatched up even faster. Almost immediately afterward Desmoulins was openly attacked by Robespierre himself.

Battle was joined—clemency versus terror—and Chaumette began to consider (as the more prescient Joseph had earlier) where the alternatives might lead. Obviously, either Robespierre or Danton had to die. Danton seemed the weaker of the two, but if he managed to turn the tables, the reign of the *sans-culottes* would be finished. Perhaps the republic would be maintained, but more likely the bourgeoisie would hold power, and it was not impossible that they would seek the reestablishment of a limited monarchy. That would mean the boy Capet—the dauphin—would be king.

On the other hand, Robespierre was far more likely to triumph. That would mean more and more executions—but they could not go on forever or there would soon be no people left to execute. When the flood of blood receded, there would be a reaction. Chaumette did not forget how, a few months after the massacres of September second, everyone wanted to blame someone else for them and be dissociated from what had happened. If the reaction were strong enough—again the result might be a reestablishment of the monarchy.

Chaumette pursed his lips. In either case, whoever held Louis-Charles Capet would hold the balance of power. It would be best if that essential pawn were not available to anyone but Chaumette himself. The first step in this direction was for Chaumette to complain in public to Simon that he was coddling the young Capet too much and then, in private, confide that he was being urged to use harsh, even cruel, measures to destroy the boy's health. He was rewarded by an expression of horror. Simon had, as Chaumette believed, come to love his charge. In a short time Chaumette had convinced Simon that the only safety for Louis-Charles lay in hiding him where "certain others" could not get to him.

Circumstances—or perhaps circumstances assisted by a word here or there—came to Chaumette's aid. On January 3, 1794, the commune suddenly decided that it was not right for any commissioner to hold two jobs; Simon could not be both the elected representative of his district and mentor of the boy Capet. Several other commissioners were involved, and they resigned the positions they held in the Temple at once. Simon followed suit with very little delay, although now he was utterly convinced that "enemies of the revolution" desired Louis-Charles's death.

On January fifth, Simon moved out of the rooms he had been occupying in the Temple itself, although he had not yet officially resigned his post. He was, despite de Rocheville's remarks, a man of shrewd mind and considerable manual dexterity. Most of his time was spent in fashioning a special vehicle to transport his "belongings" from the Temple to his own house and in mending a pasteboard horse for young Capet to play with. No one was surprised that Simon was unusually taciturn or that his expression was particularly grim. Several people had heard the boy pleading to be taken along, sobbing, "Simon, my dear Simon, take me with you to your shop. You can teach me to make shoes, and I will pass for your son."

Thus, on January seventh, having made all the other arrangements that would serve his purpose, Chaumette was in Roger's shop, asking about Roger's acquaintance with Breton fishermen. This question, coupled with the previous question about his horse and carriage, could have only one meaning. Roger's hand relaxed and he let go of the gun he was holding as he nodded. Either Chaumette wished to escape from France himself or he wished to arrange for someone else's escape. Nonetheless, it was necessary to be careful in what he said.

"You have heard more than was true in one way," Roger replied. "I was, at one time, friendly with one man who owned a fishing boat. I have not heard from him in a year. However, I am almost sure that my friend will have spoken of me to his friends, so perhaps it would be true to say that I have friends among the fishermen."

"What is his name and village?" Chaumette asked. "There have been disorders in Brittany. I will inquire about your friend."

Roger's hand gripped the pistol again. "He is a clever man, my friend, and not likely to be caught by trouble. I will not tell you his name or the name of his village or the name of his ship. If you have business that requires a horse and carriage and the use of a Breton fisherman who carries cargoes other than fish, I will try to discharge the business for you, but I will *tell* you nothing."

Chaumette was accustomed to power by now and very accustomed to dealing with accused and imprisoned men. He did not bother to try threats or promises to obtain the information he had requested. Something in Roger's eyes, in the set of his jaw, announced that either device would be useless. Besides, Chaumette did not need the information now. It would come to him in the natural course of the events he had planned.

"Yes, I have business. There is a child I wish to have removed to safety." Before he could control his expression, surprise flashed across Roger's face, and his breath caught a little. Chaumette frowned. "You are quick to perceive what I would have preferred you did not notice. Well, you will be just as quick to perceive that too much has already been said for me to take any chance. There is nothing to fear. Just do as you are told and you will be richly rewarded."

Wordlessly, Roger nodded and released the gun. Doubtless if Chaumette had planned to broach this topic, there were already men watching the shop, and at the same time it must be true that there was no present danger for him or for Leonie. Later . . . Roger set that worry aside. It was immediately apparent that Chaumette was a man who regarded his own interests as paramount. Whoever held the dauphin, held one last trump card in case all went awry. Roger was sure he would have no chance to betray this plot—not that he wanted to. As long as Chaumette did not know Pierre's name or village, Roger would have to take the child there himself. He only half-listened as Chaumette confirmed the facts he had already deduced, adding that Roger should go on with his business in the ordinary way, except that when he left his house he would be accompanied and that a man would remain in the house during the day to be sure he did not, by accident, let slip a word about the trip he would soon be taking.

"There is one thing," Roger said. "I know nothing about children, but my wife has young brothers. It would be best, I think, if my wife accompanied us."

"Oh, certainly," Chaumette agreed instantly. "I always intended that—a family party."

"And you have not said where you want my friend to take the child."

"As to that—perhaps nowhere. You will be employed by this friend, you and your son—or your young brother-in-law, whichever seems more reasonable. You will wait in the village, or go out on the boat as necessary, until you hear from me or until I come. If there are searches of the village by official parties, you will take the child on a fishing trip."

Roger bit his lip. "This is a bad season for such things," he growled, trying to seem a little unwilling.

Actually, he was terrified that the joy he felt would somehow show through the guard he was setting on his face and voice. Doubtless Chaumette intended to send guards along; the men might even have instructions to kill him and Leonie as soon as they made contact with Pierre, but Roger doubted they would go that far. Presumably Chaumette realized that such an action would hardly make Roger's friend cooperative. Whatever Chaumette planned, however, it was almost certain that the guards he sent would know nothing about the sea. Even if they did, Roger would lay heavy odds that Pierre knew a lot more. Accidents could happen very easily to those who were unwelcome passengers aboard a ship, and then—heigh-ho for England!

CHAPTER 19

The eagerness with which Roger accepted Chaumette's proposal was a measure of his growing need to escape from France. He should, of course, have been more suspicious, but he assumed Chaumette would depend on his trusted henchmen to enforce obedience. Certainly those who watched him now were far more attentive than those Toulon had set upon him. Since Roger had no intention of saying a word or making a move that would be suspicious, and since he had given up the idea that Leonie could be forced to escape without him, he was not much troubled by the man who sat in the kitchen listening to every word he said to his customers and, through a crack in the door, watching his gestures.

Leonie found the presence of Chaumette's watchdog far more annoying. He seemed to be directly in her way, no matter what she wanted to do. Moreover, it made her feel ridiculous to have a man tagging along at her heels when she went out shopping, and to need to speak loudly enough so that he would hear when she bargained in the market. Also, it made her neighbors afraid to talk to her. Nonetheless, she accepted the inconvenience without protest. Roger had told her the whole story after they were in bed. She was not enthusiastic about the rescue of little Louis-Charles because she was sure the boy was in no danger where he was. It was wrong, she thought, to drag him to England where he would become a pawn to be used against his own country, to become detested by the people he would be set to rule over if France was defeated. As long as Louis-Charles was in France, it was possible republicanism would become abhorrent and the child would be made monarch by the desire of the people he would rule. Then he would be loved and he would be able to do some good.

Unfortunately, the choice was not theirs. To refuse

Chaumette was to die—Leonie knew that. Therefore she accepted the situation and, with a psychological twist typical to herself, dwelt on the happy side: that she and Roger would escape from a situation that was growing intolerable. Roger explained the final bit in writing—even in bed with the listener out of the house for the night, he did not dare so much as whisper his intention of ridding themselves of Chaumette's men and taking Louis-Charles to England.

By January twelfth, Leonie, Roger, and their watchers had settled into tolerance of each other. In the afternoon Roger stuck his head into the kitchen to tell Leonie he was on his way to pick up a shipment of gun barrels he needed to finish some urgent repairs for the gendarmerie.

"Will you take Fifi along?" Leonie asked casually, ignoring the man in the kitchen. "She could use a long walk. She's getting fat since we go out so seldom."

"Better not," Roger replied. "I don't know how long I'll have to wait, and I don't like her running around loose. I should be back before closing time if anyone wants to see me, but not much before that. Citizen Vincent's gun is right on the counter, if he should come in. I've written out what was wrong and the bill. Is there anything you want me to bring back?"

"No, thank you—oh, yes, there is. The baker is holding a loaf for us. Will you pick that up? My watchdog," Leonie tipped her head toward the door to indicate Chaumette's man outside, "looked a little weary after following me all over the market this morning."

Roger laughed and went out, looking over his shoulder to make sure the man trailing him would not get lost. As soon as they were away from the immediate neighborhood, he stopped and gestured the man forward, asked his name, which was Garnier, and suggested that they might as well walk together. After his initial surprise Garnier agreed, and they strolled along, chatting agreeably enough about general things, like the high price of everything and the way the war was progressing. This last was a safe enough subject, France having expelled the British from Toulon and holding its own on other fronts.

Meanwhile, Leonie had moved into the shop. She was aware, after a few minutes, of men's voices at the back door, but she paid no attention aside from an irritated hope that they would not eat all of the potted chicken she had prepared for dinner. In another few minutes the back door closed and the voices stopped. Then the bell attached to the front door jangled. Leonie automatically stood and looked toward the door, ready to answer a question or serve. The front door opened part way, as if someone were holding it from the outside and speaking to a companion or looking at something in the street. Naturally, Leonie's attention remained fixed on the door as she waited for whoever was there to enter. She heard a soft movement in the kitchen behind her, and assumed it was the watchdog coming closer to the door so he could listen better. Thus she had no warning at all before a shout of "No!" and a simultaneous explosion in her head submerged her in blackness.

"You fool!" Chaumette spat at the man who now supported Leonie in his arms. "I told you to seize her, not to strike her. Imbecile!"

"I'm sorry," the henchman stammered, his eyes wide with terror. "I was afraid if I only held her, she would cry out."

"How could she cry out if your hand was over her mouth?" Chaumette asked furiously. Then, shrugging his shoulders, he added coldly, "It is too late to mend it now, but the blame for this lunacy had better not come upon me. You had better convince the lady that this was an accident, your fault, not mine, and that I mean her only well. She must be made to understand that I would not for the world have had this happen. She must be sweetened so that when I come, she will be willing to write a letter to her husband that will convince him she is well and happy, surrounded by every luxury, kindness, and comfort."

"Of course, of course," the man stammered.

Chaumette stared at him for a moment, then ground his teeth. "Danou, you are a jackass! I can read in your face what you intend. Do you know nothing of women? You think you can knock her around a little and she will agree to anything. Well, you are wrong! Somehow she will write a word, a phrase, that will betray what you have done. What she writes of must be *real*."

"No, no, I never intended—"

"Let me make myself perfectly clear, Danou. To be sure I am not blamed for anything you do—and that I get the truth of it—I will tell *Citoyenne* Saintaire that I am furious with what you have done, and I will assure her that you will not be her keeper now that I know she was ill-treated. If she does not *beg* that you be set to guard her . . . Remember, Madame la Guillotine grows hungrier and hungrier every day—and what will happen to you before you get to her maw will make you think her kiss a sweet one. Do you understand me now?"

"Monsieur Chaumette—"

"Don't you *dare* call me 'monsieur.' I am Citizen Chaumette, just as you are Citizen Danou. We are equal—remember it! And do not waste my time with pleading. You have done enough harm. Take her to the house we have prepared for her. Here, I will hold her while you wrap her in that rug." Then his rage rose again. "Stupid imbecile! Now you will need to bind her and gag her in case she wakes while you are transporting her. And remember not to let the horse go above a trot. The last thing we need is to draw attention and have someone find a woman bound and gagged in the fiacre."

By now Danou was completely quelled. He removed the kerchief from around his neck to bind Leonie's hands and used a strip of towel from the kitchen to gag her, then wrapped her in the rug he had just brought in and slung her over his shoulder. Meanwhile, the man he had been speaking to in the kitchen previously came down with some of Leonie's clothes in a sack. Fifi looked up but at first did not move from the corner in which her bed lay. She recognized the scent of this man. He and the other had been in and out of the kitchen many times, and although they had never been named "friend" to her, which meant she must avoid them if they tried to touch her, the god and goddess spoke to them without fear or anger; therefore Fifi did not growl or think of biting.

The little bitch came to her feet, however, when the sack passed her. Faintly, there was the scent of the goddess. Then Danou walked by her with his burden. Intriguingly, it smelled powerfully of the goddess, mixed with other, less appealing odors. Fifi followed, slipping out the door as the man with the sack held it wide open so that Danou's rug-wrapped burden would not bang against anything. Down toward the end of the alley, where a fiacre was being held by a casual lounger, Fifi followed, sniffing and sniffing and greatly puzzled by what had happened. Her instincts told her it was not right that these men should remove things that smelled of the goddess. On the other hand, it had been made clear to her that these men were to be tolerated, even though they were not "friends."

At the end of the alley Fifi hesitated. The sack was thrown into the carriage. Then the man who had carried it seized the thing that smelled like the goddess and yet did not smell like her. Just as the other man lifted it into the carriage, it gave a jerk and a muffled sound emerged. That was enough. Fifi bounded forward, but it was too late. The door on the fiacre had shut, the horse began to move. Fifi barked twice, but the carriage did not stop, and the little bitch gave up that useless protest and began to follow. As muffled as Leonie's moan had been through gag and rug wrapping, there was no chance Fifi would not recognize her voice. It was not merely the scent of the goddess that was being carried away, but the goddess herself. She had disappeared once from Fifi's life, and the little bitch had no intention of permitting that to happen again.

The moan had been heard by Danou also. If Leonie had remained unconscious, he might have watched behind to be sure that no one was following them. It was far more important to Danou's mind, however, to pacify Leonie. Let his companion, who was driving, watch for followers. The second man did glance back several times, but he was looking for men or horses and carriages. In any case, at first Fifi followed so close that the body of the fiacre hid her from view. She was able to keep up in the beginning because the horse was not being urged to produce speed; however, she was a small dog. She had to run hard, and she had no breath left for barking.

Inside the carriage, Leonie's first connected thought was of the pain in her head. Her next, even before she realized that she was bound and gagged, was annoyance at the insistent voice in her ear. It was so urgent, although low, and so annoying, that she had to listen even though her poor head resounded like a drum and every thump produced a lance of pain.

". . . forgive me, *citoyenne*. It was an accident, I swear it. I will explain everything. I beg you not to be afraid. It must seem terrible to you, I know, but you will pity me when you understand, and you will forgive me. Don't be angry because you were ill-treated. I swear no harm will come to you. I am so sorry it was necessary to tie you and gag you, but . . ."

The voice continued, but the sense of it was lost to Leonie as she realized she *was* bound and gagged and in total darkness. Instinctively, she fought to free herself. The voice in her ear responded, trembling with fear.

"Please, please don't struggle, *citoyenne*. You will hurt yourself. Have patience, please. You will be released as soon as we arrive."

The terror in the voice was so apparent that Leonie became momentarily more concerned for its owner than for herself. She had not yet had time to feel frightened. The pain in her head and the complete inexplicability of what had happened had produced confusion rather than fear. Now the assurances she was being given and the fact that she was being supported gently so that the jolts of the carriage—as the word came into her head, Leonie realized she was being abducted. Again instinct conquered, and she writhed and tried to scream.

"Madame Saintaire, please, please be still. No one intends you harm. Everything will be explained. Please!"

This time it was less the assurance of the voice than a conviction of helplessness that quieted Leonie. Her struggles had brought a terrifying sense of suffocation upon her so that she had to stop. With her mouth bound she could only suck air through her nose, and that was enveloped in the folds of the rag. For a time no thought could pierce the need for breath, but as her laboring lungs provided for the needs of her body while the agony in her head, which had been heightened by her struggles to move and breathe, subsided, her mind began to catch up with what had happened.

She had been in the shop. The door had half-opened—yes, but no one had come in from outside and attacked her. As she thought about it, the pain in her head could be localized to the back right. So someone had struck her from behind. But Chaumette's man had been in the kitchen. There had been voices there. The door had closed. Could someone have overpowered Chaumette's man? She thought that over carefully, fighting down the fear that threatened to set her choking again. No, there had been no anxiety or warning in either voice, no sound of a struggle or a body falling. Perhaps—no, Fifi was in the kitchen. If one man struck the other in a surprise move, Fifi would have barked. The little dog did not like violence.

Then it had to be one of Chaumette's men who abducted her. But that was mad! Roger had agreed to do everything Chaumette asked of him. What good would it be to— Leonie did not even need to complete that question to herself. Chaumette was cleverer than either she or Roger had realized. As had happened before, they had been blinded by their desire to have what Chaumette offered. Fear gripped her then, but not the kind of fear that would make her struggle against her bonds. She was a weapon to make Roger obey, to prevent him from escaping to England. While she was a hostage in Chaumette's hands, Roger would never rid himself of the guards or try to escape.

The conclusion she had reached seemed the only possible answer, and as Leonie again became aware of the careful way she was being steadied inside whatever she had been wrapped in, that answer fit what the voice had said. But the attempts to save her from being bruised recalled to her mind that she was in a carriage. Where were they taking her? How far? Panic welled up inside the shell of rational fear and threatened to suffocate her again. No, she told herself, *it cannot be far.* Even Chaumette would not dare remove her from the city. There was too much chance that an overly officious guard at the gate would investigate so odd-looking a bundle as she must be. In confirmation, the movement of the fiacre slowed even more, and the voice, which had been silent while Leonie caught her breath, spoke again.

"We have arrived, Madame Saintaire. Please do not be frightened. I must carry you inside. As soon as we are in the house, you will be released."

Inside she would be trapped! Leonie stiffened as she felt herself shifted and prepared to kick her abductor. However, the cocoon surrounding her prevented her from bending her knees much, and she thought better of the idea. First of all, the kick would have no effect, swathed as she was, except possibly to annoy the man who was about to lift her. Second, even if she hurt him, what good would it do? Bound as she was, she could not unroll herself and run away. She could not even scream for help while in the street. She was as effectively trapped now as she would be inside—more effectively. If she seemed passive and they did release her as the voice had promised, she might have a better chance to escape later. Accordingly, Leonie did not resist when she felt arms slide under her.

However, she was not lifted. A fusillade of sharp barks erupted. An unfamiliar voice cried, "Damn that dog! I'll kill it." Leonie, who had recognized Fifi's bark gave a convulsive wriggle, which brought her to her feet and, even gagged, managed to utter a muffled shriek. The voice that was familiar bellowed, "No! Don't hurt the creature. Quick, carry this—this rug inside. Quick, I say."

Now fear for Fifi made Leonie lunge and twist and cry out behind her gag so that the second man could barely grasp her.

"Stop!" the known voice whispered harshly. "Stop! I will bring the dog in to you safe. Stay still!"

It was not an easy decision to make. The voice could be lying. It occurred to Leonie that she could cause great trouble by squirming. If anyone was on the street or looked out of a window, a violently animated rug would certainly arouse suspicion. On the other hand, anyone who saw would probably be afraid to interfere. The best a person might do was report such a happening to the Section leader. But, if the men were Chaumette's, such a report would probably be ignored. Besides, she simply could not struggle for long. Already her head throbbed ten times as hard, and her lungs felt as if they were on fire. Leonie allowed herself to sag forward into the arms that had been seeking to restrain her.

As she was lifted and carried, she heard the familiar voice calling, "Come, Fifi, come. Don't be silly, now, you know me. Come."

No, Leonie prayed silently, *no. Run, Fifi. Run home to Roger*.

That prayer was not answered. Although Fifi would not have come to Danou, since she had never been told he was a "friend," the scent of her goddess, the muffled voice and movement that proved the goddess herself was attached to the scent, that it was not merely clothing, was being taken inside the same place where the man who was not a "friend" was urging her to go. That was too complex a problem for the little dog. She only knew that it was right for her to be with the goddess, even if the goddess chose to shroud herself in a thing that smelled unpleasant. Nonetheless, Fifi did not like it. She followed the man carrying the goddess, but she barked her protest all the way, and when Leonie was set on her feet, Fifi rushed growling to pull at the covering she disapproved of so much.

Danou hastened to satisfy the dog's desire, although he was not thinking of Fifi. The other man, however, launched a kick at her, which Fifi managed to avoid although she yipped in protest. This drew a shout of rage from Danou. "Damn you, Panel, get out! Didn't you hear Citizen Chaumette say that Madame Saintaire was to have everything she wanted? You fool! Is it the way to please her, to kick her dog? Get out!"

The rage in the voice was clear enough to make Leonie reasonably sure that what was said was true. Her deductions must be correct. She was to be a hostage for Roger's behavior. And for some reason she could not yet understand, she was to be well treated. The rug was coming off. Leonie trembled with the desire to run, not because she was frightened but because her capture was the ruin of all their hopes. Don't be a fool, she told herself. You can't get away now. You must seem to accept whatever they say. You must be quiet, docile—*stupid*—as you were for Louis. Perhaps you can fool them, escape later. The rug fell away completely.

"Do not scream," the man said, "and I will take off the gag." Leonie could see that his face was twisted with concern. "Believe me, no harm will come to you, but you can't escape. The doors are all locked."

His voice was raised, but only to be heard over Fifi's barking. Leonie nodded and he went behind her and undid the gag.

"Hush, Fifi," Leonie ordered as soon as her lips were free.

"Thank you, madame," the man said with heartfelt sincerity. "I am Jacques Danou, and I am sorry, very sorry you were hurt. It was a misunderstanding—a complete misunderstanding," he went on as Leonie raised a hand to her throbbing head. "Will you sit down? Would you like some wine? Perhaps you would like to lie down and rest for a while?"

"Yes," Leonie said faintly.

The pain in her head seemed to have been greatly inten-

sified by the light, and she felt sick and dizzy. She had
quieted Fifi to spare herself, not to please Danou, for each
bark had been like a knife-thrust. In fact, his voice, although not as sharp, was also painfully unpleasant. Leonie
felt an urgent need for quiet. She hoped she would be able
to think and decide when the pain diminished, what, if anything, she could do.

Danou sidled to the door with his eyes fixed on her and
called over his shoulder that Madame Saintaire was going
up to the bedchamber. Wine should be brought.

"And cold water and a cloth for my head," Leonie whispered.

The order was relayed at once. Then, looking at her
greenish pallor, Danou asked if she wanted him to carry
her. Leonie barely repressed a shudder and insisted she
would walk. She managed to do so, but the effort of climbing the stairs brought on an attack of vertigo so that she
barely managed to reach the bed before she collapsed. She
lay nearly unconscious, hearing distantly Danou's strident
yell that Panel should bring the wine and other restora-
tives. The thought of him touching her, ministering to her,
was so repellent, however, that she roused herself when she
heard him approaching the bed.

"Go away," she mumbled. "Go away and leave me to
myself."

"But madame—"

"Go away," Leonie wailed.

The anguish in her voice brought Fifi into immediate
action. She growled and rushed to nip at Danou's ankles.
Restraining his immediate impulse, which was to kick the
dog's head in, he retreated, closing and locking the door
behind him. Briefly, he considered leaving the house, leaving the city, even leaving the country. But that would mean
losing everything he had so recently gained. He had been a
carter, dressed in rags, barely surviving, before Chaumette
had employed him. Now he took what he liked, where he
liked, and no one could say no to him. He ordered Panel to
sit in the room opposite Leonie's and listen for her voice
and then went out. It was nearly dinnertime. He would
procure the best dinner that could be found. That would
give him another chance to approach that unreasonable
Saintaire slut and try again to ingratiate himself with her.

The prompt response to her demand for privacy soothed

Leonie. She hushed Fifi again and managed to soak the
cloth in the water, wring it out, and apply it to her splitting
head. The pain receded a little, but the dizziness remained.
Thoughts jumbled and jostled in her brain. She wept a little, grieving over the lost opportunity. They would never
escape, she thought, and then pushed that despairing notion away. She would get away and get back to Roger, she
would! But later, not now. Now she was too sick, too
dizzy. Later.

As it happened, Roger did not need to wait long for the
gun parts. The package was made up and he paid. It took
him longer to find a carriage. It was one thing to walk
across the city empty-handed, another to carry back a
heavy load. Roger signaled Garnier and asked whether he
wished to ride home with him.

"If not," he said, "I will wait while you find another
carriage. I do not wish Citizen Chaumette to think I am
trying to avoid his watchdog."

He might not have been so polite if he had known that
his efforts to avoid Chaumette's suspicion were in vain.
However, he had no way of knowing that, and he did not
even suspect it when he entered his shop and found Chaumette seated in a chair taken from the kitchen. If Roger
felt anything, it was a faint hope that Leonie had not been
stubborn and argued. He did not think she would be so
foolish, because he had explained that Chaumette was a
real power in the revolutionary government and not to be
slighted, but . . . His thoughts were interrupted when
Chaumette said sharply, "Please do not resist, this is only a
precaution," and simultaneously his arms were seized from
behind.

Roger jerked convulsively in spite of the warning. One
man staggered against him, but the other held firm and
Chaumette said even more sharply, "No! I only wish to
speak to you."

"Why should a man be held down to be spoken to?"
Roger snarled, but he did not continue to pull at his captors. It would not be possible for him to take them both
when they were completely on guard.

"Because I am about to tell you something you will regard as unpleasant, something that will make you very angry. I assure you there is no real cause for alarm or even

anger. You will see that I have done no more than take a necessary precaution."

"No!" Roger shouted, guessing at once and beginning to struggle. "No! Leonie! Leonie!"

"She is perfectly safe. Quite unhurt. Not even frightened," Chaumette roared over Roger's protests.

"I'll kill you," Roger hissed, his eyes blazing. "I'll kill you."

"No, you will not because you do not and will not have the slightest *cause* to kill me. I tell you your wife is quite safe. She is aware of what has happened and why. She is comfortably lodged, not imprisoned."

"You lie!"

Chaumette took in the glaring eyes, the cords standing in Roger's neck as he strained for freedom. The two burly thugs that held him were barely succeeding in controlling him. For a moment Roger's life, and Leonie's too, hung in the balance while Chaumette considered whether it would be possible to quell so deep a violence. However, the very strength of Roger's reaction marked his devotion to the woman. Thus, the deeper the anger now, the more abject would be Roger's obedience when he came to accept the situation. However, Chaumette realized he would need to be very careful. He must not hint that Roger's wife had agreed with what was done—that might make a too-loving husband jealous. He was also proud of his own foresight. The girl was silly. If they convinced her she was comfortable, safe, and would be richly rewarded for compliance, she would be able to allay Roger's doubts so that he would not even contemplate betrayal.

"I do not lie. I did not say *Citoyenne* Saintaire came willingly. She *was* abducted, but she was not hurt in any way, and the matter has been explained to her so that she is not afraid. She has been assured that you are safe, that we mean neither of you any harm, and that she will be returned to you as soon as you place in my hands the—the package—"

"You mean h—it is gone?" Roger cried. "But I do not have it!"

"No, no," Chaumette soothed. "The package will be delivered to you just as I told you before. However, I find I will not be able to travel with you as I thought I would. You will need to store it for me for a while. I need assurance that you will not tamper with the contents, however, or use them for your own purposes. Oh, I know you to be an honest man, Saintaire, but some temptations are *too* great. It would be unforgivable on my part to place such a temptation in your path without providing you with an even greater inducement to ignore it."

By the time Chaumette finished speaking, Roger had stopped struggling and merely glared. After a moment more, he dropped his eyes. "I see," he muttered.

"I am sure you do, and you will see more clearly every moment. I have sworn your wife is safe, and living in complete comfort. You have no reason to believe me, but I will prove what I say is true. You may write a letter to her, ask her any question or questions to which only she would know the answers, or any question about her situation. The only restriction on her answer will be that she will not be able to hint at where she is being kept. You may write to her every day, if you like, even after you take the package away with you, and you will receive her answers. No one will read your letters. Hers must be read, of course. I am sorry to intrude on your privacy, but you will understand it cannot be helped."

"We can write to each other?" Roger breathed, his eyes lifting to Chaumette's.

"Certainly. Depending on your behavior and hers, it may even be possible to arrange a meeting between you—if there is a delay in obtaining the package. In any case your separation will not be for very long. I may need the package returned, or may come to get it, very soon. If I come, I will bring your wife, of course. However, at the most it will only be a few months—before summer certainly she will be returned to you."

Roger was standing perfectly still now. Reason had replaced rage. There was no way he could get free of the men who held him, seize Chaumette, and wring Leonie's hiding place out of him. For now, he must seem to accept the situation. "You can tell your men to let me go," Roger said quietly. "I am not angry anymore, except," he raised his eyes so that Chaumette should not think he was trying to hide the expression in them, "I agreed to care for your package in good faith. I did not even tell my wife about it." That was a safe enough lie. Roger had told Leonie to pretend she did not know why they were watched except that her husband was engaged in special business with the commune. "I felt it would be soon enough to know when the package arrived. I am not so pleased that I cannot be trusted."

Chaumette shrugged. He had already signaled his henchmen to release Roger and they had done so. "It is no special suspicion of you, I assure you," he said, "only that the package is so precious that I almost wish I did not need to trust myself. And I want you to understand that I am not holding your wife in order to deprive you of anything I have promised you. That will be exactly as we agreed. To show my good faith, I will leave you a small token of what will be yours when your service to me is completed."

While he spoke, Chaumette pulled a packet from his coat and laid it on the counter. Then he walked toward the door, Roger and the men who still flanked him turning slowly also. Suddenly, Roger shrugged and moved toward the counter, but a single sidelong glance told him that although the guards had not followed and were moving toward Chaumette, he could not pull the gun from his pocket or reach the one behind the counter in time. Besides, what good would the pistol do? He could not kill all three, and Leonie's life was at stake.

"I will keep our agreement," Roger said. "I always intended to do so, as you will realize if you question the guards who were left in the house and who followed my wife and me. However," he hefted the packet as if estimating its value, "however, I do understand what you have said. I do not like it, but I understand it."

"Good. When you have written your letter, you just hand it to Garnier, who will be in his usual place. You will have an answer tomorrow, about noon. You probably will not see me again before the package is delivered. The man who delivers it will have final instructions for you. Please obey him exactly, and all will be well."

Then he was out the door. Roger stood like a statue for a few minutes. Finally he dropped the packet of gold coins on the counter and rubbed his hand frantically up and down his breeches as if to rid it of a corrosive slime. After that, he leaned forward against the counter with his head in his hands and struggled with his rage and his grief and his hopelessness. Fool that he was! Fool! Fool! How could he have been so stupid as to accept Chaumette's hasty assur-

ance that first afternoon that it would be best to have a
woman accompany them to care for the child. He should
have realized from the very speed with which Chaumette
accepted the idea that he had no intention of fulfilling the
agreement.

Roger's hands writhed through his hair, tugging at it. He
must think of something, some way to find Leonie. No,
first he must write to her. Whatever Chaumette said, the
poor child must be terrified. Roger bit his lips. What if they
beat her and threatened her to make her write as they
wished? He must tell her to be quiet and obedient, to accept what had happened. He must find a way to give her
hope without implying that he intended to find her and free
her. He did not believe for a moment that his letters would
not be scrutinized most carefully—that remark of Chaumette's was only another trap.

It was now clear to Roger that Chaumette was far cleverer and more ruthless than he had guessed. This was
scarcely consoling. It was as likely that Chaumette would
have Leonie and himself killed once the poor little dauphin
was returned to him. That would be their reward. Roger
shook himself. He must not think of it. He must try to
believe that he would find Leonie before any harm came to
her. But that was impossible. He was watched every moment. The first suspicious move he made would produce
retaliation. They would do something to Leonie to punish
him. He began to shake.

Finally, he drew a deep breath, knowing he must get
himself under control. He must not display his fear and
suspicion either to Leonie or to Chaumette, and he must
write at once so that she would receive the letter as soon as
possible. Blindly, Roger began to feel around under the
counter for a sheet of paper and the bottle of ink. He drew
his knife to mend the pen, but seeing how his hand was
shaking, he walked into the kitchen and poured half a glass
of brandy. Having knocked that back in one gulp, he
glared around—and realized there was no one to glare at.
The man who had sat in the kitchen watching and listening was gone.

Although he could see no immediate way in which that
could help, the absence of the listener made him feel a little
better. It pointed out one little hope. Chaumette must be
short of really trustworthy men. Roger returned to the shop

mulling that over in his mind, trimmed the quill, and began to write. Running through the letter after it was done, he felt he had succeeded in hiding the panic that still rolled over him in waves. He explained what had happened, why Chaumette (without naming him) had done what he had done—carefully writing of a precious package to be delivered—and urged Leonie to be calm and obedient. Also, because he knew Chaumette would expect it, he told Leonie he was permitted to ask questions to which only he and she could know the answers. He would, he said, ask one such question in each letter—and he asked what lay behind the warped cask.

He had tried to think of a way to include some secret communication in the letter, but he was still too upset to concentrate. Besides, he thought as he folded the paper and ran wax over it—pressing on the wax the tool he used to mark the guns he worked on—it was too soon to begin to cheat. Let Chaumette come to believe he was hopeless and would not attempt to find Leonie. Let him think they had both accepted the situation and were blind to the ultimate end to which it must come. Since there was no longer a man to listen in the shop, perhaps . . .

The bell of the shop jangled, and Roger jumped nervously. It was almost dark, but he had forgotten to shutter the place and lock the door. He gritted his teeth. The last thing he wanted was one of those damned commissioners, yet he did not dare turn one of them away. That would be out of character. Taking tight hold over the urge to shout, "I'm closed, go away," he rose to finish the business as soon as possible. However, he never asked a question. His mouth dropped open. His eyes bulged.

"I was told you were an honest gunsmith," Pierre said to him, raising his brows questioningly.

CHAPTER 20

Leonie had slept for several hours after Danou had locked her in the room upstairs, exhausted by pain and nervousness. When she woke, her head was much better, although it was still tender where she had been struck and ached a little when she shook it. Her initial confusion at finding herself fully dressed in bed was soon resolved by her memory of what had happened. She rolled to her side to slide out of the bed, rolled back abruptly as something hard and with sharp edges dug into her hip, and then clapped her hand hard to her mouth to prevent herself from shrieking with laughter.

Her pistols! She was still wearing the pistols she always carried. Pain and shock had blanked them from her mind. A whole series of emotions chased across her brain: gratitude that there was obviously no woman in the house, for surely a woman would have tried to remove her clothing to make her more comfortable; amusement that the men who had abducted her had never thought to search for weapons; exultation at the knowledge that she could escape any time she wanted.

Then the thrill faded. The pistols made escape possible but certainly did not assure it. She could fire them, but her ability to aim was nonexistent. They were useful as a threat or as a defense against a crowd—if you did not hit one you were likely enough to hit another, and no one could be sure at whom you had aimed. However, the threat was useless against two men who could come at one from different directions. For a woman alone, who was not skilled with pistols and whose captors were desperate to keep her, the guns were no certain key to freedom.

Leonie lay quite still considering what she really had and the odds she faced. She did not wish to move around for fear she would make some sound that would attract Danou or the other man—Panel, Danou had called him—until she had decided what to do. Admittedly each pistol carried extra balls and powder, but she was so slow at loading that when both guns had been fired she would be virtually defenseless.

If there were only one man in the house, it might be enough. She could call and, most probably, he would come and unlock the door. If she stood close by with the pistol hidden by her skirt, she could almost certainly raise it and fire point-blank, too close to miss, before he realized what she was doing. Even if the first shot did not kill, the second would. Leonie shuddered. It was one thing to fire into a raging crowd. You never really saw the person you hit; and you had never known that person, either. It was quite another thing to contemplate killing in cold blood a man who, although he had abducted you, was himself acting out of fear on the orders of another. Danou had been as gentle and considerate as possible, under the circumstances.

Leonie struggled with the thought for a while and then remembered with some relief that Danou was not alone in the house. That other man had wanted to kill Fifi. Where was Fifi? A whisper settled that question. The little bitch crawled out from under the bed and leaped up to lick Leonie's face. She tucked the creature into the curve of her arm and went back to her problems. If both men were still in the house, the plan would not work. The sound of the first shot would warn the other man. He would either get help or find some way to deal with an armed prisoner. Certainly he would not walk up to her and let her shoot him too, and she could not aim well enough to shoot him at a distance.

Then there was the question of getting out of the house. The doors would be locked. Leonie could not imagine her captors taking a chance on her beginning to scream for help if someone accidentally walked in. The keys would not be in the locks. Even if the man she killed was the one who carried the keys, she would need to search for them, run down the stairs, open the door. . . . Again, unless the man she killed was the only one guarding her, it would not work. The first necessity, then, was to be sure there was only one man in the house with her—and, of course, keeping the fact that she had the pistols a secret.

It was so unusual for a woman to carry a pistol at all

that no one would think of searching her. But finding out
how many men were in the house, Leonie feared, might be
very difficult. If she were to be kept locked in the room, for
example, there might be no need for more than one guard.
But how would she know? She sighed. It would not be possible to act at once. She would have to discover how
strictly she would be watched, by whom, the routine of the
household—one man might regularly go out to fetch food,
for example. It would also be useful to try to find out
where she was.

Leonie shooed Fifi off the bed and got up herself. It was
very dark in the room, but she could make out the window.
Could she get out the window? She shivered again. It
would be better to escape without killing anyone. She went
to look out and saw only a walled garden with a high,
wrought-iron gate—and the window, she saw, was nailed
shut. Even if she could get the nails out, tear up the sheets,
and climb down, there would still be the wall to get over—
the gate would certainly be locked. There were spikes on
the wall, too. Leonie sighed again. If she was locked in the
room with no chance to find out who else was in the house,
she might have to try that route, but it would be best to
explore other possibilities first.

One thing was immediately apparent—she was closely
watched. Someone had heard her get out of bed. While she
still stood at the window, the key turned in the lock.
Leonie whirled to face the door, but to her surprise there
was a scratch and Danou's voice asked permission to enter.
That was a pleasant relief. Leonie remembered the repeated
adjurations not to be frightened and the assurances that her
wants would be fulfilled as quickly and completely as possible, but she had not been sure whether that was only to
induce her to enter her prison quietly. It seemed, however,
that courtesy toward her was still the order of the day.

"Yes? Come in," Leonie called.

Danou entered carrying a branch of candles, his face
wreathed in smiles. "I hope you are feeling better, *citoyenne*," he said, "but I have here something which I am sure
will make you well, even if there are some lingering effects
of the sad mistake." He held out a folded sheet of paper.
Leonie could not imagine what it was, and did not move at
once. "Take it," he urged. "It is a letter from your husband."

"From Roger?"

Danou nodded, but Leonie still did not reach out. She could not, would not, believe that Roger had arranged this abduction. Yet how else could he know where to send a letter? Even if he had done it to keep her safe . . . No, Danou had said Chaumette. Could Roger have made some agreement with Chaumette? . . .

"I swear I will not touch you, *citoyenne*," Danou was urging. "Do not be afraid of me, I beg you. Come and take your letter."

He could not decide whether to tell the stupid woman that his master would have him killed if she did not stop being afraid of him. He thought the delivery of the letter would solve all his problems with her, but the little ninny seemed to be afraid even of the sheet of paper. And women were so unpredictable. Some would rush to his defense, if they knew his danger; but others would take a spiteful delight in getting him into trouble.

Leonie was hardly aware of him as her mind raced over the possibilities. She came to the conclusion that the letter could not be from Roger. Possibly Chaumette did not think she could read, or perhaps he thought she was fool enough not to recognize Roger's handwriting. Finally what Danou was saying penetrated her brain. He was apologizing again for the "accident" in which she had been hurt, but then he went on in a positively tearful voice to tell her that she was to choose her own keeper and that, if she did not choose him, his master would have him killed.

"Please take the letter. Please do not be afraid," he urged.

Slowly Leonie came toward him, considering what he had said. She took the letter but did not look at it. "When can I see Citizen Chaumette?" she asked.

"He came while you were asleep, *citoyenne*. We did not wish to disturb you because—because of the accident to your head. He will come again tomorrow to take your answer back to your husband."

"I may write to my husband?" Leonie asked incredulously.

"Yes, indeed, only—only you may not describe the house or what you see outside it. You may say anything else—anything at all."

"How nice," Leonie said flatly, but then she smiled,

trying to wipe out the sardonic inference. For now she must be stupid and docile—especially stupid. "But I cannot read in the dark," she complained.

"No, of course not. I will leave the candles if you like. And I have a meal for you—but it may be a little over-cooked because you slept so long. Shall I bring the food up, or would you prefer to come down?"

"I may come down?" Leonie sounded tremulous and hopeful, but her heart sank.

"Yes, indeed, *citoyenne*. I have told you and told you that we want you to be comfortable and content."

If she were to be permitted the freedom of the house, there had to be more than one jailer. Leonie swallowed her disappointment. She had better find out just what the situation was as soon as possible. "I will come down. May I come down now?"

"Certainly."

Danou stepped out and held the candles high. Leonie followed, glancing around curiously. There were three other doors in the small hallway into which the stairs rose. One was open and a man, whose regular features would have made him very handsome except that they were spoiled by a self-conscious leer and filthy garments, was sitting on a chair in the doorway. He rose when Leonie stepped out of her room and followed her down the stairs, a few steps behind but quite close enough to grab her if she should try to push Danou and make a break for freedom. He murmured something under his breath, but Leonie was too wrapped in her own thoughts to make out what it was. The closeness with which she was guarded confirmed her disappointment at being given the freedom of the house, but her spirits lifted a little when Danou guided her into the parlor on the left of the stairs. The lower floor had an "empty" feel to it. If there were only the two men, something might be managed.

There was a stove giving out a comfortable heat. Leonie realized that the pipe from it must have gone up to the roof through the room in which she slept and warmed that also. This room, then, was also at the back of the house, and there could be no question of getting to a front window. After the candles on the table and in the wall sconces had been lit, Danou went out. Panel remained in the corridor by the open door, watching. Leonie had expected that from the way he had followed her down the stairs, so that she felt no additional disappointment and was able to give full attention to the letter Danou had handed her. What leaped to her eyes was Roger's gunsmith's mark on the wax that sealed the folded sheet. Leonie barely suppressed a cry. She had convinced herself that the letter could not be from Roger, but that conviction was badly shaken. Would Chaumette think of using the tradesman's mark? How could he get it? That was one tool Roger locked away most carefully; it was the symbol of his pride in his craft.

Hastily, with trembling fingers, Leonie tore open the seals. It was Roger's handwriting! Had he . . . No. *First read it*, she admonished herself. Having done so, Leonie stared blankly at the wall for a few minutes, more frightened than she had been since she regained consciousness in the carriage. What he told her exactly confirmed what she had deduced for herself, but the stiff, careful phrasing, the strict admonitions to be obedient—that was not Roger.

Anxiously she scanned the writing itself. It seemed uncertain, a bit tremulous, as if his hand had been shaky. *He must be under restraint*, Leonie thought. Perhaps Chaumette had hurt him or threatened him—both most likely. Her lip drew back in a snarl. She would kill them! Somehow, she would manage to kill them. Sooner or later one of the men would have to leave the house. She would kill the other, hide the body, reload her guns, and kill the second when he came in. No quiver of reluctance disturbed her now. These monsters obeyed Chaumette, who had given the orders to hurt Roger. They deserved to die.

"Citoyenne?" Danou's voice held shock.

Leonie turned her head away sharply and covered her face. All she could do was pray that the man would take her expression of hate as a grimace of weeping.

"Here is your dinner, *citoyenne*," Danou said, struggling to keep his voice smooth while his fingers twitched in a desire to beat the lachrymose bitch silly. "And a sheet of paper and a pen and ink. You will wish to write to your husband. Citizen Chaumette would like to bring him the letter before noon tomorrow. You would not want him to worry, now, would you?" he wheedled.

"Yes, I will write, but please leave me alone," Leonie whispered.

It was apparent from Danou's expression that he was not

pleased with Leonie's attitude. Nonetheless, he complied, setting down the tray he carried, which bore the writing materials as well as the dishes. The new evidence of obedience to her wishes in anything that would not facilitate her escape calmed Leonie somewhat. It must be of importance that she should seem satisfied with her situation—at least as satisfied as possible under the circumstances. Then she *must* seem so, to allay suspicion. Leonie went to the table and began to eat her rather dried-up dinner, feeding Fifi what she could not get down her own throat, while she considered what to say to Roger.

Finally she drew the writing things to her. "My dearest beloved," she wrote, "I received your letter. Do not worry about me. I have been well treated and no one has threatened me or done me any harm. I was very frightened at first, but now that you have explained why I was stolen away, I am more at ease. I do not wish to remain here and be parted from you, but since you say I must I will try to endure it with patience. Fifi is here with me and keeps me company."

At that moment, Fifi rose and pawed Leonie's knee, whining softly. Leonie looked down at her, puzzled, and then realized that the poor creature had not been out for many hours. She got up from the table and went to the door. Panel blocked the exit, smiling.

"My dog must go out," Leonie said to him.

He seemed a bit disappointed by what she said, which was puzzling, but after a brief hesitation he shouted, "Danou! The *citoyenne* says her dog must go out."

This time when Danou appeared from a room a little farther back and on the other side of the corridor, Leonie smiled at him. "Please," she said softly, "the dog must be let out to relieve herself."

"How is that to be managed?" he asked irritably.

"I saw a garden from the window," Leonie suggested. "Can she go out there?"

"Very well. Come, Fifi," Danou called.

But naturally Fifi would not go with him, although she whined and ran back and forth. At last Leonie asked if she could come to the back door. "My husband has told me I must stay here," she assured Danou. "I will not try to run out or make any noise."

The men were not enthusiastic about the idea, even with

Leonie's assurances, but Fifi began to bark and Leonie continued to plead, and finally they agreed. With a man on each side holding her by the arms, Leonie was allowed to go to the back door. Fifi followed, and when the door was opened, ran out readily. She sniffed here and there, trotted about, and then suddenly slipped through the bars of the gate. Danou uttered an obscenity.

"It is not my fault if she gets lost," he said angrily to Leonie. "You told me to let her out. And you need not ask to go after her or expect either of us to chase her."

"No, no," Leonie said as calmly as she could. "She won't get lost. She will return in a little while. You can close the door. She will bark or scratch on it when she wants to come in."

The spurt of excitement that Leonie was struggling to control had nothing to do with fear of Fifi being lost. In a strange place, the bitch never went far. If she had not gotten lost during their trip to Paris or because of the moves they had made in Paris, she would not get lost now. However, Leonie had been struck by an idea the moment she realized Fifi could get through the gate. She was by no means sure it would work because she had no idea over how great a distance the little dog could find her way. However, it was worth a chance. Tomorrow, after Chaumette had come and gone, she would tell Fifi to "find Roger."

A few minutes later the dog came back, and Leonie docilely allowed herself to be led back to the parlor. There she seated herself at the table and finished her letter to Roger, telling him how much of a comfort Fifi was, how she had licked her tears away and been so well-behaved, had gone out and come back quite faithfully without getting lost, so clever was Fifi she never got lost. It all seemed innocent enough, but Leonie hoped that the emphasis on Fifi and her powers of remembering where she belonged would convey some meaning to Roger. If the dog showed up at the house after her letter had been delivered to him, surely he would understand that she could lead him back to her mistress.

In the end Leonie had barely enough room to answer the question that was supposed to confirm her identity and that the contents of the letter were genuine. What was behind the warped cask? For a moment Leonie could not remem-

ber any warped cask. Then she realized it must be the one
that hid the entrance to the tunnel in the château. She considered and rejected the idea of a false answer. There was
no sense in making Roger frantic; he might do something
desperate.

"There was a broken jug half-filled with water left behind the warped cask," Leonie wrote. That was true. Roger
would remember they had left the water jug in the tunnel,
and she need say nothing of a hiding place, which might
bring unwelcome ideas to the minds of whoever read the
letter before it was delivered.

When she had folded this missive and handed it over,
Leonie professed herself ready to go back to her room. "I
wish I had some sewing or some knitting," she said to
Danou on the way up the stairs. "When Citizen Chaumette
comes tomorrow, do you think I could ask him to allow
you to bring me something to sew?"

Danou perked up at this clear implication that she expected him to continue guarding her, and assured her that
he would be happy to get anything she wanted, if Chaumette agreed. With that Leonie was quite content. She
smiled at Danou again when he pointed out that there was
clothing for her in the sack lying on the chest in the corner,
and he readily agreed to leave her some candles so that she
could put it away. When the door was locked behind him,
Leonie smiled again. She continued to smile as she hung up
her dresses, even though the idiot who had grabbed her
clothing had failed to bring any extra underlinen or night-
dresses. Danou would not have been so content with this
smile if he had been clever enough to read the expression,
for there was a deep satisfaction in her eyes that boded no
good for her captors. Once Leonie had sent Fifi out so that
Roger could find her, she intended to separate the
guards—she was now sure there were only the two men
and herself in the house—and disable or kill them. If one
device did not work, another would.

While Leonie made plans, Roger crouched in the attic of
the house sweating with anxiety and waiting to hear Pierre
on the roof so that he could open the trapdoor and let him
in. Pierre had remained only a few minutes in the shop,
just long enough for Roger to tell him it was not safe to
stay, that he was being watched, although not as closely as

before, it seemed. Pierre had not argued, only asked, "How can we talk?"

Roger had stared at him blankly. Too many shocks and too much worry were slowing his normally quick wits. He had shaken his head helplessly. "I dare not. They have my—Mademoiselle de Conyers. If I do anything suspicious, they will kill her."

Pierre had grinned. "In a mess again, eh? I knew it. That is why I came. But it is not like you to let yourself be trapped. Surely you have a bolt hole."

"Hole!" The word had reminded Roger of the trapdoor in the roof, and he had described it quickly. "I can get out, but—"

"No," Pierre had corrected. "It will be better if I come in. Here we can talk and plan."

"But how will you get to the roof?"

Once again Pierre had grinned at Roger. "My friend, this business has addled your wits. If I can climb a mast or a line in a storm, will I have trouble with a house or the roofs in between?"

With that, the smuggler had left before Roger could protest. In the two hours that had passed, he had plenty of time to imagine a hundred things that could go wrong, but the truth was that he had seen none of Chaumette's watchdogs for some time. It seemed that the surveillance had been considerably lessened since Leonie had been taken hostage. Apparently it was assumed that Roger would do nothing to jeopardize her safety.

Still, Roger waited anxiously until he heard a tapping. Then he climbed on the stool he had brought from the bedroom and lifted the door. It was fortunate that he had accompanied Pierre on his "deliveries" or he would not have recognized him. In fact, he hardly saw him; blackened hands and face melded into black garb, all scarcely visible in the unlighted attic. However, he was immediately enveloped in a warm embrace.

"*Eh bien, mon vieux,* what sort of trouble have you fallen into now?"

"None of my own choosing, I assure you," Roger replied, but when Pierre laughed, he laughed too.

It was incredible how his spirits lifted, not because he thought Pierre could help but because he would at least be able to talk. He led Pierre into the bedroom, where he had previously tacked a blanket over the curtains on the window so that they would be sure no gleam of light would show, and told him what had happened.

"I don't know where she is," Roger finished, "and I daren't even go looking—not that looking would help—because if I made any move at all . . ." His voice began to shake, and he stopped speaking abruptly.

There was no need for Pierre to ask whether Roger would be willing to leave the girl behind. First of all, it was quite clear to Pierre that his friend was more deeply involved than merely as the rescuer of the heiress of Stour. Even if he had not been, Pierre doubted that he could convince Roger to abandon to certain death a person for whom he had assumed responsibility. He would not have done so himself. There was a subsidiary problem, however, that needed to be solved.

"Leave that for a minute. Tell me instead whether you feel you must carry the little king out of France?"

"No," Roger answered at once. "The child is in no danger. Chaumette merely wants to hide him to increase his own power or to use as a bargaining counter to protect himself. In fact, Leonie was much opposed to taking Louis-Charles out of the country. She thought that he would be hated if he were imposed on the people as king by France's conquerors—if France should be conquered. It is only Chaumette who will benefit, and as you can imagine I have no special love for Chaumette."

"Good! Then we only need to find Mademoiselle de Conyers, and—"

"Only!"

"It is not so impossible as you think. If letters go back and forth, someone carries them. No one here knows me, and I have trustworthy men with me. Among us we can follow whoever carries the letter—"

"They are not likely to walk through the streets with the thing in their hands," Roger interrupted, his voice shaking again.

Pierre cocked an eye at him. "Since you cannot do anything, why don't you leave this end of the matter in my hands. If one thing doesn't work, another will."

"No! Don't you understand, he'll kill her? Don't you see, anyone can do my part of this. At the slightest hint, he'll—"

"My friend," Pierre said, gripping Roger's shoulder, "what I see is that you probably have not eaten today and you probably have not slept soundly for a year. Can we go down and find what there is to fill that hollow in your belly or are Chaumette's little helpers below?"

"No one is there," Roger replied, "but, really, I'm not at all hungry—"

Despite Roger's frenzied objections that he could not eat, Pierre made his way down in the dark. The windows had heavy curtains, which Leonie had made and hung soon after they had become a way station in de Rocheville's escape route. It was safe to light a candle, so long as no one could see that there were two men in the room. A gleam of light would rouse no suspicions. There was nothing unusual in someone coming down to get a bite or a drink in the night. In a covered pot Pierre found the meal Leonie had prepared. He set this to heat and then convinced Roger to eat it.

When they were finished, Roger had to admit that Pierre's diagnosis of his condition had been accurate. The sense of overwhelming panic diminished, so that he was able to discuss the ways and means of following his letter more rationally. It was decided that Pierre would try first to follow Garnier, or whomever he gave the letter to, and if that failed as it likely would, to keep a watch on Chaumette. Leonie's letter was promised before noon. After he had read it, Roger would go out the back way to shop or deliver merchandise, drawing with him the watcher at the back door. Then Pierre would slip out, make his way to the front, and establish himself in the café across the street in which Garnier kept watch on Roger's front door. When Roger returned, he would write to Leonie, then call Garnier to give him the letter. This would both identify the man for Pierre and permit Pierre to know when he received the letter so that he could watch for its transfer.

"Only I don't think the man Garnier gives it to will carry it direct," Roger sighed. "I'm sure it will be carried first to Chaumette to read. Then, like as not, still another man will take it to where Leonie is held."

"Perhaps. I have an answer to that also." Pierre smiled at Roger. "I am not unpracticed in the methods of detecting betrayal and the passing of secret messages, you know, and I told you I have some good men with me."

Instead of looking relieved, Roger looked even more worried. "Pierre, if you stick your neck out so that your head gets chopped off . . ."

The smuggler laughed heartily, if softly, and clapped Roger on the shoulder. Then he poured a tumbler full of brandy from the bottle that was standing on the table and pushed it toward his friend. "Take that down, all at once, and then to bed with you. When you begin to tell *me* how to be careful, it is time you were asleep."

CHAPTER 21

It was a good prescription. Roger slept quite soundly, but so had Leonie—and without any brandy. Her soporific had been planning in detail for all the contingencies that might arise. Each time she thought of a new circumstance that could interfere with disposing of Danou and Panel and worked around it, another layer of tension fell away. By the time she was quite sure she had planned for every circumstance, Leonie was quite completely relaxed and ready for sleep.

The morning light and the clear head resulting from a good rest showed more problems than solutions. If she disposed of the men before Roger was able to follow Fifi back, where was she to go? She had no cloak or hat and did not know where she was. To wander the streets wearing only a dress—and not rags but a decent middle-class dress—would certainly arouse curiosity. To imply she did not know where she was would arouse suspicion. In addition Leonie knew she was not ordinary looking. Her blond hair made her easy to remember. Thus, she dared not ask for directions to some well-known landmark near her home, like the Temple.

The easiest answer, of course, was just to stay in the house and wait for Roger to come after she had disposed of the guards. Stay in the house with two dead men? Leonie shivered, then told herself severely that it was silly to be afraid of Danou and Panel dead when she was not afraid of them alive. Still, there might be other reasons why she should not stay in the house. She would have to devise a cloak for herself and perhaps a hood to cover her hair. Leonie began to look around for materials, but Fifi wriggled out from under the bed and went scratching on the door. Leonie followed her, knocked, and called for Citizen Danou. It was Panel who unlocked the door for her and stood blocking it. Leonie, not willing to seem aggressive, stepped back a little and said civilly that she was ready to have breakfast and the dog needed to go out. She even managed a smile.

Panel looked at her for a long moment and seemed about to speak when a door opened below. Then the man shouted for Danou, and a scene similar to the one the previous evening was enacted, except that the men did not this time hold Leonie's arms when she let Fifi out. She took no foolish advantage of this freedom, only watching as Fifi made a quick circuit of the garden and then slid through the gate. Leonie closed the door and suggested she have her breakfast in the kitchen where it was warm, which would save the men the trouble of carrying the dishes of food into the other room.

This proposal also received ready agreement, as did her next, which was that she be permitted to brew her own coffee. Leonie's face was thoughtful as she prepared the drink. Her violent rage of the previous night had faded; she now realized that many things could have made Roger's epistolary style stiff and his handwriting shaky—fear for her being the most obvious. She was no longer quite so eager to kill Danou and Panel. Pots and pans were not ordinarily thought of as dangerous, but a kettle of boiling water could disable a man and a heavy frying pan render him unconscious quite as effectively as more conventional weapons. Now smiling brightly, Leonie consumed her croissants and coffee, talking affably to Danou while she considered where it would be best to hit him.

Of course, in order to use the pan as a weapon, it would be necessary to obtain the right to use it for its normal purpose first. Leonie sighed deeply and deliberately and, as she hoped she would be, was asked why. It was so dull for her here, she complained. At home she was always busy. Here she did not have enough to do. Before Danou could reply, Fifi came scratching at the door and, simultaneously, the bell rang for the front. Danou hurried to answer the door while Leonie rose to let in the dog. As she passed his chair, the other guard seized her arm. Docilely, Leonie stopped, thinking he did not want her to open the door while Danou was out of the room.

"I can arrange for you to have something to keep you busy," he said softly. The leer on his face made plain enough what was in his mind, but he did not intend to leave Leonie in any doubt, and gave one of her breasts a quick squeeze.

Color flamed in her face, and she twisted away, but she did not cry out. A woman not accustomed to insult would have screamed; a woman inured to it would have responded in the hope of using her insulter. Leonie did not feel the shock an innocent and sheltered girl or wife would feel, but Roger had restored her full sense of her own worth. Instead of fear, rage and revulsion seized her, so furious a rage that after her instinctive wrench to free herself she was stricken mute and paralyzed.

To the guard such behavior—a blush but no protest; pulling away but no withdrawal—could only mean a playful coyness that would lead to yielding. He had said from the beginning to Danou that he was treating the woman wrong. Any girl torn from her home should have wept and screamed no matter what assurances were given her. She should have shrunk away from her abductors in fear rather than smiling and chatting with them as soon as she was over the effects of the blow on her head. Obviously, now that she had recovered from the shock and realized she would be away from her husband for some time, she would like a little servicing from a new man. It was always so with women. Danou had resisted Panel's advice violently, but Danou was an ugly brute, Panel thought. He would just try his idea out on his own. Women never resisted him for long.

Whether Leonie could have controlled herself when the seizure of rage passed was not tested. Chaumette and Danou entered the kitchen before Leonie could do more than gasp for breath. On the instant, her mind began to function swiftly. If she complained, Panel would probably be removed but not punished. That could not be permitted. No man would ever touch her again without her permission. At least, no man would do so and live.

"What is wrong, *citoyenne*?" Chaumette asked, seeing far more in her flaming face and glowing eyes than Panel did.

"I am angry," Leonie snarled. Then she made an effort and checked herself. "I have given my word to Citizen Danou that I will not try to escape or make a noise or do

anything to draw attention, and this man would not let me
open the door for my dog."

"You must try to forgive him, *citoyenne*," Chaumette remarked, his eyes narrowing.

It was obvious to him that such violent emotion could
not be generated over so small a point. However, he really
did not want to remove the men he had assigned to this
task. Danou was too aware of Chaumette's power to cross
him, and Panel was too much of a fool even to wonder why
the woman had been abducted. As the day for the little
king's escape drew nearer, the situation became more and
more dangerous. The fewer people involved the better.
Thus, Chaumette was only too pleased to overlook Leonie's
complaint.

"Please understand," he said, "that what Danou has told
you is true. I wish you to be content here. However, to
ensure your husband's behavior, we must keep you safe,
and thus Panel was within his orders when he did not wish
you to go to the door."

Meanwhile, Danou had let Fifi in and she ran to her
mistress.

"How did the dog come here?" Chaumette asked
sharply.

"She followed the carriage," Danou replied. "I can kill
her," he added with relish. "I did not do it when I first saw
her because you told me . . ."

Leonie snatched Fifi up and uttered an inarticulate cry.
Panel put a hand on her back, and she gasped and went
rigid with disgust. Chaumette did not notice what Panel
had done, but Leonie's protective gesture and rigidity were
a clear warning. He shook his head at Danou. He did not
like the presence of Fifi in the house, but he knew how devoted childless women were to those useless little pets and
he realized that, in a sense, he had outsmarted himself. If
he permitted Danou to kill the dog, the woman might be
driven to desperation; certainly she would write of her grief
and her loss—that first stupid letter, which Danou had
handed him, was all about the cursed creature. And the
gunsmith might also take fright from their killing the dog.

"No, no," Chaumette said, reinforcing his headshake, "if
Citoyenne Saintaire finds comfort in her pet, we will do
nothing that could distress her."

Danou's face fell. He had hoped, when Chaumette defended Panel, that the delicate treatment of the woman was no longer necessary because she had already written a letter, and he had already almost tasted the joy of beating her into agreeableness. Chaumette had also seemed to ignore Panel's hand on Leonie's back, and that brought Panel's advice to mind. Danou had wondered for a minute whether they might be able to use the woman as they saw fit. But the definite order to let the dog alone . . .

"I am only doing my duty to my master," Danou said hastily. "Remember what—"

"Shut your mouth," Chaumette snapped, then turned to Leonie. "Has he threatened you, *Citoyenne* Saintaire?"

"No," Leonie whispered. Panel had taken his hand away, but she felt as if a load of slimy night soil had been smeared on her and hate was rising in her, choking her so that she found it hard to speak.

"Perhaps you are afraid to tell me what you really feel," Chaumette remarked with spurious sympathy. "Come with me into the parlor. There you may tell me privately whether either of these fools has offended you in any way. If you are dissatisfied with them, they will be sent away— and punished—before I leave this house, and other guards will be chosen for you."

The walk across the corridor was brief, but it was long enough for Leonie to regain control of herself. Chaumette walked behind her, wondering how he could insist that she permit Danou and Panel to remain and yet not arouse her resentment. He need not have worried about it. Leonie would not have parted with either of those men even if they had beaten her. She was, right now, far more intent on revenging herself on that filthy Panel and that bestial hypocrite Danou than she was on escaping. Vaguely she heard Chaumette defending his henchmen and asking her indulgence for them, explaining that neither of them was accustomed to dealing with respectable women like herself, but he would speak firmly to them and make sure they were more careful in the future. Would she give them another chance? He would soon return, and if she still did not like them . . .

"I do not dislike them," Leonie said softly. "Citizen Danou has been most polite, and I see little of Citizen Panel, which is just as well. His manner is *crude*, but I am sure if you tell him I do not like it he will be more careful.

I do not wish to make any trouble for you, Citizen Chaumette. My husband has explained that, owing to some important business he must do for you, I must stay here to ensure his safety and mine. As long as I receive his letters and know he is well, I will be quiet and obedient."

If he had not been afraid he would frighten and offend Leonie, Chaumette would have kissed her. She had said exactly what he wanted to hear, exactly what he had planned she would say. Apparently his plan of treatment had been right. Both husband and wife would be passive and compliant as long as the other was safe.

"I have only one small complaint—or, rather, request," Leonie continued, taking swift advantage of Chaumette's smile. "I am so bored. Would it be possible for Danou to buy me needles and thread and cloth so that I could sew? And could I do the cooking? It is so very dull to sit all day in one room. I begin to think strange thoughts and grow frightened."

"We must not have you frightened by your own imagination. I will see about the sewing. As to the cooking—please yourself."

"Must I wait until you return for my needles and thread?" Leonie asked wistfully. "I have no nightdress nor any clean linen."

"No—oh, very well. Danou or Panel will get something for you, but they will not know what to choose."

"I will tell them what to ask for. Anyone serving in a mercer's shop will give them properly matching cloth and thread—and Roger will pay," Leonie added ingenuously, wishing to remind Chaumette that she was very dear to her husband.

Chaumette nodded. He did not need any reminder of Roger's devotion. He remembered all too vividly the blazing blue eyes, the cords standing in Roger's neck as he strained forward, hissing, "I'll kill you." From time to time he wondered if he had seized the tail of a serpent that would turn and bite him, and he considered giving orders that man and wife be killed. Most of the time, however, the violence was the best guarantee Chaumette had that Roger would obey implicitly his orders regarding the young king. The woman, at least, would be no trouble; she was docile and not too clever. Chaumette uttered some meaningless platitudes, assured Leonie that her letter would be delivered to her husband, and went to have a few final words with Danou.

This conversation put Danou into so good a humor that he was quite in charity with Leonie and willing, for the time being, to satisfy her requests. Since the first of these was for supplies to prepare a decent dinner for all three of them, Danou did not hesitate before he sent Panel out to buy the makings for the meal. This time he did not even suggest Leonie go to her room but sat chatting with her in the kitchen. Leonie did nothing to spoil this growing trust, although her mind was busy with the next step in her program.

Her problem was to find a few minutes to tell Fifi to "find Roger." If she went to her room, Leonie could say the words, but she was not sure Fifi would remember if she was not sent out immediately. The little dog might think Roger was hiding in the house, as Leonie and François had hidden to play the game on rainy days. She racked her brains desperately, knowing she had only the little time before Panel returned, but no answer came. Then, as so often happens, the problem solved itself. By the time the front doorbell rang, announcing Panel's return, Danou was so lulled by Leonie's passivity that he went to answer it without either taking her with him or sending her up to her room. As soon as he was out the door, Leonie sprang to her feet and seized Fifi.

"Find Roger," she hissed, with all the emphasis she could place on the words without shouting. "Go to Roger! To Roger! Go find Roger!"

It was the best she could do. As she heard the front door slam, she opened the back door and pushed Fifi out, crying softly, "Roger! Find Roger!" Then she slammed the door shut and stood with her back to it, hoping she could delay Danou and Panel from going out if they had heard her. At first she thought that all was lost. Both men burst into the room with expressions of fury, but they stopped short when they saw her.

"I heard the door close," Danou snarled.

"Yes," Leonie replied, her voice trembling. "The dog wanted to go out. Was that wrong? I didn't step outside, I only opened the door for her."

Danou came forward and touched the cloth of her dress, but there was no chill on it from the winter air outside.

Apparently she was telling the truth. Still, he was uneasy, although he could not put his finger on the cause. He just felt something was wrong, not realizing that Leonie's nervousness was communicating itself to him. He looked out the window into the garden.

"Where is she?" he asked.

Between hope and fear, Leonie found herself trembling. Now that she had done it, she regretted it bitterly. Could Fifi possibly find her way home? Such a little dog, such a long way? Leonie was suddenly sure that they were very far from the shop; she remembered that the ride in the carriage had seemed to take forever. Even if she discounted some of the time as being exaggerated by fear, it must be a terribly long way to such a small, helpless creature as Fifi. Tears rose to Leonie's eyes as she, too, went to the window and peered out. Had she killed the poor, loving animal by sending her away on a hopeless quest? The streets were full of carriages and carts. Fifi might be caught under their wheels or crushed against a curb. More likely she would be hopelessly lost, to wander alone, starving, and frightened until she died of weakness and loneliness.

"What is wrong?" Danou growled, growing more and more suspicious.

"Nothing," Leonie gasped, "nothing. You frightened me when you rushed in like that."

But the answer was not convincing. Danou was not stupid, although Panel was, but both men remembered that Leonie had not shed a tear nor seemed so distraught even when they had first abducted her. Neither considered that she had been numb with shock then, and the obvious conclusion—that Leonie's agreeableness and camaraderie had an ulterior motive—leaped into Danou's mind.

"I do not like this," he said between his teeth. "I do not like it at all. Panel, go out and look for the dog."

"No!" Leonie cried.

"Why not?" Danou asked.

"Because I do not trust you. You will kill her and say she was hurt in the street."

When she saw the expression on both faces, Leonie realized how stupid she had been. She had made a mistake, a very bad mistake. She had counted too much on Chaumette's assurances that he wanted her to be content. All the men had been made uneasy by Fifi's presence; Chaumette had even considered doing away with her. He had not given the order because he realized they would have to overpower her and perhaps hurt her before they could get the dog away from her. Now she herself had told Danou and Panel how to be rid of Fifi without any blame. They had not thought of it; they had only intended to look for the dog. She had killed Fifi! She had given them the excuse they needed.

"Go out and find the creature," Danou ordered, seizing Leonie by the arm. "And you, *citoyenne*, you have not been quiet and obedient as you promised. You will go to your room and stay there."

"No," Leonie shrieked, "do not hurt my dog. She does no harm."

"Naturally we will not hurt her," Danou said, smiling viciously. "I would not *dream* of doing such a thing. As soon as she is found, we will bring her to you—never fear."

A good night's sleep was of some help to Roger. He no longer felt his insides shaking with fear for Leonie, but he was worse off in another way. Rested and fed, his body now called for action, inciting his mind to a restless search for something to do to free his love. He could hardly concentrate on his work, and after nearly spoiling a delicate mechanism by unseating the spring in it and pinching his own fingers by an incautious squeeze of the pliers he was wise enough to restrict himself to polishing finished work—and this did nothing to calm him.

By the time Chaumette's messenger arrived at midmorning with Leonie's answer to his letter, the only thing that prevented Roger from seizing the man and choking information out of him was the certainty that the ragged, dirty creature had no information to give. He devoured the letter, seeking for some hint, no matter how small, as to Leonie's present whereabouts. He knew Leonie was clever enough to conceal information within innocent-seeming nothings, but read and reread, twist and turn the words as he would, he could find nothing. He cursed aloud, startling an incoming customer, and controlled the urge to tell the man to get out. Fortunately, he was only calling for finished work, and seeing Roger's black scowl, took his gun, paid the bill, and left without any attempt at conversation. Unable to contain himself any longer, Roger latched his door and went upstairs to Pierre, who was lounging patiently in the bedroom.

"Nothing," he burst out. "There is nothing in the letter. You would think the girl was an imbecile. Surely she could have given me a hint of where she was."

"Likely she doesn't know," Pierre pointed out calmly, a little amused because he understood the basis of Roger's bad temper. "Do you think they gave her a view of the streets as they went by? What could she tell you?"

"She could have found something more sensible to say than maundering on and on about the damn dog," Roger exclaimed unreasonably. "Fifi is so good. Fifi is such a comfort. Fifi is so clever—" His voice checked suddenly and Pierre sat more upright, a look of interest on his face.

"Do you dislike the dog?" he asked Roger.

"No, of course not," Roger replied, thoughtfully now. "She is a pretty, clever little creature. I'm very fond of her."

"Then there must be some meaning to all that adulation," Pierre said, echoing Roger's thought.

There was no immediate answer. Roger was rereading Leonie's letter yet again, trying desperately to think of something connected to Fifi that would give a hint of Leonie's whereabouts. Eventually he shook his head and handed Pierre the letter.

"I'm not thinking clearly," he sighed. "Maybe you can see what I can't." Then he cleared his throat awkwardly. "You must disregard what she says of a personal nature. Naturally, as we have been pretending to be husband and wife, she was constrained to write fondly. . . ."

Pierre's black eyes danced with laughter. The double bed he had shared with Roger was sufficient evidence that the pretense of marriage had gone a good deal deeper than the mere use of Roger's name. It was plain enough that Roger was head over heels in love, and the "dearest beloved" was surely not necessary to a pretended marriage. The girl could have written "dear husband" or a number of other less passionate phrases. However, Roger was not in the mood for teasing, and Pierre said nothing, giving his attention to what Leonie had written. He also reread the letter twice but was forced to shrug his shoulders in the end.

"I still think there is something about the dog that is

important, but I can see nothing more than that. Of course, I am not very familiar with Paris. Is there some marking on the animal that looks like a well-known place? Did you take the dog to run in some special area? Did she get lost and was found somewhere?"

The questions were perceptive. A positive answer to any of them would have been most significant, but Roger had already thought about them and there was no positive answer. Under Pierre's urging, he thought again about Fifi's splotched black and white coat, but there simply was nothing special about it, nor could he remember Leonie ever making any comment about the dog that could be applied to the present situation. He shook his head sadly.

"We will just have to let it go," he said at last. "Perhaps Chaumette's men will be careless and you will be able to follow my letter back. If not, tomorrow I will have another letter from Leonie. Perhaps she will be able to make her hint clearer. I'll go out now. Be ready to go as soon as you see the man follow me. I can't bear to sit still any longer."

"Now don't be a fool," Pierre said softly. "I tell you I know what I am about. We will find your—Mademoiselle de Conyers. Only don't give yourself away. Try not to look so worried."

"I can look as worried as I like," Roger snapped, "since my excuse for doing the shopping is that my wife is not well."

Pierre sighed, but he gave no more warnings. It was a dreadful thing what a woman could do to a man. Ordinarily Roger had the sweetest of tempers no matter what the circumstances, and no more regard for danger than a goat for a thistle. Thanking God that he had never permitted himself a greater interest in any woman than as a simple source of pleasure, Pierre shrugged himself into one of Roger's coats and followed him down the stairs, watching cautiously from behind the window curtain to be sure Chaumette's watchdog followed Roger.

In spite of Roger's certainty that this day nothing would go right, everything seemed to be as usual. He pretended to lock his door—Pierre would actually do that later—waited for Colurel, the man who waited at the back, and walked out through the alley, raising a careless hand in salute to the fishmonger as he passed him. He slowed his pace then, not wanting Pierre to come out while the fishmonger was in the alley, but the man went back into his shop and Roger strode forward, quickening his pace, without a backward glance.

That was a mistake. Pierre had watched Roger and his shadow as far down the alley as he could see them and judged how long it would take them to reach the end. He did not notice that Roger had slowed down because he was, at that moment, cautiously opening the door, counting the seconds in his head until he could safely whip out. Just as Roger reached the corner and turned right, the fishmonger emerged from his back door again with a pail of slop. Simultaneously, Pierre came out. The fishmonger cast out the slop in a silver arc and straightened his back. Turning, Pierre saw him, but it was too late to go back. The best he could do was leave the door unlocked and get as near the middle of the road as possible.

"Who the devil are you?" the fishmonger shouted, much startled to find a man nearly atop him when he had glanced up and down the alley before he threw out his slop.

Colurel was just at the corner, but had not turned it yet. At the voice of the fishmonger, he turned his head and saw Pierre. Since he, too, had been glancing regularly down the alley, Colurel was well aware that Pierre must have come from one of the houses in the street. He knew it could not have been from the house opposite Roger's, because that was where he lodged, and although he could not be certain he did not think it could have been the house beyond Roger's. He hesitated momentarily, torn between his desire to rush back and seize Pierre and his orders, which were most emphatic that he not let Roger out of his sight. Colurel leaped forward, his heart in his mouth. He had been warned that there was a chance Saintaire would do something desperate.

To his relief Roger was still in sight, but he was a long way ahead. That in itself was suspicious. Until yesterday Saintaire had been extremely cooperative, waiting if Colurel fell behind, raising a hand to wave in a crowd so that his watchdog would not be lost. This time he had moved very quickly. Perhaps he hoped that seeing a man come out of his house would distract Colurel enough so that he could disappear. Colurel began to hurry and then hesitated again. If this was a deliberate trick and Saintaire thought he was alone, what would he do? Perhaps he thought Colurel knew that would not save him. If Chaumette were betrayed, he would drag his henchmen down with him. No, it was better to be on Saintaire's heels so that he could not make a wrong move. And to be on the safe side, Colurel thought, he would report exactly what had happened.

After Fifi slipped through the gate, she was confused. She knew who Roger was, of course; that was the god whose odor so often mingled with that of the goddess. She understood the order to "find Roger" also. That was a dear and familiar game. But these were not the woods near the château nor even the town, where she had often been sent to fetch someone out of a shop. Two separate problems bewildered the little bitch.

The first of these was immediate. The alley on which the garden faced was not the route she had taken when she followed the goddess. That was down the street at the front of the house. The direct way to the route home was blocked by the house. Fifi knew she could not return there. It was against the rules of the game to go back to the starting point before the objective was achieved. If she did that, the goddess would be angry and say "No! No!" and send her away again with the same order.

Fifi ran along the wall until she found an opening through which she squeezed. This, however, led only into another garden, blocked from the street by the back of another house. She went out the way she had come in and ran farther. After several tries, she came to a lane where her sense of direction pointed her toward the street on which the house fronted. She turned up that, sensing its familiarity, knowing now which way she had come. Back along the route was Roger. When she found the god, she could come back to the goddess where all love, all warmth, all food and security were centered.

Trotting steadily, she came to the front of the house, which she recognized. Here, she hesitated a moment—the draw of the goddess was strong. Her little head turned just as the door opened.

"There she is!" a voice bellowed. "Fifi, come here!"

Galvanized, Fifi streaked up the street, running her best. She knew that voice and that man and she disliked both intensely. The goddess had smelled of hate and fear while that man touched her. He was no friend, and Fifi would

avoid him if she could. However, she was a small dog and
the man was running very fast. She could hear his footsteps
pounding closer, his ugly voice, filled with rage, bellowing
commands for her to stop and come to him. Desperate and
terrified, Fifi dodged into another lane. The distance between her and the man who followed increased, but he was
soon on her heels again, and again she twisted away, running blindly right and left, sensing that if she were caught
she would be hurt.

When her heart was pounding, her tongue dangling, her
eyes blinded by exhaustion, she saw a darkness and fled
into that, collapsing, panting, her little sides heaving with
effort and her whole body trembling with fear. Later, when
she had caught her breath and realized that the voice was
no longer shouting at her, the trembling stopped. Eventually she crawled out of the hole in which she had sought
refuge and stood sniffing the air.

Now the second of her two problems overwhelmed her.
"Find Roger," yes, but where was Roger? Time meant very
little to Fifi. Her happy years at the château were over-
lapped by the months of misery and loneliness there atop
which lay the few days of happiness—which seemed to Fifi
just as long as the preceding years—when she had found
the goddess again. Find Roger where? At the château?
That was where the game had usually been played. At the
many inns in which they had lodged? At the house with the
garden? At the house where there was no garden but where
there was, down the alley, the lovely smell of bad fish? Fifi
continued to sniff the air and began to trot slowly straight
ahead. She had a more immediate, more devastating problem. Where was *she*? This place was completely strange.
She was lost!

CHAPTER 22

In the commune and in the convention, the balance still swayed between Danton and Robespierre, but the scales tipped more and more in Robespierre's favor. Chaumette did not dare absent himself long from the center of action. At any moment St. Just might rise and begin to cry for Danton's arrest. Chaumette had never been of his party and did not expect to be included in the lists of those denounced along with Danton and Desmoulins, but one could never be too alert.

After his morning interview with Leonie, he had returned to his office and carefully reread her letter to Roger. Satisfied with what she said—obviously she was a silly thing and doted on the ridiculous dog—he sent the letter on with a messenger and dismissed Roger and Leonie from his thoughts. He went to the convention to mingle with the deputies and listen to what was said—and even more closely to what was whispered or only hinted at in half-words with sidelong looks of the eyes.

What he heard gave Chaumette no comfort. Just before dark he went to the Temple to visit the young Capet, who was unhappy and pleaded to have Simon restored to him. Chaumette answered him vaguely but promised that Simon would come to visit him and he should be sure to obey him. Perhaps matters could be arranged between Louis-Charles and Simon himself, Chaumette said softly just before he left. Then he went to see the shoemaker and urged him to be ready.

"The work is near done," Simon replied, and beckoned Chaumette into a shed at the rear of his house. "My wife's cousin," he whispered, "is looking for a suitable boy. He will be brought in inside the horse."

Simon showed Chaumette how the saddle lifted off, its overlap concealing the join. "It looks solid enough to ride," he remarked with pride, "and with the child inside will weigh about what a wooden one would weigh. It is my farewell present to Louis-Charles."

"If it is a present to the child, how will you explain taking it out again?" Chaumette asked.

"Many call me ignorant because I cannot read or write," Simon snarled, "but I am no fool for all of that. I must not seem to take anything that is not mine. Look here." He pointed to a large wicker basket. "That will be filled with my clothes and my wife's, but there is room under the bottom for the boy, and it will not be dark or stuffy in there because it is wicker. After I have shown Louis-Charles to the commissioners, I will take him back to his chamber. Then I will say good-bye to him while my wife puts the other child in the bed. She will come back, say the boy is in bed, and stand by the door, blocking the view of the guard and urging me to put in the clothes and go. It can be done in a minute. We will wheel out the basket, carry it downstairs—"

"Is your wife strong enough?" Chaumette asked anxiously.

"Love gives strength," Simon answered. "She will be strong enough."

Chaumette accepted that because there was no choice. He hoped the device would work. If it did not, it would be far more difficult to spirit the child away another time. However, he had little fear for his own safety. If Simon were caught, he might try to involve Chaumette, but he had his defense all prepared. He would accuse Simon of trying to drag him in out of spite. Witnesses were ready to testify that Simon had begged Chaumette to allow him to retain his post as the boy Capet's keeper, which was true, and that Chaumette had refused—which was also true, but the witnesses did not know of the substitute Chaumette had offered. It was he who had insisted that Simon display the boy to the commissioners on guard before he left the Temple for the last time.

When he had taken his leave of Simon, Chaumette's long day was not yet ended. He went to a quiet café, not known to be a haunt of his, to meet certain gentlemen with whom an ardent revolutionary would not be expected to consort. Thus, when Colurel was relieved by the man who kept the night watch, he did not find Chaumette either at his office or at his home. Colurel was more tired than usual, for he had done a good deal of worrying about what he had seen and what it meant, and was in a foul humor by the time he trudged back to Chaumette's office to leave a message. Even then he could not fully unburden himself, because all the men he knew to be trustworthy were gone and he had been told not to mention the gunsmith if he could avoid it. All Colurel could do was growl at the man in the office that he had something to tell Chaumette and then go home to bed with the fear that he would be blamed for what was none of his fault.

Roger was in no better a humor than his shadow. He had returned from marketing to find Pierre gone, as planned. When he brought his answer to Leonie out to Garnier, he had seen the smuggler drinking at the counter of the café where Garnier spent his time watching Roger's front door. After that his day had been a nightmare. His work could not hold his mind, which had been filled with anxieties and regrets, all *if I had only . . .* and *if only I had not . . .* drifting from one horrible situation to another. First he imagined that Pierre would be caught, imprisoned, and executed; then he became convinced that Chaumette would discover his attempt to rescue Leonie and have her killed.

Although dark came early on January thirteenth, Roger was nearly mad by the time he heard Pierre tapping on the trapdoor in the roof. A leaping flash of relief passed back into fear as soon as Roger saw the expression on his friend's face.

"Sorry," Pierre said grimly, "not only did I lose the man Garnier gave the letter to, but I was seen coming out of here."

"By whom?" Roger asked, white-faced.

"The fishmonger. We must have come out the doors at almost the same instant. He didn't actually see me come out, but suddenly there we were, looking at each other."

"Oh God," Roger groaned, "and he *knew* you were not in the street before, because he had just been out. We exchanged greetings."

"Now, don't lose your head," Pierre urged. "That won't accomplish anything at all. We will just have to go about this in a different way. Later tonight I will go down to my ship and get my men. Then, just before dawn, we will pay a little visit to Chaumette. I will soon enough find out where Mademoiselle de Conyers is, and—"

"Good!" Roger gasped. "Yes, of course. We will pay Chaumette a visit. Why the devil didn't I think of that last night? In fact, why wait. Let's go now."

"Don't be a fool. Go where? Do you think these men who work plots seek their beds at seven of the clock in the evening? And there is the little problem of wringing the direction of his home out of the men who are watching you without rousing the entire neighborhood. We must wait until after midnight, and I am not sure you should . . ."

Pierre's voice faded as Roger turned his head and looked at him. There was no sense in arguing, he knew. Roger could not be talked out of going along, and actually, he might as well. Once the watchdogs were pulled in and questioned, Roger would be safer prowling the streets and raiding Chaumette's home than sitting still in his own house. On second thought, he did not even want to suggest that Roger—who was known and might be a danger to them all—stay in hiding. He could not dim the light that was now leaping in Roger's blue eyes. The glaze of hopelessness had left them, and Pierre realized that most of his friend's trouble had been the need to wait passively, helplessly, for things to happen.

That conclusion was quite correct. Now that Roger knew he would be able to *do* something, a tremendous weight seemed to fall off him. The terror and depression that had been muddling his brain lifted away. All at once he was able to think and plan.

"Our worst problem—after we get off the roof—will be the patrols in the street," Roger remarked thoughtfully.

"We will be careful," Pierre replied. "It is not the first time I have dodged patrols."

"In a city?" Roger asked, but his voice was absent.

Something was teasing his mind, something connected with danger and the commissioners of the commune, but not something recent. It was something to do with Leonie, too, something very pleasant. But what the devil connection did Leonie have with the commissioners that could be pleasant? Pierre had begun to protest that a city was not so different from the countryside, but Roger signaled at him brusquely to be silent. Yet what Pierre said was also tied in with that elusive memory—something to do with getting past patrols in the street. Suddenly Roger smacked a fist into his palm.

"I have it!" he cried. "But where did she hide them?"

Naturally enough, Pierre looked at him as if he had gone crazy, but Roger did not stop to explain that he had remembered Toulon bringing two commissioners' scarves to the house when he had plotted the escape of the entire royal family. Leonie had taken the scarves and hidden them. The men's suits were still hanging among Roger's clothes in the closet. He began to rummage there but stopped, remembering that Leonie had disposed of the scarves first, before she had run upstairs, and before they had quarreled because Leonie thought he was trying to get rid of her to make room for another woman. Roger laughed aloud. That was why the commissioners were connected with something pleasant in his mind. Then he flushed slightly. The lovemaking that had followed their quarrel had been something more than just "pleasant."

"Roger, what's wrong with you?" Pierre asked sharply.

Roger laughed again at the troubled look on the smuggler's face. "I haven't run mad," he assured his friend, and explained his thought processes.

"Marvelous!" Pierre exclaimed. "If we have those scarves, we can walk all over town with my men tagging openly at our heels and no one will question us." Then his face clouded. "But she would have disposed of them, no? It would be dangerous to have such things, and women are fearful creatures."

"Not Leonie," Roger said, "and I think she would have spoken to me about it before she threw them—Oh, by God, I remember! That's just what she did."

"Too bad," Pierre comforted, thinking it was just like a woman always to do the wrong thing. "Well, we will manage without—"

"No, no," Roger interrupted. "That was how Leonie—I mean, Mademoiselle de Conyers—hid them. She put them down at the bottom of the bag of cleaning rags. They must still be there."

Both men nearly jostled each other getting down the attic ladder until Pierre drew back, realizing he didn't know where Leonie—he smiled inadvertently. Roger was certainly doing his best to imitate that fabulous bird that hid its head in the sand when danger threatened, thinking if it could not see, then no one else could see it. Where then, did Mademoiselle de Conyers keep her rags? Fortunately, it seemed that Roger knew. By the time Pierre got down the stairs, Roger had the scarves out and was waving them triumphantly.

"Now all we need is a story in case we meet a patrol that knows we don't belong in their Section," Roger said.

Pierre looked at his fever-bright eyes and then at the untouched food lying on the kitchen table. Obviously Roger had forgotten to eat again. For that matter, he was hungry himself. He eyed the ill-assorted purchases and sighed. It was also obvious that Roger had no idea how or with what to make a meal.

"You think of a story," he said. "I'm hungry. I'm going to try to prepare some sort of a supper that won't poison us out of this crazy stuff you bought."

Roger examined the wilted greens and drying meat on the table with mild surprise. "Leon—Mademoiselle de Conyers attended to the food. I didn't know what to buy and—and I wasn't really thinking about it either, but . . . You know, Pierre, you're right. I'm starved."

He watched Pierre for a few minutes but then became restless and began to fidget. After another minute he said, "I think I'll get everything I want to take with me. I won't be coming back here ever again, no matter what happens."

Fifi was also starved. She was very cold and very tired, too. All day she had run up one street and down another, sniffing and looking and listening for anything familiar. She was too footsore, too frozen, too frightened now to think of the game of finding Roger. All she wanted to find was a way home—any home. Even the dreadful months alone in the château, stealing garbage from pig sties and killing mice and eating dead birds was better than wandering like this. There she had at least known where she was.

The failing light did not trouble her much, but a fine drizzle that wetted her coat and made her even colder had begun to fall. Wearily she plodded on, her silken tail draggled with mud and filth tight against her rump in her abject misery. If it had not been so wet, if she could have found a dry hole to crawl into, she would have given up. Still, she sniffed hopefully, and at last she was rewarded. She did not smell home or the god or the goddess, not so great a joy as that, but she did smell food.

She turned into an alleyway, her pace increasing, the tip of her tail beginning to curl hopefully. The odor intensified; Fifi's nose twitched and wiggled. There was a warmth mingled with the food odor too. There! Fifi hurried to a pile of offal near the back door of a food shop. Eagerly she snatched a mouthful, then another. There was noise, which made her nervous, but it was dim and dull, separated from her by walls and a door. There was a bone with fat and gristle, but it was too large for Fifi to drag away. Still, it was so delicious that Fifi's caution diminished as she wrestled with it. Suddenly the sound intensified and simultaneously a woman shrieked and a glittering object flew at her, barely missing her.

Terrified, she leaped away, tiredness forgotten as she ran with all her might to escape the clattering threat. In her fear she did not stop but ran headlong into a wide avenue at the end of the alley. All day Fifi had turned away from such streets, knowing that "home" was not on such thoroughfares and that she was not allowed to go on them unless accompanied by the goddess or the god. Startled by the openness, Fifi hesitated and turned to run back; but fear seized her and she began to tremble, hearing in memory the shriek and terrible clatter. Fearfully she turned into the wide street, slinking along as close to the buildings as she could get.

Terror and guilt notwithstanding, Fifi's nose continued to work. Suddenly she stopped and lifted her head, her tail came up and began to wave slowly. Vaguely she remembered that she had been frightened, but now she could not remember why. What a long walk she had had! The goddess would be very angry. She must hurry home as fast as possible. Perhaps the goddess would not know that she had come, all alone, to that place that smelled of leather and ink where the god talked to "friend" Fouché, who fed her bon bons.

Fifi ran her best, but she was wet and cold and tired. It grew darker and colder. Then memory of warmth and comfort and food applied a spur, and she ran again. There was a steady encouragement for her too. As she ran along the broad rue de Rivoli, turned left into the rue du Temple, the way grew more and more familiar. It was very dark now; there was no moon, and Fifi could barely see the way at all. However, she really did not need to see now. All the scents were familiar. She had run these streets often at the heels of the goddess.

At last she uttered a happy little bark. There was the sweet stink of bad fish. Next, only a few steps farther, was home. Her tail high and waving madly, Fifi jumped the step and scratched at the door. She stood waiting impatiently for a while, then scratched again. Sometimes the god and goddess were slow about opening the door for her. Still no answer. Fifi barked once or twice and scratched again, but the door remained closed. Her tail drooped a little. She was very, very tired. One more halfhearted scratch, and she lay down on the step. She was still cold and wet and hungry, but this was home. Soon someone would come.

Leonie's day had been no better than Roger's or Fifi's. Danou had pushed her, none too gently, up the stairs, and just as she had reached the door she had heard Panel shout, "There she is," and then command Fifi to return to him. Leonie did not think Fifi would obey Panel, but she might accept the invitation of the open door hoping to get back to her mistress. Even if she ran, she was such a small creature that it was not impossible that Panel could outrun her or corner her somewhere. Before she could hear any more, Leonie was thrust into her room and the door was locked.

Since then Leonie had had nothing to do but regret her own idiocy. Why, oh why, had she wanted to drag Roger into this? Her plan to dispose of the men did not need his cooperation. She could have made a rough cloak from a blanket and asked for the Salle de Ménage—that was not near her present home, but she knew well how to get home from there. Why had she sent poor Fifi out to her death? It was her own weakness, Leonie knew. Danou and Panel deserved to die, but Leonie shrank from killing coldly and deliberately, perhaps needing to shoot a second time to finish a wounded man and later needing to handle the dead bodies. She shuddered and began to sob. She could have forced herself to it, but she wanted Roger, wanted to know he was coming, that he would approve of her, comfort her. That was why she had murdered poor faithful little Fifi.

Tears dried in fury at herself, Leonie paced the room,

her eyes as golden as her namesake. "Coward," she hissed at herself, "did you not learn in those horrible months in Saulieu to depend on yourself?"

Now, the bitter thought continued, *you have ruined everything.* Even if by some miracle Fifi should survive and find her way home, what could Roger do? He would never dream the little bitch could lead him back—even Leonie was not sure now that she was clever enough for that. Leonie began to cry again. All she would have accomplished was to increase Roger's misery, and for that she had probably ruined her own chances of escape. The men would never trust her. They would never come alone to her door. She would never be able to convince them that she no longer cared about Fifi and would be a passive prisoner.

She cried herself to sleep and woke, hungry and desperate, to find that Roger's letter had been pushed under the door. Reading it made her cry all over again. Hopelessness and fear breathed through every line, although the words were all of comfort, all urging her not to worry, not to be afraid. Everything would soon come out right; this period of trial would soon be over and they would be together again. A complete giveaway of Roger's dreadful mental condition was that he had not even asked the "significant question," the answer to which was supposed to identify her.

Again rage and tears racked her alternately, now and then made more intense by a little hope. At last, after many hours had passed, the hope died, and Leonie acknowledged that the miracle she had longed for had not happened. Roger had not come; therefore, Fifi was either dead already or as good as dead. Leonie rose from the bed on which she had been lying, resolved that she would save herself. Then she realized she was shaking with weakness. Nonetheless, she gritted her teeth and drew one pistol, then went to the door and knocked firmly. Quite soon Panel's voice answered, asking what she wanted. Leonie swallowed hard.

"Whatever you think I did or did not do," she cried, "I am sure Citizen Chaumette would not like it if I was starved. I am hungry. Either let me cook or bring me food."

"It is there," Panel shouted back, "on the dresser."

Leonie bit her lip hard. Now what was she to do? She went over and looked. The food was ice-cold and the coarsest fare the nearest *cafetier* provided. Leonie called complaints through the door, but there was no answer this time. She was about to start pounding on the door, when she realized it would be better to eat first and regain some strength. She knew there were no writing materials in the room. They would have to bring paper and pen and ink if she was to answer Roger's letter. Whoever brought the materials, she would kill at once inside the room. Then she would slam the door shut, possibly she would be able to roll the body across it to block it while she reloaded. Then the other one . . . Leonie shuddered and nearly choked on her mouthful of food. There was no sense in feeling sick. She *had* to do it, *had* to escape. Roger did not know where she was. He could not save her again.

When the food was gone, Leonie rested for a while. Then she drew her pistols and checked the priming and loading. Finally she went and knocked on the door again. No answer. Could Panel have gone down to eat? Should she blow the lock off the door? No, that would discharge one pistol and place her in even greater danger. Leonie knew she could not hope to hit anything except at point-blank range, and once the men heard the shot they would be warned. She waited a few minutes and knocked again.

"You might as well be still," Panel said. "I heard you the first time."

"Please take the tray away," Leonie said. "I do not like the smell of stale food. Also, you have forgotten to bring me paper and pen to write to my husband."

Panel merely laughed at that, and Leonie ground her teeth. Danou had not forgotten the writing materials. He did not want her to write, expecting she would complain about her dog and her treatment. They intended, she supposed, to say she had taken advantage of Chaumette's leniency, tried to escape, refused to write . . . anything to discredit her. Furious, Leonie pounded on the door, but Panel only laughed again, enjoying her frustration, and she finally stopped.

The slow hours passed. Leonie tried one device after another without success. When she asked to go to the jakes, she was told to use the chamber pot in her room. When she asked for water, she was told there was a jug of it on her tray. When she begged for the needle and thread promised to her, for a book, for a candle, she received no answer at all. She thought of trying to break the lock with the butt of one of the pistols, but she was afraid to use the gun that way while it was loaded, and to unload it would place her at the same disadvantage as shooting off the lock. It would warn the men that she had found a weapon of some kind.

Rage and frustration brought tears again, and she cast herself down on the bed, exhausted with tension. The house was utterly silent, the room dark as pitch. Leonie thought wearily that it was just as well no one had responded to her last few attempts to get the men into her room. She would have to wait until the next day to escape now. It was very dangerous to be out on the streets after dark, especially for a woman. Robespierre, with his mania for "purity," was particularly violent against ladies of the night. If they were caught plying their trade, they were executed. She must stop being foolish, Leonie admonished herself. She must go to sleep as soon as possible so that she could wake early and be ready. Danou *had* to bring her food.

Resolution, which can accomplish many things, is unfortunately of very little assistance in obtaining sleep. Although Leonie removed her clothes and tucked her pistols under the pillow, she did not find any rest. She tried one position, then another, tried to keep her mind blank because she knew her thoughts would not be conducive to sleep. Still, frustration and misery take their own toll, and at last Leonie drifted from miserable images of what she might have accomplished if she had not urged Fifi to escape, into uneasy dreams filled with images of the past. A recurring dream of escape, which had not troubled her since Roger's rescue, took hold of her again. She heard the stairs of the Saulieu Hôtel de Ville creak under surreptitious footsteps, heard the snick of the lock as the door opened. Her hands reached out to wake her mother—

"Eager, aren't you?" There was a leer in Panel's voice. "You don't have to hurry. We have all night."

A rough hand seized Leonie's breast. She was still half-asleep, and her dream switched to nightmare. The bed-clothes hampered her limbs so that she felt held down, as she had been that night her virginity was torn from her with such violence. Terror laid an additional weight on her so that her struggles were mere twitches and her throat was too dry to scream.

* * *

Deep asleep after her enormous exertions, Fifi also dreamed little dog dreams of hunting and playing. The house was dark and quiet for several hours while Roger waited in the attic for Pierre to arrive. Then, very faintly, voices invaded the dreams of play, but Fifi's name was not mentioned and she was accustomed to voices around her while she slept. However, she did drift closer to waking, that special sense that brings dogs instantly alert when they are called. But the voices stopped, and Fifi slept again. The worst of her exhaustion was over, though, so that when the odor of cooking oozed around the cracks in the door, her nose twitched and quivered. Then, dimly, there was the voice of the god. Instantly, Fifi was aware of hunger, of cold, ills the god could cure; she leaped against the door, scratching and barking.

Roger, who had just taken a large mouthful of food, very nearly choked to death at the sound. Gasping, he lurched to his feet, almost overturning the table in his eagerness, and wrenched open the door. Fifi bounded in, draggled tail waving high, and he swept her up into his arms, regardless of the wet and mud, hugging her so tight that she yelped in protest.

"Fifi," he gasped, "Fifi! That was what Leonie meant! She sent Fifi for us. Let's go! Pierre—"

"Stop squeezing that poor dog," Pierre exclaimed, "or Mademoiselle de Conyers will find her pet dead when we release her. And what do you mean, go? We have just agreed—"

"But we don't need to force Chaumette to tell us where Leonie is. Fifi can take us to her," Roger interrupted, caressing the little dog more gently.

Pierre stared at his friend and then began to shake his head. "It is a miracle that the dog found her way home. It is impossible that she should find her way back to a place she does not know well." Roger's grip tightened, and Fifi grunted with the stress, but forgivingly stretched up to lick the god's face. Pierre shook his head again. "Have some sense, my friend," he urged. "Look at the poor animal. She must have been wandering for hours."

It was impossible to deny that. The wet from Fifi's fur had soaked through Roger's shirt. He exclaimed, got a cloth and rubbed her somewhat dryer, and then scraped nearly all his own meal into her plate. The enthusiasm with

which Fifi attacked this largesse confirmed Pierre's conten-
tion, implying that the dog had not been fed for some considerable time. However, Roger would not accept this as
proof that Fifi did not know the way. He leaped, instead, to
the ridiculous conclusion that Leonie was being starved,
and nothing Pierre said had the slightest effect on him.

When it became obvious that Roger would go alone if
Pierre continued to argue against the project, the smuggler
agreed. He had realized that it would not actually be a
dangerous enterprise nor waste much time. Two commissioners walking together in the street probably would not
be questioned. He would go with Roger until his friend
could be convinced that Fifi was wandering at random.
Then they would go to the ship, collect the men, and pro-
ceed with the original plan. He won a little delay by convincing Roger to let Fifi rest awhile after her meal, but
the little bitch's alertness as Roger picked up everything he
wanted to take showed she was no longer exhausted.

Another delay was caused by trying to decide whether it
was safe to let Fifi out by herself while Roger and Pierre
made their way over the roofs. Fortunately, before it was
necessary to do that, Roger remembered the sling that
Leonie had prepared to carry the dog when they first
thought they might need to escape that way. Fifi did not
like it. She protested with wiggles and yelps, but Roger
managed to quiet her, and he and Pierre made their way
safely over the slippery slates and down a knotted rope
looped around the chimney of the last house into the end of
the alley. Here Roger released Fifi, cautioning her again to
be quiet.

"Find Leonie," he said, his heart thudding sickly between prayer for a miracle and disbelief.

To Fifi, such a command was perfectly logical and fitted
all the rules of the game she knew. She now remembered
that she had been told to "find Roger." She had done it and
had been rewarded, as was proper, with a delectable
treat—Roger's dinner. Of course, Fifi did not know that,
nor was she confused by any memory of being lost between
the time she was told to find Roger and the finding. Now it
fitted perfectly that she should be told to go back to the
goddess. Tail high, she trotted out of the alley and uner-
ringly turned in the direction taken by the carriage she had
followed. Roger looked at Pierre, his eyes full of such

pleading that the smuggler could not bear to destroy his hope.

"Well," he temporized, "she seems to be very sure of where she wants to go."

Hastily the men knotted the illicit scarves of office around them, lit the lantern they had prepared, and set out to follow the dog. For all of Roger's brave words, he was almost as surprised as Pierre at Fifi's steady trot and purposeful manner. Naturally, as hope grew stronger, he tried to depress it, telling himself that Fifi might merely be following a route she had often taken when walking with Leonie. But the little dog did not stop to sniff or leave her mark. She forged steadily ahead until it was obvious they were beyond any reasonable walk for a dog or even for shopping. Pierre slapped Roger gently on the shoulder.

"By God, I think you were right. I think your Fifi *does* know where she's going. Listen, Roger, do we dare to stop her, or will it mix her up? We can't simply walk up to the house and knock on the door. We must plan something, some way to get in."

"I won't stop her," Roger replied quickly, "but we don't have to knock. Fifi will."

Pierre looked puzzled, then grinned and nodded. Of course; the dog would bark and scratch at the door until someone woke to let her in. He and Roger would only have to wait out of sight beside the door. When it opened, they would burst in. Content with this plan, the men followed Fifi, their hope growing stronger as the little creature began to pick up speed without losing a bit of her determination. In fact, they had a bad scare when Fifi broke into a run and darted down an alleyway. They had to run too, and would have missed her altogether, except that an errant gleam of the bobbing lantern picked up a splash of white on her coat as she wriggled through the gate.

Fifi knew nothing of the dangers surrounding her mistress. She was totally unaware of the plan Roger and Pierre had to get into the house. She was only delighted at having played the game of "finding" so perfectly. Dimly she was aware that the distance for finding had been unusually long, and this added to her joy because she knew the goddess always made a bigger fuss than usual when she found someone far away. The god had been very pleased. He had caressed her almost too much and had given her a marvelous dinner. Thus, Fifi was most anxious to get to Leonie. She wiggled frantically through the fence and galloped to the door, barking shrilly.

"Stop, Fifi!" Roger ordered in an agonized tone.

What a fool he had been! He should have grabbed her when she began to run. He should have tied a rope to her or had some way to control her. There was no way for him or Pierre to get over the wall in time to surprise anyone who came to the door. Nonetheless, Pierre dropped the lantern he had been carrying and both of them leaped desperately, trying to get a handgrip between the spikes on the wall to pull themselves over. Fifi might not be heard immediately, or whoever was in the house might be slow to answer her summons because it was so late.

CHAPTER 23

To Leonie, each second that had passed since her rude awakening had seemed like an eon of torment. She felt that the hand on her breast had squeezed her nipple forever, that the stinking breath had choked her forever, that she had been paralyzed by sick loathing and fear forever. The thin yapping that came through the closed window jolted her mind out of its numb horror. Fifi! Fifi was not dead!

Time and place whirled and then steadied into reality. Leonie recognized that she was only held gently by the blankets, not forcibly restrained by Marot's henchmen. In the same moment Panel's head lifted as he, too, heard Fifi's barking. He hesitated, knowing he had to let the creature in to silence her but reluctant to leave the delights he had only begun to taste. He was a stupid brute, wholly unable to recognize any emotions he did not himself feel, and wholly convinced that he was irresistible to all women. He had easily convinced himself that all of Leonie's actions had been inspired by a desire for him.

Throughout the day he had not responded in any way that would give Danou cause for suspicion. However, Danou had gone home—or out—for the night. During the day both were on duty so that Leonie might never need to be left alone, but at night, when she was locked in her room, one man was allowed to go off duty. Panel was thus alone in the house and did not fear interruption from Danou. Neither did he fear that Leonie would reject him. His hesitation to leave her was solely because of his reluctance to break the rising sensation of lust that was gripping him. But at the same time he knew he could not permit the dog to go on barking. That might arouse the neighbors' curiosity.

"Lousy bitch," Panel groaned, and began to heave himself away from Leonie.

Hatred and disgust were already boiling in her. Now terror for Fifi was added to the mix. Leonie was sure that Panel would kill the little dog as soon as she came in. Her hand slid under her pillow. As she withdrew the pistol, she cocked it, pushed it right against Panel's head, and fired. He was dead before he fell forward atop her, but Leonie did not know that immediately. To her frightened mind it seemed as if he had dodged the bullet and was attempting to restrain her. She struggled wildly, striving to grasp her other pistol and throw off the limp weight that was crushing her.

Roger and Pierre heard the shot as they came over the wall. Each crouched instinctively for a second or two, both assuming that a guard had fired at them. For Roger the movement was only a momentary shrinking. He was far more afraid of the reprisal that might be taken on Leonie than of whatever danger threatened him. Accordingly, he sprang to his feet almost at once and ran through the dark in the direction of Fifi's yapping. Pierre shouted at him to wait, then realized that no second shot had been fired and rushed to follow him. To Pierre the silence was proof that their enemies were wily. They did not waste ammunition shooting into the dark. Plainly they were saving their balls and powder for shots at a surer target.

He called a warning to Roger, who paid not the slightest attention. Cursing all women and their effect on men, Pierre followed his friend as swiftly as caution allowed, dodging and weaving but moving fast. When he heard the explosion of another shot much closer, he cursed aloud. It was very difficult to see in the dark, but it seemed to him that the door had opened just as the shot rang out and Roger had fallen forward into the greater darkness within the house. The dog's yapping stopped simultaneously. Pierre fairly leaped forward, throwing caution to the wind, only hoping to get to the door before Roger was dragged inside.

The sound of that second shot, which Roger had fired to break the lock on the door, and the cessation of Fifi's barking drew a wail of bitter anguish and rage from Leonie. She was still pinned down by Panel's body because she had been struggling single-mindedly to get at her second pistol. Now, galvanized by rage, she gave a frantic heave and the limp corpse rolled aside. The lack of resistance told Leonie what she previously failed to notice—that her shot had been effective. However, at the moment she felt neither satisfaction nor horror. She was intent only on revenging poor Fifi, who, she believed, had returned from the dead only to be more finally destroyed by Danou's pistol.

Half-mad with rage and grief, Leonie pulled her second gun from under the pillow and rushed out into the corridor and to the head of the stairs. A dark form was just turning from the lower hallway to mount the staircase. Leonie had the alternative of waiting until she could discharge her pistol at point-blank range or firing immediately. If she waited, she could not miss, but if her pistol misfired or she only wounded the man, there would be no escape for her because she would be within his grasp. If she fired immediately, there was only a small chance that she would miss her target completely. He could not dodge and he was below her in a straight line. She, however, could run back to her room, perhaps block or lock the door, and have time to reload her guns.

Without more ado, Leonie pulled the trigger. However, in the second or two it had taken to make her decision, Fifi, who had stopped barking when Roger opened the door, now scented the goddess and let out a shrill yap of joy, darting up the stairs between Roger's legs and causing him to stumble forward. Leonie had aimed for the broadest part of the body, the chest, hoping that even if the man climbed more quickly than she expected the bullet would still hit him. Roger's fall saved him, the bullet merely creasing the top of his shoulder. Nonetheless, the shock of tripping and the sudden, hot stab of pain wrung a resounding English oath out of him.

"Roger!" Leonie shrieked, casting away her pistol and nearly falling down the stairs herself in her anxiety.

The English oath had made the whole situation clear to her. Fifi, against all expectation, had found Roger and led him back—*and I have killed him*! Leonie thought. Hysteria rose in her, but before it could break, Roger's head lifted.

"Leonie!" he exclaimed, and then he gasped, "Leonie!" She was stark naked.

"Have I hurt you, beloved?" she cried.

Pierre, rushing down the corridor after Roger, had cowered aside instinctively at the sound of Leonie's shot and raised his own pistol, but had to jerk aside again when he

was nearly brained by Leonie's flying gun. By then the
voices had made clear that there was no immediate enemy
and he started forward, only to turn his back. It was dark
in the hallway, but the white gleam of Leonie's body was
unmistakable. Still, the shot—and Roger had fallen. . . .
Pierre was wondering whether he should go to his friend's
assistance at the risk of offending Leonie's modesty, when
Roger answered the girl's question in a voice of such
strength, which displayed only mingled relief and irritation,
that he felt it more expedient to stay where he was.

"What the devil are you doing with that gun—and stark
naked?" Roger roared, getting to his feet.

"Thank God," Leonie sobbed. "Oh, thank God I
missed."

"Yes, never mind that," Roger growled, ignoring the
ache and the trickle of blood from the slight wound, and
struggling out of his coat. "I have been dying with fear for
you, and I find you defending this house. Did you agree to
play this game of Chaumette's?"

"No," Leonie gasped, but she scarcely heard what Roger
said. In the relief of knowing herself safe, the horrors of
this dreadful day—which had culminated in Panel's attack
on her, his death, and Roger's miraculous escape from
death at her hands—was too much for her. She felt herself
being wrapped in something, and that made her whirling
mind fix on Roger's question. Why was she naked? But
that was a crazy thing to ask. Roger must know that her
abductors had brought no nightclothes or linen with them.
Of course she was naked. She could not sleep in her shift,
which she had worn all day. It needed airing. Besides, there
were other things to worry about that were far more important than what she wore to bed. Where was Danou?

That question checked for a moment the dizzy spinning
in Leonie's brain. Her eyes searched the corridor and fastened on Pierre, who was just turning to face them, having
judged from the sounds that Roger had covered his woman.
To Leonie that slow movement spelled doom. She was sure
it was Danou, who had been lying in wait in one of the
rooms and now had them trapped. Uttering a choked cry
of warning, Leonie tried to throw herself forward to protect
Roger. To him it seemed as if she were trying to get past
him, to escape him, and the agony of the last few days

exploded into raw rage so that he slapped her, forehand
and backhand.

The pain, coupled with the belief that they would both
die in that moment, pushed Leonie past the hysteria that
had been rising in her, directly into unconsciousness. She
toppled forward limply, right onto Roger, who staggered
back down the few steps he had climbed. Pierre was enormously surprised at what he had heard and seen, but surprise had never slowed his reflexes. He would have been
long since dead if it had. Now he leaped toward them
just in time to save Roger from falling over, and between
them they eased Leonie down. Although Roger had not
fainted, he was as little use as Leonie who had; and Fifi,
dancing around the pair of them yelping with excitement,
added to the confusion.

All the noise, Pierre noted, had produced no reaction.
There had been plenty of time after the three shots were
fired, the dog's barking, and the noise of Leonie and Roger
shouting at each other, for someone to come—even if that
person had orginally been asleep. Thus, Pierre deduced
that they were alone in the house. He mentioned this to
Roger, who paid him no attention, alternately agonizing
over his own cruelty and Leonie's unfaithfulness. Shaking
his head sadly over the degeneration a woman had produced in a previously cool and clearheaded companion,
Pierre went to block the back door against intrusion. He
did not expect any, but leaving the door open was asking
for trouble. Then he ran upstairs to find a more effective
covering for Leonie than Roger's coat. The garment did not
conceal a great many essentials—which explained pretty
clearly to Pierre what had turned Roger's head—and it
seemed to him that both Roger and Leonie would feel
much better when she was adequately covered.

The only open door was that of the room in which
Leonie had been imprisoned, and Pierre naturally tried that
first. Inside, the candle Panel had carried was still burning.
The light was not bright, but the scene that met Pierre's
dark-adjusted eyes cleared up the puzzle of Leonie's behavior. He whistled softly, his eyes skipping from Panel's un-
buttoned breeches to the discarded pistol to the horrible
wound in the dead man's head. Such a woman! Perhaps
Roger was not such a fool, Pierre thought a trifle wistfully.
Perhaps if he had met a woman who combined such loveli-

ness of form with such determination of character, his head would also have been turned.

Of course, Pierre was crediting Leonie with rather more than she had really accomplished. He thought she had somehow wrested the pistols from Panel. This small detail was corrected when he came down carrying a blanket. By then Leonie had recovered her senses, and, as her first words to Roger had been a warning against Danou, Roger's suspicions had been reduced enough to permit him to listen to what she said. What he heard then made him mute with shame, so that instead of apologizing and explaining he said nothing.

Pierre's arrival temporarily settled Roger's problem because he gave them no further time to talk. Since it was possible that Danou would return to the house at any moment, he sent Roger to get Leonie's clothes. She refused, with a convulsive shudder, to reenter the room where Panel lay dead, and dressed in the parlor. Then Pierre hurried them out of the house, the blanket serving Leonie in lieu of a cloak. The commissioner's scarves stood them in good stead, as did the weather. The streets were empty, even of bands of thieves and the night watches—in some cases a distinction without a difference—so that they made their way through the freezing drizzle without interference to the docks on the Seine where Pierre's boat lay. Once there, a sufficiently haughty manner, coupled with the official scarves, overawed the two miserable guards who were standing watch.

Even when they were aboard there was no time for explanations. Roger was needed to help man the ship and to stand guard in case they were challenged. Unfortunately, these duties did not fully occupy his mind. His offense against Leonie assumed enormous proportions, and he had more than enough time to dwell on a series of most unpleasant facts. That he had behaved abominably might not have been much of a problem. Roger had a glib tongue and an agile mind—when he had a clear purpose and a clear conscience. He could devise both reasons for what he had done and arguments for why he should be forgiven. More difficult was the time and place in which to present these reasons and arguments. During their walk to the ship there had been more pressing things to discuss, such as whether it would be better to sail directly for England in the small vessel or return to Pierre's base and transfer to the *Bonne Lucie.*

The decision had been to sail directly. The weather was wet and cold but not at all stormy, and Pierre was relatively sure it would hold for the short passage across the Channel. Whether the calm would continue long enough for them to sail against the prevailing winds to Brittany and then cross was much more doubtful. In ordinary times Pierre could have guaranteed Roger's safety in his own home town if they had to wait out a winter storm, but in the present political situation he was not sure. All in all it seemed a lesser risk to cross immediately in the small but sturdy fishing boat. However, *small* was the operative word. There was barely room aboard to find a sheltered corner for Leonie. There was certainly no place that would provide the privacy necessary to the soft explanations and affectionate caresses Roger thought necessary to comfort her.

Having got that far, the third and only insurmountable problem presented itself. Roger began to wonder whether it would not simply be better to allow Leonie to think the worst of him. He knew it would not be fair to press his love on her at this moment. She was a great heiress; she was young and beautiful. She could marry where she chose—a younger man, wealthier, of greater rank than his own. It would not be fair to bind her to him before she had seen men more suitable to her age and station. Roger remembered quite well that he had argued this subject with himself previously, remembered his rationalization that Leonie might be pursued and taken in by a fortune hunter who cared more for her purse than her person. He saw now that the rationalization had only been a salve on his guilty conscience. The guardian appointed—and most likely it would be his father, who was already the executor of her uncle's will—would take good care that she did not marry unsuitably.

Thus, when they were at last clear of the river and out into the Channel, relatively free of danger, Roger made a stiff, formal apology to Leonie for striking her and for his unjustifiable suspicions. Until that moment Leonie had been very happy. She had not given a second thought to the slap Roger had dealt her, understanding without explanation what must have passed through his mind when he saw her apparently unrestrained and armed instead of a helpless prisoner. She had not taken umbrage at his lack of trust. After all, she had accused him of worse on less evidence.

Nor had it troubled Leonie in the least that Roger had not spoken to her except to ask after her physical comfort. Leonie realized how dangerous their situation was. It would not have been safe for a "witness" to be tenderly embraced by or gaily conversing with a commissioner on the street. And it was obvious, once they had reached the boat and started out, that Roger had duties to perform that could not be interrupted for "sweet nothings." Leonie concentrated on keeping herself and Fifi out of the men's way so that they would not endanger their rescuers.

The voice and manner in which Roger addressed her was, therefore, a horrible shock. Unbelievingly she listened to him say that he was very sorry for the misunderstanding, that he hoped Mademoiselle de Conyers would find it in her heart to forgive him, although he acknowledged that what he had done was inexcusable.

"What you have done? What have you ever done me except good?" Leonie whispered, aware of the men around them who, because the boat was so small, could not help but overhear. "You have saved my life again and again. There is nothing I cannot forgive you."

Roger winced. She had said in the past that she loved him and had called him beloved, but she might have been fooling herself, confusing love and gratitude. This certainly sounded like it. If so, he was lucky he had not pushed her into marriage or into promising to marry him. Unhappy as he was now, it was nothing compared to what he would have suffered if Leonie had fallen in love with someone else after they were married.

"Thank you," he replied, his blue eyes as blank as marbles, "that is most generous; but I beg you to think no more of the matter. I mixed myself into your affairs quite voluntarily. I assure you, you owe me nothing. My friend Pierre will tell you that I have a nasty habit of intruding into other people's affairs."

"Roger," Leonie murmured, "why are you so angry? What have I done?"

"I am not angry at all," he insisted. The pain in her eyes caught at his throat, and he had to pause a moment to clear his voice. "I assure you, mademoiselle, that you have done nothing wrong, ever, nor ever displeased me in the smallest way. To know you has given me the greatest joy I have ever experienced, but your welfare is no longer my responsibility. I—have no claim on you. We are safe now—except for the possibility of a storm at sea, but I cannot protect you from that."

"What are you saying?" Leonie gasped. "Are you going to abandon me in a strange country in which I know no one, where—"

"Of course not, Mademoiselle de Conyers," Roger said, stressing the name. "Pierre will take us to a port only a few miles from my father's house. My stepmother will receive you. She is a most delightful woman, kind and sensible. She will tell you just how you must go on and present you to the *ton*—that is, the best and most elegant society. In no time at all you will have more invitations than you can manage, and so many friends—"

"And you?" Leonie interrupted, "Will you be there too?"

Roger's eyes dropped. He could not look into her pleading face. He would end by promising to accompany her, escort her, and he could not. He would not be able to endure watching her slip away from him day by day as her circle of friends enlarged and more and more men courted her. Every word she said made it clearer that it was a mixture of gratitude and need that bound her to him. When she needed him no longer, she would realize that she wanted a younger companion. The gratitude would last longer. He could hold her with that, he knew. Desire flicked him, and he hated himself for thinking of imprisoning Leonie in that disgusting trap.

"You will not need me," he assured her. "You will be so busy—and I will be busy also. I must try to reestablish my business—I am a barrister, an *avocat*, you would say. And I must get to know my son again. He will have changed from a boy almost into a young man in the years I have been gone."

Leonie stood mute, her eyes brimming with tears. She wanted desperately to plead with Roger not to desert her, to cry that she loved him, that she would rather have him than *ton* invitations and casual friends, but she knew that would be wrong. She had already robbed him of more than two years of his life, separated him from his child at a crucial time, possibly ruined his business. . . . How could she ask more of him?

Perhaps if the voyage had been tedious or dangerous, some incident might have occurred to break either Leonie's or Roger's reserve. However, it was a perfect crossing, swift and uneventful. In addition, the weather did not encourage idling by the ship's rail, which would have made conversation almost obligatory in so small a vessel. The sleety rain fell steadily so that anyone without specific duties tended to huddle silently into whatever protection could be found.

Arrival did nothing to improve matters for Leonie. During the voyage Pierre told Roger that he would set them ashore and leave immediately. He did not wish to be trapped in England, perhaps for weeks, if a series of winter storms began. His parting from Roger was warm and emotional. It was a terrible contrast to Roger's manner toward Leonie. In an effort to guard her reputation from the smallest hint of scandal, he adopted a manner of icy formality. He did not even enter the private parlor he engaged for her at an inn until a carriage could be obtained to take her to Stonar Magna. Leonie's numb despair deepened.

She was hardly aware of the storm of excitement and joy when they reached the house. She stood silent, even when she was enveloped in a soft, scented embrace. The tone of the soft voice changed from welcome to concern. Leonie struggled with herself, trying to respond, but a sense of isolation, of utter distance from everyone and everything around her, bound her tongue. The soft voice sharpened, orders were given. Leonie, resistless, found herself being helped up a flight of stairs, undressed, given a warm, sweet drink that had an odd, bitter flavor, and tucked into a warmed bed. Leonie would have wept, would have cried out for Roger or not to be left alone, but she was sleepy, so sleepy.

When Leonie's breath came in the long, even sighs of deep sleep, Lady Margaret left the room to rush downstairs and join Roger and her husband. She had done little more than kiss and hug her stepson when he arrived because it seemed to her that Leonie, a stranger in a strange land, needed more comfort and attention. However, her first real look at Roger made her draw a sharp breath. The light was gone from his expression again. She told herself that it was

only exhaustion, but the concern in her husband's eyes
when they met hers briefly warned of a deeper trouble.

"Roger tells me," Sir Joseph said, "that the situation in
France is terrible. There are hundreds of executions every
day in Paris alone."

"How dreadful," Lady Margaret murmured, but she did
not believe that the execution of strangers, no matter how
numerous, could have brought that look of suffering to
Roger's face. "Mademoiselle de Conyers is asleep," she
said. "Poor child, it must have been terrible for her."

Not a muscle moved in Roger's face, and yet Lady Margaret knew at once that she had touched the source of his
pain. She was shocked: part furious, part incredulous.

"Terrible is not the word," Roger was saying. "You
wouldn't believe the agonies she has suffered, and without a
complaint, with hardly a tear. . . ."

He went on to describe the happenings of the last few
days, and Lady Margaret's rage and amazement began to
diminish. She was even more sure now that Leonie was the
seat of Roger's trouble, but it certainly did not seem to be
the girl's fault. There was a note of warmth and tenderness
in Roger's eyes and voice that had never been there, except
in the beginning, when Roger spoke of Solange. Lady Margaret waited for her husband to ask questions, but he did
not. She was annoyed, although usually she agreed with Sir
Joseph's refusal to interfere in the lives of his adult children. He would listen if they wished to tell him something
and then offer help and advice, but he did not ask questions.

Somehow Lady Margaret felt that he was wrong this
time, and when Roger refused to spend the night, she burst
out, "What is wrong, Roger dear? No, Joseph, don't say it
isn't my business. Something is very wrong, and I think it
is Mademoiselle de Conyers's fault."

That was a trap, and Roger fell into it headlong. "No,"
he protested. "She is the kindest, sweetest . . . Oh, for
God's sake, I am twice her age! And what the devil would
people say if I married the heiress before she ever had a
chance to meet any other men?"

Sir Joseph pursed his lips at the latter statement. Lady
Margaret shook her head at the first. She was far younger
than her husband, but except for the knowledge that he
would probably predecease her, she had never regretted her

marriage. She interrupted Roger's catalog of Leonie's perfections to state this fact. A muscle in Roger's jaw jumped.

"Don't make it harder, ma'am. I know what you say is true, but—but you were a woman who knew something of life when you chose my father. Leonie is a girl without any real experience—and she has a strong obligation to me. It wouldn't be fair to her."

"Would she be willing to marry you, Roger?" Sir Joseph asked.

"Yes—I think so."

Again Sir Joseph pursed his lips. Roger held his breath. If his father said it would be best to marry Leonie . . .

"Perhaps it is as well you did not," Sir Joseph said slowly. The muscles jumped in Roger's jaw again. Lady Margaret bit her lip. Sir Joseph held his son's eyes steadily as he continued to speak. "I don't think nineteen is so young, and I don't think you should worry too much about what people will say—they will always find *something* unpleasant to say when they see someone else snap up a prize. Still, the atmosphere in which you were living could not have been conducive to clear thought on either your part or that of Mademoiselle de Conyers. Both of you need a period of calm and stability."

Lady Margaret opened her mouth to protest, then shut it. She was a great believer in striking while the iron was hot, but in this case her husband was right. Another mistake like his first marriage would kill Roger. Lady Margaret determined that *she* would measure Leonie's character, and if it was not all it should be, Roger would soon have his eyes opened. On the other hand, Lady Margaret thought, smiling a little, if the girl was worthwhile she could manage so that there would be no chance for Roger to lose her.

"Your father is right," she said, patting Roger's hand. "And now you come up to bed. No, I'll not hear of your traveling home, exhausted as you are. Philip is at school—you can ride over to see him tomorrow—and the house itself has managed to stand for two hundred years and more. It won't fall down if you don't live in it for another day or two. And there will be no need to see—we might as well give her her English name—Lady Leonie," she added in a lower voice as she drew him from the room. "You will be gone long before she wakes."

"Be kind to her," Roger urged softly as he parted from his stepmother. "She has lost everything, every person who was ever dear to her. Life has been so cruel to her. . . ."

"Go to bed, Roger," Lady Margaret replied, almost sharply. "I assure you I am not wantonly unkind to anyone."

Moreover, there was not the slightest need for Lady Margaret to be unkind to Leonie. It became obvious within hours of the girl's wakening that Roger was the lodestar of her existence. She was not interested in her inheritance, beyond the need for reassurance that she would not be a burden to anyone. Lady Margaret tested and probed, but she could find no flaw in the girl's character. Balls and parties? "Yes, oh yes," Leonie replied absently, and then with animation, "Will Roger be there?" Dresses and jewels? "Will Roger like it?" Within days Lady Margaret found that the only way to get Roger out of Leonie's head and off her lips for even a few hours at a time was to assure her that she could have Roger whenever she wanted him.

"May I write to him to come and get me today?" Leonie asked immediately, eyes brightening.

"No!" Lady Margaret exclaimed, and laughed. "It is not decent! There are two hurdles to get over before you can marry. First of all, people will say it was a conspiracy to swallow your fortune into our family. Very nasty things will be said about Roger, and about my husband, who is your Uncle Joseph's executor, if you are not presented and given an opportunity to receive other offers. Then, too, Roger is afraid you are so grateful to him that you do not realize he is much older than you. He wants you to have a chance to meet other men so that you will be sure—"

"I am perfectly sure. I am not such a fool that I do not know love from gratitude."

"I think you do, my dear," Lady Margaret said. "The trouble is, you must convince *him*, and he will never be convinced until he knows you have had a choice and still prefer him."

CHAPTER 24

Lady Margaret had convinced Leonie that she had to do it the long way. She introduced her to English fashion and English manners, made sure she knew the steps to the latest dances, gave her experience in local balls and assemblies, and then took her to London in the Season and introduced her to society. The only thing she did not bother to explain, because she could not imagine Leonie would be ignorant of it, having come, as she did, from the French aristocracy, was how Roger might occupy himself while Leonie was being displayed on the marriage market. She did not herself mention that Roger had a new barque of frailty in tow, but other members of the family were not so reticent.

April passed into May and May into June. London got hotter and stickier. Sir Joseph complained that he was getting hoarse first presenting offers of marriage to Leonie and then explaining to the disappointed suitors that he had no power over Leonie's choice and could do nothing to force her to accept a proposal no matter how advantageous. Leonie had waited happily in the beginning for Roger to begin his formal courtship, then wept and grew furious over his indifference. To her it seemed clear that Lady Margaret had been mistaken. Roger did not wish to marry her—or, probably, any woman. Lady Margaret herself had been somewhat puzzled by her stepson's behavior, but then she called herself a fool. Naturally Roger would not wish to be one among the mass of Leonie's suitors. After she had rejected them, he would approach her in the decent privacy of his father's home and settle the matter.

It was a pity that no one except Sir Joseph verbalized his complaints. Leonie did not dare speak of her doubts, partly because she did not want them confirmed and partly because she did not want to place Lady Margaret and Sir

Joseph, who were always so kind to her, in the position of pressing their son to do something he did not wish to do. She thus had no outlet for her fear and her frustration. Always now, when she thought of Roger, he was talking to, laughing with, caressing a shadowy, indistinct form. That shadow tormented her, until at last she decided she had to meet Roger's new inamorata.

Events played into her hands only a few days later. One of Roger's half-sisters complained bitterly to Lady Margaret that Roger had refused to escort a woman-friend of hers to the opera that evening, and when she had asked him what better he had to do he had replied that he was going to Vauxhall Gardens. Lady Margaret had changed the subject so abruptly at that point that Leonie realized Roger would take his mistress there. She pretended she did not understand at the time, but she had slipped away from the ball she was attending that evening with a rather wild young gentleman, whom she had convinced it would be a great "adventure" to go to the Gardens and get back before the ball was over.

She did accomplish that, and by insisting on a restless wandering "to see it all," she even managed to come face to face with Roger and his woman. She did not pretend disinterest or indifference. She examined Roger's mistress swiftly from head to toe then looked questioningly at her former lover. He had gone as red as fire when they first met; now, seconds later, he was as pale as ashes. Leonie began to put out her hand to him, but he pulled his companion roughly away.

Although her absence at the ball was not detected, the adventure was not without repercussions. The following afternoon Lady Margaret burst into Leonie's room and remonstrated quite heatedly with her for slipping off to such a place without a chaperon and, even worse, being so vulgar as to confront Roger and his mistress. Respectable women with proper upbringings did not do such things. It was their duty to remain blind and deaf to the casual sexual promiscuity of their males.

"But I wanted to see her," Leonie wept. "She is *very* beautiful. And if Roger loves her—"

"Roger does not care a farthing for her, nor she for him," Lady Margaret snapped. "Don't be such a ninny! Men have needs and must satisfy them. It has nothing to do with you. Oh, why were you so foolish! I was just about to tell Joseph to complain to Roger that you have rejected every offer made, but now he is so furious—"

"Sir Joseph is angry too?" Leonie asked faintly.

"Not Joseph!" Lady Margaret raged. A good part of her fury was that her husband would not take the matter seriously. He had nearly had a fit laughing over the confrontation, chortling that the girl showed a fine spirit, and it served Roger right. "It is Roger who is in a temper. Who do you think told us of this insanity of yours?"

Leonie's tears dried. "Roger is angry? But why? I would have been civil. If he does not want me—"

"Oh, you silly chit! I've told you already that a casual *amour* has nothing to do with you. Men—"

"Not my man," Leonie said quietly.

Lady Margaret opened her mouth to scold again, then closed it and swallowed. She had often wondered whether Roger had embroidered Leonie's adventures out of the same doting fondness that had made him, in the beginning, turn all Solange's faults into "charming ways." Leonie had been so placid and docile, so sweet and biddable, all the time she had been with them that Lady Margaret found it difficult to believe she could face a riot or shoot an attacker in the head. Now she doubted no longer. The yellow eyes were as bright, fierce, and merciless as a she-wolf's, and the sweet lips were hard and thin. She said nothing else, not even when Leonie rudely turned away from her. Without another word, Lady Margaret left the room.

Leonie was not conscious that she had been rude. Her own words had sparked a decision in her. If Roger was her man, she had waited long enough for him—but was he? Leonie reconsidered her whole relationship with him and came to the conclusion that either Roger was being singularly (and idiotically) quixotic—it had never occurred to her that he might feel ridiculous courting her among a crowd of other suitors after what had existed between them—or he was utterly cruel and depraved. If the latter were true, it was time she knew it and stopped longing for him. That was easy enough to decide, because Leonie could not believe it. She had lived with Roger for more than two years, and in all that time no single spark of cruelty had marred his actions. On the other hand, she had evidence enough of his willingness to tilt at windmills.

Leonie sighed. Lady Margaret was right. She had been a fool to make Roger angry. The last time she had made him angry . . . A blush suffused Leonie's face as she recalled the lovemaking that had followed their quarrel. Then she grew pale and then red again. Had Roger taken out his temper on his new companion in the same way? Leonie snarled like her namesake. To waste himself on a slut Lady Margaret said did not care for him! Idiot!

The more she thought about it, the more Leonie became convinced that Lady Margaret was quite right about one thing. Roger was almost certainly avoiding her to prevent even a breath of scandal rising about her rescue. As for the mistress, she served a dual purpose: She was a sign to Leonie that Roger was not lonely and Leonie need not worry about him; and, of course, men did have needs. That made Leonie grind her teeth with rage. Idiot! What about her needs? Did Roger think a woman could turn her body off and on as one could snuff and relight a candle?

The Season was almost over. When it was, Roger would be out of her reach. Lady Margaret would take her to Bath or to some popular watering place for the summer. Philip would be home for the long vacation, and Roger would be with the boy. Leonie had not the smallest wish to separate Roger and his son. Far from it! She had very much looked forward to Philip's company. She liked boys. It would have been a little like having François returned to her.

Now the dreary summer stretched ahead—more balls, more card parties, more meaningless flirting and gossip. No! Leonie did not care if she never saw a member of the *ton* again. She had had enough of Roger's foolishness. He *had* loved her. Even if Lady Margaret was not right about his continued desire to marry her, even if his passion had cooled, Leonie could see no reason why Roger should waste himself on a succession of indifferent, expensive women. She could provide everything they could—and she would cost less. She wanted him; they wanted only his money. Whether or not he loved her, it was obvious that Roger did not want to marry anyone else. Therefore, Leonie decided, it would be best that he should marry her, and without any more nonsense.

The decision made, the rest was both easy and complicated. Leonie knew that Sir Joseph had a set of keys to Roger's rooms. She also knew that Sir Joseph had very reg-

ular habits. For an hour before dinner he would be safely
sequestered in his dressing room. Leonie rang for her maid
and told her she had a sick headache. She would take some
laudanum and sleep. She did not wish to be called for dinner. Naturally enough, this brought Lady Margaret
anxiously offering comfort. Leonie was not to fret herself.
She was sorry she had scolded her. Roger had the sweetest disposition; he would soon be over his temper. No
real harm had been done.

Leonie accepted these assurances with simulated drowsi-
ness and said she was sure she would feel better after she
had slept. Having disposed of Lady Margaret, Leonie
sprang from the bed with a hushed trill of laughter, locked
her door, and began to alter a bonnet and light pelisse for
her adventure. When she was sure everyone was busy either dressing for dinner or with duties connected with it,
Leonie stole from her room and down to Sir Joseph's study.
He was a most methodical man, and Leonie found Roger's
keys neatly labeled in the drawer with all the others.

Then it was simple enough to walk out of the house. On
the main street that passed the square in which Sir Joseph's
London house stood, Leonie hailed a cab. Twinkling with
laughter, she told him to take her to the nearest posting
inn. There she knew she could obtain a meal without raising remark. Young ladies of the best quality did not travel
unescorted, of course, but less fortunate females—
governesses and ladies' maids, for example—were often
constrained to do so. Thus, no eyebrows were raised when
Leonie entered the inn, seated herself at a table, and
ordered a meal.

It was not the elaborate dinner that would have been
presented at Sir Joseph's table, and the surroundings were a
far cry from the quiet elegance of his dining room; nonetheless, Leonie enjoyed herself hugely. She had not realized
how much her uncertainty about Roger had weighed on
her spirit. Now that she was determined to have him—and,
honorable idiot that he was, she knew her trap would
work—everything she saw and heard was a delight. She ate
her dinner with excellent appetite, quite slowly, pleased
that the bonnet, from which she had removed all trimming
and stiffening, gave her so seedy and dowdy an appearance
that no one even glanced in her direction.

When she had finished, she paid and then thoughtfully

purchased two newspapers that were being hawked in the
inn yard. Probably it would be some time before Roger
returned home. It would be just as well to have something
to read. After that, she hailed another cab and gave Roger's
address. It was unlikely he would dine at home—single
gentlemen seldom did so. Perhaps he would be already
dressed for the evening. That would mean his valet would
be free, too, and the rooms would be empty. If Roger intended to come home to change, the valet might be in the
apartment. Leonie hoped she could let herself in silently
enough so that she would not attract his attention.

Actually, the better of the two chances was true—Roger
was dining and spending the evening with his eldest half-
brother—so that Leonie's plans moved without a hitch. She
was able to let herself into Roger's lodging quietly, and it
was quite empty. She had plenty of time to examine the
whole apartment, to determine where the servant's quarters
were and where she could best conceal herself if the valet
should return. This event did occur, but it did not discom-
mode Leonie. Her bolt-hole was quite secure, but she
scarcely needed to have concealed herself since the valet
did no more than turn down Roger's bed and fill the
carafe on the bedside table with fresh water.

Poor Roger had had a far less pleasant day than
Leonie, even if one included the scolding she had received
from Lady Margaret. No comment Lady Margaret made
on Leonie's behavior could compare with what Roger said
to himself about his own. Although he had been telling
himself for some time that he had no chance, that Leonie,
besieged by offers from far more appropriate suitors, would
soon settle on one among them, he had never really given
up hope. And, as he saw men previously courting Leonie
begin to avoid her and realized they had been rejected, that
hope had started to grow. *As soon as the Season is over,* he
told himself, *if she has not accepted someone, I will ask if
she will have me.*

Now he knew it was finished. He could not guess what
evil fate had brought them face to face under such circumstances—if Roger had guessed Leonie was looking for him
he would have been much angrier (and much happier).
Unable at first to blame himself—and incapable of laying
the blame on Leonie where it belonged—he had turned on
his mistress, quarreled with her, slammed a substantial roll

of bills into her hand, and bade her a final good-bye. She was neither surprised nor distressed, having realized from the beginning of their affair that Roger's mind was elsewhere, whatever his body was doing. It was rather a relief than otherwise. Her pride in her work had been sorely tried by Roger's indifference, and her nerves had been set on edge by wondering whether each day she saw him would be the last.

The next morning, equally naturally, Roger was furious with his useless and expensive gesture. He had parted with a prize pullet for no good reason—it was not the sort of thing he could tell Leonie he had done, nor, furious as she must be, would she care. He remembered sickly how he had assured her, when she had been jealous, that there would never be another woman. He would never be able to convince her that this had meant nothing. Sure he had lost Leonie, he tried to block her out of his mind, and he lay abed alternately cursing himself for becoming involved with a presentable lightskirt—he could have contented himself with whores—and for dismissing her after the damage had been done.

Then he began to rack himself for not acting faster in Vauxhall when he first saw Leonie. Perhaps he could have avoided her, but he had been so surprised, so struck with longing when she suddenly turned into the path he was walking along, that he stood stock-still, staring at her instead of getting out of the way. The only effect of these useless regrets was to make Roger late for his first appointment of the day. That had been unpleasant enough in itself, because he had refused to defend a so-called gentleman in a breach of promise suit. This friend of a friend was now insisting on making Roger explain his refusal. Since he had himself told Roger he was guilty, in a rather drunken conversation they had had at the common friend's house, the situation was unusually delicate.

The interview was even more unpleasant than Roger expected. His would-be client simply refused to understand why Roger should care that he was, in fact, guilty. The girl, he said pointedly, was a nobody. He grew quite abusive when Roger at last convinced him that, in his eyes at least, the law was not subject to class differences. If a man were guilty, he was guilty no matter who the injured party was.

The day had not improved after that either. Roger found

his clerks idiotic, his colleague vapid, and his friends annoying. It occurred to him, after nearly choking on a superlative dinner in his half-brother Arthur's house, where he usually enjoyed himself greatly, that the fault was not in the day but in himself. Acknowledgment brought a kind of release. The image of Leonie flowed into his mind, and he welcomed the pain it brought. Even pain was better than the emptiness he had to impose upon himself to exclude her.

"What the devil's the matter with you, Roger?" Arthur had asked. "If you don't want to stand for parliament, then don't. I thought after your experiences in France you'd have some valuable ideas for that crowd of half-wits in the Commons, but it's nothing to look so tragic over."

"Sorry, Arthur, I didn't even hear you. I don't—I've got something on my mind."

"So I see," Arthur replied. "In fact, you look as if whatever you've got there is pretty indigestible." He drew Roger from the drawing room into the corridor beyond. "Look, don't stay if you don't want to. No one will notice you've gone in this madhouse. We can talk about it some other time."

"Thanks. Good of you. I think I will go. I'm not adding much gaiety to this party anyway."

"Do you want me to see you home?" Arthur had asked, suddenly aware of the gray bleakness of his brother's expression.

"No, of course not." Roger had tried to smile. "I'm all right. Just—just worried. I'll stop by tomorrow. Perhaps parliament would be a good idea."

He was conscious of his brother's eyes following him out but he simply could not make any further attempt to relieve Arthur's anxiety. His attempt to bury grief in activity had failed. He had to be alone. The logical place to go was home, but Roger was afraid that his solitude there would be short-lived. If Arthur did not come chasing after him— or send another of his brothers or sisters to make sure he was all right—any of his numerous friends might drop in. Softly cursing all well-intentioned busybodies, Roger made his way to a disreputable alehouse where he could drink himself unconscious without a single kind, worried glance cast in his direction.

Even that went wrong. No one interfered with his attempt to get blind drunk, but he could not. The liquor would not bite. At some hour early in the morning, carrying sufficient gin to float a moderate-sized ship of the line, Roger walked home. He was still steady enough on his feet to discourage the cutpurses who had been watching him out of the corners of their eyes, expecting him to keel over at any moment. He was not aware of the time any longer, only that it was late enough to discourage visitors.

The odor of candles that had guttered out eliminated the slight impulse Roger had to start all over again on his own brandy. It was simply too much bother to find fresh candles, and he had no intention of waking his servant. He did not even want to talk to him. He made his way in the dark into the bedroom, slowly undoing his neckcloth. Midway in his untying, he stopped, surprised. The room was quite bright, bathed in silvery moonlight. He had not seen a room lit by the moon since he had come from France. How odd that his man should forget to draw the curtains. Roger could never remember him forgetting before.

He looked around bemused, more drunk now than he realized, his mind's eye conjuring up Leonie's face as he had seen it so often asleep in the moonlight. She had loved the moonlight, and the earliest light of the sun, too, ever since that first night they had made love in the tiny room that had had no curtain on the window. Whenever she could, after they were ready for bed, Leonie had opened the curtains so that the moon and sun could shine in. On days that they could sleep late, she would get up at dawn and close the curtains. Often they would make love in the first light of a new day and then sleep again.

"Leonie," Roger whispered, "Leonie."

"I am here," came the soft-breathed reply.

Roger's lips twisted. That was quite a freight he was carrying. He could remember being drunk enough so that his vision acted peculiarly, but this was the first time his ears had played him false. He started toward the window to close the curtains, trying to ignore the painful wrenching in his breast.

"Leave them open, Roger."

Roger stopped, his hand raised to pull the draw, his insides lurching. He had heard of bad gin, which could blind men and drive them mad, and, God knew, the stuff he had drunk had tasted awful enough. Only he didn't feel sick, and he also knew the bad stuff made you awfully sick.

"Roger, say something," Leonie begged. "Aren't you surprised that I'm here?"

She was here! No she wasn't! He was mad. If he was mad enough to be hearing logical questions, he would probably die. That wasn't such a bad idea, but he didn't feel sick. . . . He realized he was still standing, rooted to the spot where he had stopped when Leonie's voice told him to leave the curtains open. The voice was coming from where the bed stood, but he was afraid to turn and look—afraid equally that he would see her and that he would not see her.

"You can stop pretending to ignore me." Leonie's voice now had the kind of sharpness it had held when she had called him a lecher. "I'm not going away. It's too late anyhow. I've been here since dinnertime. My reputation is doubtless shot to hell, so you will just have to marry me."

Roger turned slowly. She *was* there. She was sitting up in the bed, holding the bed curtain back so that the moon shone full on her face. It was bleached colorless, but it was her face. He put the heels of his hand to his eyes and rubbed them hard. Then shook his head. That was a mistake. The room reeled. Roger staggered forward and had to catch at a bedpost to keep upright. But when the room steadied, Leonie was still there.

"I cannot see what right you have to be so angry you will not speak to *me*," she raged. "*I* have not been cavorting publicly with loose women."

No, Roger thought, *no. I may be mad, but could I be mad enough to make up that sentence? Only Leonie would say such a thing. Every other woman I know either pretends the muslin company does not exist or is a member of it and does not call its other members "loose women."*

Roger would now have liked to ask whatever he was listening to whether it was real, but his tongue, lips, and jaws were recalcitrant. He could do nothing more than cling to the bedpost and stare. Leonie, misunderstanding the bug-eyed glare bent upon her, popped out of bed and confronted him with blazing eyes.

"Oh, have I shocked you?" she hissed—and then relieved her feelings with a masterly dissertation on Roger's crude taste in women, lack of intelligence, lack of perception, and general stupidity, ranging from English to French and back as each language failed her.

He listened with owlish solemnity, and at last finding his voice, announced with considerable dignity, "I am a drunkard, too."

Checked midflight, Leonie peered at him. His back had been to the moonlight ever since he had turned to look at her. Now Leonie realized she had not really been able to see his expression and had been reading her own ideas into the shadows on his face.

"You mean you are drunk?" she wailed, horrified at the thought that all her effort had gone for nothing. "But you are never drunk!"

"Yes I am," he replied slowly and carefully, his tongue seeming to have developed a life of its own and an unruly desire to insert unwanted sounds into words when it did not refuse to operate at all. "When I am unhappy, I get drunk quite often."

It had by now occurred to Leonie that it did not matter whether Roger was drunk or sober. In fact, it would be much easier to handle him drunk than in full possession of his reasoning power. She came closer, put her arms around his neck, and murmured, "Poor Roger, have you been unhappy? So have I."

"You are naked," he announced next. "You have recently taken to appearing naked at very odd times and places."

"It is not recent," Leonie giggled, unloosening one of his hands from the bedpost and dragging his coat off on that side. "And this is *not* an odd time or place. One cannot be expected to take along a portmanteau to a clandestine meeting, so I could not bring a nightdress with me. I was asleep in bed. There is nothing odd in being naked in bed if one does not have a nightdress."

Roger's eyes widened in horror. "Have I got into your bedchamber?" he croaked, letting go of the bedpost and nearly falling on Leonie as he attempted to turn around.

"No," Leonie soothed, taking the opportunity to push him down so that he was sitting on the bed. "I am in *your* bedchamber." While he digested this piece of information, she drew off his coat completely and undid his waistcoat and the buttons on his breeches and shirt.

"What are you doing?" Roger asked as his shirt slipped

off his arms and he became aware that he would soon be as naked as Leonie.

"I am taking off your clothes," she confirmed, choking on laughter. "We have just agreed, have we not, that it is quite proper—not at all odd or out of place—to take off one's clothes to go to bed. You are about to get into bed."

"Yes!" Roger agreed emphatically.

So far, that was the only thing that sounded right in this whole conversation He remembered that he had come home with the intention of going to bed. However, as his shoes and stockings came off, it occurred to him that something was wrong even with this idea. It was not really possible that Leonie was in his bedchamber taking off his clothes. They were not together in France. They were separated—forever—in England. Leonie would never speak to him again, much the less take off his clothes. He was imagining things. He closed his eyes.

"Laval?" he said weakly, naming his valet just as Leonie pushed him backward, so that he was flat on the bed, and began to tug at his breeches.

Leonie did not pay too much attention to the slurred word. It began with the first consonant of her name, and she answered tenderly, "Yes, my love, I am here," and kissed Roger's knee.

Roger shot upright, shoving Leonie half across the room. "I never knew you were a pederast," he roared. "I am not so drunk as that!" Since Leonie did not know what a pederast was, and since Roger still had his eyes tightly shut, it was fortunate that he continued, "You are dismissed. That fault is too dangerous in a valet."

Leonie burst out laughing as she picked herself off the floor. "Idiot," she cried, "open your eyes. I am not your valet. You cannot dismiss me. I am going to be your wife, and wives are not subject to dismissal. Look at me, you fool. Is this a man's body? I am Leonie."

Well, it could not be Laval. Roger's whirling brain fixed on that. He had never mentioned Leonie's name to his valet and had never mentioned his feeling for her to any person except his father and Lady Margaret. But then who had taken off his clothes?

"Open your eyes!" Leonie cried, coming forward and shaking him gently.

"It cannot be Leonie," Roger said aloud, this time with

the fixity of purpose of the very drunk. "I have offended
Leonie and she will never speak to me again. Leonie would
not take off my clothes. I am only seeing and hearing her
because I want her so much, and the gin was so bad that it
had disordered my brain."

Leonie stared at him in a mixture of frustration and joy.
It was wonderful to be reassured that Roger did love her
and still wanted her—he was obviously too drunk to lie—
but how could she convince him she was real if he persisted
in believing everything she did was his imagination? Then
she began to laugh again.

"Then why worry. If I am not real, you may do what
you like with me. It can do no harm to anyone."

At that, Roger did open his eyes. The logic, he felt, was
faultless. Then he thought he had perhaps accepted that
conclusion too quickly because it was what he desired.
While he considered it, he reached down and drew off his
breeches and underpants. Then he realized he was naked.
Leonie (or whatever it was) he could see standing just in
front of him and watching him—she (it?) had not touched
him. He lifted a hand toward her, realized it was clutching
his underpants, and dropped them hastily with a feeling of
embarrassment. In the next moment, he was smiling bea-
tifically. He must have taken off all his own clothes himself.
The—image—whatever it was—was right. If the bad gin
were causing this delusion and killing him, it was already
too late to save himself. He might as well enjoy his last
moments or hours of life.

"My darling," he sighed, holding out his arms to Leonie,
"my love, heart of my heart, well of my life, my precious
jewel—come to me."

She did, half-smiling, half-crying, wondering if he would
remember in the morning and not really caring. Roger's
body was a little slow to respond, in spite of the inflammation of his mind, because of the desensitization caused by
overindulgence in alcohol. Leonie did not mind. She was
delighted to be able to display her skills, and they were not
displayed in vain. Roger surmounted the effects of drink
quite adequately to please Leonie and far too enthusiastically for coherent thought on his part.

Their first union was quick and explosive. It was delightful but by no means enough to content Leonie, who had
nearly six months of starvation to make up. They did not

talk in the interval. Leonie was too afraid that something she said would divert Roger from the satisfactory track he was in now. Roger had a new puzzle with which to muddle his drink-dazed brain.

He was not unacquainted with the techniques women used to stimulate and heighten their lovers' pleasure, but the women Roger used all did pretty much the same thing in the same way. This was not surprising because they were all professionals who had received similar training from the procuress who had launched them on their careers. Roger patronized one particular procuress almost exclusively. He had found her to be reasonably honest and to specialize in clean, high-quality wares. Thus, it was understandable that the repertoire of his mistresses was limited. To add to this, he generally needed little encouragement, being a passionate man who had come to a woman for a particular purpose.

A few of the things Leonie had done were familiar, of course, but she was no professional following an established pattern. She was a woman deeply in love, expressing that love. Thus, much of what she said and did was completely new. That meant something, Roger was sure, but thinking of how she touched him and what she said stimulated his body far more than his mind, and he turned to her and reached for her lips. They were yielded readily, as were her breasts, her belly, her thighs. Roger's caresses were returned in full measure and overflowing. Gentle fingers plucked and stroked, squeezed, scratched, tickled. Roger writhed and groaned, but she held him off, laughing, teasing, until his passion made her own fever too intense to resist.

That was a much longer session. Roger really sweated holding back until his partner's satisfaction was complete. By the time they were finished, his efforts had burned some of the alcohol out of his system and cleared his head a little. He lay limp, staring at the join of the bed curtains, while a series of ideas drifted around in his head. He snatched at them mentally and pinned them down firmly with numbers, like points in a lawsuit.

(1) He had never even thought of some of the things Leonie (?) had done to him. Therefore, those things could not have come out of his imagination.

(2) Neither he nor the bedclothes were spattered with semen. One thing he was sure of was the convulsions of pleasure that had twice racked his body. The result of those convulsions had gone *somewhere*.

(3) Except for the delicious fatigue that naturally followed lovemaking, he felt fine. Obviously he was not going blind or dying from bad gin.

(4) Ergo, the being whose warmth he could feel, whose soft breathing he could hear, was not a simulacrum bred in his mind but a real being.

"Leonie," he whispered, turning his head. "Is it really you?"

She smiled at him sleepily. "Have you come to your senses? Yes, of course it is I—really and truly, in the flesh. Do you think you will manage to remember in the morning so—"

"Morning!" he exclaimed. "It must be nearly morning now. Good God, Leonie, are you mad? What time *is* it? How did you get here?"

He had sat up and was preparing to get out of bed. Leonie sat up too, watching him warily. "I got here by cab," she said. "If you mean how did I get in—I stole your keys from your father's desk. I don't know what time it is, but it doesn't matter. I left the house before dinnertime, and I have been here ever since. Surely I have been gone long enough to create a scandal."

"Not at all," Roger assured her. "My stepmother is not such a nitwit as to raise a hue and cry. Unless—you didn't give her reason to believe you intended to run away with someone unsuitable, did you? Come, Leonie, get up and get dressed. I am sure I can get you back into the house—"

"I haven't the smallest intention of leaving here. Lady Margaret knows perfectly well that the only man I would run away with or to is you—and she does not consider you unsuitable. Neither do I."

"Now, Leonie, listen—"

"No, *you* listen. I don't know whether you don't wish to marry at all or whether you don't want to marry me in particular, but I no longer care. There is—"

"Leonie, don't be silly. I—"

"There is nothing those whores can give you that I cannot!" Leonie shrieked, overriding his voice. "You don't love them, but you take them places and talk to them and couple with them. Well, I ask no more of you—and you will save a great deal of money by having me instead—"

"Leonie!" Roger bellowed. "Hold your tongue."

"I will not!" she screamed. "If you don't marry me, I will tell the whole world that I was your mistress for more than two years in France. I will not go back to your father's house. I will stand outside your door and—"

He grabbed her and clapped one hand over her mouth. "Of course I will marry you, you fool. By special license, tomorrow if you wish. I am dying to marry you. I have wanted to marry you from the first day I clapped eyes on you. *Now* will you let me take you home?"

He removed his hand from her mouth cautiously.

Leonie eyed him with suspicion. "Why do you want to take me home if we are to be married?"

"Because I happen to be in love with you, and I want you with me all the time. Naturally my—my—"

"Your whores?"

Roger raised his eyes to heaven. "Whatever. They were not received by my married friends, but I would hate to have to give up all society because my *wife* was persona non grata."

It was very suspicious, Leonie thought, that Roger should yield so quickly. All the other times they had disagreed about something, the argument had continued a long time before he gave in—if he ever did. She got out of bed, but instead of dressing she lit a candle and brought it where it would shine on Roger's face. He was just tying up his stockings and raised his head to look at her.

"I do not trust you," she said. "When you think you are saving me from my own folly, you are deceitful as—as a revolutionary. If you insist, I will go home, but I have made up my mind. You *must* marry me."

"I will. I assure you. Tomorrow—no, today. As soon as I can get—" Roger suddenly put a hand to his head. "Perhaps not today. The day after. I have a feeling," he said, "that I will not be a very satisfactory bridegroom today."

"Backing out already? No! Here I stay—"

"Leonie, please. I do not wish to back out. If you had been a little more patient, I would have asked you in due form as soon as the Season was over. If you are in a hurry, I will marry you as soon—as soon as I am sure my head will not fly off. I merely do not wish to attend my wedding with the great-grandfather of all hangovers."

"Why not? It is customary in England, I understand, for men to have a bachelor party. No, I do not trust you. I don't understand why you have changed your mind so suddenly after avoiding me as if I had the plague for six months."

In spite of two little black devils, each engaged in hammering a long spike into one of his temples, Roger found his mind clear. "It is because I have suddenly discovered that you are mentally incompetent and that my father and stepmother are not capable of controlling you," Roger replied, taking the candle from her hand and putting it on the floor. Then he kissed her long and thoroughly. "Yes," he went on, "you are a sad case if you prefer me to all your other suitors. However, I promised your father when he was dying that I would take care of you, and I intend to devote the rest of my life to that sacred promise, since you are incapable of caring for yourself."

The kiss had stifled Leonie's initial gasp of outrage, and the rest of what Roger said was perfectly satisfactory. She understood that he was joking, but she thought contentedly that he was more serious than he himself realized. He did not really think she was insane, not that, but he had been shocked by her behavior. There had been a certain sharpness in his voice when he said his father and stepmother could not control her. He felt they had allowed her twice to come to the brink of ruining herself, and his sense of responsibility had taken firm hold and vanquished his silly qualms about the differences in their ages and fortunes.

How lovely! Leonie smiled mistily. A whole lifetime of shocking and enraging Roger—just a little. He did make love so superlatively when he was angry and forgot to be careful. And a triple benefit each time—the fun of whatever scrape she devised, the joy of "making up," and the assurance that the mischief would spur her responsibility-minded husband to a deeper interest in her with each escapade.

A native New Yorker, Roberta Gellis has had a dual interest in science and historical literature since early childhood. She began her writing career twenty-one years ago as a diversion from new motherhood and has been writing historical fiction ever since. She has a B.S. in Chemistry, an M.S. in Biochemistry, and an M.A. in Medieval Literature. Some of her best-selling novels are *The Sword and the Swan, The Dragon and the Rose,* and *The Roselynde Chronicles*. Ms. Gellis presently lives with her artist-photographer husband, Charles, and her college-age son, Mark, in Roslyn Heights, New York. *The English Heiress* is the first novel in the Heiress series, set in France in the turbulent 1700s.

Once you've tasted joy and passion, do you dare dream of

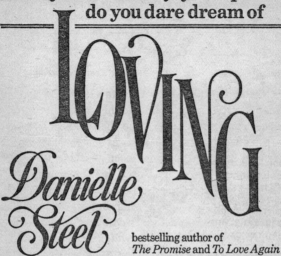

LOVING

Danielle Steel

bestselling author of
The Promise and *To Love Again*

Bettina Daniels lived in a gilded world—pampered, adored, ador-
ing. She had youth, beauty and a glamorous life that circled the
globe—everything her father's love, fame and money could buy.
Suddenly, Justin Daniels was gone. Bettina stood alone before a
mountain of debts and a world of strangers—men who promised
her many things, who tempted her with words of love. But
Bettina had to live her own life, seize her own dreams and take
her own chances. But could she pay the bittersweet price?

A Dell Book $2.75 (14684-4)

At your local bookstore or use this handy coupon for ordering:

| **Dell** | **DELL BOOKS** | LOVING | $2.75 (14684-4) |
| | **P.O. BOX 1000, PINEBROOK, N.J. 07058** | | |

Please send me the above title. I am enclosing $_____
(please add 75¢ per copy to cover postage and handling). Send check or money
order—no cash or C.O.D.'s. Please allow up to 8 weeks for shipment.

Mr/Mrs/Miss_____

Address_____

City_____ State/Zip _____

Class Reunion

RONA JAFFE

author of
The Best of Everything

"Reading Rona Jaffe
is like being presented
with a Cartier watch;
you know exactly
what you're getting
and it's just what you
want."—*Cosmopolitan*

Annabel, Chris, Emily and Daphne left Radcliffe in '57 wanting
the best of everything. They meet again 20 years later and discover what they actually got. Their story is about love, friendship and secrets that span three decades. It will make you laugh
and cry and remember all the things that shaped our lives.

"It will bring back those joyous and miserable memories."
—*The Philadelphia Bulletin*
"Keeps you up all night reading."—*Los Angeles Times*
"Rona Jaffe is in a class by herself."—*The Cleveland Press*

A Dell Book $2.75 (11408-X)

At your local bookstore or use this handy coupon for ordering:

| **Dell** | **DELL BOOKS**   CLASS REUNION $2.75 (11408-X) |
| | **P.O. BOX 1000, PINEBROOK, N.J. 07058** |

Please send me the above title. I am enclosing $ _____
(please add 75¢ per copy to cover postage and handling). Send check or money
order—no cash or C.O.D.'s. Please allow up to 8 weeks for shipment.

Mr/Mrs/Miss _____

Address _____

City _____ State/Zip _____

"The Hollywood novel by just about the hottest screenwriter around."—*Wall Street Journal*

by William Goldman
author of *Marathon Man* and *Magic*

William Goldman—Academy Award-winning screenwriter of *Butch Cassidy and the Sundance Kid* and *All The President's Men*—has written a shattering, nationally-best-selling novel. He has seen and learned a lot of Hollywood's best-kept secrets. In *Tinsel*, he tells a story only an insider could.

"Scathing, witty, merciless, and a fast enjoyable read. The film colony may squirm, but the rest of us will lap it up."—John Barkham Reviews

"No-punches-pulled slashes at the business. Complete with names named." —*Kirkus Reviews*

A Dell Book $2.75 (18735-4)

At your local bookstore or use this handy coupon for ordering:

| Dell | DELL BOOKS | TINSEL | $2.75 (18735-4) |

P.O. BOX 1000, PINEBROOK, N.J. 07058

Please send me the above title. I am enclosing $ _____
(please add 75¢ per copy to cover postage and handling). Send check or money order—no cash or C.O.D.'s. Please allow up to 8 weeks for shipment.

Mr/Mrs/Miss _____

Address _____

City _____ State/Zip _____

The first of six magnificent sagas

The Australians

The EXILES

WILLIAM STUART LONG

They came from England—thieves, felons, murderers, justly and unjustly accused—human cargo destined to hack a life from the harsh Australian wilderness. A turbulent saga of love and lust, of loyalty and betrayal on the Australian frontiers.

A Dell Book $2.75 (12369-0)

At your local bookstore or use this handy coupon for ordering:

Dell   **DELL BOOKS**   THE EXILES $2.75 (12369-0)
         P.O. BOX 1000, PINEBROOK, N.J. 07058

Please send me the above title. I am enclosing $_____
(please add 75¢ per copy to cover postage and handling). Send check or money order—no cash or C.O.D.'s. Please allow up to 8 weeks for shipment.

Mr/Mrs/Miss_____

Address_____

City_____   State/Zip_____